John Schuster ...ig
340 Un...
Gra...

M000187394

By Joshua Cohen

The Quorum (Twisted Spoon Press)

Cadenza ∫or the Schneidermann Violin Concerto

Cadenza ∫or the Schneidermann Violin Concerto

a novel by

Joshua Cohen

fugue state press
new york

Fugue State Press
PO Box 80, Cooper Station
New York NY 10276

www.fuguestatepress.com
info@fuguestatepress.com

Let my style capture all of my time. This should make it an annoyance to my contemporaries. But later generations should hold it to their ears like a shell in which there is a music of an ocean of mud.

~

Music laps at the shores of the intellect;
only those with no firm ground under their feet can live for music.
— Karl Kraus

Cadenza ∫or the Schneidermann Violin Concerto

An epigram is only a wisecrack that's played at Carnegie Hall.
— Oscar Levant

CADENZA, Italian, from the Old Italian *cadence*, meaning much the same as it does in this language, a musical term (excluding the military definitions), a noun.

A solo passage intended to feature a performer's virtuosity.

A parenthetical pyrotechnic flourish, a tangent without meter, a brilliantissimo *flight of fancy*.

Now understood as a section of a concerto, conventionally situated toward the end of a 1st movement, a section reserved for the soloist and the soloist only, the orchestra having stopped, leaving the soloist unaccompanied to display his instrumental proficiency.

Then the CADENZA ends, the soloist often signaling his finish with a long trill, and the orchestra reenters to finish the movement.

Though originally a CADENZA was a vocal embellishment, a practice that later extended itself into instrumental music.

In opera, a CADENZA was improvised by a performer on a cadence in an aria — performance practice allowed three CADENZAs in an aria, or *melismas* (as they are known vocally), the third being the most elaborate.

What initially interested me in the CADENZA was that it was defined to me, in the course of idle conversation, by my friend the pianist Alexander Wald — to whom I dedicate *Schneidermann* — as "an extended solo passage in an *improvisatory style*," italics mine.

Meaning — Wald went on to explain — that the CADENZA was improvised, ex tempore, up until the advent of Romanticism (and so the advent of the famous virtuoso personality), during and after which composers wrote them out, in an *improvisatory style*, a style that derived many of its parameters from instrumental technique.

Meaning that the CADENZA was focused more on instrumental showmanship and less on a soloist's exploration of a work's thematic material.

Eventual third parties — the famous virtuosos themselves — also wrote their own CADENZAs, many written as specialized practice material for themselves, or for students, and a handful of these became so widely played, and appreciated, that they, today, seem like they were written by the concerto's composer into the original score: a prominent example being Joseph Joachim's

CADENZA for Brahms' *Violin Concerto*, overthrown later, at least to my ear, by Heifetz's.

Today, very few virtuosos perform the CADENZAs of Beethoven or Mozart — which themselves had their genesis in improvisation, in the great tradition of the composer/performer — instead preferring the CADENZAs to these composers' concerti written by their instrumental forbearers: examples in the piano repertoire should include those by Busoni and Reinecke.*

Today — according to my friend Wald — outside of *modern* or *serious* aleatory music (which is as deaf to the world as the world is to it), and excluding possible analogies in *popular*, *ethnic* or *world* musics, almost no virtuosos improvise their own CADENZAs.

---

* Ferruccio Busoni, 1866–1924, was in his day, according to Wald, an ultra-modernist: a composer, conductor, theorist and pedagogue, he was also a virtuoso pianist of great power; indeed, according to Wald, some of Busoni's ideas regarding the limitations of human ability — both in musical execution and perception — prophesized the rise of electronic music. Today, however, according to Wald, he is considered at best a historical phenomenon, his name alive only in footnotes, his achievement largely reduced to his prolific piano transcriptions and CADENZAs for the works of classical masters.

Karl Reinecke, 1824–1910, was, according to Wald, the Germanic opposite of the Italian Busoni: whereas Busoni was a progressive, a direct precursor to the serialist future, Reinecke was an unabashed Romantic, whose lush compositions and piano technique had small audience, and almost no influence, after the First World War. Today, according to Wald, Reinecke's more serious contributions are almost wholly forgotten, with the exception of his CADENZAs, which remain in the repertoire only to provide contrast with, or service to, the greater works of the canon.

~ MUSIC ~

Good evening!

Distinguished virtuosi, acclaimed virtuosos and virtuosas of this the greatest orchestra in the world, members and memberesses of this fine ensemble, tuxedos and dresses of the New York Philharmonic Orchestra, you behind me I've stooped to rehearse with for far too many seasons now and have yet to conquer, consider this your cue! to draw out the long bows: downbows for the 1st violins, upbows for the 2nds — the bowings are as necessary as they are Schneidermann's, written into your parts, yes, believe it or not, in his own hand, and such hands! (though I helped some, because among his many other lacks in this country was a publisher) and, yes, let's have the final cadence, drawn out to the last and stiffest hair, to the frog and to the tip of the bow as they're called,

okay! gasp, we don't want anyone asphyxiating on us, now do we?

Will

Will the orchestra please stop? desist?

    Everyone finished?

    Gasp, it's okay! If you all just remain seated, and listen, I promise that no one will get hurt. Trust me, everything's going to turn out fine.

Good evening!

Sehr trotzig   Good evening ladies and gentlemen,

p ———————— *f*

good evening kids of all ages, good evening my exwives and my
wife and prospective wives, good evening some of my own children
out there in the audience, good evening my lawyer, my agent, my
accountant, good evening my recordlabel execs, good evening my
podiatrist (who just last Thursday she told me that my onychauxis
it had developed into onychogryphosis, had a professional trim my
nails),

good evening my proctologist (the mother to my thrombosed external hemorrhoids, don't ask), good evening my ex-
inlaws, my inlaws, my prospective inlaws, to you aspiring musical
professionals out there, to the would-be musical professionals only
if, the musical amateurs and the failures, good evening to that most
notable of moguls Mister Samuel Rothstein Jr. just sitting out
there dumb in row one two three four FIVE, good evening to my
poolboy also let's call him my unofficial psychopharmacologist,
good evening also to an exwife's poolboy who let's call him her
poolboy, good evening to my great colleague the violinist Maestro
Jacob Levine ladies and gentlemen, everybody give him a hand! a
warm round applause!

good evening my students, to those who want to be my
students, those who'll never be my students, good evening my hair
& makeup homosexual, my Thai masseuse, my rabbi, my S & M
dominatrix, good evening my grandson who he fixes my electronics
and gets them to blink and chirp like new, not to forget my
therapist PhD and if I did what repression would that imply? and
so a good evening to my therapist's therapist too, a most good
evening to the harpist who I lust after though in professional quiet,

my orchestra, good evening.

Thank you all for the pleasure of your attendance. It
means the world to me that you all showed up.

Listen: I am standing here onstage, under the proscenium
arch, in the world's most famous and honored concerthall. Having
finished performing for you the 1st movement of the Schneidermann *Violin Concerto*. The 1st movement of two movements of the
first, last, and only violin concerto my friend Schneidermann he

ever

ever wrote. And addressing you instead of performing its cadenza.
Understand. Or this is my cadenza. Understand? A parenthetical
pyrotechnic flourish. A tangent without meter. A brilliantissimo
solo of souls and so on. In matters of art, you decide, and while
you're deciding,

take your time, all you need,

you've paid all too much for that privilege — allow me to
wipe the sweat from my bow and my brow with a handkerchief I
pocketed from my hotel, Uptown, from the maid's pushtray, that
bounty on coasters in the hallway of my accommodation,
ultradeluxe, hotel name of Grandsomething, you should look it up
sometime, God it's gorgeous! everything's marble: bookmatched or
is it matchbooked like a violin's back the whole lobby it's like a
hulking revetment of Proconnesian cippolino marble all of it
aching huge-veined as if the stone itself is perpetually aroused and
the maid, well, she's some sun-skinned, indigene ingénue with the
sweetest two loaves, ready for sanctification, tucked away under
that pink as a tongue uniform that it fits her as tight as her name
does: María, or at least that's what her fantasy-fulfilling nametag
has it as, just María because we're just old friends, a mother of one
and one's enough he's so smart (demanding), a mixed-race genius
kid with enormous as-if-for-myopia glasses at least in the grey-
wisped school snapshot she showed me his mother's twice-
divorced the third guy he dropped dead (heart), first love in Sing
Sing for three strikes he's out of the armed robbery racket but
that's a whole other spiel, other lives altogether and I'll know more
tomorrow, I hope, or I won't know anything more tomorrow, I
hope, but I'd have filled the most Stradivarian of her F-holes
anyway, varnished her good and hard forever and ever:

ewig, ewig as that great Christian Gustav Mahler would've
had it, but only if Schlesinger's conducting, or Leonard Bernstein
— and they're not. I am. Sort of. Me.

But who am I?

the resident European in America, the only sane American
in Europe.

Who do I think I am?

everywhere an international genius, a bearer-of-conscience-
and-culture, once loved as much as respected.

But I'm no one, really.

Don't be shocked! The cultured are so easily shocked!

Don't whisper! Don't gossip! Don't ask-around!

You'll never find answers in music, only more questions and so, yes, I have a speaking part, not quite notated, not quite mentioned in the program you've glanced through and idly referenced, riffled through the least piano of my pianissimos and are now manically flipping through to see if I have a history of mental instability, some schizoid personality disorder that would serve to explain this away.

My decision to address you with my voice instead of with my violin.

Allow me then to assure you all of my — relative — sanity, to promise you all that I am relatively sound (ask any of my doctors, all ten of my chiropractors who they've received complimentary tickets for this evening).

And don't see, *listen*. Hear that it's not as if Schneidermann he was oblivious, not like the Lethe it flowed in one ear out the other: Schneidermann he was the iconoclast even the iconoclasts worshipped and so it's not as if he didn't forehear this, that my friend, that my only friend the failure that was my Schneidermann he didn't in some sense expect this. Maybe even wanted this. Intended it and set it in motion. And anyway Schneidermann he's left no explicit instructions as to my address being unwanted, left no even veiled directives as to my address, this, being unnecessary.

Because he, in the end, the finaleless finale, left nothing.

Except this *Concerto*, a sizable body of piano compositions, string trios and vocal music, some ephemera, memento mori, occasional and souvenir pieces, a heap of juvenilia and life entire, which is now up to me, and my lawyers as much as I pay them, to sort out: to scrounge around his refusal for either an on-paper or a spiritual Will, some indication or instructions and given over at any expense as to what the hell I'm supposed to do with the so-much-of-everything, the Nachlass it's said that Schneidermann himself left unfinished, incomplete as his life unlived, fallen short of its fullest, unresolved to what I know is his destiny still.

And as his, then yours from mine.

Because from the very beginning,

my mother's curtains up,

I was a soloist. By the year I left Europe I was already the

world's

world's famously renowned virtuoso. And it's tonight and tonight only that I am yours, fully, truly, away from the music, away from my instrument now and so forced to go under, descend, into life, to the world and the midst of those who suffer it. Among whom there are some, a select few, a mere handful it sometimes seems, who they find solace, find peace, in me, in my instrument, in my music,

might be hard to believe it but there are some who in listening to me, to my instrument, to my music they end up and maybe for the first time ever hearing themselves. Hear also that there are those who praise me, whether they praise me for profit or out of some psychological need it doesn't much matter as there are many (though less and less of some and more and more of others with each passing season), who praise me as less a violinist than a virtuoso and less a virtuoso than a musician, in the words of Zeitblum always a critic and here tonight, and hello! quote a *pure* musician unquote (*pure*: shades of Pythagoras and, yes, shades, Orpheus), though Zeit he'd be the first — or the second after Schneidermann if he was still around — to admit that such critical commendation, such raving recommendation of my greatness with just the faintest note of the aloof, the requisite snob is by now nearly 20-30 or more years outdated, more or less applicable to any other concert's play, fitting almost to a previous career and not to the geriatric violinist you hear before you tonight:

praise has no use for me now, all washed or is it dried up as I am, forsaken by those unworthy of even forsaking me, left for old by Schneidermann, broke by my wives present and ex, betrayed even by music: it dying too — and perhaps dying with Schneider-mann — and not even having the most modest modicum of respect to say goodbye. To finish out its movement. Goodluck. To realize its possibility, to resolve and so Godspeed to the soul! the life and conscience of the public bound now in wires, in wireless wires and wrapped in repurposed manuscript like the domestic practice of Maria Anna Keller, Frau Haydn using her husband's compositions as butcherpaper — she's the model, the patron saint of all you patrons:

no, it's not that none of you are affected, that none of you feel, it's more Elemental as Schneidermann he always said, more Fundamental as Schneidermann he always insisted, it's that you

don't even know from music, that you don't even know what music
is anymore, no one does and what to expect? like just last week a
man on the subway, an old thin-lipped gray-goner out on the Q
train who he must have recognized me or maybe not but still
addressed his need, anyway this mass-transiting-dead he just
turned and with shatter all over his face, his ears dangling like
pierogies stuffed with testes he asked me and simple enough what
music was, asked me what is music? and what did I do? I answered
him as fast as glib allows with that old proverb popularly attributed to Louis Armstrong that if you have to ask you'll never know,
that if you don't know, you never will but know that when I arrived
at my ladyfriend's one bedroom with kitchen-corner (a Polish
woman out on Brighton Beach), and had taken care of my Schneidermann would say *conjugals*, I got myself up off her aureolian
futon folding myself out in skin and sweat, went over to her
packed if never understood wall-length walnut shelves and plucked
her Webster's dictionary (the first possession she'd acquired upon
arriving in America last decade is a detail she furnished me),
thumbed away and for the virgin time ever at my age and level-of-
success to MUSIC, to the entry for and of MUSIC and there
standing in midmorning sun, drip and pink-paisley socks I suddenly lost my faith in words too:

    not only wasn't my picture in there but Schneidermann
he's not in the *Grove* either, you understand? or at least not in the
edition I own, lacunaed from the volume *Riegel to Schusterfleck* — a
tragedy,

        a travesty,

    unconscionable, and so allow me the opportunity to rectify
your ignorance, will you? official ignorance too but we'll begin at
the begun, allow me to fill in the gaps in every melody ever spewed
through this great hall, yes: might I take a moment of your evening
and of my solo to recall Schneidermann? an artistic decision that
might allow his ghost, if ghost he is, to rest easier with this liberty
I'm taking and, sure,

        what's to be expected? you're grumbling again! already!
shouting at me as if I could hear you with all this music in my
head, all these memories of memories of,

        me just another voice in the din, all this heteroglossolalia
verging on ipsissima verba in here (Schneidermann), so that I can't

for

for the life of me remember that which is most important,
        the chaff from the,
        the forest from
        the forest in Poland where Schneidermann he — no, only
what I want to, what I myself know will I remember: first-off this
great man and our friendship,
        our kinship,
        the ship that my father and I took over (the Leviathan,
unfortunately my real father and not my Schneidermann), steaming into this great golden orb that sets on my neck, shining down
over New York and yet giving no warmth.
        If you would just listen you would hear: about my life,
about his life, about our lives and our life,
        and this violin you only 15 minutes ago were so tuned to,
a violin actually owned if not played by Hitler — actually, no, it
wasn't but for a moment you believed me, for a moment this
artifact it deepened us, made everything different. Schneidermann
himself though played this violin (though not too well),
        Schneidermann who maybe died insane as he ever was as
you all — should — know the long-story-short, maybe read of his
disappearance last and laziest Sunday on the rearmost page of the
newspaper of record or in the few as elite glossed magazines that
they printed up his posthumous fame — his 14 minutes and 59
seconds of post-mortem renown, his not even quarter-hour resurrection of which this concert, commenced at my own request, my
own pull, my own financial outlay and insistence as shrill as any
wife ex or present is almost certainly the final act, the 2nd and last
movement and then what?
        died insane, maybe, died exactly how though? and where?
died anyway or at least this late afternoon I buried him, Schneidermann who he gifted me this violin — which itself was a gift to
him, a Baron's accolade of a Schneidermann's earliest and onlyest
success, the opera — as if to reward me for my or my father's
foresight in fleeing Hitler (me with my father, me without my
mother or my Schneidermann), and so Hitler in the poetic sense
which causes love and wars might have owned it had I and my
father not been lucky and smart in that order.
        A question! From among the orchestra ingathered behind
me to stare at my soloing tush, 107 souls, 108 for the 2nd and

final movement if we ever get to it when the harpist punches in —
she's just sitting there lovely now, gorgeous, remote, manicure
folded in lap and all of her mortified — from among you, how
many actually understand what you're playing, really, truly, I ask
rhetorically? because everything the soloist does is rhetoric, in fact
— or, as one of my lawyers always says,

> *in point of fact*, which I've never quite figured out — every-
thing nowadays is rhetoric,

> not rhetoric as one of the fine arts,

> as Plato would have had it,

> as an essential instrument, as a staple of every fine not to
say total education but in the sense — or senselessness — of these
bitch-boos, heckles and jeers that some of you are now giving out,
sounding without first listening as I attempt to steal Schneidermann back, to claim him for art from the posthumous encomia
and their economy, yours, imprudent in your sounding without
first listening, as if to prove your own existence, as if my addressing you here, now, doesn't prove it already! and so just go ahead!
feel free!

Good evening, Mister President of this hall soon to fall.
Just take a seat. You own them all. We'll be here for a while.

As long as you're at it someone might as well go around to
a bodega near here and pick up some overripe migrant-picked
Trenton-fresh tomatoes from José or Manuel, or María if she's
here? if you got those tickets hopefully just for you and your dear
mother, or was she dearly-departed-dead? and so besides her (with
her excuse, being a member of a minority, 60 million-strong), how
many of you out there know what you're hearing when you're
listening? know what you've heard? and without anyone telling you
first, providing your reaction, vetting your opinion? Let's elect
someone then — aren't democracies great? except in art — and
then have him appoint someone else to get those rotten veggies,
and even if no one ends up throwing them it's okay because I'm
sure at least one of my women knows how to make soup.

Because initial misunderstanding, at-first unununderstanding,
is okay. Is fine. Is permissible. To-be-expected. But ignorance is
not.

Even I, myself, well-trained from three years, had no idea
what to think the first time that Schneidermann he played this, not

this

this but his *Concerto* for me and in the piano reduction in which
nothing at all was reduced, first day of harmony instruction at the
Music Academy in Budapest — a strange discipline, the study of
harmony, and even stranger to begin it with this composition on
the first day of that first study, but such was Schneidermann, that
was his genius, was his total need for total attention, for validation,
his method stranger even than this, than his *Concerto* which Schneidermann he explained, this piece we've paused in, thusly as he
paced the room,

      and Schneidermann he paced like an inept attempt at
tuning a string: tight, nervous vibrations and then gradually, after
hours of exercises as physical as mental, gradually loosening,
slackening every day toward a nap's 5 p.m., loosing pitch, becoming
not music but gut, pure gut and

      gut luck as Schneidermann he always pronounced it explain-
ing that to Helmholtz, Hermann, the acoustic scientist of Bonn
and Berlin who he also believed, Helmholtz did, that life it was
brought to the earth by meteorites from further stars, or at least
according to Schneidermann who he was my instructor in much
more than music, in art too, in the lowest discipline of history, in
the highest discipline of philosophy (metaphysics),

      in life,

Helmholtz who's dead, 1894, as is Mahler, ditto
Schlesinger who he died however as Bruno Walter because how can
you hope to die well with a Jewish name? Schneidermann he often
asked no one and least of all himself, Jewish dirt dug with a Jewish
shovel is fine, yes, sure, a Jewish stone too with a Jew under it
under some Jewish trees with no names, understandable, but a
Jewish name on the stone? that might be asking too much, might
be too evident, out-in-the-open, in-too-many-faces Schneidermann
he often said over coffee and coffee and coffee and coffee

      (wherever Schneidermann and I went, pre and post the
matinee movies, wherever there were free refills, BOTTOMLESS
CUPS) — amber-voiced Bernstein's gone and, well, maybe even
Schneidermann too, yes, maybe he's dead, dead as all the others, as
all the other Jews, maybe even more so, forgotten, my real father
who he wanted to be my Schneidermann passed long ago and me
soon enough. And gut, cat gut, is what they used to make violin
strings from if you didn't know or forgot — that's what cats are

for, ask my friend the newspaper editor Katz who he owns ten
street versions of them, and then of course the initial stages of
violin domestication are often likened unto a cat's screeching,
      and what hack composer was it anyway who he transcribed
his kitten tripping across the piano keys and had himself a fugue
subject? Schneidermann he once told me and I forgot, he always
told and I always forgot, like who for that matter lining a birdcage?
Frau Haydn again? who she was also so religious that,
      or a litterbox with scores of whom, Herr Baryton? yes,
Schneidermann he would know, would have known, always knew
and me? I've never owned animals for the simple reason that
they're dumb, dumber even than humans, than people, but Schneidermann he kept spiders in a jam-jar (as Spinoza, an intellectual
pretension), spiders he'd pit against each other in death-duels, and
once — but you could never tell if he was joking or serious, or just
old — but once after we'd left an undifferentiated matinee Animated movie together Schneidermann he told me that he would
have no problem owning a cat (Bast, an Egyptian goddess), that
he'd invite a cat into his home (his apartment, his room), no
problem, but only if he could charge it rent, that rent it was the
one condition for the cat's tenancy, then asked me how much I
thought he could charge a cat rent, how much did I think a cat it
was ready, willing or able to pay for a manuscript-laden corner and
Schneidermann's heart-intentioned hospitality? but it was not pets
but Schneidermann though I was explaining (though I am, in a
sense, also Schneidermann's pet),
      but if I was to explain Schneidermann to you I'd first have
to explain his work to you, to explain this piece to you, this piece
we've paused in, in my wild caesura of his *Concerto* but of course
Schneidermann he was not at all an explained man, in no way open
to explication, nothing programmatic about him or just the
program it's as long as unknowable: man and work and work and
man, same thing, one and the same, inseparable,
      holding fast to one another,
      each saving the other,
      inter-refugees if you will, both fleeing the terror of popular
inquisition
      (but does that sing to a grave-shaped ear beyond this
vale of

meres

meres?), and don't send in your responses, don't care what you think,

if you even could and at this remove — it's all at best a mystery wrapped in an enigma strangled by a questionmark as stooped as his posture.

Enigma, the word, so used, slips, slinks into its own definition, after some thought is internalized, turned inward but the word in my own language, my first language, word I learned young, wrapped tight in my white alpaca sailorsuit:

it's *Rätsel,* a near anagram on my own name, surname of Lästerer which has or had the meaning of *mocker,* now Laster, a *vice* and anglicized as subsequently Americanized as all things are and without an umlaut — Immigration, ROTHSTEIN management and my promoters to thank for that — prefixed by *Gottes* — , as in *Gotteslästerer,* and I mean *blasphemer,* word-for-word a *god-mocker* and, living up to my name, or down, I mock through my music and, as a naturalized Laster, I last all night, just ask me tomorrow and I'll answer just as I did when the newspapers and magazines they called in response to my calls, left messages because I always screen and who doesn't in this city? called back again and again,

wanting to know,

not to understand but just to know,

to *fix the facts* as one editor she said as if the facts they could be fixed and how?

Born in either Buda or Pest — I forget which — on New Year's Day 1910, Schneidermann was.

Schneidermann to me: on November 11, 1911 which does seem too late in Kisvárda, Hungary.

Schneidermann to me: New Year's Day 1906 in Bohemia, later Czechoslovakia but of Hungarian parentage (where their name it would have been Šnajdrman).

Schneidermann to me: 1902! in Máramaros-Sziget, Romania, of Hungarian parentage.

Schneidermann to me: 1904 in what's now Ukraine of Hungarian parentage (Schneidermann, when there was another word he never said JEWISH).

Schneidermann to me: Užhorod, Christmas Day 1909.

Schneidermann to me: on the date in question in Košice.

A hairless man who he never had to shave despite claiming

he shaved three times a day,

    a bald man like Pan with a bony skull and bumpy forehead that might remind Americans of a dinosaur, Jews of a prophet like Jeremiah or Moses, and which the Europeans — if there are any left — once referred to as *un double front.*

    A bald bone of man who he took to wearing a ladies' wig he found on the street,

    dumpster-diving Schneidermann he often said, it should be recognized as an Olympic sport,

    Schneidermann he was always thinking of the Greeks,

    a man who once when he was walking and because his shoes they were too large as too wide for him and so they would always fall off him was once and in Midtown bitten on the heel of which foot I don't remember by a snake. Which race of snake I don't know. He lived.

    Schneidermann to me: I was born in Miskolc, but we lived in Nyíregyháza, in Debrecen, in Békéscsaba, in Orosháza — stop me when I'm getting warm I always thought, the past is the past and who wants to remember? I always thought,

    when you're born a musician you're born to the world as Schneidermann he always said.

    Schneidermann to me: we had no money.

    Schneidermann to me: we were poor.

    Schneidermann to me: after my father died.

    Schneidermann to me: my first composition,

        my Opus I,

            to tell you the truth, I don't consider it part of my output,

                well, the first piece I ever composed it was scored for four voices, SATB, a chorale — I was four years old, I was five, Schneidermann he once said he was three — on a text of Mother's,

                his mother she died in childbirth, twins,

        a Rudy and a Schneidermann they were, on a text of Goethe's,

on

on a text of my own, in my most primitive Hebrew, which
I learned from a renegade melamed who:

Gar manches Herz verschwebt im Allgemeinen,
   Doch widmet sich das edelste dem Einen which would translate to:
many a heart wanders (this was the bass and the tenor, in canon) / *and
is lost in too wide a love* (the alto) / *but* (the soprano) *the noblest devotes
itself to one object alone* and I, Schneidermann the object he once told
me over three of my mentholated cigarettes to one of his
triskaideka-filtered coffees, I sang the eunuch soprano, his father
the alto with an aunt on tenor, an aunt on bass and Schneidermann
at the world if not universal, intragalactic premiere he was leading
them at the piano, bashing as thrashing, all-forearm strum-thump-
ing as he doubled them on the old upright, on the asthmatic mold-
splotched spinet they had before Schneidermann he turned 12 and
they the aunts they got him the grand, sacrificing all they had for
his art which was after all all Schneidermann he ever asked of
himself — sacrificing his health (it was an Asian flu-day for him
at an age when an Asian flu-day it could be your last) to play this
first ever piece of his for me and from memory as the manuscript
it was lost in the War which Schneidermann he always, often
referred to as
         what happened or as
         that which happened — this was six-seven years ago down at
my old place in Midtown (west, I'll never live in the east again),
now an exwife's, actually a husband-in-law's when we Schneidermann and I we were rehearsing together and for no purpose I
understood yet another violin-piano sonata that Schneidermann
he'd never finish and after interrupting my second entrance at
m. 94 to play this piece of juvenilia for me (because the melodies
they were related),
         my Opus -1, my Opus Prehumous if you want, if you will
Schneidermann he said:
         so shoot me! I was young!
              and to put up with that trauma,
                   with *what happened*, with
         what had happened,
              witnessing my then-wife being beaten to death in
front of me (Poland, 1944), you'd have to be crazy to rank it with

his mature work, to set this work — play — alongside those late
great masterpieces comparable to if not completely surpassing their
models:

the three infamous hammerblows of Mahler's *6th Symphony*
of 1906: his enforced Jew-resignation from the Vienna Opera, the
death of his four-year-old daughter Maria, the diagnosis of his own
fatal heart condition by a certain Doktor Marianus — is anyone
else in the house? paging posterity! all transfigured, revivified,
remade and incarnated through Schneidermann's never acknowledged thefts, treatments, borrowings like for example the eight bars
note-for-note in the upcoming if ever 2nd and last movement that
were taken, sans scoring though without acknowledgment, thanks
or even a postdated personal check to Arnold Schönberg, from the
Master's 1926/7 *Der biblische Weg* prefiguring his later operatic
masterpiece *Moses und Aron* with the two tablets of brothers bound
into one character, one Max Aruns which was a name he used, the
alias Schneidermann he gave at the roach-ridden rat-shit-spackled
Westside SRO he lived in throughout the 50s and 60s before I,

and how Schönberg over there, legally Schoenberg over
here in Los Angeles, Californ I-A how he couldn't finish the thing,
couldn't bring himself to finish his last and only opera, couldn't
despite all complete the 3rd and final act, as no-poetry-after-
Auschwitz Adorno pointed out himself falling victim to silence,
formlessness and void, nullity the punishment for violation of the
2nd Commandment against the making, even remaking of graven
images that Moses he smashes sometime in there somewhere as for
years! years! — in America, on the Pacific, the wrong ocean —
Schönberg he hesitated to set to music the first and only scene of
Act III and Act Final and how a bit before his death he consented
or was it relented? anyway allowed this 3rd act of his masterwork
"to be performed without music, simply spoken," in the event of
his being unable in his final days which he was and they were to
complete its musical setting,

the first two acts of which work though and to my ears at
least (or to my memory, from the first, last and only times I heard
either, one from Schneidermann and the other at the Met at which
I was sleeping with a bovine extra in the Golden Calf scene)

sound like an absolute and absolutely non-ironic, entirely
ill-intentioned rip-off — if my memory serves, as Schneidermann

who

who oftentimes was my memory he once in a rare moment of
strength insisted: that that opera entire indeed it was largely a
measure for measure and often a note-for-note-for-note theft of
his, Schneidermann's, own and only opera, his *Die Ziege* of 1932/
33,

  The Goat for those who may need opera translated it was
his own one and only, first and last opera: a huge hit which
changed everything for him which would change yet again in a few
years, seven, six, which won him a heap of acclaim and money
which the War it quickly lost him, on a libretto by a certain Zed
Hofmeister (one *f*, he'd remind you), a bloated-to-beautiful man-
about-town, Berlin, who he would let Schneidermann engage his
sister and then his wife while Hof he was out sucking anuses,
indeed out doing anything but working on *The Goat* (through the
mails, it took him three years),

  his libretto on a well-worn if not by then already totally
hackneyed Jewish theme as all themes are and absolutely everything
is Jewish if you're that type of Jew, and so you have to understand
that even then which must seem to at least most of you out there a
forever ago we — they — were exploiting from a high as mighty,
Sinai-summit of universal Kultur the whole shtetl aesthetic,

  the schmaltzified as did Chagall,

  as later did the Noble Singer,

  using it to our own ends, mocking our own superstition
while out-moderning the goyim in the process, destroying their
nationalism, at least condemning it while clinging fast to our own
throughout all four 10-scene acts of *The Goat* and beyond into
world (its popular overture, often performed separately in its day)
in which, I hate summary and you should too:

  in which a rich, womanizing Duke and is there any other
kind? no, he's a Baron, van or von Something or Other,

  might as well be half-German, half-Austrian minor
nobility with a name like Gregor van Vonvon as that was the
maturity of the thing, the libretto in which,

  the Baron van or von Baron who he loses his virility, the
guy just wilts, can't-get-it-up and this needless to say is way before
the little blue pills, an immensity prior to 100mg in one share or
is it tablet of PFIZER? and so he's unable to perform, nothing, no
cure works and in the very first act he tries them all: prayer, prayer,

the ingestion of variegated roots and tubers, primitive suction treatment involving the muted use of an offstage trombone, the curtain going up on the whole spiel with him in bed with one of his many women, a peasant girl just laughing at him, laughing, laughing, "laughter billowing the damascene canopy of the oaken four-poster into clouds purpling the setting's sun" — and so much for Hof's stage directions! Indeed, this is the first and to my knowledge only purely laughing aria in or out of the repertoire, an aria in which a woman, A Peasant Girl (in this instance, the debut, a wide-eyed, equine-mouthed mezzo-soprano with knuckles for nipples), she just laughs along, assuredly on specified pitches, to the music in what has been the only aesthetic as well as technical advance on so-called *Sprechstimme* since Schönberg's pioneering *Pierrot Lunaire* of two decades earlier,

indeed not just this aria which it represents the technique's technical if not aesthetic height but all the lines, the role entire of this bronchial, consumptive, starved-limbed mezzo is just laughs, in point of fact all the lines of all the Baron's women (except his wife, the Baroness), and there are many (women), are all just pitched laughs, Hof he didn't like to work too hard and so all this laughing, laughing, laughing, God I hate opera! and a strange as old Jewish doctor, no, a rabbi convincingly debuted by a man named Hans KIforget who he's out walking one day let's imagine to visit his ailing sister or to do a Shabbos gig in let's say Kasrilevke and is nearly run over, almost flattened by the Baron's carriage, his coach less a kocsi, which was the Hungarian source of our word — MADE IN KOCS — and more a Germanic Landau at Schneidermann's insistence en route to some therapeutic seraglio that Hof he left rather unfleshed-out as he had to abandon revisions for an urgent appointment he had with death at Davos, premature and so it of course transpires that the Baron he — after of course not apologizing to the rabbi for the near-fatal near-accident, and only after let's say sexualizing the whip on the person of his own, Moorish, postillion — instead confides his little tiny impotence problem to the rabbi who in turn advises him to get a goat, yes, a goat and to put it in the room with him, to sleep just him and the goat in the baronial bedroom in the baronial bed until the advent of the, Jewish, month of Nisan, around Eastertime the rabbi explains, three months or so hence from the nearly vehicular

homicide

homicide incident and then he'll be cured, and so the Baron he
complies — like how can't he? — and orders in a goat from his
stables, a goat raised, lovingly raised, a goat indeed the only friend
of this poor stableboy who all day he just plays a flute (panto-
mimes playing a flute actually sounded in the pit by a piccolo, a
normal flute, an alto flute and in a memorable 24-bar solo by a
flutter-tongued bass flute, an instrument perfected just the year
previous by Rudallo Carte & Company working on the Böhm
system whose patent-holder he was the premiere flautist's in-some-
way-inlaw),

     anyway this poor as young fluteplaying stableboy who he's
in love with the Duchess (who puts the *tart* in *Entartete*),

     as the Baroness is in love with him, the two have of course
been carrying on and in open secret for years,

     and so you can already almost fill-in-the-blanks: the Baron
he sleeps in his bed with the Goat, and because this is just-pre-
WWII German (not to say displaced Weimarian, or just held-over
Austro-Hungarian) Modernism, there's a transference of a whole
lot more than temperament going on here as a Baron and a Goat —
played by Jew Hans KIforget who he also played the Rabbi —
through gradual, subtle and for their time near-miraculous lighting
fx. with of course a trifle heavy-fisted musical suggestion thrown in
(each to their own motives), wholesale exchange existences: the
Baron he becomes the Goat and the Goat it becomes the Baron, the
former Baron, the Goat, going back into the care of the Poor
Farmhand or Stableboy who he marries the Baroness after the
former Goat, now the present Baron, casts her off, away, and more
than capable now of ahem performance he commences with a truly
great, bang-up finale, indeed a finale to end all finales and cardiac-
arrest all the censors, a real crowdpleaser this actlong scene of
intense and unrestrained fornication:

     and so okay, Schneidermann he hated the libretto even
after his own, hasty, revisions after the initial Berlin run but he
made good money on it and, anyway, it's still X times more
intelligent than *The Magic Flute*, all that Masonic *mishegas* that it was
one of Schneidermann's favorite words,

     or *Der Rosenkavalier*, admit it, music by that great Nazi
Richard Strauss who to make amends, ends meet at the end of his
life that it was the end of the War he goes ahead and composes that

paragon of total restraint, his late *Oboe Concerto* for an American
G.I., John de Lancie of the Philadelphia Orchestra then occupying
the Strauss estate at Garmisch-Partenkirchen and, again anyway,
The Goat, curtain down after nearly 80 heckled-from-shock performances Schneidermann he'd conducted and directed himself, earned
for its composer a not insignificant fame or is it notoriety? a name
which is all that matters in the end, no integrity here though the
score it was reported — by Schneidermann, by forgettable greater-
Reich-musicologists — as destroyed, thankfully lost in the war,
     in *that which had happened* according to Schneidermann,
     if you took out all the words, the music it was exquisite, I
remember from his playing and singing, nasaling to me of snippets
and from memory one day up in my at least ducal penthouse at the
Grand,
     or at least Schneidermann he once told me: purge the
words and the music it speaks its own name, speaks to its time
much more, much more deeply than for instance did the
Rosenkavalier — 1911 its premiere in Dresden, a city that was to be
worthlessly exploded to 30 pieces of silver only a bit after the Old
World it died in 1914 or 1918 take your pick with the War and
the only opera that emerged, that escaped the world's anus gaping
let's say subito esophageal after that it was by Puccini if you didn't
already know, would never have guessed, Signor Giacomo's never-
finished turn-of-the-century and yet 1924 throwback creampuff
Turandot, the one with that thrice-riddling Asian ice-princess like
which exwife?
     with Ping, Pang and Pong doing verismo in trio in Peking,
a work pretty much ensuring *Nessun dorma* for an audience like
yourselves,
     a perennial mainstay playing probably tonight, right now
just a short subway for you taxi, hackney-horse-drawn-carriage ride
Uptown as successfully as it did then in 1926 at its belated
premiere once the composer's student I forget his last name
Schneidermann he would have known had finished it (if you leave
right now, you might still make it),
     the only work in that idiot's idiom that captured
anyone's — lack of— imagination after the big-B Birth of huge-
M Modernism,
     and in our version, our adaptation, let's say that the

tethered

tethered Baron who's now a roped Goat he has to witness his
Exfarmhand screw his Exwife's brains out, just aria-braying his
stained ivory keys like crazy as, or that the Farmhand he has the
Goat, the exBaron, do his Exwife or at least try to while the
Farmhand he prods them both and in every hole with a rusty
pitchfork that's surely just a prop:

    that was my idea, for an update, for a *Goat* Version 2.0, a
revival, new production of the opera but Schneidermann being
Schneidermann Schneidermann he said no and no and no again and
again, refused to listen, couldn't, Schneidermann he disliked any
input, indeed regretted the composition of this opera entire, his
first and only and last opera, always disowned it, at every opportunity or rather it's that Schneidermann he never talked about it or
more accurately never liked to, avoided mention of it, really, or else
forgot about it altogether or said he did or really tried to (American whiskey, American matinee movies, American whiskey at the
American matinee movies), denied any knowledge of its existence
whatsoever was his method or lack of method, ignorance or else a
deflection, attributed it to another Schneidermann, a similar young
success whose promise was fortunately or not fulfilled by the War,
the Second World one: death in the East, in one account Buchenwald in an immunization experiment, in another, Dachau and
freezing,

    Schneidermann to me: my cousin.

    Schneidermann to me: no relation.

    Schneidermann to me: actually, only the librettist's name
it was Schneidermann, which was of course only a pseudonym,

    though a pseudonym perhaps not as mindnumbing as
Larry Lee, as Lawrence Lee — the American alias of my communist
concertmaster just now exiting stageright.

    God! it's absolutely impossible to trust an Asian —
they're all so diabolical, inscrutable, and so, what's the word?

    placid! Well, alright Wang-Lee, suit yourself you hack! you
have no taste, you have no tone, you have no touch, no feel, you'll
never work in this town again, which is all wet with the winter
we've been having of late.

    I've forgotten that it's almost X-mas. Though most out
there don't observe. A Merry-merry to you and yours.

    Because I've taught all those people, those Asians Ping,

Pang and Pong. Because they think they can play but they can't. Because they think music and they play math. Not Puccini. And certainly not Schneidermann. But if I would've been born an Asian, life would've been that much simpler.

You rote monkeys! half the string-section's Asians taking scarce musical jobs away from all the musical Jews! You deserved Einstein's bomb! What do you know from ecstasy? What do you believe in?

I myself believe in death. But that's because I'm supposed to do something with my life, because I have greatness' birthright,

charge of representing the world,

chosen people, a light unto the nations and you know the rest:

setting an example even unto the ultimate, a martyr to the end, not yet — still have bills to pay, checks, debts and tabs to honor, so I need to do it, this, not this, need to keep this medicine-show on-the-road, snake-oiled, traveling season to season inevitably premiering with Mozart and postmiering if you will with Beethoven, with not a few more accompanying:

Mozart's *5th Concerto*, yes, Beethoven's one and only, sure, but also Brahms', Berg's, Bartók's *1st*, Busoni's even if I'm feeling generous, Shostakovich's *2nd* and,

need to keep it going, perpetual motion machine on the eternal return tour, the eternal tour to infinite nowhere and why? engaged to play Shostakovich's *2nd* 17 times and one time more this upcoming season, from here to the hall of Lenin's hometown, Shostakovich's *2nd Violin Concerto* written a year early for the virtuoso David Oistrakh's 60th birthday and before the composer he could make the mistake of presenting the score to his friend and interpreter to commemorate the day Shostakovich he realized his miscalculation and so went home and wrote his wonderful as weird *Sonata*, that idiosyncratically dodecaphonic Op. 134 which I play as well, which I also often played with Schneidermann but in private but Schneidermann he,

who always wrote so fast, Shostakovich did, though he finished that score the *Sonata* a month too late for the virtuoso's true 60th birthday the year later: the strange tragic year of 1968 and so that's not only very absentmindedly artistic, yes? and very Russian actually Stalinstyle-entropic, right? but it's also almost

totally

totally servile: composer to performer, whereas my
      relationship (I hate the word, and mistrust it above all
others) with Schneidermann it was quite the opposite, diametric: I
served *him*, performer to composer, I appealed to *him*:
      I'm Schneidermann's true wife, his sweet-singing daughter
hanging his laundry-whites out on my longest line,
      don't you know that I'm Schneidermann's performing
monkey?
      that I need to keep it going and going to gone? A perpetual
motion machine, yes, this Shostakovich-style passacaglia perpetual
motion machine on the eternal return tour, yes, that I'm the eternally
touring wandering Jew to infinitely returning nowhere? and why?
      Because just like you I've got debts to pay and tabs to
honor, nth mortgages, alimony, all my money: a million denomina-
tions of support, wives present and ex to keep in ever-increasing
dress sizes like 5000 SMALL,
      children and even grandchildren on the dole, parental
welfare: first wife's children, second wife's children, third wife's
children, a whole children's chorus of empty as hungry mouths
      but calando! calando! calando! as Schneidermann he
always said (I always limped Downtown too fast for him) —
calando meaning, yes, in musical Italian *a diminishment in volume and
speed*
      but also an anagram on Doc Alan, my first-call personal
physician, my prostate-feeler, hands of an artist that they should be
cast in bronze or plaster take your pick, watch your budget except
for that gorgeous watch of his, Swiss, his wife, Indian, she got him
for his golden birthday or was it anniversary? anyway his or their
50th so that he can tell me that my time it is up, but tell me
instead, Doc: are you disappointed that I've given up my famous
cadenza in favor of this improvised piece of what at least the
mothers out there would call poop? kaka? dreck (all the language
of maternal subversion, intended to mitigate our horror at the
inevitable quality, universal absolute, of life, which is *shit*)?
      come Doctor, come prima, come sopra you can answer me,
tell me how you feel about this soon infamous soon to be
nonpiece of worthlessness — mine and not Schneidermann's —
spewed out unto this famous soon to be condemned hall?
      and one can only hope, right?

this rightly or wrongly most famous and honored
Carnegie concerthall named after a man who'd exploited even his
own charity on the way to the top, this hall once built on the backs
on the aching spines of immigrant Atlases, railroadmen and
steelworkers the federal government they didn't just happen to
shoot dead on strike once the Hippodrome it gave out and now
being held up and kept in operation only with benevolent grants
and bequests, digging money right out of the grave — how soon
until it's shut down? how many 1000-persons half-capacity
concerts left? how many more times will you leave your Dress
Circle seats for the restaurant at intermission (though your
reservations they aren't for another 45 minutes)? before you just
stop sending your checks in favor of supporting something
advertised to you as more worthy? marketed of-the-now if not the
nowest? how many more unsubscribed seasons, programmed-by-
rote, until all is, and finally, maybe even thankfully, condemned?
just boarded up?

like CBS' famous 30th Street recording studios (you
played here and you recorded there), that old Baroque church,
rather that wonderfully non-denominational Temple of all the great
virtuosi including yours truly, red-lit for my first American
recordings of the Mozart *Concerti* in 1955, same year as Glenn
Gould's first recording in the same facility and who do you think
got all the press? as the studio it was sold in 1981 to the multina-
tional whim after the last official recording session there and what
was it? what do you think? it was for Baroque if not Classical
symmetry's sake Glenn Gould again, Glenn Gould even in his
misanthropic seclusion unavoidable, inevitable Glenn Gould
inevitably recording BWV 988 — that's Bach's *Goldberg Variations*
— his second, you might say encore recording or rerecording of
them after his famous 1955 sessions in the same space, the last
recording ever sanctioned in that hallowed, sacred house before it
died into the future:

as a glo-in-the-dark-disco, last trend's nightclub or
whatever it is now (I never walk by it because I never walk in this
city),

but that's okay because Glenn Gould he escaped back into
hiding, unscathed, back to Toronto, never had the same problems I
did because Glenn Gould he never married and I did, there was

never

never a Misses Gould besides his mother and yet there are probably a hundred million Misses Lasters (ask my lawyers, or theirs),

and they're probably all out here tonight! whispering,
tsking, gossiping, comparing rulings and settlements, God maybe
even breastfeeding each other! an entire audience of former and one
present but probably not for long Misses Lasters just doing
anything besides listening,

you never listened,

ever which is nearly 50 years ago now, north past an
exwife's house up around Danbury, actually now after her second
divorce my ex-husband-in-law's property if you will up in Ives'
neck-of-the-woods, the Housatonic at Stockbridge, yes, outside
Charles Ives' town up there in let's say pastoral Connecticut on the
way up to Boston is the route, in the old wrecked MERCEDES M-
CLASS I've driven it a thousand and a half times in my sleep to
play those quick, tight one-nighters at the city's almost acousti-
cally-perfect Symphony Hall where RCA VICTOR in the winter of
1954 they pretty much invented multi-track recording as Charles I
knew him as Chuck Munch and the Boston Symphony Orchestra
they were performing, interestingly enough, Berlioz's huge *The
Damnation of Faust*,

RCA engineers getting the performance down on both
mono and 2-track tape — these were the first ventures into the
WORLD OF STEREO, stereo sound that everyone has installed
in their toilets nowadays, leaving monaural behind, flushed, to
capture the nuances of Heifetz (might as well speak his name),

Piatigorsky, Reiner, yes Munch, Rubinstein, Fiedler and so
on, all those Europeans in America, all anticipating that, and one
day soon, home sound technology

(or, in German, *Homesoundtechnology*) it would eventually
catch up, and catch up it did the year later, the Year of Glenn
Gould, 1955 in which ¼" 7 ½ ips stereophone tape players they
were finally introduced to the market, made available to the general
public and now everyone — or everyone willing, able, to drop the
money — had stereo in two tracks, one for each ear, in three tracks
soon enough and more, in more and more and more until now,

in the studio like I was last month when you just punch in
a sound and then punch in another, recording note-by-note, all on
the gray bubble of computer and instrumental skill it's decidedly

not required (*we'll patch it up in post-production*),

even shunned by those who would guard their fortunes as their ineptitude.

Understand that we are not qualified to take risks anymore, according to Schneidermann. Understand that we no longer bear papers entitling us to make mistakes, according to Schneidermann. Understand that there is no longer any understanding, that we as musicians used to improvise fugues: improvisation as free as possible within absolute discipline as Schneidermann he often said, rules not to be broken but to be reflected (Schneidermann he above all coveted a pair of mirrored wraparound sunglasses we'd once seen star in a matinee Search & Rescue movie, I bought them for him when I was out in L.A. but Schneidermann he never wore them,

said I'd gotten the wrong pair) — and then they go and use popmusic in serious music and serious music in popmusic, grafting strains to the point at which the modifiers they mean nothing anymore according to Schneidermann who he was always listening, ears always open, agape, and so neither does their orchestration of history seem to sound when you think about Verdi and how many people put in an appearance at *that funeral* (thousands upon thousands according to Schneidermann!),

when you think about Verdi's music as the favorite music of the organ-grinders and their monkeys from Milan to Paris Herself,

apegutans and chimprillas a choir of them that they were mad squealing and lowing amongst themselves all the origins of man's distress, through pinkest salivafied gums just discoursing upon the difficulty if not the rank impossibility of ethical communication, moral colloquy all the way Uptown at the Bronx Zoo: this was last year in late summer's animal rape of early autumn, around the Jewish New Year and the Day of Atonement when Schneidermann he asked me to break his involuntary fast, poverty, and buy him a cottoncandy and then — as Schneidermann he leaned in to gum down on the gossamer sugar — Schneidermann he slipped me and behind his back as if in some matinee Espionage movie, or Spartakiad spectacular some wetted lichened papers, a manuscript I thought only to hold while Schneidermann he indulged but it was instead his way of giving me, of gifting me a

composition

composition, for me as it was written for me or was finally finished or unfinished for me as it was and as it is, dedicated too:
indeed it was the manuscript of this *Concerto*

we've finished only one movement of,

and if you want to know how the next movement begins,
how the 2nd movement and the last last movement of
Schneidermann's last masterpiece if only, his 1st and only *Violin
Concerto* that won't ever begin again, how it begins, then I'll tell
you: it's with three notes,

dumb dumb dumb if you'll excuse my humming lip-numb,

numb numb numb I sing it to the stone eye of my Grand
teevee at night, these three pitches sung high and sweet into the
whirring hum of the mute, indeed these three notes they limn a
major triad to begin the last and ultimate movement of this major
non-tonal — not to misuse the term *atonal* — work, the notes
being G,

E a sixth up and a

C to resolve it all in the middle: an arpeggiated C major
chord in second inversion if you want, if the theory of music's
your brand of banality, if we have any Schenkerians out there in the
audience tonight and all sounded on the oboe,

not on the xylophone like the NBC theme you didn't say
— indeed, it is the NBC theme! as I told Schneidermann at the
Zoo as I flipped through the pages in front of the penguins,
they're the same notes! to which Schneidermann he replied in that
mafioso picked-up-at-the-movies American idiom he often sought
refuge in only when he was angry, with me, Schneidermann he
replied:

I don't know no MBC (Schneidermann he was always half
decorous, Old World-immigrant and half from-the-matinee-movies
and so you never knew, what was irony or just senile strangeness, or
what just wasn't at all).

You can't use that! I said to him in the aquarium, everyone
knows that! it echoed, even a prehistoric icthus agreed. It's the old
NBC sign-on/off theme, I said, though they don't do much signing
either way anymore.

Schneidermann to me: but that's a triad, a major triad, in
2nd inversion, fifth, third, tonic. Any Bach used it more times than
you've breathed.

But it's the NBC theme! as I insisted all the way to the reptile pavilion. My tongue a serpent's fork to eat his lean pride.

Like it's the three famous chimes I said: like This (in my best announcer voice, like General Sarnoff or Paul Whiteman or)

is the National Broadcasting Company, BONG BONG BONG.

People will laugh (and I laughed like the emphysemic ape that I am).

Schneidermann to me: but they're not supposed to (laugh).

Don't use it! You can't! It's under copyright anyway, patent whatever, registered trademark the in-perpetuity intellectual/musical property of the National Broadcasting Corpse. They'll sue you! it's theirs!

like in the 20s after the end of a program, the NBC announcer he would announce all the call letters of all the NBC stations carrying the program (I didn't know this then, wouldn't have mattered, as if Schneidermann he ever listened to history), and like with more and more affiliates this was soon impractical, would cause some confusion as to the end of network programming and when the stationbreak it should occur on the hour and every half-hour and so some sort of coordinating signal it was invented as I only later was told by a prominent musicologist in Basel for whom Americana it's just an embarrassing hobby,

a diversion, a naughty sideline though ostensibly legal and so three men in NBC's Music Division whose names this musicologist he said I'm sorry, I forgot they after much trial-and-error and error-and-trial, and which comes first? came to the simplest solution or what it seemed to them then like the simplest solution which was this, this *G-E-C* I was told only later when I asked,

answered that though *B* and *C* they are notes that there is no note for *N* and so that they scrapped that idea as I was told only later, that they went for the C major chord as a musicologist friend in Basel he once told me, a plangent solution, rich, at-peace, though now I only told Schneidermann (not knowing any of this, just concerned with the absurdity of the appropriation whether conscious or not):

That music is the music of an American business! A band of lawyers will set up camp in your hair!

Schneidermann

Schneidermann to me: I'm bald and it's music. It's
music's.

But it's so identifiable! artistically, you can't use it! as an
aesthetic decision it's indefensible! It's even in the same key,
octave, everything. N. — I sang (emphysemically aped) — B. C.
Jesus God they'll bankrupt you!

Schneidermann to me: I'm already bankrupt.

Schneidermann was bald, yes, and already bankrupt,
always, in perpetuity yes, that much is true, and though he owned a
television, an old Zenith job, and kept it on all day (when I paid
his cable bill), Schneidermann he kept it on on mute, the
WEATHER CHANNEL or QVC like an abbreviation of philosophical discourse and so how was he supposed to know? so bald
that you couldn't tell where his head, when unwigged and dehatted,
ended and the sky it began, so bankrupt that his shoes they were
Joe the Turk Salvation Army and three times his size, twice his
width and they'd fall off him at every opportunity: on the way to
the subway, to the MWhatever bus I never remembered when his,
137th Street / City College, stop it was out-of-order which was
often,

all on the way, on his way to the movies, the M5 or 11
bus it was to the American matinee movies, which was the last
place, the last time I saw Schneidermann: was at the movies as
usual, at a matinee, as usual, not up on the screen, no, but in the
seat one over from me, the seat most next, our jackets errant idle
steaming jizzum in the middle, on the one seat between us,
unoccupied or just occupied with my fur and his rag raining humid
stickiness up, us seated a sprung spring apart as was the tradition,
the norm,

the *už* as which exwife she often truncated it? to familiar-
ize the assurance of *usual*,

us seated a seat away enough to be together when it didn't
embarrass us to be together, and to be apart when it did (love
scenes, sex scenes, sex-with-love scenes, sodomy scenes, that scene
in which the adolescent he shoved a lawnmower into the anus of
his alter-cocker-spaniel),

as was our habit, two grown-old geniuses of the liver-
spotlight huddled as together as our dignity allowed and to see this
movie, to audience this one last matinee movie the same as all the

others that we saw together over the almost 50 years that Schneidermann and I we went together in which we saw them all (dreck),
we must have (a waste),
it was our *thing*
this matinee-movie-going, Schneidermann and I above all
(beyond and besides being musicians, artists, geniuses, Americans,
Europeans, Jews) we were matinee-movie-goers — matinee which
is from the French at least according to Schneidermann, as in let's
take in a matinee in the morning as opposed to a soiree which it's
undertaken in the evening (at my penthouse at the Grand, American whiskey, Spanglish turndown service and),
matinee from the French *matin* meaning *morning* as Schneidermann he just once and idly mentioned to me one June day
around Maturalia as it happened after one matinee movie or
another about 25 years into our 50-year-run, *matin* from the Old
French Schneidermann he said *matines* meaning *morning* as well
though a morning older, also the first Office with lauds of the day,
the first canonical hour of seven canonical hours of the Church's
perpetual day perpetuating what exactly? dawn, sunrise though
Schneidermann and I we always went, always matineed or matinee-
movied after lunch (sometimes French, sometimes Italian or deli,
Hebrew National hotdogs or the torturous goo of pretzels off the
saltless street),
French from the Latin according to Schneidermann that
June afternoon around Maturalia as it happened as Schneidermann
he later reminded me after that matinee movie about 25 years in
that it's from the Latin *matutinus* or *matutinae*: the morning vigils to
honor Matuta the Roman Goddess of Dawn, patroness if you
didn't know it of newborn babies, oceans like the Atlantic and
harbors like New York at least according to Schneidermann — and
Schneidermann, well, he just left in the middle, in the middle or at
least near or around the middle of this last matinee movie of
almost 50 years of matinee movies (hundreds upon hundreds!
thousands unto thousands!), Schneidermann he just got up and
left in the course of the movie, in the course of the movie's life, in
the course of the movie's lives, about one hour and a few minutes
in,
say 18 is what I told the police,
around 4 p.m. plus or minus the ads and the previews and

that

that MGM Metro-Goldwyn-Mayer Leo the starred lion of Samson just roaring out that motto of theirs that Schneidermann he loved to doubt, was perpetually unsure of, that ARS GRATIA ARTIS writ wreathed around the filmstrips with which Schneidermann he had to agree and how not to? *with their numbers?* like copia iudicium saepe morata meum est, you know? Schneidermann he often admitted, asked, with all this art gratifies art, art for the sake of art, art-for-art's-sake-stuff that wasn't even famous old Latin, just a modern-day rendering by some MGM honcho Schneidermann he still, always wanted to be a purist, indeed that was his greatest ambition, like does anyone really believe that the greatest art is an art that serves itself? and itself only? Schneidermann he always asked himself and I think not only himself, quoted Ovid to answer: spectatum veniunt, veniunt spectentur ut ipsae and so on, they come to see as much as they come to be seen Schneidermann he would never say *we* — this was three weeks ago and Schneidermann he went, I'd assumed, to take a piss (his piss organs they always troubled him, often he just pissed into his empty sodacup — we always patronized the concessions, I always flirted with the spray-on tannest concessionaires),

or maybe I'd assumed to haggle for yet another free popcorn or soda without gas so more like refill of liquid slug (Schneidermann he always patronized the concessions, and with my money, believed also that free refills they were America's greatest contribution to world culture, always loved the phrase BOTTOMLESS CUP),

and but Schneidermann he never returned, just disappeared, no one ever saw or heard from him again, or since, apartment — if you could call it an apartment, a studio, a room — left untouched, and don't think I wasn't hauled down to the precinct for autographs, interviews and photo-opportunities.

But I wasn't. I went on my own, reported it and myself on my own accord, for and despite the manifold urgings, urgent warnings I received from my lawyers, and their lawyers whom they consulted in one of these what-if, I-have-a-friend-of-a-friend scenarios that we all have to plot, steer by — went despite my husbands-in-law and my exwives out there: their entreaties, pleas and please, all those why-do-you-want-to-do-a-stupid-thing-like-that's? from all these women who they seem still to care and why?

Sentiment's not required to cash my checks. No need to ID your hearts.

Why is it that whenever I play this original sin Apple at least all of you are in attendance?

Stand up, dears. Or not. At least do me the favor, or is it the honor? of listening, of at least trying to listen. I have something to say, to you, to you who resented Schneidermann, to you who always resented

my Schneidermann as you always put it and steadfastly refused to make him ours, to all of you,

but first, someone get me some water! — without gas! Jews hate gas! — someone speak to someone more important, or else go out to the Park and hit a rock or something, maybe descend to the Styx with a commemorative cup.

Thank you to no one.

Some questions: which one of you played Eurydice to my Orpheus (assuming I am one)? Which one of you did I most rescue or did I do the utmost to rescue? from poverty, from misery, from first husbands and seconds and leftovers, from lack of U.S. citizenship, from lack of talent?

Yes, who was my Eurydice?

Or your-Id-is-she, and don't you out there, you undistinguished mass, pity my violin-shaped women. As I did to marry them. Because no one beautiful or rich should be pitied, and you don't believe me? If you don't then let's have the houselights, please? maybe? no? so I can see who's leaving through the doors I hear slamming?

and there goes half the brass section behind me,

trailing thick spit out into the wings,

definition of *optimism*: a tuba player with a business card, just like my visiting card for which I paid double for embossing it just says GENIUS — I give them out to spite,

and God! all the oboists gone too! those tuning sirens, the touched heads of the orchestra: all that air backed up, traffic-jammed, gives them inevitable maybe even enviable brain lesions, didn't you know that? how could you, lesionaires? no less than six of whom are required for this *Concerto* I've now hijacked, for this *Concerto* I've now ruined, this *Concerto* I've now failed.

I suspect my wife, which one? all of them, of playing the

oboe

oboe: those lips like pillows, and that absolutely perfect stupidity, the perfectly absolute stupidity of all of them — of my first wife who she'd loved me for my music, my second for my fame, my third for my money, as did my fourth who she was also my first, and my fifth who she was just my fifth: divorce, divorce, divorce, divorce, divorce and now I'm on my sixth,

no,

seventh, or is it? not legally actually, well, out-of-the-country (Canada, but it seemed like Switzerland), fifth I'm only separated from, or, maybe,

I should stop talking, order a gag, ask my lawyer, or my lawyer's lawyer. Or my shrink. But what does she want me for, number six? My shrink's shrink might suggest that she wants me for all the reasons previous.

Wife Number Six is a soprano. She even has the T-shirt that it says across her udders: DIVALICIOUS, don't you dear? and what's the difference between a Lamborghini and a soprano? She wouldn't answer you that most musicians they've never been inside a Lamborghini and hahaha,

but don't let my cough worry you! it's had me for years and yes, Doc, I know I need to quit, at my age and all that, should stop this smoking — anyone got a light?

No?

Yes?

Thanks for the help. A hearty round of applause for the mensch in the front row, center, with a book of matches from the bistro around the corner, the place it's called *Giorgione's*, on 50something & Mad. it's a Zagat-vetted, Michelin-overstarred, good good good spot — anyone want the telephone number? What did you have?

Everyone, he — what's your name?

Great.

Everyone, Ari Feingold of New Haven heartily recommends the salmon tortellini.

Everyone, thank Mister Feingold, great — you have something in your teeth, is that the appetizer's spinach or your dessert's poppyseed glaze?

but I'm just kidding or no one will notice, just as you were all too polite or were you too stupid? to notice that I've executed,

with just one minor mistake in my between me and you absurd
second entrance, m. 18 — the bow does not break like that —
that I have executed thus far all on my lonesome: yes, ladies and
not so gentlemen (Mister Feingold excluded of course), heathens
and nominally affiliated Philistines of all ages, one suit and one
suit only has held together our first half entire. Because tonight,
your eminent musical director who he's the heir to Leonard Amber
and Mahler, your foreign Maestro Laureate (because even now
most geniuses are, have to be foreign), he's in his penthouse —
one of his four penthouses worldwide to be less precise —
engaging in sex oral and anal with under-aged males, members, yes,
members of your youth chorus, and your regular on-retainer Guest
Conductor,

this I have on good authority: a janitor in the wings, name
of Jimmy or I just call him that, tells me and janitors, maintenance
men, sanitation engineers, no irony or slumming, they know
everything and Schneidermann, well, it's not that he wouldn't have
indulged (though only out of his fetish for all things Hellenistic:
Schneidermann and his Griechendeutschen ideal that was less the
escapism of Weimar than the idolatry of Judaism though it must
be related that Schneidermann he and only once placed a palm and
its five fingers on my 7-year-old I think it was inner-thigh, to hold
as if to weigh my taboo hindquarter but I just glanced at it, told
him that his five fingers they were stained all over and with ink and
Schneidermann he removed them and it, the palm and that's that,
the end of it, all it's worth, all-she-wrote),

but understand that it's acceptable, permissible to even
laugh now (but make sure it's warmheartedly),

and it's okay to feel joy, why? because they do, because all
homosexuals they're essentially optimists just as all heterosexuals
they're essentially pessimists, the reverse of that first lemma
holding just as well as those who'd do anything, well, they're
merely normal — let me tell you that those who swing pendulum
to any pits, half-filling and half-emptying are essentially the only
sane ones out there,

to resolve your question of how to spend the rest of your
night, but at least answer me this (something that Schneidermann
he once asked me after a matinee movie I forget, maybe a matinee
Homosexual Acceptance movie which have been so popular the last

three

three-five years):

why are homosexual people never poor? (you ever meet a homosexual homeless? he would ask, a lesbian maid?)

Schneidermann to me: I'm thinking about homosexuality as a way to increase my earning potential.

Schneidermann to me: if I become fully, actively gay then I'm sure to get into a good tax bracket — like why are they always well-fed, groomed and dressed? or is that just the movies and teevee?

just another stereotype (Schneidermann he had mine, PANASONIC, never plugged it in),

like yes, why do homosexual people, no, at least homo-sexual males, why do they always seem more free than I am? more happy and honest? natural? well-adjusted?

and don't dare give me the feminine, the effeminate argument as epitomized in so exemplary a fashion just now by the House Manager waving his manicured hands manic on the Second Tier as if he's last year's Miss America, the Pope, or on a train departing, pulling out now for the 19th century,

Leon, I love your hair! you wear that suit so well!

What do you want? you're doing what? I can't hear you nearly as well as I can myself.

Like listen, I first heard of him,

decided to speak this tonight instead of the two cadenzas previously written for this work,

Jesus! is my elbow shit tonight,

got my first break when Szigeti he got ill (oysters), when I substituted for him and at the last proverbial minute in the Beethoven *Concerto* with,

you who are leaving, getting up off your stubs and going to coat-check, engaged in the business of getting-out-of-here, I, I know that I'm wandering, making senselessness but wait! please, but a moment! langsam,

shtum,

psht: we all know how much you paid for this, for me (I get 10%), so why don't you remain seated and try to enjoy the show if you haven't already exodused, refugeed? and I don't know if I'd blame you if you did, because I did

(though IT,

what had happened it had to be worse than I am now),

because I myself got out, got away, de-Europeanized myself just in time and with my father but without my Schneidermann (who he should have been my father),

because Schneidermann he was as stubborn as a Jew, and without my mother because by then she was dead, as dead as a Jew, dead like my older ever younger sister in infancy, dead like a child of mine too (but that was later, and I, I don't want to talk about it),

dead like maybe, probably, Schneidermann is now, I don't know but I buried him,

dead like I'll be soon,

dead like this woman she isn't because I, I saved her life, because according to her though maybe not her husband I saved her life, because she claims my music (which really isn't mine), that it saved her life — this woman I'd like to share with you, actually just a letter from her, a mother, a wife, never mine, not all of them are, a letter here in a pocket of my pants, allow me to unfold it in my defense.

Where are my glasses?

It's from a woman I've never met, the letter — my present wife, which and whomever she is, has no grounds whatsoever for any of her accusations ever-prepared

and is her lawyer present?

probably intermissioning, out having drinks, scheduled probably for tomorrow a.m. for 18 holes with *mine*

and mine's mine when I'd like to put 18 holes in *her*!

links always pursuing links (roll up the sleeves)! and so suffice it to say that I received this letter just three days ago from my agent who, while he does not-much, does receive my mail. Did pass on this letter. Did accept my thanks for it. And of course takes his commission.

I'll leave off the salutation, spare you some odd personal details, possibly touching in all the parts you don't want to be touched in and so the crux,

originally from Latin's *cruciare*,

to torture at least according to Schneidermann it reads:

Following the loss of my managerial marketing position I went through

like

like the worst of depressions:

Pam — that's me! — did PAMELOR, PARNATE, PHENELZONE SULFATE, PROZAC,

SELECTIVE SEROTONIN REUPTAKE INHIBI-TORS,

and not eating at all except for toothpaste (COOL GEL, BREATHBOMB),

and chocomocha ice-cream, a half-gallon of rocky-road every now & then and so putting on weight, not sleeping at all despite doing handfuls of thinking serious about suicide and you,

your Beethoven Concerto, *which I caught in Los Angeles last week when my husband of one year he just decided to drag me there, in a mink over T-shirt and sweatpants,*

it might sound crazy but it made me want to live again, you did and for that, well, God bless you.

God! who writes letters anymore? who knows how to write? who reads anymore? who even knows how? has-the-time? especially when you're at the movies, which is the only place and time that Schneidermann he ever read and Schneidermann he read much, all, and not only but mostly in his later years at SPIELBERG movies,

indeed STEVEN SPIELBERG matinee movies they were the only times and places that Schneidermann in his last decades he could find enough quiet, internal, headspace quiet in and during which to do his reading, and always in the original:

Damaskios during the movie with that archaeologist in the hat,

Herodotus during the movie with that Jew Dreyfuss and the aliens,

indeed all the great *H*'s of Hellenism while he was at it: Herodotus and Hesiod and Hekataios and Hieronymus (and Hellanikos),

Herakleides (of Pontus), not to forget Herakleitos and Hermesianax

(the Alexandrian poet, a departure from such cosmogo-nists as I think Herondas during the trinity of movies about that

war in space and some undefined FORCE like God that it doesn't
make any sense),

Hesychios during the sequel to the movie about that war
in space and some undefined FORCE like Art that it doesn't make
any sense,

Hippolytos during the sequel to the sequel, or the prequel,
is it? to the movie about that war in space, among the stars and
some undefined FORCE like World that it at least didn't make any
sense to me and to Schneidermann, well, who ever knew? Homer
and Horace Schneidermann he also read at the matinee movies, the
Attic orator Hypereides and Hypnos who had him rhapsodic,
anything but riveted to the screen and no matter what empire was
striking and why,

no matter what dreck it was that might have been, that was
smeared all over it,

no matter what negligible dreams our eyes they might have
projected up,

indeed Schneidermann he did all his reading in the light of
the most SPIELBERGIAN of SPIELBERG's fire/explosion
scenes, his reading of all the *H*'s of Greek thought, philosophy, of
Hellenistic poetry and theology, theogony too and all in the light
of an actress — any actress, they're all the same after Hair &
Makeup, even the director's wife — who she couldn't tell you even
with a last-draft script wilting on her knees the difference between
Cosmology and Cosmetology,

the difference between Good and Evil,

between High and Low,

between the matinee movie music accompanying all their
90 minute ascensions and failures, their love affairs and their
kidnappings and our own Johann Sebastian Bach who — as
Schneidermann he reminded me after the NBC incident — signed
his own name into his final fugue and only a moment prior to
death or near enough for our cinematic purposes, signed his BACH
with a *B♭* and an *A* and a *C* and an *H* that among the Teutons it
stands for *B natural* as my one German once wife now ex she always
advised me immediately prior to any interviews or media appear-
ances that they didn't involve playing instead talking, junketing,
interviewage, but advised me in this language, with all the stale
humor a healthy sexlife would excuse but without an irony that's

lost

lost in translation and how I'd just laugh anyway as she'd sing me
the note, the *B natural*, sing it to me sinus-high, in her most perfect
pitch (she was, is a pianist, so not famous that she's never even
heard of herself, and despite my half-efforts)

and then I'd invariably and almost as happy punishment,
Schadenfreude if you know her I'd push her from the taupe hallway
into the hotel's nearest service stairwell to have my way with her,

what she, in her most earnest American slang with that
Köln roll, would call a *quickie* more like a *kvik-ee* — to have all the
ways I would with her to calm myself prior to descending to that
underworld of manicured-in-nicotine-journalists, reporters who do
the ARTS because they can't write straight copy and their eye-tired,
flash-mad photographers and how, and always just before I could
attain orgasm, she would stop, pull away, wrap herself in that
mauve woolen shawl you always,

and claim that she was too frightened of being caught,
Angst haben.

Women, because what are they worth? Men, because what
are they worth? Music, because what is it worth? and, more importantly with music, what exactly *is* the *it*?

Music, because what can you say with any certainty about
music except that, yes, it exists, indeed it is? Because you can't say
anything about music, about music as music, music qua music, the
old tapdancing about architecture routine you can't talk about
music, about music gratia music let's say, no, instead and of
infinitely greater worth you can only talk about the personalities
involved, yes, about those who have been touched by music, those
subservient to it, the people in and of music, the musicmakers and
in doing so hope, just hope, that music itself it comes through.

Because when you begin — and we all have — just begin
to talk about music you are in point of fact immediately talking
about musicians (even if you didn't want to, even if the personalities they don't interest you nearly as much as the art that it shaped
them and so was shaped by them),

and that such an unconscious let's say modulation or
transposition of intent it's always there, irrevocably so, unavoidably
present as much as it's understood, accepted without hesitation,
without thought one as to its why, its meaning, without an interro-
gation,

because this we know,

of its reasons,

like remembering Schneidermann when I should be playing
him,

like and but the answer is that the work and the man
they're all one, of-a-piece (and Schneidermann he would've agreed,
like all my ideas it was his first and always), that Schneidermann
is, was himself Schneidermann's own greatest composition. His
monument to our time. Yes, that's possible. Within the realm, the
real of the maybe.

Schneidermann, whose morality was just sympathy.

Schneidermann, whose sympathy was all pity.

Schneidermann, the utterly portable man: who had no
habits, required no maintenance,

he-of-no-plans,

who required only subsistence, the barest minimum of
contingencies (*Existenzminimum*, a word Schneidermann often said
Walter Gropius stole from him),

who had almost nothing whatsoever to do at all with any
conventions (musically and in-person),

especially not in any of his compositions, in any of his
enormous output, in any of his homogenous work-product, the
immaculate body that reached its highest if not most let's say
public perfection in this *Concerto* only now — and at its American
debut performance, its New York premiere and the first time this
version of it has ever been publicly presented in the whole entire
world! — only now to host what is undoubtedly the worst cadenza
of any career.

Yes, there have been others.

While this work is only now, and thus far partially and
poorly, performed, you should know that it was written through
the years 1939 to 1989, throughout the years 1939–1989, that
indeed it took 50 years of effort however distracted, effort however
intermittent, interrupted by war, detainment, imprisonment,
attempted genocide, immigration or was it exile? you know the
spiel and so the need to remember (feverishly), or rerember
(fevered), to rework, rescore the work and from memory again and
again all through loss, poverty, the geriatric toll I know all too well,
though Schneidermann he often bragged, claimed that the actual

composition

composition of it, the actual hunched-over-desk ink-and-paper composition of this composition, that it took him no longer than six total — if dispersed, however shattered — months in all those 50 years of what seemed like an eternity. And so though Schneidermann he finally decided to give me the manuscript that day at the Zoo at the monkeyhouse, the primate lager as Schneidermann he always said and only a few weeks prior to his disappearance at and from the matinee Holocaust movie, when Schneidermann he must have finally decided that the world it might be ready for this music and so for his disappearance (as they might mean the same thing),

    it wasn't as if this work, which is dedicated to me, was indeed also written for me, fit to my fingers, was an express dedication let's say, no, won't let my ego interfere with posterity — yes, there were others:

    Kohn was the first, a virtuoso violin consultant to Schneidermann, author of the first cadenza for this first and last *Concerto* in an earlier, more reserved as it was incomplete — as it might always be incomplete — version, Kohn a too-earnest, all-serious man, a would-be modernist Schneidermann he knew well from Conservatory days in Budapest who supplied Schneidermann not only with ample ampoules of over-pure morphine from his doctor-brother but also with a six-seven minute pyrotechnic travesty for the as-yet, always-yet unfinished work that Schneidermann he anyway had been publicizing to anyone who would listen since 1929 and that's at the latest,

    Kohn followed by one Raubitschek (later Roubíček), a didactic, academic violinist who he also fancied himself a composer if a dilettante who has maybe two-three volumes of etudes still listed in *Patel & Son's* (if just for the historicity of it all),

    Raubitschek also Kohn's rival both artistically and for the love of some salon-happy, heavy-lidded bourgeois heap of anemia who it wouldn't be worth it to mention her or here (a silent masturbator with gnawed nails, the daughter of a proofreader for a local Salonblatt),

    his Raubitschek's offering heavily derivative of Kohn's, though a dumbing-down, an explanation scholastic and dry, but if you ask me, which you haven't, I'd say that both cadenzas they're too sweet for anyone's sense of irony nowadays, lace and velveteen anachronisms that less imparted than wantonly displayed only either modernist, Kohn, or else sentimentalist, Raubitschek, ego, in doing so rendering no respect whatsoever for Schneidermann and/or Schneidermann's art, not at all,

and if you asked them — which you can't because they're dead, one of the heart and one of the War — the art itself it didn't matter as much as their claim on their! composer's talent did, indeed what mattered was only their cinnamon-schnapps, chessplaying friendships with the man, Schneidermann, whose talent they only had to suspect prior to that talent suspecting them.

They were his angels some days (loans), his devils on others (interest), who they had no idea, neither of them did, of their influence on Schneidermann, influence more like their anti-influence, their power to deter, their sway — they were his Shakespeare-companions, his Timon-buddies, false-comforters to his Job, they,

walking each other to the tram stop, arm-in-arm from the never-fashionable Kesten salon neither would quit without the other (that strain-of-anemia-with-a-vagina),

they were absolutely worthless except in the examples they set only to be denied, discredited, avoided at all costs (usury, they sent Pest's only sober Russian to collect),

they were Romantics on the concertstage and equally worthless Classicists in bed,

Apollonian in their conversation and Dionysian in their mirrors,

Romantics after just one glass of schnapps and me, I've got one of those love/hates with the two poles, Romantic and Classical, but not the Poles:

I hate them all except for a certain Jadwiga (Hedwig), who she lives at the end of the D Train, but that's almost the whole history of a world I only half remember — and I've recorded my own version of this, not this, twice, just last week and for a European label, a German recordlabel:

once privately just last Thursday for an insane, insanely rich Singaporean gentlemen who he's obsessed with quote unquote *modern music*

and once previous a month ago for a small European,

German

German label with terrible distribution, almost inextant, accompanied if you could call it that by some thrown-together-at-the-last-
possible-moment, overworked if underpaid orchestra of pan-Slavs
(and don't even ask as to the quality of the liner notes, the translation I had to perpetrate myself),

and both with my true cadenza (not this) — it's as yet
unpublished, but two students of mine, hacks, are polishing their
modern on it and for further information,

if you're interested,

to hear more about our product then, and please, consult
your local media conglomerate for impertinent details:

Kohn, who I once studied with him at the Music Academy
in Budapest before,

and who once when I was 10 I played his father's *1st, Last
& Only Sonata* for him at his funeral (his heart), was in point of
fact more than a Romantic, much more, indeed he was an Excessive:

an obese man who in later life devoted himself, his career
and even the careers of his weaker students, his reputation such as
it was, to the music of his father (János Kohn, 1860–1917, who
Schneidermann he said was once the most promising student to
emerge from the studio of that great if nonexistent composer
Arkady Kitsch)

and beyond, indeed devoted himself to gargantuan-
German-M Modernity or at least to what he thought was Modernity, because in sad truth Kohn he wasn't talented or was it disci-
plined enough to handle the Classics? faked the modern no one
knew what to expect because Kohn he couldn't be true to the tried
everyone already knew and loved,

but I shouldn't talk: because to be honest as a husband I
listen to no music, indeed I own no music not in paperform, not in
fingerform, not in headform and when I do lately, listen, it's been
to Felix Mendelssohn, Mendelssohn only and I can't explain why,
listen to him in my head, with what those who wouldn't know
better refer to as the *inner ear*,

hearing itself, reception right through the fuzz, gunk and
the wax though my agent — Adam, are you still here? — the
schmuck, he gifted me a stereo last X-mas but he calls it the *holiday
season*,

like now — a huge stereo that it looks like a mutant brain

or at least a cerebellum thrice-cancerous: a multifunction polymodular whatever Asianmade stereo that I never plugged in, instead I gave it away to Schneidermann and still in its box, cardboard and its glittered tongue of bow and Schneidermann he went and used it for a coffeetable (covered it with an EL-AL airlines blanket I stole for him, used it to seep the leak of his gunmetal teapot),

       which is not much more ridiculous than the present my son Noah he presented me with last Hanukah: a pair of Asian slippers that they also weigh you when you initially step into them, your weight displayed in digits, LED, across the scuff of the toes, my son a maven of technological, health-minded footwear — what's it going to be next year, Noah? With any luck I'll be dead.

       What else you got in your ark out in the suburbs? what bounty? what booty? Mister Rothstein of your multinational pharmaceutical and sportswear interests, what fruit basket/gift certificate largesse are you giving away for this X-mas holiday?

       the most wonderful time, of the year as it's said, as it's sung,

       O how I love X-mas in Exile!

       that's been my most amenable, receptive hall, Exile — excellent acoustics though perhaps it has too much capacity for reverb,

       and about capacity:

       where's the Fire Marshal when you need him? why are there suddenly so many law enforcers in our midst? who called? an entire squad, almost, in my sanctuary, and welcome!

       who tore their tickets? coat-check anyone?

       check your guns?

       what and not who exactly do you serve and protect?

       Not Schneidermann you didn't when last Purim his room it was broken into but thank God there was nothing to steal. Not Schneidermann you didn't when because for once he was dressed nicely for Passover (in an old defiled suit of mine), he was mugged and when the mugger he found out and much to his amazement that his sartorial-minded mugee he had no money on him he just went ahead and knuckled another tooth out. Not Schneidermann you didn't when you fined him a hundred and who knows how many more dollars I paid worth of money that Schneidermann he definitely didn't have for smoking half a cigarette, hand-rolled, he'd

bummed

bummed and politely as Schneidermann he told it off an — AIDS-riddled — prostitute on the job in the line at the Unemployment Office day-long,

and how when he complied with your request by putting it out, Schneidermann he just dropped it to the floor and stamped on it with his old shoes, ship-sized, under his new Italianate suitpants you went ahead, littering! and arrested him!

Schneidermann to me: the cops are after me.

Schneidermann to me: the cops are after me because I'm an artist.

Schneidermann to me: they only come after the transcendent ones.

Schneidermann to me: they want to silence me.

Schneidermann to me: they have silenced me.

Schneidermann to me: I can't compose anymore because that's just what the cops they want me to do.

Schneidermann to me: where and how do I apply to become a cop?

Schneidermann to me: if I was a cop, they'd give me new clothes.

Schneidermann to me: they'd even give me a car.

Schneidermann to me: sirens are the most effective instruments of musical truth yet engineered by modern urban society,

and it's thanks to him that and among my many other talents I can name them all, can identify all the sirens, all by ear, all these sirens shattering this winter:

last night, lying atop my bed under the canopy the height of 21st century ostentation,

second-millennium gaud,

melting icecubes on my chest and belly bared, on an endtable the shallow white roomservice plate

of melt wrung out, old water with my hair floating atop reddest-gray,

curls like sails,

naked to the waist, the huge natural sponge, an exwife's loofah I never travel without dripping pool down to my navel,

yes, I have a navel, I'm not a God — I keep it to remind me of my mother who,

sponge nested in the nude valley between my breasts,
dripping down to the bedspread, soaking my sheets out of stain,

hell should be as hot as my suite was! with everything
maxxed-out, except the enormous overhead fan fancy like a
constellation of plums,

a real fire in my fake fireplace you just have to flick the
switch like a dark nipple,

sex-high radiator gasping overtime,

mini-fridge whining a metropolitan melos in A minor or
thereabout as the shades they kept it all in when day rose over ice,
with the sirens slicing through, wailing!

and me not being able to help myself:

horns! honking! blare and bleat! horns in my day in
Europe tuned to a minor third now here in America retuned,
pitched higher, wider and more discordant, horns on this side of
the ocean tuned almost to a tritone! the interval of the devil!

and the sirens, too! yes, God the sirens! their blast! I just
couldn't help myself:

the police siren, a positive identification, the fire siren, yes,
the ambulance siren, well, the siren indicative of a heart-attack, the
siren indicative of cardiac-arrest, an infarct, the siren indicative of a
fatal shooting, the siren indicative of first-degree murder, second-
degree, the siren indicative of manslaughter, the siren indicative of a
passion murder (husband's murder of wife sounding different from
wife-of-husband), the siren indicative of a burning "accident",

the siren indicative of a chemical "incident",

the siren indicative of a car-crash,

of a five-car pileup on the George Washington Bridge,

of terrorist activity on the morning news,

the air-raid siren deep in my memory, the monthly tests
scaring the Kultur out of everyone and I knew them all,

even knew a man who he claimed his mother had either
slept or studied with Doppler back in his Prague days,

indeed I knew all my European Humanism assbackwards
as Schneidermann and I we'd heard once in a matinee movie and
repeated, repeated, repeated Schneidermann did who he loved the
matinee movies,

loved America as he loved to slum,

and so it's probably from that great pedophile Socrates

that

that I had this idea, the idea for this oration, the idea for this
address, the idea for this outburst or testimony, this this, last
night as I,

couldn't sleep, wouldn't sleep, anyway didn't and so was
up, awake and dulled, daze-ached just off the red-eye, in from L.A.
and God was I jet-lagged! mucous in my mouth I was passing the
evening naked, nude and reading aloud, idly, in first the nightstand
drawer's King James Bible and then in one of Schneidermann's old
leatherbound books I'd redeemed from his jacket pocket,

liberated from Evidence this account of that great
pederast's Socrates' final hours, Plato's report in his *Phaedon* which
was Schneidermann's favorite *Phaedon* after the *Phaedon* of Moses
Mendelssohn it must be remembered and (Schneidermann he often
considered composing a cantata about the Mendelssohns in three
parts, Moses and Felix the outer movements, the middle section of
Abraham Moses' son and Felix's father to be left silent, tacet if not
incomplete and),

all about Socrates' last attempts at speechifying, it describes and how when Plato who he wrote the thing in the third
person like God gave the Torah he says and so touchingly:

"I think, perhaps, that Plato was ill," in order to free
himself you would think from that discipline of psychology while
simultaneously — indeed, with this very line — inventing psychology that non-discipline,

in order to be free though not as free as his master
Socrates he was soon enough (Xanthippe's haw, the hem's lock),

and but I'm most definitely here, in good enough health
for my age-group as my doctors will vouch, and what's more is that
I have the nerve to serve as my own Plato, my own witness,

last night tanning to ripe melanoma under the lamps and
the sconces, infinite artificial suns to be snapped on and off with a
clap of the hand,

me not to be confused with Dionysus, me not to be
confused with Xenophanes who he was never to step over the
horizon,

the quivering string, the setting fingertip,

thinking, Xenophanes did at least according to Schneidermann, that there were many suns just passing over the horizon like
the infinite fingertips of infinite hands and so maybe we do have

the time allotted for me to massage your heads with my callous
calluses. Xenophanes the rhapsodist of Colophon, dimmed by the
Homeric verses, according to Schneidermann who would know he
denounced poets for giving Gods men's traits, anthropomorphizing
them if you will and so gave to the Greeks a single God, proposed
to them in the form of an eternal sphere:

    the earth's goatskin drum just blare, bleating tragedy,

    at triple-forte through the expanded percussion battery
that ends this work that will never end,

    that resolves this edifice that will never be resolved,

    and I'm a rhapsodist too, but with no new innovation, no
improved goods & services, just abusing trusts public and private
and all for what? for you? for your sakes?

    I'm your somehow father? guide? Virgil? lover? More like
you're all my orphans and I, ladies and gentlemen, I'm just a liar
with a lyre thrumming away, a Nero or near enough

    to say that it's not all about the imagination and the
received, the free and the strict, the ear and the serial or now
whatever they've managed to mask the serial as, that it's not Apollo
on one hand and Dionysus on the other — Apollo the bow,
Dionysus the fiddle — no, anything but:

    it's Orpheus, Apollo and Dionysus are Orpheus, abso-
lutely, Orpheus from the toes to the head disembodied, singing
still as it floats down maybe the Hudson.

    And Jesus was an Orpheus, yes, his music the sermon
mounting, and King David son of Jesse too, harpist of the *Tehillim*

    you Reformed Jews in the midst of the encampment
would refer to as the *Psalms,*

    yes, he was also modeled on Orpheus, as was that most
pagan Paganini, his legend that's also the Faust legend that it was
stolen off Orpheus, the cult of all virtuosi in essence the cult of
Orpheus, a sect of priests and prophets and not just a few dead
white men.

    Priests and not a God, me and not Schneidermann.

    Schneidermann, the last of the great unphonies and
euphonies.

    Schneidermann, the last of the great composers.

    Pythagoras to Schneidermann. Schneidermann to
Pythagoras. Pythagormann. Schneidoras the last of the great.

Schneidermann

Schneidermann the last,

     me, who deserves only to be torn apart — *sparagmos* I think it is in Greek, or maybe *omophagia*, Schneidermann he would have known — rend, ritually, this victim or maybe I'm to be melon-scooped out by the women in my life?

     murdered by them as Orpheus he was in one account — I forget which, this Schneidermann he knew as he knew all — with the implements of domesticity, like the hollow rollingpin you fill with water for weight, the pitiless Oriental knife that a friend of which exwife she once sold in kitchen demos and door-to-door?

     and, you know, I've read that this very same Plato he hints at a cult of wandering priests who they took money to relieve laymen from neurotic guilt (check your ticket stubs),

     that these were the Orphic priests, and so please feel free to think of this as an initiation into manifold secrets,

     a schmeck of the Mysticism Schneidermann he would think (Schneidermann just like Hölderlin they were almost pathologically against anything that anyone else they were for),

     and all that metaphysical Schwärmerei Schneidermann he would say once you'd embraced it,

     of last Reich Schneidermann he would insist above all and all its Theosophism that destroyed all of Europe and Art or at least — or so Schneidermann he'd insist and lament — the option of taking it all to heart, in-all-seriousness, as a life.

     But, as Schneidermann he'd always say, that's just the movies talking.

     Because — with Schneidermann gone and possibly, probably dead — we have to think this is ritual, must insist, not a whole society's madness, not the setting of the West with our flight-of-fancy too misguided to even approach too near to the sun.

     Because given our loss this must be necessary, not some gross mistake (like marriage, children, being born and).

     Because within this hall, within this violin, within me is the secret of

     the stuff of transcendence,

     of,

     excuses they say and I say reasons,

     Stuff happens Adam my agent says,

     No accounting for taste say my recordlabel execs,

Time marches on and I say ensuring that the next generation they don't drool a next Flood on the planet,

Original Sin it's written but I prophesize in retrograde a sense of loss from the very first that many of my landsmen, my dead or dying without-a-countrymen explained much better than I could ever hope to (Schneidermann he'd always recommended the cultivation of a negative canon),

and so I see that now you're listening! but I'm no Isaiah, no Jeremiah, this isn't Ezekiel 14:1-11 (Schneidermann's favorite to set), this isn't an apology, or at least not yet,

not to you, not to Schneidermann who — and from among the living I'm not naming names unto any commission (as did your father, Mister Rothstein, who he ruined the Party, Spring 1950),

because as the ancient Egyptians believed naming is owning, according to Schneidermann is possession, is 10/10ths of all divine Law and,

anyway, it's better to have every name, whatever people, the press syndicate, your wives ex and present, your children they all want to call you: Polyonymous, schmuck as I'm going to tell you what you can and what you can't do,

because someone has to but first let us welcome this new influx of police, S.W.A.T., this army of lusty young men on-leave from private, livingroom wars: overreact and it's fine with me, to welcome the Chief of Police of this fine urbis and the President of this wonderful hall now coming down the center aisle and in lockstep as if for binding consecration at my hands — but I'm the one to be bound, no?

Good evening, gentlemen, no irony in that, no — from me? Perhaps you know the work, Chief, of that great Hellenist Ulrich von Wilamowitz-Möllendorf, no? but you should.

Because Orphism was not a religion, the Orphica not a worship, Orphism not a theology but an art, understand? Because at bottom religion is art is philosophy is

WHATEVER SATISFIES, maybe, like the slogan on the candybar I like to eat, like the candybar I like to eat but shouldn't, like the candybar I'd then share with Schneidermann at the movies (nougat the only offering worthy of SPIELBERG, nuts and caramel for anyone else),

WHATEVER

WHATEVER SATISFIES the slogan on the candybar I'd
buy for us at the matinee movies but Schneidermann he'd just
unwrap ahead and eat the whole thing,

and the JOHNNIE WALKER RED LABEL WHISKY I'd
bring for the COCA-COLA CLASSIC I'd buy, for him, and the
popcorn larded with something passing for butter (ejaculate,
Schneidermann he always suspected)

on top of which was always propped in seep the book that
Schneidermann he would at least try to read throughout the
matinee movie — certainly, Mister Rothstein are you listening?
certainly a symbol of our times:

a man who reads in a movie theater, a man who reads a
burning book in a movie theater on fire — or maybe a better
symbol it would be that guy who he found a creditcard on the
street and who tried to use it but it was cancelled and so who
ripped it jagged in half so that it had a sharp point and with this
primitive weapon stabbed a shopclerk in the throat, shived her,
killing her to steal whatever he would? it was a shoestore in
Queens I think it was, yes, that guy I read about in yesterday's
paper will do, would serve to represent our world, our here and now
or maybe an AIDS-conscious rapper, who knows?

or that actress who she makes this season's — high —
living off doing topless work only in artistic B & W pictures?

or the black judge in all the climactic scenes in courtroom
dramas because all judges in all movies nowadays they have to be
black, African-American, Conga-Tongan-Franco-British-Hispano-
American just like I'm an American-German-Hungarian-
Ruthenian-Ukrainian-Jew and how far back — to the Philistines?
Phoenicians? Paphlagonians? — do you want to go in our *relationship*?

being something of a connoisseur, me and Schneidermann
too, though connoisseurs weren't the only things European we were
(Schneidermann he was once also a répétiteur at the Hungarian
State Opera in Budapest, but that's another life, a whole opera's
worth of not worth going into it),

as I was trying to establish the credentials for our connois-
seur-ships, our cinema-connoisseur-ships, to tell you all how
Schneidermann and I we knew all the ins and outs, the loopholes
and plot devices, relationship formulae, the ropes and the tropes,

all the gestures to our attention deficit, how Schneidermann and I
we knew all the disorders so well that they MORPHED I think is
the word into our order,

how we'd spoil for ourselves as much as for each other all
the endings, surprises and twists, the whodunits and those mul-
tiple-personality matinee movies in which the bad guy and the
good guy they and only at the very end turn out to be the same
guy,

then roll the CREDITS,

how Schneidermann and I we and with sacred if fallen
irony knew all the lines, could indeed hold whole conversations —
and often did, with sarcasm of the most extreme strain — using
only dialogue from movies, from the same movie, from many
different movies:

like Schneidermann and I we'd sing to one another (in
worthless voices), as if we were doing Musicals, would walk, pose
and talk, walk, pose and talk like in those DeMille Biblical epics
just like in those operas that they used to do out in Bayreuth,
Schneidermann and I we knew all the pickups and turndowns,

every line of entertainment of everyone's rained-on or
rained-out late Sunday afternoon known as life,

knew all the zingers from a life of an audition for what
exactly? death? knew all that Schneidermann and I being geniuses
we never had to rehearse,

scenes that became altered only when our screen memories
faded,

or when our failures they became memorized,

when old lines they became new from ever newer younger
mouths or newest lines they preempted our own old expressions of
what? love, lust, grief, yes, Schneidermann and I we knew it all and
we knew it: what dress she wore, what he said to her when she wore
it or took it off, and so on and so forth — how Schneidermann
and I we knew all the movietheaters as well, intimately as we knew
all the ticket-takers and usherettes worth a leer or a pinch (at least
I did), how Schneidermann and I we knew all the screens in all the
movietheaters, too: Schneidermann he often said that he knew the
squeak of each seat in each screen so well, that if he would have
heard someone (but who besides us? Schneidermann he asked as if
I could join his company in delusion) sit and squeak, Schneider-

mann according to Schneidermann he would have been able and
immediately to name the row and also the seat number,

unconsciously and possibly even Schneidermann, or so
he'd maintained, he'd know to a moment, at least to a showtime
the last time the last person he or she ever sat in that seat in that
row (though Schneidermann he knew that he'd never know that
person, not that that mattered) — how Schneidermann and I we
knew all the movies so well it's as if we'd lived them because that's
pretty much all our life consisted of, besides music.

Because we would attend up to one matinee movie per day
to take our minds off, because it was and for nearly 50 years off
and on when I was in town a ritual, and we didn't need a telephone
to fix the time as if time it could be fixed and how? but at 3 p.m.,
or around 3 p.m., or within 3 p.m.:

the dying hour,

the canonical hour of failure,

the-day-giving-way-to-winding-things-up-hour — mati-
nee-time and so at the reduced senior with presentation of AARP
card admission until 4 p.m., us meeting out in front of the
boxoffice in front of the theater (and I always paid), our almost-
sometimes-daily embarrassing assignation and don't think that we
didn't wallow in it, the-sin-of-it-all, relish the sense of slumming
in these so many theaters in the greatest metropolitan area and how
Schneidermann and I we'd settle on the one for the day, well, we
wouldn't: call it thought-transmission if you like, call it mind-
reading if you want, extrasensory whatever, intuition, geomancy,
geloscopy if you will but the truth is is that we would both
individually get the schedules from a certain newspaper you all,
should, read, and that we'd both, individually, red-circle the
matinee movies we intended, again, individually, to attend, probably
on his part as much as it was on mine in order from

1.) what we wouldn't mind seeing down to

2.) okay, something to pass life and we'd both — individually because at least Schneidermann he was an individual —
show up in time wherever it was at whatever theater to loiter there
in front of the boxoffice, me always with the fifth of whiskey and
two tickets and Schneidermann always with nothing and none to
act as surprised as it humored us to meet each other just idling
streetside or in the lobby,

sometimes.

Like didn't expect to see you here. Like just imagine that.

But to my point. Get to my point. Mustn't lose ear of the point,

which is that the last and final time that I and Schneidermann we individually decided to get together it was at the movies as usual, at a matinee as usual, not that I saw him or that Schneidermann he saw me up on the screen, God forbid! but that we saw each other first in the lobby by the boxoffice and then proceeded, in a silence art-inspired, to theater 7 to sit in Row S Seat 17 and 19 always, to sit a seat apart, a seat, #18, away from one another in the middle, interjacent, our jackets stinking jizzum-infused rain in the middle, the mezzo termine this seat number 18 separating us seasonally occupied by my faux-ermine atop his vomitous schmatte, us seated a sprung spring apart as was our custom, our habit, as was our ritual, tradition and to see this matinee movie, to audience this one last matinee movie, this final film of the maybe five-six thousand that Schneidermann and I we had attended and together over the last half-century and in the course of the thing, in the suspended middle, in the reeling mesial what did he do?

Schneidermann he just got himself up, struggled tush-first, dodderteetering as much from old age as from the OLD GRANDAD whiskey Schneidermann he'd consumed through the row stepping shoes and cerebrum-shaped popcorn to the aisle and out.

Never to return. Ever. About one hour and a few minutes in. 18. Around 4 p.m. as my Statement it should reflect Schneidermann he went, I'd assumed, as I told the police against all advice I'd unsolicited, to take a piss (Schneidermann he had a war going on in his urinary tract, often he just relieved himself into his half-full sodacup I then had to remind him not to drink from, pinch his loop-de-loop straw, take-it-away),

or to the lobby to Jew-around as he always said for a free and yet another refill of stale,

popcorn like whitehead tumors,

or a soda refill,

without gas as Schneidermann like all Jews he hated gas and so just medicinal goo, as syrupy as dark and as dry as a Tokaj wine Schneidermann he always said (Schneidermann he was a

longstanding

longstanding concessions customer, on my dime),

and as Schneidermann he left he left too this book behind: his favorite (second-favorite),

most precious (second-most-precious),

anyway treasured book behind, left in one of his jacket's pockets Schneidermann he also left his jacket behind and so its pockets in one of which he'd left me a Plato's *Phaedon* in the original I have trouble with and always will,

never to return,

ever, absolutely disappeared, pulled a vanishing act and gone, poof! no one or just I never saw or heard from or about him since or again, his room — if you could call it a room, more like the squared torso of a straitjacket — left as it was, as disarrayed, wrecked, as pretossed by the unidentified Intelligence Agencies as ever (Schneidermann he often after matinee Thriller movies maintained that the NSA it was actively recruiting pianists who they didn't want to eliminate, those who didn't as he always said stick-with-the-program),

and don't think I wasn't taken Downtown, actually cross-town for questioning because I wasn't. Against the how-intentioned advice of my lawyers and theirs, my wives ex and present, my sons and even my lawyer-son, my agent and my trusted lobby-bartender at the Grand I went and by myself on my own accord, for my own accord — but you know what you gentlemen, what you cops out there in audienceland, what you didn't ask? failed to ascertain? never did want to know?

you never wanted to know what movie it was that Schneidermann and I we were watching, what goddamned waste of a matinee movie it was that Schneidermann and I we were in the middle, that we were near the middle of — it's a long flick, actually endless — when Schneidermann he might've decided that he'd had enough, when Schneidermann he anyway decided to exit the illumination.

Incredible. Unbelievable. An oversight, I'm sure. A regret-table stupidity. A mistake not to ask and even off-the-record to protect our aesthetics and any innocence that my reputation might still have left to its name what dead winter afternoon's entertain-ment — on pain medication as I always am, dead to the quicksil-ver-screen, numbed — what dead winter afternoon's deadest, most wintry entertainment it was that it began at 3 p.m. on a weekday I forget which now but it's all in the Report that the Detective he took earlier this month, in earlier December, 2002, maybe the fourth or was it the fifth night of Hanukah? maybe a Thursday, a Wednesday:

anyway the most regrettable, most embarrassingly stupid, wasteful day of the week for matinee movies — almost three weeks ago it was now, yes, at a movietheater named after that avid theatergoer our President Abraham Lincoln, up on West 68th Street it's a Loew's of the Loew dynasty, the Löw franchise anglicized as Americanized as everything is now and without an umlaut,

and which ended for Schneidermann early when he exited an hour and 18 minutes in almost three weeks ago it is now and still you don't know, will never know whether or not I'm making all this up,

just improvising,

inventing,

interpreting,

imposing-my-will but the movie it was a movie about the Holocaust, yes it was a Holocaust movie,

and but for those of you who live in either potholes or ghettos, a Holocaust movie is a movie that addresses or attempts to address the genocide or the attempted genocide of European Jewry.

It was gray. Black & white fought. Jews died. I ate mints. My left leg it fell asleep.

It, the matinee movie, was a one month rerelease of a movie from a decade earlier, 1992 I think it was, a 10th-anniversary rerelease of a film which it won a golden idol named OSCAR for BEST PICTURE the following year (1993, I believe it was the 66th Academy Awards hosted by that African-American who she thinks she's a Jew named Whoopi I think but I always confuse her with Oprah), along with six other golden drone awards for almost everything else,

besting that movie that it was about a piano, titled THE PIANO that Schneidermann and I we saw and we hated because that bitch who she starred in THE PIANO and who she also played the eponymous piano she was terrible, according to Schnei-

Schneidermann

dermann she was hopeless, had neither ear nor technique.

Anyway, the matinee Holocaust movie that won and won huge it was a movie by a man with a beard.

Also, sometimes he wears a hat above the beard.

It was a movie by a man who he dreams so well that we all don't have to as Schneidermann he often said and was jealous,

a movie by my disappeared friend's favorite director, you might know him as SPIELBERG.

It was a movie about the Jews and the Nazis and about what the Nazis they did to the Jews, a movie about one man who was a Nazi who he made a difference as all men they make a difference in one way or another, a Nazi who he saved his own soul which as the Talmud and this movie remind us is as if he had saved an entire world — the saying the matinee Holocaust movie usurps in its titles it's actually from Sanhedrin 37A if you're interested, as my daughter the female rabbi she told me last week, in its Mishnah to be precise it actually says whosoever saves a soul of Israel and so on and so forth but that's not for audiences of the family-of-man, as Schneidermann he would say it's not something the whole family would likely enjoy.

Believe it, it was SCHINDLER'S LIST:

a matinee Holocaust movie about a man named Schindler (or Szyndler),

and his list — music by that great 19th century composer Williams, fiddle solos by my friend, that paraplegic polio prodigy Maestro Itzhak Perlman, ladies and gentlemen:

sound as huge, sweaty, gout-swollen as he is, and the music it's not even the worst of it.

Listen: I'm not going to get into the debate is it documentary — or docudrama, whatever that is? — or is it entertainment? TRUE or FALSE or is it merely Fiction as Spinoza's distinctions in the matter go? value of depicting the Holocaust by one who hasn't suffered in it, from it, of it, firsthand, for those like myself, and unlike Schneidermann, who we never experienced the terror so that all together we might approximate, inevitably misrepresent, and then share the horror up on the screen, the horror of

what happened, of

what had happened — no, I'm certainly not going to revive all those meaningless and so ageless controversies, and why? am

I afraid?

 because they're worthless, because it was a movie, because
it was as bad and it was as good as all movies are, because all
movies and especially all matinee movies they're aesthetically equal
in God's eyes, at least in mine — this movie it just occupied,
destroyed, over seven hours of my life:

 the movie's running-time plus train-time to the theater
and after the show another three hours in the New York rain
disappearing into Polish snow searching for disappeared Schneidermann Uptown and Down,

 questioning the ushers, management, ticketgirl

 and out the theater and around the block again and again
but what part did Schneidermann he leave at you ask and you
didn't?

 the scene with that lost wandering red-jacketed girl?

 the scene when Untersturmführer Amon Goeth he just up
and starts shooting people from the terrace of his house out in
Płaszów?

 the scene set on that gorgeous spring day in 1943 with the
ghetto liquidation and one SS soldier he's playing a Jew's piano
and another SS soldier he peeks his helmeted snout into the
doorway and asks, like the — scripted — idiot he is:

 Das ist Mozart?

 Nein. Bach was the answer, to be specific the *English Suite
#2 in A Minor*,

 but it was nothing that dramatic, nothing as huge in
implication as that:

 it was some intimate scene with I think he's an Irishman
and that limey skinhead Ben Kingsley doing his best Gandhi in
typing up the list, that's when he left.

 Hudes, Isak the LIST listed,

 Feber, Ludwig the LIST listed and Schneidermann he left,

 like why did Schneidermann have to view this? He had to
live it. He had to survive it to live it. But a couple in the back —
no, not heavy-petting — the only other audience there, they didn't
live it and so its incarnation up on the screen it was horrifying,

 and but don't hope for edification, no, I won't enable even
my own pain:

 Schneidermann he wasn't in tears, no, Schneidermann he

wasn't

wasn't even emotional — the fact was was that Schneidermann he
got up and left, the fact was was that we were the only two people
in the theater,

  matinee-junkies,

  the two witnesses required by the Talmud for the successful prosecution of an offender (but one had left, and SPIELBERG
he lives out in L.A.),

  the truth is is that the couple in the back, that they were
created by me to create a reaction, an Other: we always need an
audience.

  Schneidermann and I we went to it, the last matinee movie
we, individually, attended and together toward the end of its 10th
anniversary run, when it was brought back to selected theaters I
don't know how exactly they select them but,

  to celebrate its 10 years as a movie, its 10 years of
movieness, of movietude, its 10 years as a work of art, as an
OSCARWINNER,

  OSCAR, same name as Schindler by the way, just different
spelling, is copyrighted, trademarked, whatever — nine years after
it had won and won huge, swept everything, or almost everything I
think, even won for MUSIC I think or I'd like to think because it
would serve the purposes of my argument, would establish mediocrity as the standard,

  establish dreck, shit as not only expected of us but even
awardworthy,

  and indeed this might have been what killed Schneidermann, if in point of fact he's dead: the 10-year virus of this music,
indeed of all matinee movie music, which Schneidermann he
thought ridiculous, all equally ridiculous, (obviously) infinitely
worse than his own eager earnest and yet still genius attempts,
efforts which they indeed were, efforts which Schneidermann he
undertook in his inkstain of a room and from his inkstain of a
memory, all alone — composing if not just recomposing the music
to a matinee movie that Schneidermann he, we, had seen, just
screened earlier that afternoon, O God how he did this all the
time! having scored or rescored whether on paper (dairy product
packaging, one dollar bills, porno magazine subscription post-
cards)

  or in his own head in the endless end probably hundreds

upon hundreds of matinee movies and so maybe Schneidermann he actually left this movie, this last matinee movie, to go (but where?)

and work out an idea it had, and so urgently, suggested, an idea inspired by or in reaction to its original music (but what?)

and how Schneidermann he would every time we left a matinee Whatever movie immediately disregard my admittedly oftentimes deranged, hypercritical, censorious pronouncements on the plot, dialogue, acting, sets and so on and so forth, and instead — he would — just begin discussing, rather discoursing on the matinee movie's music and almost always only on the matinee movie's music, dissecting it, humming it, singing it in his terrible voice (his diaphragm it seemed somehow to have been transplanted to mediate between his nasal columella),

demonstrating how he'd reharmonize specific if unworthy passages on a piano keyboard suspended in the Midtown air always a step ahead of his limp,

and God in heaven! how Schneidermann he's not around anymore to do it the same, not there afterward at around 6 p.m. when the matinee movie it let out to rework to my amazement the music of and for this last matinee movie, the last matinee movie I also attended and the last movie matinee or not I ever plan to attend (I'll stay in and order-out, I'm millennial now),

and so it falls to me, O God now it's my responsibility to deal with this music, with this American Williams' music for this the most Jewish movie of SPIELBERG's (who Schneidermann he always referred to as SHTEVEN SHPIELBERG),

this music for SCHINDLER'S LIST,

it's my lot now, it's now my responsibility, to explicate, to parse, interpret,

though don't expect anything Schenkerian (Heinrich Schenker, Schneidermann he said that he once stole a pen off him, from his reserved table at Berlin's Café Canard),

no, I won't play it, I'll just talk it, analyze it, subject it to fair & balanced critique

as they say, well-reasoned assessment — like in the movie, we have these let's say GHOSTED, LIMNED violin figures, figurations, these schmaltzy overextended lines, a technical term:

SOL like the name of my tailor whom I also tried explain-

explaining

ing all this to,

 that in the real, this is post-War and post-Socialist Poland
trying to integrate into the West they were shooting the movie in
and that in the movie,

 this is Wartime Europe: musicwise, Webern's soon to be
shot dead by some American G.I. way the hell out in provincial
Mittersill, von Webern to you while Schönberg his teacher he's
playing tennis out in Beverly Hills, in Californ I-A with Stravinsky
playing on a tenniscourt purpose-built into what was then the
world's largest martini glass outside the Poconos, Alban Berg —
third member of the Viennese trinity — well, he's already dead,
Mahler, their spiritual father, already long dead in that grave
Schönberg he LIMNED (history-speak,

 critical-cant),

ADUMBRATED so well in that painting of his,

 yes, he painted too, the man he served as many masters as
himself — Mahler's grave a deep timehole, a Zeitloch of Celan's
falling us back to a rainy day in the German world, 1911, with
Alma (maiden-named Schindler, no relation) probably fellating the
second-string priest behind a headstone as all the students they
mourned (students mourn the most), with Schönberg still owing
Mahler money and did anyone even wear a yarmulke to the funeral?
say a Kaddish? which leaves Alma Mahler née Schindler his wife
who she's still sleeping with anything that walks and calls itself an
artist free to forsake the discomforts of National Socialism,
emigrate to Los Angeles and but

 like listen, it's simple:

 Schönberg, the Holocaust music for this Holocaust
movie, Webern, the music for SCHINDLER, Berg, the music for
SCHINDLER, Mahler, the music for SCHINDLER, Stravinsky,
the music for SCHINDLER — and this is fair because they're all
playing off the same score, because they're all dealing with the
same material, because and it's too funny not to be.

 Like listen, it's simple:

 Webern and the music for the movie with the alien who it
looks like a penis,

 Stravinsky and the music for the movie with that Tyranno-
saurus Rex who even though it's ferocious its little arms still make
it look like a homosexual,

Mahler and the music for the movie with the shark in it
that you never get a good look at it because it's always underwater,

like *Da da, Da da, Da da* do you get it? the shark's ap-
proaching schmuck! Schneidermann he screamed when we first
screened,

but there's nothing a quick cut can't solve, fall fate to a
previous frame, the editing floor in a film that'll never be made
(unless you're interested in financing, Mister Rothstein),

a film of Schneidermann's life, in fact just title the thing
SCHNEIDERMANN'S LIFE, we'll do a treatment and I'll try to
nail SPIELBERG down — the last hour and 18 minutes of which
film has to include the first 78 minutes of the last film that
Schneidermann he ever saw, so if Mister Rothstein out there you'll
be so generous as to lay out the money for the rights all we have to
do is begin the PR campaign,

all we have to do is fluff the casting couch and allow
ourselves to be seduced by talent:

and so, because the music it's almost unknowable (and it
might have been composed that way), then what about the man?

a hedgehog in foxfurs to Babel his enemies Schneidermann
he wanted to be but lacked the funding,

a Trojan Man in America not like those ads that they sell
high-grade prophylactics Schneidermann he'd add,

Schneidermann, as difficult to place as Zeus: was He both
Chtonios and Olympios? who He changed names like Schneider-
mann he changed shirtcollars? and changed names too: first
Schneidermann, and then later, over here in the underheated
Schneidermann he always said *flat*

that I have to sort out one of these lifetimes, *Schneiderman*
at least that's how most of the police they spelled it: two *n*'s to one
n on the Missing-Persons Report and so which one was it or two?
and once even on a concertprogram in Vienna three *n*'s,

a typo that Schneidermann he rectified himself in a speech
to the audience (two-plus hours long), and then what? did the
letters, the naming, make him any less of a mann or a man?

Capricious as Mozart Schneidermann was, a composer he
loathed because everyone loves, at least loved him, Jesus! even
musical idiots they know him — Mozart, a composer Schneidermann thought an inferior imitation of God. But you have to

forgive

forgive a friend his idiosyncrasies, don't you? especially a friend who was raised, after his father died young at heart and his mother in labor, by his nine musical aunts.

Women who were his real instructors I told the police that Schneidermann, he had Beethoven's hair. In my description perhaps too-detailed and so worthless-to-any-authority, I stated that Schneidermann, he had Sinai's nose. Schneidermann, he had Asia's eyes as I told the sketch-artist (all two billion of them, the eyes, none of which saw or would see anything coming). Schneidermann, he had Mozart's glands (ears). Schneidermann, he had America's lips, but — and in a paradox we must expect — they really truly did have every intention of speaking the truth,

just as I did when I told the Detective that Schneider- mann, he was once mistaken for the Turkish Ambassador (though I don't know that the badge he believed me), that Schneidermann, he was once mistaken for a John soliciting a prostitute for directions to a new multiplex off 10th Avenue and that Schneidermann, he was never mistaken,

had them put into their Report all about Schneidermann's tooth and Schneidermann's ear,

went home which nowadays and with the wife-situation what it is is my hotel, this was Thursday I believe, or Friday, anyway the next day at around 3 p.m., it was 4 that I sat myself down on the sagging leather thongs of the luggagerack and thought, just tried to remember everything that had escaped me down at the fog-laden Precinct:

all about Schneidermann's pockets and Schneidermann's pockets' holes I always teased him about.

About that which fell out of Schneidermann's pockets' holes. About those who found that which fell out of Schneidermann's pockets' holes. About those who loved those who found that which fell out of Schneidermann's pockets' holes:

like a cola-eroded tooth,

a clip-on tie burgundy-ugly with blue corporate stripes, a clip-on abaloneous earring,

a postcard print of Man Ray's 1924 *Le Violin d'Ingres*,

a transvestite/transsexual named Ingres' newspaper ad scissored-out (*erotic role-play, no limits*),

a novelty watch, stopped, dead, casing cracked, second and

minute hands missing,

a $10 casino rebate voucher on a bus ticket down to Atlantic City on Greyhound from Port Authority Gate 70something,

a bus schedule of shuttles, piss-aisled from Port Authority down the parkway to the casinos in Atlantic City (gambling, Schneidermann he always said it was the closest *human* approximation of artistic creation said Schneidermann who he loved to gamble on money other than his own),

actually, I have all his lists in my pockets now,
somewhere,
here,

WHAT	WEIGHT	HOW
tomatoes	2	———— .99
cheese	pack	———— 1.75
bread	loaf (day-old)	———— .99
cigarettes	pack	———— too much
generic coca-cola	2 liters	———— .79
whiskey	enough	———— forget it
paper	ream	———— 7.99
ink	57 ml.	———— 6.99
pornography	110 pages	———— 5.99

a grocery list, for the week — forgot to tell them the police that Schneidermann he often spelled his name, in private autographs, in autographs to me that he often paid for his lunch with Schneidermann he more often than not spelled it

$chneidermann the *S* replaced with a dollar-sign (which Schneidermann he always said *thaler*, the West's earliest mint out in Joachimsthal where),

NEW YORK	NY	————	12:00a
ATL CITY CAS NJ		———— 02:31a	
NEW YORK	NY	————	01:00a
ATL CITY CAS NJ		———— 03:31a	
NEW YORK	NY	————	02:00a
ATL CITY CAS NJ		———— 04:31a	

NEW

NEW YORK	NY	————————	03:00a
ATL CITY CAS NJ		——————— 05:31a	
NEW YORK	NY	———————	04:00a
ATL CITY CAS NJ		——————— 06:31a	
NEW YORK	NY	———————	05:00a
ATL CITY CAS NJ		——————— 07:31a	
NEW YORK	NY	———————	06:00a, and so

on and so forth,

     or,
     and,
like a shard shattered sliver of an old LP record (someone
and the Imperials slicing a pocket's lining),
     Johnny Walker and the Imperials,
     Lil' Jimmy & the Beamers slicing his pockets' linings in a
tallis-looking jacket that Schneidermann he found in the trashalley abutting his building and redeemed though without washing,
a jacket in which he had actually exactly five pockets, in one of
which he kept a scissored-out list from a national magazine —
stolen off my Grand toilet — listing the names and teenages of 68
known proven suicides,
     68 teenagers who they imitated a rock idol to his very end:
a shotgun blast to the temple on a three times lethal dose of —
over-pure — heroin, and some are still trying to prove it was a
murder and maybe it was, and if so then what does it matter at all?
because the initial cause — Schneidermann he'd always tell me,
Schneidermann he'd always insist — because the initial cause,
Schneidermann he'd always say touching engrayed tongue to nose,
is not as important, not as practically important as the effects
initialed,
     because God is not as important as your fellow man and
because — to further flesh out his idea as skeletal as he was —
history is not as important as the present it has destroyed:
     that the 1st movement of this past 20th century is
unlistenable as it is unplayable, that the 1st movement of this past
20th century shouldn't even be acknowledged by its composer as
part of any corpus and we all know who that is, its Composer, that
artificer, that pseudo-artist whose skill or lack of skill, whose
talent or lack of talent depending on whose side you were on axis

or allied it culminated in that enormous, technically terrifying or
just terrifically inept, mid-century Cadenza of History,

that improvised history, that went-with-the-flow record
that almost but not quite set me against all Romanticism, my
beloved Romanticism — because you need to understand that
when the world it's Romantic, the art is Classical and vice-versa,
and that they each think themselves the other, read your Nietzsche
with sunglasses that aren't your prescription but Schneidermann's:

who though he and desperately needed specs Schneidermann he never owned nor wore them except, once the mirrored
wraparounds they were forsaken, when Schneidermann he wore a
drugstore magnification pair at the matinee movies during the last
year or two,

Schneidermann whose memory it was great because his
eyesight it was terrible, Schneidermann who he remembered or at
least said he did all the antecedents, the precursors and yet saw
nothing coming, blind to the black & white,

deaf too if you can believe it, but selectively deaf, which we
musicians we have to be to the tattoo on the drums,

the march into Märchen,

unaware or just stupefied I believe by all these clumsy
crazy orchestrations, entr'actes, intermezzi and overtures, by
history *in an improvised style*:

one egoist just soloing on the instrument of humanity,

or sawing away? like a magician?

one soloist hogging all the attention, high above the rest
and playing with all of us in an improvisatory style, and not just
that: but *really improvising*,

inventing,

on-the-spot playing and with all the tropes: round up,
deportation, selektion, invasion, occupation, mass-death and so on
and so forth deep into Poland,

one full-of-himself man improvising forever long, playing
with history with insufferable panache, with incredible, enviable
technical apparatus, virtuosity even unto an overload, a superabun-
dance of brilliance, which is disaster — because don't you feel, not
you, don't answer, that some periods, eras, are just made up on the
spot? extemporized and that you're the material being used, bent,
twisted? we, me and Schneidermann, being high notes in Hitler's,

in one European's Cadenza of History, in the world's
Concerto the reckless upper spectra of the uppermost tessitura —
though Schneidermann he went through the camps, went through
all the camps, camp after camp after camp after camp and I, I went
through Amsterdam and then London, ultimately went through
nothing,

      while Schneidermann he descended into nine-and-a-half
hells accompanied not even by slide trumpets or valve trombones
(B♭ minor) but only by his brassy then-wife and then-daughters, I
descended and with only my dying father — who he shouldn't even
have been my father — into this world we know of as America, yes,
how in the 1950s I was plunged into purgatory with all the
amenities whereas Schneidermann he received the total European
education, I only gleaned and saved what I was able to while my
father he,

      since I was 3 he my father and not my Schneidermann
took me from lesson to home to lesson to home to lesson to home
and since I was 7, since my demi-semi-public debut recital in
Budapest substituting for my musical cousin Ziggi at the casino at
the Leopoldstadt for which I received as fee 10 gold coins worth
10 kronen each (5 went to Ziggi)

      it was schlepping from home to lesson to recital to home
to lesson to recital to home to lesson to recital, and so never
finding the time — not even in transit, not even in my later
virtuoso peregrinations, amongst all my sexual messianism,
requisite sightseeing, audiences and interviews — for any true,
measured and quiet study of the past to know the future, for any
true learning that didn't have to do with four strings and a bow
(like I didn't read Chaucer until I was 57, in piebald diners
throughout Middle America, didn't know the poems of Celan until
I was 60, picked them up in paperback in translation at a Midtown
megastore on the recommendation of Schneidermann, $17.95),

      no time for any true humanities so that I could develop a
humanity of my own, and so that's why everything I know it's
glossed to Schneidermann's experience who as a composer he was
compelled to train for music as well as to train for life,

      to train for music as much as for life, for survival,

      to train to Poland as I shipped myself over to America,

      whereas everything I know is on-the-fly, is fly-on-the-wall:

gossip, the overheard and nth hand, lies and predictions, condolences, confessions and praise,

my knowledge of my people can be reduced to a knowledge of dirty jokes, three recipes and the prayer for the dead, my Hebrew is a reformed idiot's Yiddish and though I've been around,

traveled from Poland to the Pole almost, Warsaw to Warsaw, Texas off Route 148,

I know nothing, though many may think me an avatar, a mandarin's mandarin I'm just a man who's lived, who's lived easy, who's survived (nothing),

and who's survived easy (it was nothing),

who's kept his ears and his mind open,

his mouth too for poulet frites in Paris, I've sipped Kaffee in Berlin, done guláš in Prague, БОРЩ in Moscow (for years menus were my only reading),

yes, kept my mouth and ears open to inept Hebrew, filthy Yiddish, formal German, musical French and Italian, I have a 10-year-old's grammarless Hungarian by now with memory being,

smatterings of Czech/Slovak/Polish/pan-Slavic from snippets of Russian, enough, this language and my true tongue which is music — music the true Latin of the world whereas my Latin ARS GRATIA ARTIS it's just guesses educated or at the very least educable, my Greek execrable as was my Shakespeare's who I didn't read in the original until I was 30 (and slept with an actress who she was botching Cordelia in the Park where,

but it was I who couldn't *heave*

my heart into my mouth), so that Schneidermann he had to translate for me from let's say Hesiod who he teaches that Orpheus, he was the son of a Muse:

her name to me was Eva once and María tonight, and Frieda and Jadwiga, Akira and Naomi and,

Orpheus and me, the "fathers of lays"

as glossing Pindar but you don't want to hear about him, about Pindar that perpetual revisionist of perpetuating myth but instead about my women, those shriekers out there in the audience who they took to my myth and instead of remaking it, revising or revisioning let's say they just ran with it and in high-heels down metro streets, gave it new life and purchase though you won't know them until you misunderstand me:

that

that this *Concerto*, and its true cadenza that it's less about
art than about me, less about itself than about myself, which might
after all be the so-called tragic flaw in music, in performance, in
the soloist, the so-called Classical "tragic flaw" (*hamartia* in Greek
according to Aristotle according to Schneidermann in the Torah it's
translated as *sin*) in any music I play, that I'm more important than
you (God, that's Romantic!) — you think I paid to listen to
myself play? you think I play for you and not for myself? you
think that this cadenza, this false cadenza, is about purging
myself? is about imparting something to you? about inheritance?

this cadenza nested in a greater cadenza and that within an
even greater cadenza and so on (the Gnostics whom Schneidermann loved), and even unloved Schneidermann just a flourish —
but still you'd know me,

know my head separated from my stalk, floating in the
midst name-perfumed, singing still,

still you'd recognize my voice only if you'd listen, but
instead some of you are talking, insulting, gossiping, planning
futures and happiness (where-to-have-dessert, who-to-marry),

giving out talk in all its most, maybe least stupefying
varieties: far-talk, near-talk, nose-talk, side-talk (Upper Eastside-
talk, Upper Westside-talk),

small-talk, large-talk, that-talk, this-talk,

over-talk, under-talk,

nth-talk, x-talk,

gossip unto the apocalypse, a pack of lips, a mass kibitz-
ing, orbits of noise ringing my planet of head:

you people always discussing weighty matters (you
think)!

doing deals of Creationary proportions, scams of Biblical
scope (you hope)!

names dropped and then picked up, dusted off, returned to
sender, dinner-plans preempted by a sneeze or a cough, matches on
and off and then on again as empires they plot themselves and
disintegrate as offhand as possible, isn't that right, Mister
Rothstein?

your wife as all wives sorting the onyx innards of her purse
and you,

if you're not all drinking the Reception already, but

langsam, ritardando:

you'll have your opportunity for rebuttal, for crossed-over examination when I'm good and dead.

Because *I* knew Schneidermann. Because I studied under Schneidermann. Because I lived with Schneidermann. Because I live without Schneidermann. Because I watered his houseplants when he was away concertizing. Because I watered his daughters (dead in Birkenau) when he was away concertizing and lecturing.

Who are you talking to, Chief? No one wants your megaphonics!

No, *you* listen to reason! Because *I* watered his wife (dead in Birkenau), and his daughters (dead in Birkenau), when he was away concertizing and lecturing and teaching and, no!

I won't come down from my mountain until I've had my tablets! and because I watered his wife and his daughters and sometimes I must admit all of them,

and at the same time when Schneidermann he was away concertizing and lecturing and teaching and conducting: this was my practice, what this Russian girl I've been keeping company with lately

(a prodigy, much fire, lacking technique, unpolished and hot as wild, body boyish up top but bulging below, 19th century thighs, red-hair dyed with dark streaks but she's gorgeous in that frumpy concert dress of hers when the straps they fall in the midst of a fast passage to expose her sweaty nibs), what this émigré girl who I also water her at our weekly lessons most private she calls my *practicizing*,

and yes, I took my meds, my pills, yes I remembered and no, *that* diagnosis has nothing whatsoever to do with it! I expect more from you, Doc Alan! come on!

and the rest of you, well, keep smelting away at that calf now that I'm mixed like my meds weren't, O where was I?

that I knew that I would never understand Schneidermann is what, but I also and equally knew that not to understand Schneidermann was to essentially understand him.

Enigma. Friendship. Guilt were three words that Schneider-mann he scribbled down in a spiralbound notebook, going through the dictionary, Schneidermann he was learning the language, April 2, 1954.

Emigrant

Emigrant. SEE *Immigrant.* First of May, 5714.

Admittedly, I would never fully know Schneidermann but I understood that not knowing Schneidermann, in part, was in itself knowing, absolutely, totally, wholly knowing Schneidermann is what I wanted to explain to you (it's difficult),

as an opinion of his would soon be, would soon become, consciously or rather not, an opinion of mine: as for example if he held X in high regard (liked his tone, his touch, his whole approach to the music),

then I would hold X in high regard, however and oppositely if and when I held X in high regard (for his interpretation of my interpretation, let's say),

then Schneidermann he immediately held X in the worst possible regard, regardless of my protestations which, indeed, had the exact opposite effect than what I had originally intended (to sway him to X's solo sonata playing stolen off my example),

and merely invited, permitted, Schneidermann to regard X, poor poor poor X,

me for example who I often reversed my own opinions to reverse Schneidermann's and not like he didn't know, do the same or adjust accordingly,

me or even himself to retract, to regard whomever as even less than he had initially regarded, disregarded or despised him before unto the point, of course, obviously, when X's pure regardless state would suddenly seem to Schneidermann as pure — intentional — genius, regardless or is it irregardless? of previously held opinions, which were previously held only to be eventually, patiently, overturned,

converted to their diametric, polar opposite — but such is art, as in the case, say, of me,

of my childhood, less a true childhood than a prodigyhood salvaged only in intimations of a deeper, higher, glory:

like here kid, play this violin and you might get somewhere in this life, get out of the ghetto and stay out, like practice your piano and you just might make something out of yourself after all, you know, earn all the accolades and acclaim of youth overachieving, which will only mature if you live that long, are allowed to outgrow them, mature past them into embarrassment and regret and then, well, you'll know, only then will you understand,

say like me, when I first presented myself to him, Schneidermann, in Budapest at the Conservatory, like when I first and
without knocking entered his spare studio and took out my violin
from its coffin of case, when I first and without further introduction that then even I understood would have been superfluous to a
genius such as Schneidermann, tuned my violin to the four tones
always in my head, *G D A* and *E* and played for him a then popular
prodigy/virtuoso piece almost all on harmonics that it imitated,
maybe, Pope Gregory's nightingales on helium,

that I probably shouldn't have played and for him, Schneidermann, and at my very first and only audition but which I
anyway did, though only on the advice of my — false, true —
father,

unaccompanied by anything but the ground bass of my
ambition.

I was young. It was all I knew.

Schneidermann to me: you're worthless, just another
ghetto hopeful with technique and an eager parent (I'm translating
half from the German and half from the Yiddish that Schneidermann he inadvertently slipped into).

Schneidermann to me: your technique is incredibly, evenly
matched by a depth of expression that's quite rare for your age. For
any age. For anyone at any time. Ever.

Schneidermann to me: give up the fiddle and live a normal
life.

Schneidermann to me: you're the greatest violinist I've
heard since Szigeti,

or fill in your own favorite here.

Schneidermann to me: the greatest potential I've heard of
all time, the greatest I've heard of all time, already polished,
finished, ready for the Valhalla Fame and don't think that I didn't
live by these opinions (*the only opinion*),

don't think I didn't die by these opinions,

opinions voiced daily, voiced hourly, revised by the bar,
revised by the note, by the bowstroke, opinions of an opinion
added-to and subtracted-from in perfect inverse, in the harmony of
absolute opposites, just by a tug on a low-lobed ear,

a tug on either pineapple-lobed ear,

any ear and even on one of mine as Schneidermann he

accompanied

accompanied me on a death-rattling grandpiano he played coin-on-
the-wrist as if to parody me as I then played book-under-the-arm
into a mirror, playing so that my musical faults (because I had
significantly fewer technical faults, enough), all of my musical
faults and there were many in those days, enough, all a million of
them they had something to reflect on and echo off in bare, pitiless
benevolence through poor posture, awkward elbow positioning,
either too loose or too tense, undersexed-adolescent-tight, too
mechanical moto perpetuo, too expressionistic, emotive, seduced-
by-the-seduction, ignorant of or too occupied with the phrase as
the fundamental unit of musical thought phrase-depending, unable
to interpret in any context apart from my own earnest ambition,
unable to play with any contingency other than the counsel of my
own ego and though I'm sure that I sounded great, already then at a
EUROPEAN and so at an INTERNATIONAL LEVEL, even
perfect to any and everyone else, Schneidermann he was the only
one who knew, the only one who listened, the only one who heard
— ultimately I understood that he was the only one who would,
even who could at our thrice-weekly private lessons in that grave-
spare studio in that rotting Conservatory in that decaying capital of
that dead country in the middleless middle of that European void.
    As every morning I woke early,
    I was always Schneidermann's favorite,
    at the Conservatory I had no friends,
    music was the life of me.
    The death of my potential as a person. As a human.
    I met Frieda in the greenest park, the management of my
time was always of the greatest importance to me, I kept a wish-
bone in my pocket, the music of Mozart is not known to induce
diarrhea as my landlord once told me when he had new pipes
installed, the other Frieda she was already soaked and waiting and
enlisted me to help her find a lost umbrella.
    As every morning I woke early, at least earlier than Ziggi,
        and practiced,
    then off to the Conservatory in the afternoon for my
lesson with Schneidermann,
        then back to my room where I practiced,
    then over to Schneidermann's house for further instruc-
tion.

Life.

Schneidermann to me: I'd be honored to teach you.

Schneidermann to me: I'd rather have a violin string tied around my penis, the other end tied to the studio's doorknob and ask you politely to slam the door on your way out.

I'd rather have a violin string tied around my penis,

the other end tied to the chandelier on the ceiling,

stand myself up on a piano made out of ice,

and wait until summer for my sex to tear.

Schneidermann to me: have you asked the Director about studying with me?

Schneidermann to me: the Academy it hasn't paid me in a month.

Schneidermann, he was my first teacher. Schneidermann, he was my only teacher. Schneidermann, his first teacher he was a man also named Schneidermann, his father as it happened and a pianist of no renown until he died and then even less and Schneidermann the younger he became adopted by composition and his father's nine sisters, the nine — barely, bourgeoisly — musical aunts who they raised him from the age of 5,

from the age of 7,

of 10,

12,

muses too and, yes,

yes, I'm implying incest not of Krafft-Ebing's idealized sort but dirty, dirty, dirty origins of this *mystagogue* (one of his favorite words, Schneidermann he spent much time in the Webster's M: *Matricide, Millionaire, Modernity*),

this crafty man whose craft it never ebbed,

this synoptic man and his synoptic religion of art: a kind of Gesamtkunstwerk of huge-German-L Life in the face of all opposition, attempted genocide, poverty, the whole gig *heimatlos* — how are your chops, foreign-tongued, feeling tonight?

like the time when I grew up and out of Yiddish and had to learn, to study grammatically-true Hungarian, had to perfect in speech, comprehension and composition my formal Hungarian (which never happened), Hungarian I think the most difficult of all the languages outside Africa and the Orient and Music and the language of the women of my new hometown or hometowns of

Buda

Buda and Pest (all the men I met they all spoke German to me as I
was a foreigner, a musician and a genius),

    but the women, O the women! they would either accept
your proposals, suggestions, innuendoes or else reject your advances, feels, gropes and all in Hungarian, and it took me at least a
year of study in Budapest at the Conservatory to understand
enough Hungarian and of its nuances, shadings to know if these
dark-eyed, dark-haired, moon-skinned women who they were just
girls were outright saying yes (IGEN),

    were outright saying no (NEM),

    or else saying a yes that meant a no (just frustration later,
the taste of tease in your unkissed mouth),

    or if they were in the end saying a no that meant a yes,

    a please (KÉREM),

    or else a please-do-it-to-me-now-against-this-wrought-
iron-railing,

    against all appearances this humanist hemisphere we're
living in would have me maintain — and how I'd then bring them
back to their rooms or to an empty pianoless practice room at the
Music Academy and have my way with them, have any way with
them they'd let me in those days, metronome-regular I'd pierce
their menses as slow as larghetto with them moaning in E♭, as
neither major nor minor, just a fact, evident, there as I couldn't
bring them back to my room, a room I then shared with a cousin

    (Jews just like the African-Americans they have cousins
everywhere, I've noticed), a distant dark-as-a-shvartze cousin
actually whom we all called Ziggi as a diminutive as he was for
Zigeuner, which is German for *gypsy* though he wished he could play
like one but instead was hopeless, fiddled like Nero unto the ashes
of the Holocaust that he probably welcomed, that relieved him
though privately,

    because Ziggi he'd practice the violin all day and for
nothing, no reward except more fault, more debt to life lived in the
one spareless room we shared in the roominghouse of some obese
Swabian dentist, also an amateur recording-artist for whom I made
my virtual debut, Schubert, on cardboard disc, an over-mustachioed
man named either Schöller or Schnöller I forget which now and so
between the two of them, between Ziggi and the Swabian, what
hope could I have of dragging a willing woman, girl, home with

me? but I remember that Ziggi,

far from being unsexual, as far on foot from Minsk to Pinsk or Omsk to Tomsk as Schneidermann he always said just unsatisfied, yes:

it was that Ziggi he would examine various pictures both illustrated and photographic of breasts, of mammae of various sizes and shapes, of various varieties let's say to get I think an idea of what pleased him, aesthetically, to get an idea of what he should seek in waking life, Ziggi he would hoard these pictures, obtain them from an antiquarian bookseller and — curiously — an outwardly respectable petshop, would spend all his money on them so that his parents they'd always and monthly have to send, wire like puppetry more and more that Ziggi he swore to them he spent it on partitur, also on violin strings that's how many he'd snap in a given month from all that emotion, frustration, pent-up aggression unpent in practice,

for nine months we lived together, under the roof of the Swabian, in the attic, a garret if I must, two thin beds across the room from one another, two beds up against opposite walls, actually his against the window because he'd arrived second and I was always considerate, self-denying if not pitying his scandalous — that we were related — lack of talent, though it didn't prevent him from sleeping well,

maybe it actually helped him but I never did,

didn't help me,

never could sleep well ever, I always woke when it was still quite dark,

stygian (Schneidermann he loved that word),

Umbrian too, but Ziggi he never moved in his sleep, though he wasn't quite like a corpse:

he slept fully, as if he fully deserved the rest from the day's worthless exertions,

his neck slept (mine was always maniacally veined, 10-tensed),

his shoulders slept whereas mine were always deeply entwitched,

his toes slept as mine they danced unveiled, nine different mazurkas in eleven different time signatures,

while I was as awake as restless and there was this one let's

say

say tradition that I had, which was that I'd examine the pictures, my distant, dark cousin's collection he soon about five-six months in willed to me, actually he soon forgot all about it, forgot all about his former fetish-mania and so I stole the whole stash when he Ziggi he got himself a consumptive Christian for a girlfriend with a deaf-mute for a mother and mammary-traits, the girlfriend's, that we would like to assume met his own exacting specifications.

When I pulled them out from under my mattress the pictures they were voids, patches or holes in the dark air, outlines of nullity — everything else in the room existed in form, shapes of Ziggi's clothes like the Ziggi-coat he wore,

the Ziggi-gabardines,

the Ziggi-underwear stained with wisps of Ziggi,

and his socks draped over Doktor Schnöller or Schöller's starving furniture as I wouldn't turn on the light,

it would wake Ziggi, and Ziggi he would see me looking at the pictures, his pictures, my pictures,

not that Ziggi he didn't know, he obviously knew all about the pictures but maybe he didn't know that he knew or at least didn't admit it to himself — myself — that I'd stolen them

because I was the good one, the promising one, the one-who-promised, the one with the talent, who was talented, I who at least knew and admitted to myself that I didn't want to know exactly what Ziggi thought or knew regarding *me* and *looking* and *pictures*,

in truth to assert an adolescent image I didn't want to know for sure that Ziggi he didn't think that I looked at them is what I was trying to say,

and so I'd spread the pictures out on the wrinkled sheets,

pulled off the mattress in my tempest-tossing, lying on the floor like a swirl of vanilla softserve if my image is to be American (Ziggi he loved the *Eis*),

and I'd support my head, the Europe atop my neck with one hand, with the other I'd

as in the cheap curtains' far dim with the sun just coming up, peaking, I'd gradually assemble the pictures:

the naked, awkwardly posed bodies filled out with the light, as the chintz curtains they got more and more transparent, see-thru (like all my intentions),

light enough for me to wake the pictures (which was the
only reading I did in those days, the genesis of my sexual obses-
sions),

not light enough to wake Ziggi and but shortly before the
alarm rang — it was a new model his parents had sent up, only the
best for their boy, rousing him to practice duets with his girlfriend
a mediocre pianist though more talented than he would ever be
even after the two together and finally relinquished, gave up and
opened a music shop whose debt and the distance it put between
them, Christian-Catholic and Jew, it would have killed them had all
those musical Nazis not thoughtfully, thankfully, intervened,

and Auschwitz it relieved them of their burden just a
month before circumstances they would have become totally dire.

I kept one eye on the pictures and another eye on him and
the alarm next to his head, almost wedged in the void of his ear,

would quickly shove the pictures under my mattress and
feign sleep and then his alarm it would ring, sound and wake him
up and Ziggi he'd jump across the room in one jump to lean over
my form falsely-sleeping,

then fling the curtains open all the way and open the
casement windows as he lit his first cigarette of 12 for the day —
the whole room it would fill with season and the suits and dresses
they were already outside,

but there aren't any pictures left anymore, are there?

no more flat, static images, no more paper-porn, now all
examination occurs off a screen and skin-periodicals themselves
they're now specialized fetishes: no more foldable foldouts, mourn
the erotic accounts that Schneidermann he always loved and said
that he learned the American language from — its obscene idiom
disallowed in the matinee movies, not-so-taboo to his immigrant's
ears — sitting for hours at a time in the most abandoned public
library up on St. Nicholas Avenue with the Webster's or
Macmillan's or Oxford's in one hand and in the other his girth just
thrust amongst all those letters-to-the-editorix:

I never thought it would happen to me, but Schneidermann, over
here on the Uppermost Westside he'd often answer the door nude,
a faddish Austro-Hungarian habit imported to Harlem if not like
an unashamed updated Wandervogel-thing that Schneidermann he
indulged while trying to schnorr free thin mints off a girl scout,

but

but no matter what it was (pure exhibitionism?), it did
little to endear him to various missionaries and the pizza-delivery
personnel I often sent his way as ambassadors of goodwill, foreign
aid or just, well, surprise!

(which was von Clausewitz's first principle of warfare,
Schneidermann he reminded me once out of nowhere after a
matinee Revolutionary War movie), when they extended their
Sunday palms and expected a tip.

Unembarrassed as the Mormons and wageslaves weren't,
natural as anything he'd admit you in. And ask you, probably, to
listen to his chest. To auscultate him.

Because — skinny as hope, a pianostring spine, naked as
hope — it was his unrattleable belief that he had somehow or
other maybe inhaled or swallowed down the wrong pipe a coin, into
one of his lungs: some days his right lung and some days his left
but always one coin in one of them and so often too often Schneidermann he'd ask you to listen to his chest, ear to the mating of
ribs and you'd listen, near him, too, smelling his smell if truth be
told

(and it should: Schneidermann he wouldn't have had it any
other way — he thought deodorant a scam and anti-perspirant a
government plot that would track among other things your *movements* and *hormones*), and he'd breathe. And cough.

Schneidermann to me: does it sound like a nickel or does
it sound like a dime?

I couldn't say. It was a rattle. As if the lung itself was coin,
with a coin inside.

Schneidermann to me: if it's a dime it might be worth
coughing up,

and then he'd sit — seemingly more naked than previous
if that's possible, tush-nude, buttocks gripping the bench — at the
piano, his BALD upright because the WIN it had been shvitzed off
long ago and I'd unlock my violin (*fiddle*, Schneidermann he always
said),

my violin worth approximately 198million times any
amount of money that Schneidermann he'd ever earned or would
altogether in his whole life overlong and yet still always too-short,
and we, Schneidermann and I we'd just go at it, geniuses in heat —
that was my best performance, one Manhattan afternoon, me and

him and this waylaid composition, his *Concerto* huddled around his piano, her, an upright as he, believe it, and a coin, a hollowed quarter, a plugged nickel maybe it was in a lung, maybe his only lung and tinkling to jangle poor around at anything surpassing even an impoverished mezzo-forte.

This was way the gehenna and gone as Schneidermann he always said up-Uptown,

this was a reduced piano, but in no way a piano reduction — hammering into the opening bars of his *Concerto*, Schneidermann he nailed down everything: after the break-in, the would-be burglary, Schneidermann he nailed down the bench, and the upright.

O the orchestra! You who have slowly dispersed behind me, off to assignations, moonlights, husbands, wives and lovers, to sip vaguely Zennish tea at a café next door, even the harpist who I love and dream of but haven't yet plucked she's wilted on home,

almost all except for the toddler timpanist who he seems to find me amusing, don't you? Well, Schneidermann, he held your whole woodwind section in the first pad of his right ringfinger, unadorned, in this nation, in this state unmarried like Glenn Gould but Schneidermann he was a more formidable pianist (as was Richter, in not only my opinion),

was indeed a more formidable everything,

and just ask the woodwinds, piccolos to bellowing contra-bassoons! the years of excruciating training, of discipline, of denial, fine honing and for the oboes the reed insanity, the suburban money that bought them, you, the leisure to fine hone because there are no geniuses here, except Schneidermann (and maybe myself),

Schneidermann he had all that well above a knuckle and so how could you,

dispersed backstage,

into cabs or subways and away,

statements to the press, the nightly news,

Downtown for rare liqueurs to watch me up on the screen if anyone's filming here,

to gossip, how could you expect to live? if you even wanted to? if you weren't staying on this thing, sticking-it-out — sweating too much, shvitzing on you, sorry,

if

if you're just staying on this road just because there hasn't
yet been a scenic turnoff,

a welcoming detour?

like the road — if it could be called a road, more like a
mud — I first took with my father from Bukovina, from
Czernowitz to Hungary, to its capital of Budapest through hitching
and walking and mudding to the Music Academy and my first
lesson with Schneidermann,

with the first note of which I played planting the seed for
this wind of a composition, seeding the air for this snow of a
Concerto,

maybe,

no, truth, trudging and mudding to my first lesson, yes,
but to my first lesson with a then famous and now unknown
violinist (that's how it was before recording, before the memory-
of-technology),

a virtuoso who he wouldn't have bled for him, Schneidermann, were it not for the — overinflated — money that Schneidermann he used to lose to him in a most hermetic, involved form of
whist of their own invention,

there to room with the virtuoso's nephew (never a virtuoso
himself),

and then with my distant, dark cousin Ziggi (never even a
violinist),

was introduced to Budapest, my first real city and its
women, was introduced to pornography and so to women who they
won't talk to say No only listen,

love,

and studied in the afternoon for only a month with the
then infamous and now absolutely forgotten violinist who he was
the only and so unworthy appreciable reason for my, false, father
mudding us from Bukovina to Budapest and the Music Academy to
his studio like India, like I thought India would be, like India it
wasn't when I finally made it there in the 70s for a UN, UNESCO
benefit concert but as it should have been and for only a month,
for only 30 or 31 days before I went and switched studios which is
something you never do, with all the nerve of youth and its
ambition switched to Schneidermann, 30 or 31 days before I
moved my person, my talent and so my destiny — with the

Director's disapproval but with the Director's consent because of
my talent or was it just my obstinacy? head-strength? — from the
virtuoso to the musician, from the hack to the artist, from the
child to the man, pledged allegiance to music over dreck, to art
over shit, God over shit, in the end which has not yet begun I and
already at that immature, hairless age opted for redeeming shit over
unredeeming shit, in the endless end I went for the transcendent
shit over the mundane shit, the meaning over the gesture, the shit
of meaning over the shit of gesture which was all my will was at
the time, a gesture to a world that I just dreamt, hoped meant
something more as there in that sparest unsparing studio there was
only one of us amongst the two of us amongst Schneidermann and
I who was not a monkey flinging around its own shit,
        who wasn't a retarded infant eating its own shit,
        dead in infancy from eating its own shit and then reincar-
nated again as a monkey, a spidermonkey flinging around its own
shit,
        a shit-stuffed lemming gone over the mediocre edge —
you ever encounter one of those? — as punishment for sins too
numerous as too grievous to apologize for just now (hubris),
        to atone for (arrogance),
        to repent for only to commit and then commit again and
again or so it seemed, then.
        We played — an earlier version of — this *Concerto* and I
improvised a cadenza,
        in that roomless room Schneidermann he improvised the
Piano Concerto he never lived short enough to compose,
        in that roomless room we played his unfinished sonatas
and I improvised them to finish,
        we studied and we played,
        we analyzed and we played,
        we concertized and we played,
        we toured and we played, through the years, through the
air, through the smoke:
        according to Schneidermann, according to two-three pack-
a-day Schneidermann, to five-six pack-a-day Schneidermann if you
were interested in his pianistic technique then I'd tell you exactly
what Schneidermann he told me, which is that the true test of
pianistic art/prowess or whatever you're having is to be able to play

the

the piano and smoke simultaneously, at the same time and by
playing I mean,

by playing Schneidermann he meant playing with both
hands (or with any # of hands that you happen to have, however
many the War it left you with), so that no hand is available to
remove/insert, ash or stub out the cigarette and so you have to keep
playing with all the smoke getting in your eyes as that old song
goes and Mister Fein,

Mister Feinberg, Mister Feingold whatever your name do
you happen to have another light?

No?

No.

Fine, have it your way Mister Fire Marshall — with ash
filling the studio, staining its strained walls, ash getting on the
keys, ash getting between the keys, ebonying everything, on your
latest-prodigy-style whitest shirt and secreted in its ruffles,
streaked down your most velveteen cerulean cravat, eyes all flood-
ing, lacrimal apparatus shutting on and off involuntarily with not a
pause in your playing, no aural

(or, Schneidermann he often insisted while demonstrating
or non-demonstrating and so demonstrating at my Grand keyboard, physical) impact on your playing evident whatsoever in a
performance practice, a keyboard style that is without doubt the
pinnacle of last century's piano century:

dark, almost foreboding but more Stoic than most — that
was him, was Schneidermann who he did this every concert, sure,
but also every rehearsal, indeed every time he sat down at the piano,
to the piano, always, a feat no less amazing than his execution of
amazingly difficult compositions that were even more amazingly
also of his own composition as was I,

who served the function, filled the honorable office — as
if we weren't serious contemporary musicians rather an endless,
Weimarian, cabaret act of lighting and stubbing — of inserting
new, fresh cigarettes for him into those lips constantly chapped to
peeling:

four packs that's 80 of them to play straight through
Scriabin's latest sonata with not a pause between cigarettes not
indicated in the score, or accompanying me — but who accompanying who? — in Shostakovich's *Violin Sonatas* without tear one,

nothing shed,

not for the music neither for the smoke, and you can bet that four packs a day it gets expensive in this America where talk is cheap but smoke is taxed as to be almost prohibitively expensive and so that's why in later years Schneidermann he smoked only, mainly Romanian or maybe they were Bulgarian? Macedonian? Albanian? just generically-Balkan? post-communist cigarettes that Schneidermann he got mailed to him from there wherever it was, mailed to him over here by colleagues and excolleagues and sons of colleagues and grandsons of excolleagues all perpetuating the memory of the man known to them or their parents or their parents' parents from before or during the War as a genius, and though Schneidermann he kept cartons of these (couldn't get over the fact that the factory it now in the American century rolled them for you, lamented the days of rolling-your-own, a rehearsal piano he ruined losing loose tobacco to the spaces between the keys),

kept cartons of Eastern, post-Roman cigarettes cheaper, much, than what you pay over here and especially now what with taxes a luxury that Schneidermann he would never afford, could, even what with the mailing costs that Schneidermann he never reimbursed them for anyway, cigarettes shipped over one carton at a time so as to avoid Customs, duties eluded — piled if not lock-and-stockpiled, as if for the Apocalypse or at least a global smokables shortage in his room (it was always a shortage with him, 28 small, 18 x 18 in his apartment Schneidermann he always said *flat*),

Schneidermann he still invariably ventured out daily or more to the corner-stand, newsstand I call it (Schneidermann he always said *tabak*),

to the stand on his corner for a fresh, new, shiny pack of LUCKIES or MARLBOROs, anything more expensive that they wouldn't kill him in the end because nothing would kill him in the end that would — indeed, in-deed — never come,

an end not so final — but they did give him some serious sinus/maxillofacial problems, upper-respiratory difficulties toward the end that wasn't an end (the half-dollar in the lung),

in the end not his end to have,

the pleasure of popping some equally serious pills:

emphysema

emphysema, on my prescription, PREDNISONE, anything on my prescription — given as Schneidermann he was to misdiagnosing and mis-self-diagnosing, dosing unto overdosing and every goddamned day after day after day on little green jealousy pills (I'm sure all my doctors they remember, late-at-night all those strange symptoms I insomniac phoned in),

on medium-sized keep-you-regular pills,

on large as an ark in the water-glass horse-pills — Schneidermann he loved defining himself in the medical encyclopedia, *The Merck Manual* that:

Schneider, C. V. — German anatomist, 1614–1680, discoverer of *Schneiderian membrane,*

Schneider, F. C. — German chemist, 1813–1897, inventor of *Schneider carmine,*

Schneiderian membrane — also *Schneiderian,* nasal mucosa, mucous membrane that lines the nasal cavity, first described by C. V. Schneider, German anatomist of the seventeenth century,

Schneider's first rank symptoms — symptoms indicating probable schizophrenia, provided that organic and toxic etiology are ruled out: delusion of control, thought-broadcasting, thought-withdrawal, thought-insertion, thought-interruption, delusional perception, hearing one's thoughts spoken aloud, auditory hallucinations that comment on one's behavior, auditory hallucinations in which two voices carry on a conversation and so on,

Schneidersitz — a typical sitting position with legs crossed in front ("Indian-style"), exhibited by severely defected patients with phenylketonuria and resembling the position commonly attributed to tailors at work (German),

with his glasses on only when he (always reading), when Schneidermann and I we went to the matinee movies and only then in the later years and not even his glasses,

just a pair of UV-protected, magnifiers and sanctifiers that Schneidermann he'd stolen off a rack at a drugstore on the way to the matinee movies, once — as the lights went down, the glasses went on, Schneidermann he got the advertisements and the previews, Schneidermann he got his glasses out:

huge, amber-tinted, round-as-thought orbs that made him seem/look somewhat odd,

professorial, yes, but professorial-sleazy, smarmy,

upperlip-sweaty.

Not that he ever taught. By anything ever but example.

Schneidermann to me: pianists who make noise when they perform.

Schneidermann to me: pianists who make noise when they record.

Schneidermann to me: they don't have the discipline to remain silent.

Schneidermann to me: none of them do, no exceptions.

Schneidermann to me: Jesus! (and then how Schneidermann who he disliked Gould though regarded him with the utmost in grudging respect,

how he'd often when we, when Schneidermann he though infrequently talked shop about pianists how he'd always and immediately touch on Richter's touch, the Richter-scale of Richter's touch and all about how in the 80s the 70something-year-old Richter who hated us, who he hated me and you and all we stand for,

all you stand for, how Richter he just said to hell with the West and that whole gone insane hemisphere! who needs New York and its Philharmonic? I'll just play Siberia! me one of the world's greatest virtuosos in demand everywhere but still and always an upright Citizen, God how much Schneidermann — a man with little naivete in all else — how much he envied that! his position!

how Richter he said sorry to the West and instead went and did his duty by the East, one-nighters strings of them in the hallowed halls of Orekhovo-Zouevo if you know it, in Petropavlovsk, Tchegdomyn and Tselinograd and how)

Schneidermann to me: dispense with the human and you have a perfect music, dispense with the human and you have no music.

Like listen to a soundless spiritless note sounding spirit Schneidermann he often heard from his heart,

like a soundless spiritless sound of spirit that Schneidermann he once told me about outside the 24/7 store near him owned by Arabs that supplied Schneidermann with all of his weekly needs, the 24/7 Arab-owned store that Schneidermann he often referred to as the ARAB STORE, or else the ALL DAY ALL NIGHT STORE, or just the STORE,

like

like listen: a typical musician has 12 notes but a typical pianist has only 10 fingers and Schneidermann he always wanted to know why,

One of those, how do you say? Unanswered Questions, Schneidermann he always answered himself, like why does the STORE always advertise a sale on toiletpaper only when the STORE it's all out of toiletpaper?

like when you hear a performer you should hear only a composer, according to Schneidermann, when you hear a performance while you should hear the music Schneidermann he often maintained,

listen to the virtuoso or virtuosa and then listen to the virtuous Schneidermann he often accused, listen to the interpreter and then listen to the interpreted was his frequent though unsolicited though never unwelcome instruction,

like hear the interpretation and then hear the interpreted were all Schneidermann's instructions to me,

all reminding me of my own stint teaching, Uptown, of my own students and their own destinies now inextricably linked to my own,

reminds me of that scandal that the school it managed to keep out of the papers, this example of musical gossip,

backstage patter,

the example of behind-the-scenes Volksmärchen,

which I heard from my excolleague there from the Caucasus: a passable pianist, a Jew who he teaches all these Asians, all these children of diplomats and executives and,

rich, young girls shipped in bulk over here,

dropped on us all like dark-eyed-bombs,

to work on marriageable talent if not a solo career,

well, my friend the professor he had them then prepping, indeed had them a halftone flat of insane with all this mad-practicing and preparing they his students did every year for the school's annual piano installment of the school's annual CONCERTO COMPETITION

which if you win it you get to play the demo piece with the school's top orchestra at a big concert attended by all the critics who would launch a name — and so with about 150 wretches passing as, paying top dollar to be piano students and all vying for this one distinction, it was a big competition, THE big one as much as they're all concerned and all of them are, for the moment,

those weeks and months of moment,

all those scale exercises and drills for finger independence, hour after hour working a single passage, a single measure over and over, a lone note struck and struck again and again again, a sound sounded to stay sounded, always, forever to sing and sing wide when called upon and for, on such pitiless command that you would think that the piano it would know after all that practice to play all by itself, to play and practice itself and for itself in that single, foursquare practiceroom:

four walls, a door, ceiling and floor, and a piano and its bald bench that's all you get, the amenities of art,

a room lonely when empty and lonely when occupied, yes, that's the stage:

a single piano lonely for a piece played through to its end, its finale, a grand tuned once a week as all of them are at THE major metropolitan Conservatory to the stars,

conserving all für all of you and even Elise, whoever she is — yes, and so we have a single piano in a single practiceroom, topfloor, shared by two Asian girls who they might have looked like a single Asian girl,

actually, the Platonic Asian girl if Asians they even know from Plato,

indeed two Platonic Asian girls if that's possible, one good, one evil, all sallow jaundiced skin, pitch hair pitched in grease dark as space, galaxies of acne,

skinny as keys, essentially titless and yet all they did with all this talent was to practice, daily, nightly on their one lone piano in their one lone practiceroom, up on the topfloor of the Conservatory's building overlooking, overhearing the Park where,

they'd practice and long into fits of mild psychosis, missed menstruations, pimple-popping extreme insomnia they'd practice until they'd switch shifts, just in time you would think not to go wholly over the edge, but — practicing what? practicing passage after passage of what virtuous test? what concerto was to be adjudged? juried? what Olympian concerto was it that they were slaving to wasting what youth they had over?

it

it was, the composition, if you can believe it, it was
Ludwig van Beethoven's *4th Piano Concerto,*

yes, that masterpiece in G major, Opus 58 and if you want
any more information those two Asians they definitely didn't
know: it was written in 1805/6 while the Master he was also
laboring in fits over his one and only opera, *Fidelio,*

and as if that wasn't enough also on his 4th and 5th
symphonies if you know them — his fourth of five piano concerti
it was that it begins with a slap in the face of every convention:

those piano as dolce five bars solo instead of the expected
orchestral tutti with the strings then answering and pianissimo
whole keys away followed by a movement, allegro moderato it's
marked and based on the same three quavers later made more
famous as the so-called fate motif or motive of the *5th Symphony:*

dumb, dumb, dumb, DUMB it goes,

numb, numb, numb, NUMB if you'll excuse my singing
deep into the work's second movement:

yes, that gorgeous, polar second movement, the shattering
extreme andante with moto movement in which the piano and the
orchestra they never play together, rather only against each other,
competing some interpret it as and maybe but the contrast is
what's more important, is actually all of it, the drama that's not in
the struggle as much as it is in the separation,

the rift,

asunder-age,

like stereo before stereo — the piano as Orpheus lulling
the orchestra,

charming the tits off the beasts:

Asians, two of them, about 150 of them and all playing
Beethoven's *4th Piano Concerto,*

and not playing more like responding to stimuli as my old
dead friend Isaac Stern he noted when he visited Shanghai in 1979,
like Schneidermann he always talked about Asians and their mania
for all this artistic mass-production,

for the once-made in the West for them to remake and
more efficiently in the true East,

these Asians who they just reproduce their instruction,
stiff as wood, synthetic even! not interpreting just sounding the
notes, getting from one dot to another and not even letting the

rests speak! the white!

yes, these are the polar roots of everything wrong, but you'd want names, right? put names they all sound Wu Fu the same to faces they all look insensate alike, want me to identify these tinkling twins? not Siamese, just Asian and under the Asian blank, bitter rivals:

atomic nerves, automaton ruthless up there in the single last practiceroom on the topfloor of the Conservatory's earless building with a view to the Park where,

with their DOVER Xeroxes or UNIVERSAL EDITIONS,

their teacher-marked sheetmusic they meccanico all.

But one, she did something amazing.

Inspired, she left.

Her only inspired performance, she went out into the open:

into Manhattan — and forget that apple propaganda, will you?

this is the land of the locust-eaters,

of the opinion-a-dayers,

fighting ground of the bears and the bulls and the stage for a waiter acting out *the best tiramisu in town,*

out among the turbaned gridlock and multitasking pigeons, she went! she walked! the world! went into a Midtown drugstore,

any Midtown drugstore, one anonymous one of one anonymous chain,

and there she bought a canister of shavingcream — men's and aloe-scented, she was nervous — and a packet of razors,

cream it was let's say $3.99, and good old straight standard as sharp razorblades, $2.99, the money from her parents,

not a cheekshaver — blades, this pianist she goes and buys 11 packs' worth, with eight blades in each pack for a grand total of she did the math:

one for each key,

the light and the dark, enharmonic equivalents of tragedy and then — as if too long out in the pulsing air — the pianist she returns, runs quickly back to her dorm, changes her costume to concert/concertowear (she always practiced in the clothing she was

to perform in according to her teacher my friend, a true dress
rehearsal daily),

    a fluffy it should have been pink-mint taffeta travesty as
I've dreamt it and goes up to practice until 7, the 2 to 7 session,
the other girl, the rival, coming in for the 7 to 12 block and then
they'd argue in whatever way that Asians they argue over who gets
the practiceroom when it's officially forbidden, the rules say off-
limits, the 12 to 8 a.m. shift, unto the morning hours with the
sun's eye appraising the Park where,

    and sometimes they'd both even sleep there, snuggled
close, under the piano, making sure that the other was as inactive,
indeed as wasteful and as unimproving as herself just dreaming
dreamless up,

    indeed they'd each always individually stopped practicing a
few minutes prior to the end of their individual practice sessions
according to their teacher my friend, five minutes before the key
and the key's practiceroom and practice piano and all its keys they
got turned over, reverted, so that the other girl she couldn't hear,

    gauge her chances,

    cop an interpretation,

    exploit a weakness,

    ridiculous according to their teacher my friend: they'd each
initially — before the CONCERTO COMPETITION it was
announced to their expectation — individually stopped practicing
five minutes prior to turnover (all this too according to their
teacher my friend, an earnest pianist but also a Jew who he just
couldn't help himself in gossiping this along),

    the two girls just meditating on a future I would guess for
those five minutes before, and maybe even mentally practicing,
fingering air but then they'd each individually arrive earlier and
earlier and so they'd each individually stop, cessate, a caesura 10
minutes prior, then 15 minutes before with this block of null
spinning, spiraling out until,

    if this tragedy it never occurred, if this unfortunate
incident it was never to progress past sublimation,

    leave the meditation-phase,

    transcend,

    then all of their days they would be passed just waiting
and for nothing in front of the piano and in jealous silence — at

least it would be interesting to imagine, secret-guarding like the four minutes and 33 second cage of John Cage, the four minutes and 33 second tacet of David Tudor's silent Woodstock performance, 1952:

hushed, and sometimes they'd even both sleep there according to their teacher my friend, wrapped tight under the piano in the rug, pseudo-Oriental and soiled, the pair flicking quick engreening tongues at each other's eyes,

but it was that night, in question,

when she, one of them at 15-10 minutes to 7 she went and placed the razors she purchased, the blades sharp edge up she wedged them all between the black keys and the white, between the white keys and the white keys at B and C and E and F, introduced the razors next to and so surrounding every single key white and black except one at the very top of the keyboard and pushed in and deep against the base of the keys, the soundboard, standing sharp as thin and almost invisible if inspected from directly above which is the position you play the piano in if you're Asian and so have impeccable posture, steel slivered in the shadows (they always practiced in inefficient light, being Asian they never complained to the Maintenance Staff which),

an augmented scale on razors spaced equidistantly, a whole tone pain on the dark keys just the perfect preparation for a B major answer in a concerto in the key of G dur as the Europeans they used to say,

the rival at the door and doubtless she knocked first, after all have to have the pretense to politesse, must preserve to the extreme all that Asiatic ritual:

when the girl, the victim, she entered the practiceroom this was the first time that the first girl, the sadist, she smiled, or according to how I've imagined it — when the victim let's call her when Sumi, when her hands they came down in a chord, well, there's all this huge globbing blood on the ivory! God! just a freest flow, three fingers of each hand (six in all, warming up on an E♭ major chord in two octaves)

with all their however many tendons severed, a wrist or two too she played so hard in an overture to the passion that she had to be taught according to their teacher my friend:

screaming void in that practiceroom! howling veins! and

the

the other, the sadist, the bitch, the anti-Sumi, what had she done? she'd barricaded the door with the hallway's upright, a spare tuneless upright piano used to accompany only the fattest and most hopeless of sopranos pushed into place to trap Sumi there, to bleed and to bleed, to bleed and to die,

but how far should I take this history? extend this tragedy? the Conservatory's cover-up? the press obliging because two members of the Conservatory's board they're on other boards too? the expulsion of the anti-Sumi followed by her deportation from the U.S. of A.? the ruining of Sumi's career, her life, returning home to some 1000-floor Zen pagoda unmarried, to her parents who, God! they were huge in the Southeast Asian financial sector just dying of grief, disappointment, scuttled ambition and all the money left her spent on an enormous heroin habit that it eventually indebted her to a life of sexual slavery?

or that she's down on the boardwalk now in Atlantic City, playing the synthesizer with her gone purple toes? or out at some Pacific Northwest VA hospital singing through her ears the anthems of the world? What's the introduction and when's the coda? Questions.

Like how did these Asians really play, besides unfairly? I asked their teacher my friend, my colleague the Jew pianist from the Caucasus to which he just shook his vaguely triangular and so almost Pythagorean head,

my friend and he wanted to be Schneidermann's too, this Jew piano professor who he related to me this gossip I just gossiped to you,

should also mention that his uncle that he had a different sort of malady, a different type of art-sickness:

which was that he lived other lives or — more accurately because this uncle his whole need it was accuracy — rather that he relived the life of another, actually and with total accuracy the uncle of their teacher my friend he relived the life or attempted to relive the life from the age of 13 (from his age of 13)

of the composer whose G major *Concerto* it figured prominently into the gossip I was gossiped and just related to you with just a few embellishments (interpretation),

to-be-expected (the smile, the sleeping-under-the-piano), this uncle who he married into a family of a very few families of self-hating, self-loathing, self-everything Viennese Jews who they formed a secret-society-type-discussion-group,

an organization whose purpose it was to secrete and discuss the life and work of one Weininger if you know him,

geboren in Wien in 1880 who he became a Christian, converted on the very same day that he received his Ph.D. in 1902, Weininger who he formulated a philosophical justification of male-superiority, who he hated women almost as much as he hated Jews like himself, Weininger the Jew who he formulated an idea that every human, meaning me, you, my me, your me, your you, my you that we are all unions (not like those in the wings soon to be on quintuple-hooved-overtime),

but are all unions, matings of male and female: male the positive, productive, logical and ethical and female the pleasure, whore, or the procreative, mother, Weininger did who he then went on to think, write and publish the idea that the Jew is not of a race or a religion but that the Jew is instead an element or force in all people, in all of us, an element of force found in people like us who they think they are Jews just as it is found in people who they don't want anything to do with the Jews, the Jewelement or Jewforce an impulse that it believes in nothing, utterly nihilist and wasteful, believes not even in the male as the female does according to my friend the Jew pianist from the Caucasus according to Weininger and so it's understood why the Jew, why the Jewelement, the Jewforce why it and with such elemental grace always gravitates to anarchism, materialism, empiricism, Socialism, atheism, Zion-ism,

Ismism and can only be cured, quote unquote cured with the absolute rejection, societal, if not destruction of Judaism and the Jews and its and their faith in nothing, in zero in this absurd but you have to admit Jewishly brilliant synthesis of Romanticism, Wagnerism, Nietzscheanism and psychology and so on in a three-sex anatomy of the soul — man, woman, Jew — which it wouldn't be lost on some later German thinkers with a National Socialist Weltanschauung but didn't necessarily win him, Weininger, many friends among Vienna's Jews at the time (excepting this family and its life-sick Weiningersalon),

and that and depression,

a general malaise, like what's-it-all-worth?

like

like I'm a Jew too and so I'm just helping out, saving the world by doing this realization it finds him and only a moment after the publication of his masterpiece

Geschlecht und Charakter if you know it up in the rooms that Beethoven he lived in in Vienna, Beethoven his idol, van Beethoven the featured composer of a million CONCERTO COMPETITIONs and there, in the Master's study, at the age of 23, Weininger what does he do? he goes and slits his throat to death,

to enable his ideas at least to achieve some semblance of immortality, to be discussed at the salon of this uncle's wife's relatives at their ne plus ultra deluxe apartment that it was on Bergstraße in Vienna where the uncle he was welcomed less for his analytical/philosophical mind than for his knowledge, his mental repository of raw data on the Life & Times of Ludwig van Beethoven:

an obsession of his that prevented him from ever attending the meetings of the salon on evenings when Beethoven's activity it has been documented, preserved and passed down and so you can empathize, I hope, with this very Jewish obsession,

an obsession not unlike an Asian obsession but with more metaphysical purpose,

not an exact as quiet, indeed dispassionate to almost mindless reproduction of an Old Masters painting,

or a whole town's reenactment of a Passion Play — every decade in thanks for being spared of the Plague, at Oberammergau deep in Bavaria,

but a recreation of the creative impetus and environment is what he the uncle had in mind, indeed an inhabiting of time and of space (use of only early 19th century technology: no telephones, phonographs, automobiles and so on),

as much as an incarnation or incarnating of a mind and so just as Beethoven he kept a copybook in his deaf days, this uncle he went around Vienna and wherever else Beethoven he toured with wool dipped in ether stuck in his ears to deafen himself unto everything except the very geniuslessness resounding inside him, and a copybook or actually a copy of a copybook tucked under his most artistic arm into which he the uncle wrote exactly what Beethoven he wrote and at the same time only 100 years later as

exactly as we humans we never manage: *1770–†1827, 1870–
1927 or rather 1883 when he, the uncle, was 13 and begged his
parents out in the Caucasus to move to this town in the West it
was named Bonn so that he their only child could then reenact,
could recompose the already decomposed first and unnumbered of
the Master's concerti in the same city the following year when he'd
be 14 and Beethoven 114 (though after 1927, after his 57th year
with Beethoven lived or relived out there wasn't anything left to do
and so),

    but this greatuncle he also kept his own copy or
conversationbook and in this one he the uncle kept not his own
thoughts (because he was as selfless as an Asian, actually looked
like one too, his people though assuredly Jews they were quite
obviously from the Caucasus),

    but contemporaneous accounts of the Master's life from
his peers,

    or maybe not his peers but at least from the people who
were around him, Beethoven, scribbled-in and on the appropriate
date as I remember, from BOOK B, some entries that his nephew
(so unlike Beethoven's nephew, that beautiful boy, cause of such
grief!),

    a few entries my friend the Jew piano professor he showed
me once when he had me up to his brownstone in the West 60s
near the Conservatory and the Park where,

    and very pleasantly didn't try to hide his disappointment
when I stood in the doorway without the Schneidermann I'd
promised to bring, and instead — because Schneidermann he
couldn't go, couldn't find his shoes, insisted yet again that he
wouldn't accept a new pair from me — brought a bottle of dead
grapes to atone, to sit on his labial, reddest leather sofa and read in
the tattered volume an entry quoting the Viennese, not Austrian,
conductor Ignaz von Seyfried:

    "In improvisation, Beethoven did not deny the element in
his character which tended rather to the gloomily somber."

    or the words of Josef Gelinek, Viennese, not Austrian,
composer who according to the uncle and so the grandnephew was
quite famous in his day: "The young man has the very devil in
him. I've never heard playing like it!"

    thinking all the while — as we were waiting for the mini-

schnitzel

schnitzel-in-cranberry-and-cream-sauce hors d'oevres to be served
by his housekeeper his mistress — but why still?

yes, I couldn't help asking then to myself as much as I did
though later to my Schneidermann who he was absent that evening,
asked why now?

like why is it that almost two hundred years after
Beethoven's death, new millennium and all, yes, why are we still
suckling the man's Schwantz? as Schneidermann he would say,

that the idea that numb trustfund Asians just off the
tarmac from Hiroshima and Nagasaki that they're still practicing
their nights away,

placticing as they'd say deep into the Napoleonic fray, it's
insane!

almost unbelievable!

like haven't we had enough already?

what's new? and the answer is nothing much since then,
nothing much since van Beethoven he became Beethoven only,
thanks, since the aristocracy it was asked and politely to go fist
itself

and fist itself it did, and tightly,

so that making money was money made and not money to
support art anymore in this age without qualities,

this age without values,

this world aged to deathless ageless death as Schneidermann he used to say,

and the tragedy isn't that we're better off now, more free,
it's that we know we're better off now, freer:
in this worldless global age,
in this proportion that's all out of proportion,
in this form-without-form,
in this inept fugue without flight into climate-controlled
void,

this 11-fingered concerto's cadenza that's all a pointless
recapitulation, an empty reprise, a summing-up ultimately of
nothing,

yes, and the year that I first heard this groan, this gas, this
hiss, this noise all around it was my last winter, yes, it was my last
Purim, my last winter and my last Purim in Europe, my last Purim
in my last Europe,

the last festival of lots in a time of lots of lasts, a time like all time before the War in the matinee movies it was winter,

that last winter I was forced to spend touring with my true father and but without my true Schneidermann: the two of us we were doing a spa-circuit, from Bad to Bad to worse and around again, my father and I we were doing the hit parade for all these bloated beasts in robes of fat playing Samson with the columns of the colonnades, yes, we were in the second city of the tuberculosis empire that day into night, that holiday's holinight we were in Marienbad, now as then under the First Republic it was known as Mariánské Lázně,

only a year or so later to become a Schutzstaffel playground, R & R for the SS,

in the hall there we were going over we were always going over some Schubertiana when this teardrop of a man he just walks right in, interrupts our unneeded but my father he always, needed, insisted upon it daily rehearsal as if he the man lived there, owned the joint the hall the Saal which maybe he did, sure, why not? didn't say anything until we'd finished the unfinished, unfinishable movement, until we had in updated stürming und dränging mit all that ineffable drum und dran played unto the posthumous end — my father at the piano, serviceable but never generous, me at me — to then and as an official of the local Jewish community cordially invite us in the softest, most lambthroated and solicitous voice I have ever heard outside of an opera not by Wagner, to invite me and my father (but mostly me and especially my violin if only it would lug and play itself without me,

without *interference*),

and so just inviting me with my father as baggage to the great Byzantine spring of the Marienbad synagogue that early evening and to hear the megillah being read,

to witness in song the history of Esther the Queen, Queen Hadassah of Persia and her brother, social-climber and confidant his name it was Mordechai and the redemption of their people, of your people, of my people and my father, Jewsensing free food and homemade pear slivovitz if not a mitzvah in the offering he agreed, accepted for the both of us and so we went an hour later, two hours before the recital it was scheduled to the grand if already falling apart inside synagogue you say or temple, shul I've always said as

my

my father he said in Marienbad,

      not as plush, as posh as Carlsbad but impressive enough
— for families let's say like the Levinskis who they changed their
names to protect themselves, to conceal the always innocent, who
they in the 50s invited me often to their property upstate but not
as a person, not as a fellow human being but as a violinist, this I
always understood that when my presence it was requested it was
the presence not of me that was desired but the presence of my
talent, my taste in deploying it when they used this ploy:

      we'd love to have you,

      pause,

      and your music for dinner at 8 — this I always understood and
more than always resented as much as I loved it, indeed thrived on
it, the effect of my true and only presence, on men, on my rivals,
especially on women, my object,

      and on the assembled there in the shul in Marienbad on
that last Purim as I played, improvised what I thought was a
Jewsounding tune, dispatched a snatch of embellished klezmer-
liturgy for a few minutes I thought high-class,

      then they clapclapped, and the rabbi's son he ascended to
the almemar and began to read, to sing the megillah (the rabbi he
was already drunk, half to sleep and my playing it lulled him the
rest of the way)

      and as we came to the first and always heart-numbingly,
seat-edged expected mention of Haman, the son of Hammedatha
the Agagite if you know him, the progenitor of Amalek whose only
mission it was, indeed is always in perpetuity the destruction of
the Jews, of us, of myself and (grandfather to Hitler, Saddam and
Osama if you follow the news),

      and yes, as per tradition, as is a mitzvah all the Jews they
all began shouting, all the Jews in anemic gingerbread Marienbad
all in ragged unison they all began shouting at this mention, at the
name, making noise as is proscribed to blot out HAMAN's name
from the earth,

      to obliterate the name of the hated people Amalek who
they waylaid the Israelites in a desert more real, less coral colonnades littered with shattered souvenir sipping vessels of those
taking the bubbling hot cure gone dead and normally, politely —
or as I was used to, my father too — on Purim and at the mention

of Haman the audience in the shul they would make noise only for
a moment and then and only then the reading, the singing it would
continue but they, then, in Marienbad and maybe just maybe it was
their local custom, their way of doing things, what-they-went-by,

their minhag, but they made such a noise! unstoppable
noise out of every hole and seam:

mouth-noise, yes,

but also nose-noise,

ear and eye-noise,

hand and foot-noise even for a full minute at the hearing,
the speaking of the first NAME, for two minutes, three,

huge booms like the American explosions they were
already delivered! arrived! ordnance from their very mouths!

in enormous bombination, thunderings for five minutes,
10 in howling, wolf-whistling insane through two-fingered fists,
with teeth smashed out, lips pursed in gummed ruin,

noise ripping throats, shredding them into red standards
strange,

reeds of voice lashing out to bind the very letters of the
hated NAME,

to bring the shul to collapse with stomping and knuckle
rasps unto 15 minutes,

20 of cool cracked leather screams!

thongs of pure shriek! until my father, in the midstless
midst of all this — in fear for my career as much as for my life, I
guess — he grabbed me and ran me out into the muzzled street
with my violin in its case in his third hand, its handle then in his
mouth and all the shortest way back we ran back to the old Hotel
Weimar and its concerthall where we sat as near each other as we
ever did on the low stage for another hour,

feet dangling gravity, almost dead but shaking life, refusing
to talk to one another, unable to, to utter mindless one, make any
sound whatsoever about tonight, about tomorrow, about our
itinerary over the next two weeks, passports and traintickets until I
would be — and finally — reunited with my Schneidermann,

and I played that night but I played horribly, all shook,
out-of-tune,

as if any sound it was that NAME,

indeed was any name which they were all equally terrible,

except

except my own up on the marquee 10-feet-tall,

but at least my father whose name one of my sons has, at least and for once he didn't whip me.

And so, noise.

What passes for thought, as thought passes — who's left to leave unfinished a Requiem for thought? what sort of grave? what sort of headstone? an epitaph?

Here lies, here lies,

when I'm supposed to be offering you some, any, enlightenment: that's my calling, my duty and so you enforcers of the Law out there tonight, you, Chief and his squad, I warn you to watch out for the noisemakers, for the peace-disturbers,

not the howling pants-pissed drunks and their tailless dogs, a two-day Harlem party but the real noisemakers: those whose creations destroy thought,

the big-building men, the financiers, anyone who does lunch with Mister Rothstein out there, the paperless polluters, watch them:

because it's because of them that I can't sleep at night — awake and mentally going over contracts out on me, stipulating who I can play with, where I can play with them, what we'll play together even out on the road when I should just take it to the streets, the rooftops,

serve and protect the needs of the thinkers, bluemen and blackwomen!

beware the silent noise too, pull it down! break out the cranes and the cherrypickers! raze the ads to their very foundations, smash in all the displays,

and the screens: because while silent noise is itself not noise neither is it so nonexistent as to be true silence,

more like a whisperweight hum Schneidermann he often said,

the self's manufacture of noise when the world around the self, the world representing the self, is for some rare moment and reason silent as Schneidermann he often maintained (in the matinee movies, as the lights dimmed, hush, expectation, God! Schneidermann that's what he lived for, died of),

because the world, our world, has conditioned us to produce interior noise when the noise of our external — worldly

— machinations somehow, somewhy, falls silent was the phenomenon that Schneidermann he often remarked upon when,

or do we all become deaf, at some point, at some fact,
become numb to the world and train our ear inward? Schneidermann he always wanted to know, offered an earlier self as proof,

molding our ears like Canaanite clay around each and every
canker of existence, auricles becoming dumb vessels for this living
discord unto the exceeding of every capacity and our heads they
just shatter out like the month of Purim?

like the month named Adar leaping itself like a mountain
on fire into a second Adar (two tablets),

intercalated flame,

exploding into waste! into noise! the din of the spring of
1938 resounding swell in my ears forever longer than months they
can contain:

God! all the rituals, laws and habits, the feather, the heifer
made of ash, my father in a three-piece suit and sweating glorious
wit, the blaring gossip of the table over the ground bass of the
Haggadah on Passover, Pesach for the purists and we'd sit, would
be shouted out down the enormous as old oak table stretching all
the way back to Egypt proper probably, table with lion paws on the
Persian probably from Shushan rug not yet stained as if the since
housebroken beast it had sinned and bad enough to be turned to
wood with a new tablecloth on top, all the family there and at
attention to themselves, each to his or her own place in order of
favor I once thought to my grandfather's right (before I understood how easily he or just his political affiliations confused us),

anyway each in his or her own relation to the head, my
grandfather who,

and how I was estranged and irrevocably so from the
Cousins as I called them (some were just children of close family
friends),

my Cousins all around my age and only because of my
abilities as if I was responsible in any way for them I was estranged, and irrevocably, because of my talents I was removed or at-
a-remove, because of my talent I was saved for great if not greater
things, greatest as music it always *got in the way,*

music it always *interfered,*

music it always prevented me,

my

my life,

my world and so the whole world, everyone's from *a semblance of normalcy,*

from relationships which would have, I'll admit it, failed anyway — doubtless, they all do, give it time — and so, final-reckoningwise, music might have to absolutely has saved me from a significant measure of pain, grief, in point of fact, yes, that's what talent does, that's what addiction it does, that's what it means *to have no say in the matter,*

an addiction to talent, to yourself:

it saves you from the wheat-high world on those Passover seder nights when the Cousins they would try to slam your fingers green, leaf-thin in all the doors' hinges to make you unto them, unto who they at least were intended to become: dead in Poland or petty, bureaucratified civil servants at worst, always super-confused immigrants at best to starve their children's children's way to the top,

but this was seder at their house, over There, in Budapest near Gödöllő, in Pest to be precise, either when and where they lived in Ferencváros or later when they moved though not for too long to Józefváros and I was 10 years old, 11 maybe, 12, 13 and all the family they were together and for the last time as I wasn't,

as I was upstairs in that fading, paling house just crying the stones out of my sockets because the Cousins they wouldn't include me, wouldn't have me in their smoking session out in the shared yard, smoking leaves wrapped in leaves, newish spring leaves, green as wet so they wouldn't burn as well as their bodies did just a few years later with me upstairs in my uncle's — and I suppose my aunt's — bedroom all damask and still,

my body spread out on the floor and un or subconsciously practicing,

practicizing fingerings: lefthand violin positions straight out of a facile, though conceptually-sound, perusal of the two volumes of Joachim and Moser's *Violinschule* (Berlin, 1902–05),

or was it Spohr's? practicing these first on the trunk of a rubbertree, a wilting as it was perennially unsunned spiderfern maybe it was and then — how it traveled there I do not know, never do — on my small, hard as death putz, moving fast to savage whirr my three purple main veins as if to explode my head up and off to the sky as a star sorely-needed

and all in the hyper, amped-up fingerings now of the Beethoven or was it the Brahms *Violin Concerto*, my father, which? he wouldn't let me learn yet but which I was learning anyway and secretly, actually by ear and then on a high note,

I forget which because sometime, when in there the fingering to keep all limber and make up for a missed session due to the holiday practice blurred, became usurped and imperceptibly to me into purple stroking full-two-fisted,

and *hard*,

I exploded up! all over my face! my shallow neck spattered, jizzum also heavy on the fake rubbertree leaves dripping tears down the ribs, globbing on the fern, jizzum spanning my cheeks, pooling in their dimples,

bubbling over my nostrils,

bursting salt over my mouth, up and under my glasses to mix with my weep of joy on the night of the first seder of the last Passover with the Cousins outside smoking leaves newly sprung from the old oaktrees and then,

wiping my seep with the edge of my uncle's — and my aunt's — bedcurtain, cleaning up and off but more like smudging my glasses into backlit white, ghost,

I heard my name among the Cousins' names being called to come in and downstairs for the seder to begin as I wiped again,

then again,

a smear,

unto a greasy red sickness as I replaced my wilted penis amid the burning crust,

and groped my way stomach-ached, to the stairhead at which I paused, and stopped.

Unable. Unworthy. Denied. Disallowed I was,

I couldn't go on, Mister Rothstein, couldn't make it, Misses Rothstein who you seem so incredibly interested out there shredding manicured nerves with your stub,

and do you know why? know that I wanted to, needed to, absolutely had to:

my aunt she was calling me and my mother she was dead so when my aunt called — my father's sister or my mother's sister, I never knew — I listened.

But

But blocking my path, the stairhead, was what I won't call
it a black or a blank screen, a white or just empty rectangle projected into air — no, this was life not the matinee movies — it
just was, there,
    and, I, just,
    plainly,
    clearly, couldn't descend the same stairs that I'd ascended
and perfectly well not an hour or more ago — not that I didn't try,
I did, was prevented, barred, blocked.
    I ran into the space and was repelled,
    twice,
    three times, thrown, landed on my tush as Schneidermann
would say, another time, and another with a run behind me and was
again, yet again, repelled, bounced hard through the hallway's
ambit back to my uncle's — and my aunt's — room, indeed
through their room and flung out the shut, many-paned window,
    and *hard!* shattering the breathing, bubbling glass, crucified
in mullion and yet landing somehow quite unscathed on a balcony,
    the balcony one of three of a neighboring house,
    onto a garden of a balcony,
    a balcony edged in boxed hanging gardens and so,
    okay,
    a bit cut up, bleeding in scrape I had landed, was on the
lap of a neighbor, a widow who she spent all her waning days
staring into the house I was just expelled from, gazing lust into my
uncle's — and my aunt's — room, observing the nothingness
testifying false to her steaming imagination,
    had landed on her lap and quick as a modulation, a mood
shift for the 1st violins (though we should have also some walking
bass and maybe muted brass swells as well)
    his pants were down (this event, Schneidermann he always
said that this event that it was the most important event of his
creative life, of his *creationary life*),
    his pants were down and she — a withered widow who she
was 60 Schneidermann he said if she was a day — she used his
own just spent juices to lube him back to length and there he was
again, proud, high as the American flag, which as the girlscouts
they always remind us should never touch the ground,
    like magic at that age which for him I believe it was 10

and so while his immediate family (his nine aunts, his revolving
accompanists in four-hand piano pieces and his unfortunate
brother Rudy),

and his extended family to cousins (on the other side),
while they were busy waiting for him and for him only to begin, to
prelude the seder with a choice musical selection, nothing too
challenging for their seder, their order (their seder which it skipped
the liturgy, the Haggadah, was only a meal) — he, Schneidermann,
was and ineptly as you'd expect at that age which when he told it
over and over again it got younger and younger Schneidermann he
was vaginally engaging his nonet of aunts' 60-year-old and widowed neighbor nextdoor,

masturbating for the first time, losing his fist-virginity
and his virginity-virginity on the same day, on the first or sometimes the second night of Passover as Schneidermann he often told
it, of passing-over, within the same hour, half-hour as Schneidermann he often maintained — that's youth, formative, never to be
recaptured, recreated, not even in the made-for-teevee adaptation
that'll never work, that'll never be in the works, that'll never then
insult the post-nuclear ratings advisory people with this scene:

Schneidermann at the age of 10 already wise in his
knowing,

engaging this neighbor's folds gray-old, for an hourplus of
eternal youth out on her alabaster, immaculately-kept terrace just a
man's soft length from his 36-limbed relatives' house,

one room for each limb it seemed (houses in those days
even in the East and if you had the gelt as Schneidermann always
said enormous, even in the center city, but spaced so unbreathably
close together and since bombed or otherwise demolished, replaced
by new housing units, concrete cementing plastic, which, in their
immaculate stupidity, sheer panel upwardness, offer nothing but
insult to what we all once knew, loved, and, most importantly,
fundamentally misunderstood as EUROPE

or at least I did, refused to understand, my generation did,
my death-generation),

among them Schneidermann doing her out on a gleaming,
wrought-iron pediment facing in,

a whorl of sanatorium white into kronk municipal green as
Schneidermann he often described it to my imagination,

bush

bush and bird masonry collapsing itself all around in jags
of fall with him, Schneidermann — and by his own account(s) —
trying to wrap his hairless 10-year-old arms around her, his hands
seeking cup,

to claw her old woman though tight flab as he sailed,

tunneled into her, again and again,

Schneidermann to me: she was missing a nipple, I think it
was her right, never asked her about it and wouldn't have.

Schneidermann to me: I couldn't find her nipples, try as I
might and I tried, couldn't find them, searched up, searched down,
not happening, nowhere to be found, the nipples, perfectly
nippleless.

Schneidermann to me: two snowed-over mountains,

two snow-covered hills,

two boardwalk sno-cones (Coney Island, Brighton),

two half-suns,

two half-moons,

smooth, perfectly smooth and I, I groped them sore as I
shtupped her Schneidermann said that he shtupped her up there
while the family they waited on me,

was made to wait for him, forced:

they sent spies out, cousins to the far fat recesses of each
room and taunting at my name, there to forage for the foreign
element, the afikomen for all they knew, that which was making
them late, prolonging the food, the meal, prolonging it longer than
any observed liturgy would have and me, Schneidermann he once
said, mentally, emotionally I'm still up there, three floors high and
shvitzing in the mid-spring,

she's holding me and whispering why Dolfi, Wolfi, like her
own personal Muss es Sein?

as my second load it hardens to her navel hairs,

like a second skin and she's moaning! won't stop moaning!
over the teevee inside on the volume setting 18 as Schneidermann
he told me this and for the nth time outside on *my* balcony,

outside on *my* terrace,

out on my Sinailike penthouse patio at the Grand, the
hotel of choice for those who actually can afford one, a choice, this
about maybe 10-12 years ago, me in town for the purposes of
concertizing (I lived in Maine then, a leafy hovel, spending much

time though teaching ex-Soviets in Jerusalem and also down with
an exwife in Florida:

fold the country lengthwise in half and you have Maine
and Florida, Maine kissing Florida, Maine going down on if not
gagging on Florida — two places I'll never go back to, can't, two
states I can never be in again, two ideas I hate and hate equally and
yet they're complete, absolute opposites, polar),

out in the winter like we're having now,

almost a Kamchatka winter as Schneidermann he always
said, with us bundled up in inebriation and furs out on the balcony, gossiping over the teevee's volume setting of 18 and I,

I had a recording session tomorrow, a recording date, that
tomorrow, what was eventually and after all too much legal hassle I
won't get into brought out but by an Asian label as the 35TH
ANNIVERSARY recording of his,

of Schneidermann's *3rd Violin Sonata*,

a mini-*Concerto* unto itself, this cadenza not included on
the record I had to after all pretty much pay the record multina-
tional to finally put out and advertise (an initial limited edition
release after which the Asians they up and obtained the rights),

had to agree to three recordings of post-post-post-Roman-
tic shit just to get that incredible *Sonata* down on tape, disc, and
pressed for those on my X-mas list (Schneidermann and) — and
Schneidermann he'd elevatored up to my penthouse at the Grand
more to socialize, schmooze as Schneidermann he always said (I'd
been out of the city a six-week lifetime),

than to talk me through that piece of his which we'd
anyway been through something like 6,000,000 times together
prior,

that work which is available wherever finer paragons of
artistic irrelevance are sold and instead of either (rehearsal or
schmoozing), Schneidermann he ended up telling me again and for
the xth time all about his Passover before the war (the First World
one),

before the War after which Schneidermann he often joked
not that you'd laugh that he was often mistaken, mixed up or just
his name was with the name of the man who he though prema-
turely declared the founding of the Weimar Republic: the Socialist
and Prime Minister Philipp Scheidemann if you know him, though

the

the two in my Schneidermann's youth they did look alike around
the neck, the President of the short-lived to almost unlived Weimar
Republic it was Ebert, the last name and intelligence of a famous
movie critic who,

all about his last Passover before the War to end all wars
but it didn't (the 3rd movement of that *3rd Violin Sonata* it's a set
of earnestly abstruse but underneath all ironic variations on an old
Germanified Haggadah tune),

all about vaginally engaging his nine-wombed aunts'
widowed neighbor as we drank glass after glass into the night of
some Bohemian Sekt an — otherwise tasteless — admirer of mine
he had sent up from the ice below.

Here the view was of Manhattan, not the backside of some
petit-bourgeois home in Pest.

Here were, are, air streets emptied above the ego-traffic,

and all I wanted to do (besides engage in a *mutual exchange
of ideas* with Schneidermann)

was to get on that bluest white airplane back to Jerusalem,
where everyone sane they were exploding the history out of each
other, themselves — anywhere but here, anywhere but Maine and/or
Florida,

any's where just away from the hippies and the retired, the
survivalists and the dead, and thank God you can't be in those two
places at once!

This was destined to be one of our *dynamic visits* (with the
Steinway grand María-polished, hauled up to my suite as per my
standing special request),

a *dynamic visit* which Schneidermann — out of his 50-year-
recent element in all this Grand opulence, out of his element
always, never knew what not to do first — a *dynamic visit* that
Schneidermann he often defined for me as one in which each party:

holds nothing in reserve,

if you want to do something, do it,

if you don't want to do something, then don't — and expressed in
this way, you understand, this hold-nothing-back,

this urge to restrain restraint and expressed in this way it
comes off as quite a quaint Old World formality, a stiff gesture, a
throwback from the time before movies when everyone anyway
acted as if they were actually in a movie and explain that,

or an opera, explain that, the frankness if not the Schneidermanness of a man lived on past his allotment (yes, I'm handing you your interpretation, that's what I do, what you pay me for, what you pay for me),

and that expressed like this, in this way, this *dynamic visit* that Schneidermann he meant and meant ironically meant also among everything, anything:

meant freedom of exchange, relaxation, was to be agreed-upon prior to the exchange, prior to the relaxation, to put all at ease, to establish the mutual understanding that now and only now is it acceptable, indeed are you allowed, asked, urged even to kick your shoes off, loosen your collar (separate from your shirt, of course),

roll up your shirtsleeves, get down to work and that and only that's how this man,

this mensch,

he, how this Schneidermann he always kept his hands and such hands! in a time that has passed us all by,

which has cut short its own, huge, dynamic visit in the most obscene, pitiless form possible (matinee movies),

or at least imaginable (American matinee movies), ladies and gentlemen,

and that once this permission's been granted, then beware,

be on guard against granting this permission to just anyone, to strangers no matter how veritable, yes, be skeptical especially of living, of existing in a society in which this permission it's in-wired, taken-for-granted because then — then you have to know too, to understand also that Schneidermann, that his sexual life over here, his 80-years-plus following his Pestilent defloration, over 50 of them spent as spent over here, in this great nation you need to understand that his, that Schneidermann's sexual life it can be reduced and without exaggeration to the wonderful phrase

mental masturbation as Schneidermann he always put it,

or *ideational masturbation* as Schneidermann he often said,

or *stroking-of-the-mind* as Schneidermann he once told me,

but I feel it relevant or just exciting to recall that there was, possibly, in this half-century of celibacy only half-involuntary, what is known as a *bag lady*,

a

a homeless older female who had allowed him, by his own
account, to penetrate her through a hole in her bag but,
    again but,
    that possibly might serve us as an example of
Schneidermann's always eccentric, always idiosyncratic to at times
like this just not very funny sense of humor,
    humor with the humor removed was what Schneidermann
he mentioned to me at least once as the guiding principle of his
work,
    or of his non-work, Schneidermann's as I now remember
— and as per Picasso I was, and as always, treating him, Schneidermann, at a finer Frenchtalian restaurant:
    at Chez Chez, Chez Giovanni, Chez Something or Other
it doesn't really much matter except to say that the mafia it
arsoned it down a few-five years ago, and how after we'd ordered
and ate and the check it came, to me who was overtimes better
dressed (Schneidermann pre-rumpled in a house-jacket, the cuff of
a pantleg ripped away, Windsor-knotted around his neck as a tie),
    and how he, how Schneidermann how he tried to foist off
a musical sketch that he'd fountainpenned (half a fugue, my pen a
Mont Blanc that Schneidermann he often called a Mont Blank,
Schneidermann who he kept always a pencap clipped to shirt's
pocket, the pen itself it was lost long ago),
    a musical sketch that Schneidermann he'd fountainpenned,
mine, on a napkin, theirs the restaurant's, to pay for our bill in lieu
of cash or credit, convinced that it would work, Schneidermann he
thought, knew it would suffice tip included to pay for it all but all
they did, the manager, maitre'deranged and the waiter all without
apology, was to add the — retail — price of the napkin onto our
bill because after all it was a fine linen napkin now ruined and how,
in walking afterwards,
    Schneidermann never apologizing, whereas I was always
apologizing, always in a state of apology, constantly caught in
apology,
    how Schneidermann instead of apologizing and perhaps
just to save face he told me that he'd received a letter,
    a *communiqué* was his word and so a communiqué it was
written on a — stained — pillowcase of and from an elderly
admirer (every season it seems that all our admirers they're

elderly),
        a pillowcase/slipcover written on in one account lipstick,
or blood,
        or burnt matchstick and but giving an address in far
Uptown New York, Uptown-Uptown verging on the Bronx and
how Schneidermann he went, and why not? what to lose? Inwood it
was,
        nothing else to do except art and we all know how much
that's worth in America, and so Schneidermann he went and
walked, Schneidermann he always walked whereas I always take cabs
everywhere in this town because like you I'm a patron of the arts
— walked higher and higher,
        and higher to losing two shoes, all of his shoes in his
progress and Schneidermann he would've lost three if he had had
that many feet,
        and maybe just maybe he'd read the address wrong,
probably, most definitely unless it was a joke, but who so desperate
as to play a jokeless joke on a 90-year-old Hungarian-Jewish
Schneidermann?
        up there where the city's deserted, a desert of desiccated
asphalt, up that high where no one can breathe without a mask or a
tank, up near the antenna-horned unicorns frolicking static at the
Cloisters, past the complimentary-mint newsstands and bundled
readerless and maybe even printless newspapers (ALL THE NEWS
THAT'S PRINT TO FIT that's what Schneidermann he often
said),
        an old man pitiless as pitiful running past the blocks
abandoned, running on beerbottle shards, malt-liquor turds, over
meridians of ash, motor oil, syringe discharge, thick food-stamp
vomit, potholes full of rainwater and globules of anal salve,
        limping in run oblivious to soon bare soon bloodied feet,
not slowing, never, not ever and all the while dripping a flower-juice
trail
        like a snail in bloom I, I come to the address specified and
but it's an abandoned building — holding these huge sweet-dying
flowers, I'm feeling especially *gay*
        in the old meaning of the term, meaning ready for love and
women,
        always ready for love and women because and at heart I'm a

staunch

staunch admirer of Western Humanism,

  but the building, it seemed condemned, a dropout, looked a ruin:

  all fall like the last tenement left standing on Olympus, all the windows boarded up to crumbling around the voids all except one, one on the top-top floor, in the middle, the center window of the 5th floor just filled by a stained-with-what? American flag hanging there vertical:

  stars atop in their close ranks absolving the logic of any constellation, stripes striping down on this old, holdover flag of 48 states don't ask me why or how I counted as I stood outside debating,

   questioning,

  less than answering myself,

  really Socraticizing as to whether or not I should try, venture, enter, attempt ingress, if then then what was it worth?

  was it worth it for an easy, quick — if probably speech-less-strange — shtup? when a baby, just a baby it went flying out of the American flag window, no more than a toddler, an infant really and wet and definitely thrown out (but by who? why?)

  and hard to fall six stories! maybe seven down! and — thankfully or thanklessly depending — just landing on a high wild hedge, unkempt bushery and without a scream as the American flag it flapped back into place and I ran, just ran as I was ashamed,

   unsure,

  ran back backwards as if leaving the presence of majesty I ran two blocks, three:

  impossible to find a cab in the neighborhood, impossible in the whole upper demographic but I found a limo just idling, of course up that forsaken high you won't find a taxi but a limousine and I tapped manic on the tint of eyeless glass until the African-American gentleman he rolled down the window and I offered him $300 to take me Downtown,

  anywhere Downtown from here and quick! and I ended up leaving the bouquet of lilies-of-the-valley in the limo's backseat,

  dripping no more, neither was I even after all that walking home that it reminds me of shoes,

  not those which my wives ex and present they love and have bankrupted me for the love of but shoes lost, those which

Schneidermann he always referred to and with not the slightest irony that's not warranted as *life*:

 understand that Schneidermann he had two shoes, that one pair of shoes they owned him, sizes too large for him, sizes too wide and that when he walked (to the grocerystore, to the matinee movies, the newsstand that Schneidermann he always said *tabak*),

 that they'd inevitably, invariably fall off,

 one or the other or both and that Schneidermann he wouldn't notice the loss or the losses until he got home (his apartment, his room),

 and tried to take his shoes off at the door (as the Old World tradition, as the Asian tradition),

 and that then and only then would Schneidermann notice that he had no shoes to take off or else one less than expected or actually unexpected and so Schneidermann he wouldn't leave the house (the apartment, the room as small as a newborn's ego I have to sort out before)

 again until I'd returned his shoe or shoes back to him because it was my lot, my mission, my sacred though I had to remember, to always remind myself unsworn duty to find his shoe or his shoes — Schneidermann he never bought a new pair, couldn't afford one or them as he got this pair from the army with the worst uniforms in the world, the Salvation,

 and so it being my job, I'd and dutifully stalk the circuit,

 the few blocks around his building searching for a shoe or shoes (and don't forget to look up, to the telephone poles, the laced lines),

 for his shoe or his shoes and then return it or them to him, hunt, pacing the six blocks up and the six blocks down and around his, Schneidermann's, ill-health or just laziness confined him to,

 except if he was heading to the matinee movies — SPIELBERG's movies especially they gave him strength,

 energy,

 emotional as much as intestinal fortitude,

 SPIELBERG's spiels as Schneidermann he always called them they always gave him the will to live because in them, well, everything's possible or if not possible because let's say of the irreversible laws of space/time, or of breathtaking cliché,

then at least everything it will and most assuredly work
out in the end,

by the time let's say we shut the window of 90-minutes'
duration:

lovers in love, at least the Jews starring in the matinee
Holocaust movie they survive, aliens returned to home planets,
neo-dinosaurs prevented from wreaking massive havoc on our
major urban areas — and that these shoes they were often scat-
tered, or shoe, against a curb from where if not when Schneidermann he didn't raise his foot or his feet, his leg or his legs, high
enough for clearance and so the curb it would pry his shoe or his
shoes off, or two different curbs, or the same curb on two different
trips in two different directions and there his shoe or his shoes
would be, lying in the street:

often soaked of dye to gray pools pleather-lined, toes
wedged in a sewer grating or gratings (never stolen, who would?
never irretrievably lost),

as Schneidermann their owner or the owned as Schneidermann he always insisted he was Schneidermann he would just go
shuffling around in his home, in his apartment, in his four-square-
with-whitewashed-walls-room

pacing around and around totally or just partially shoeless,

completely or just incompletely, and which was worse?
unshod just like a Judean prophet or a wild Appaloosa on the
plains of Jeroboam,

like a man named Jesus the authorities they took in for
just being honest, angry and shoeless, hauled in and sentenced
without even being tried by the Jews, the Romans, all the huge-
German-A Authorities

and then what did they do? they nailed him or Him up to
the North Pole,

and set it ablaze at high noon of the Fourth of July,

by the Gregorian Calendar, of course — and so now let us
praise the firefighters! the police and emergency medical personnel
who they have seen fit to assemble here tonight,

or you're all just following orders, I know that excuse:

to charm or coax me down off this perch, this frog
smoking on his perch, this frog-headed-goat, or goat-headed-frog

with the heart of a dove — I salute you gentlemen,
everyone does, and do I hear women out there, am I right?

don't be afraid but don't be too hasty — allow me my
allotted time, until the union quits or gets time and a half, which
is impossible even after Einstein,

allow me my scriptural-plus years of age, its wisdom or
lack and, yes,

okay which is my favorite word made international during
the Second World War, alright, fine: yes, so I've pissed my pants up
here,

drip, drop of water torture,

rivering past my leg hairs down to pool in my own hand-
made alligator shoes, polishing my reflection in their scuff,
preserving my dignity, squash,

squish, and no dear I won't wear the diapers! It's not my
age, not my nerves, no, not anything like that — it's more my fear
of not getting this right,

performance-anxiety from when I premeditated this last
night:

going over and over all the lives in my head, their linkages
and order, their teardrop lineages, the years and their music I knew
that I wouldn't get right, would never get straight, get across,

impossible to improvise with any sense of the real,

and so you might wonder to yourselves at least if I'd
already written something,

anything,

put something down on paper, if I'd formulated what's
known as a

prepared statement instead of just emptying my superfull
head all over Schneidermann's more than just posterity,

and the answer to your non-asked non-question is that yes,
that yes I have and that here it is, in one of these pockets somewhere, on Grand stationery, one of these,

no, this one's not slit yet — I didn't pocket this handkerchief as much as I just stole it, must have caught a cold like a
frisbee this afternoon in the Park when,

but it's not a new suit (I'm not that permissive), it's old
concert dress from a few years ago, funeral black worn to shine —
or here, in one of these interior breast pockets,

the

the slit one,
yes, here it is all crimpled and crumpled up,
stained with spill, the early vodka and late espresso:

I leave my entire estate to the human in Row AA, Seat 100.

that's the last seat in the last row of this the last hall, I
believe, the cheapest ticket — sorry, standing-room-people, only I
need someone respectable as an executor, someone who feels
passionate about something, is willing to pay, to invest in meaning
and that, that's as far as I got.

But do I really intend suicide tonight?

Answers later, to follow, at the Reception, and again: save
your stubs.

Quick! someone, some clown run in from the wings and
shpritz me down with some seltzer.

God! they really soak you in here.

Come on!

You're not picking up on it? not so much fans of audience
participation, are you? too mature? too sophisticated? wit not dry
enough for you?

You're supposed to yell:

You're all wet!

that's one half of the house, and the other half's supposed
to shout, after the first half's finished:

You're all washed up!

Get it?

Come one and come all! take subways or a taxi, get here
anyway you can, scalpers are standing-by, God! you're all welcome
to heckle:

now that the Law's in on it, now that I'm a public nui-
sance all over the 11 o'clock news you might as well get some
overripe, spic-picked Joisey-rotten tomatoes in here from the
bodega on the corner — I'm tired! and some popcorn and
jujubeans again I'm asking and how many times?

I'm tired.

Throw in your badges and your bullets from their guns.

Because the object here as much as our subject isn't as much me as it is Schneidermann, is more specifically Schneidermann's fate,

because what we're interested in here, now, are fates and fates only — because what do lives matter? Nothing. Amount to?

Efes, zero in Hebrew is one of the few words I remember (though zero, nihil it's an Arab idea)

and all prophets they should end up denying their Gods! so take a walk, Schneidermann! take a good long walk, which was pretty much the sum total of your artistic process, non-process, yes, take a good-long-shoelosing-walk!

just like you always did, hands clasped behind your back like Brahms he always did (Beethoven's battered wife, fleeing in fear),

just like that day when mid-movie, mid-matinee, when mid-matinee-Holocaust-movie you just up and disappeared — you always sitting next to me, one-over asking me to repeat the lines you missed and I'm sorry to say that you missed most, me obliging you with my English I learned in London and with my American I learned in America with the reflection of the tropes that you learned in Auschwitz:

in *what had happened*, in

what happened:

the freezing experiment,

eating the ice that was that man's ear,

waking up with a throat sore with ash — how the Selektion it still exists you always insisted, even now you maintained, that now they select only the dumbest, the stupidest, the most inept and then what do THEY do? you asked (THEY being anyone with more money than you, which was almost everyone, with more fame than you, which was most),

answered that they elevate them as high as possible, put them in positions as powerful as the imagination now isn't, and why?

and how all this matinee-movie-going, this theater-attending how it's all false you insisted, how it represents or at least represented for you and your talent a failure, a pure neglect of

true

true life and how it's all wrong! a waste of time that's not ours to
waste, indeed that wastes us and so on and so forth you went and
you raved, but how I can't help it! you said, Schneidermann did,
asked what else is there to do with a mind nowadays except to take
it to the matinee movies? you ranted — and then, yes, that's when
Schneidermann he told me all about his friend Frank was his last
name I think it was, or was it his first?

your friend Frank who he wasn't really your friend,

wasn't really Schneidermann's friend in that while Schneidermann he still thought about him and daily they — him and his
actor-friend Frank — hadn't exchanged a word posted or telephoned with one another for over a decade-and-a-half, was it?
Schneidermann he asked incredulous and then said,

God! that's an eternity in the remembering!

told me and for the last time of a million times all about
how Schneidermann he met this Frank from Prague on the ship
over, the Leviathan (like a drive-thru fish-sandwich Schneidermann
he once said, lunching down on a fast-foodstuff, after a matinee
Something movie, my treat),

and how while Schneidermann he told him Frank that he
Schneidermann intended to stay in New York and to get-in-touch,
good luck and so on,

how Frank he told Schneidermann that there are just two
letters that you needed to know, in America:

an L. and an A. they were the two letters that this Frank he
then said that Schneidermann he then said to me the 12th and the
1st letters in this new alphabet,

the only two letters that you needed in this new language
Schneidermann he already knew half of (Shakespeare),

two little letters meaning the world according to Frank,
meaning Los Angeles as he explained to Schneidermann who then
but years later explained this to me:

the metropolitan-concentration-camp-of-angels is how
Frank he explained it as Schneidermann he told me and for the
final time one day after our matinee Substance Abuse movie at one
coffee-drinking-establishment or another back in the days when
you could still smoke in this city,

I think you can still smoke in certain quarters, sections of
coffee-drinking-establishments in Los Angeles, in HOLLYWOOD

but you can't here in N.Y. — at the coffee-drinking-establishment
at which Schneidermann he told me that this Frank he was an actor
in Germany, or at least in German-speaking-films, that he was born
in Prague or Prag as he called it I guess, who was a survivor, a
through-marriage-somehow relation to Willy Haas who he was now
seeking some work, Frank was, as an actor and in Los Angeles,
   where Schönberg he went, where Stravinsky he went, where
Bruno Schlesinger who he died Bruno Walter went, where Alma
Mahler née Schindler — Klimt, Zemlinsky, Gropius, Kokoschka,
Werfel and Johannes Hollnsteiner — she went packing her anus,
vagina and mouth along for the trip, and where too this Frank
Schneidermann's ship-friend, his immigrant-friend, his long-out-
of-phone-and-postal-touch friend whom Schneidermann he said he
anyway died 10 or so years ago now, then, well, where he went too,
to seek some work as an actor and who indeed was successful
according to Schneidermann who he identified him to me,
forefingered-him-out in numerous movies we just happened to
audience together throughout the 60s, 70s, 80s and early 90s in
matinee movies as numerous as this Frank's roles they were not:
   how this Frank he invariably and always with his accent,
with his German accent, with his Prag-German accent how he was
always cast, typecast, as a Nazi, how this man Frank who he was
deported from Prague to Terezín he survived, made it through
  what had happened, through
  what happened,
   to Theresienstadt with the first transports in winter 1941
according to Frank according to Schneidermann, to that derelict
Nowhere, that purgatory-of-art, fortress-of-music walled with
unreal silence was how Schneidermann he described it to me
(Schneidermann who he'd never been there, went direct from
Europe to Auschwitz, the express train first-class),
   to Terezín, Theresienstadt it was in German Frank he told
Schneidermann who he told me:
   a concentration camp en route to Auschwitz now a barely
functioning enclave of a few thousand, many elderly, gypsies,
miscellaneous undesirables mostly resettled there by the commu-
nists is what I told Schneidermann after I'd visited there when I'd
played Prague that last spring and took a tour with all the rest of
the hyphenated-American-tourists (can you take our picture? it's

easy

easy, just press the button!),

it's there, to that town founded in the early 19th century as a fortress in tribute to the Empress Maria Theresa that the Nazis they established a so-called Potemkin-village-camp, to house the mostly Germanified Jews of Masaryk's republic I've understood,

indeed the tour guide a Terezín-survivor himself said: a stop-off for artists, the intelligentsia and the politically-minded to serve the Reich's Freizeitgestaltung propaganda aims as I've understood,

like when the Red Cross they came to tour a camp, to ensure that they were run quote unquote hygienically and quote unquote humanely they went or were taken there:

a camp where nominal Jewish autonomy was merely a pawn in the Nazi's larger solution as the survivor-tour guide said like he was accepting and from our very wallets the Nobel Prize for Peace,

as Schneidermann and I we heard from a teevee documentary we watched this fall at my penthouse at the Grand we watched the, hour-long-sweeps-week, special on the volume setting 18 — God! the Nazis they might as well have sold tickets to this camp, subscriptions! to this huge, citywide concerthall of deported musicians like Viktor Ullmann and Gideon Klein, Hans Krása and actors like Schneidermann's Frank,

Ullmann, a disciple of Schönberg over there and Schoenberg over here who he Ullmann went to his death a modernist and that's no way for a man to die, or the only way according to Schneidermann who he accorded that idea all the either/or it deserves,

Ullmann who he insisted that "Theresienstadt has served to enhance, not to impede" his music, Schneidermann who he insisted that America it has served to impede as opposed to enhance his music,

we have Ullmann who he speaking for we insisted that "our endeavor with respect to art was commensurate with our will to live," and then we have Schneidermann who he insisted that his endeavor with respect to destroying his art it was commensurate with his will to destroy his life, in New York, whereas we have Ullmann, dead in Auschwitz, 1944, on the same late fall, early winter transport as this Frank who he knew him but who survived,

Terezín that made the amateur Hans Krása focus more on

his music, made him more responsible to his talent, the vessel of
which died (was exterminated)

in *what had happened,*

during *what happened,* New York that made the genius
Schneidermann focus less on his music, made him less responsible
to his life and so to his talent — and now we have movies with a
popular soundtrack and what's called a *classical score*

as Schneidermann he mentioned to me once, nose-deep in
an orange julius:

incidental music by someone as if any music according to
Schneidermann is incidental, like just take a look — never a listen
— at how many charts they have! Schneidermann he couldn't
believe it: top of the pop charts, the homosexual charts, the #1
song on the paraplegic lullaby chart,

like the music for a Holocaust movie — according to
Schneidermann all Jewish music is, whenever a composer he wants
to represent Jews or their music according to Schneidermann it's
always just schmaltz with a minor second, then a major third (and
Schneidermann he sang or rather screeched it for me),

overdubbed shtetl Schneidermann he once said, I hear the
last 10 years has witnessed a huge revival of klezmer music in
Germany, according to Schneidermann,

like tell me all about you and Charlie Parker again, Schneidermann he often asked me, about Charlie Parker and the oboe on
the White Man's with-strings-sessions, a string section of refugee
Jews gone unionized, me among them and I only remember his
sweat,

and his perfection,

tell me about — I asked Schneidermann, on our way out
from a matinee Time-Traveling movie — instead tell me all about
the differences between rhythm and time,

about limitation,

the difference(s) between gesture and meaning and
Schneidermann he instead asked me to inform him all about this
rap music phenomenon,

about the difference(s) between the violent impulse
acted-on, and the violent impulse acted-out was what Schneidermann he wanted to know all about as we exited a matinee movie
in which a rap star he was recruited by the military for top-

secret

secret intelligence-work,

like killing a Kazakh mafioso to sleep with a post-Soviet underwear-model, like the difference(s) between:

I shot dat mutterfucka Schneidermann he sang, rapped, in that voice, rasp, of his and actually shooting that motherfucker, the difference(s) between

I raped dat bitch Schneidermann he rapped, sang, in that rasp, voice, of his from that hole above his chinbandage and below his hat and his wig, Asian eyes and Sinai's nose Schneidermann he wanted to know the difference(s) between

I raped dat bitch Schneidermann he merely said and actually, really, truly, in-waking-life finding and then following this let's say mulatto nurse just off work, a single mother of one maybe just trying to unlock the door to her Washington Heights walkup, keys for fingers and with an armful of hard-earned-groceries, then jumping her, dragging her by the hair to the nearest cinematically-underlit-alley, spilling her groceries all over the asphalt:

her kid's favorite sugar cereal as a treat for good grades, sinless apples, peanutbutterchunk and throwing her the single mother of one against the wall, and trash, taking out your penis, pulling down her uniform's skirt, grandmother underwear and then, and finally! inserting your rigor mortis penis in what is most definitely an unmoist vagina,

and all with the cameras rolling! was what Schneidermann he wanted to know:

like explain white people to me (Schneidermann he was always demanding, at pre-theater-eateries and theaters and post-theater-eateries and always on my dime, on my hundred-dollars),

like explain pain, explain usurpation, explain the suburbs where my daughter Dina she lives,

like explain that guy who he plays the guitar and sings through a nostril named Dylan,

explain why the yes Schneidermann he used the phrase *youth-of-today,*

why they wear pants so large and so low: are their penises really that much larger in length and in girth than the penises of our own generation? Schneidermann he wanted to know,

why grown men nowadays why they wear tight T-shirts exposing their — hairy or hairless — midriffs, like explain why the adolescent males on his street why they all favored sour-apple-lollipops, and were always entering and exiting his neighboring apartment, room, at all hours of the night on all nights throughout the dark 1980s,

like won't you please explain the phenomenon of monolingualism to me? Schneidermann he once asked in the American language (non-language, like I had all the answers as I had three-years seniority as an immigrant),

like explain why his other nostril is named Zimmermann,

like do you really think — Schneidermann he asked me one day on the way out of a matinee movie in which a man from the distant future he returned to the American West, to the 1880s and became a cowboy, a raygun desperado, a spaceage pistolero — like do you really think that Trotsky he ever engaged Frida Kahlo anally?

like what's wrong with two Jews sinning in sodomy on a long, hot Mexican day? Schneidermann he once wanted to know,

like explain why you changed your name in America, what's your Hebrew name? would you ever agree to be in a movie? Schneidermann he asked me that day at that smokeless, coffee-drinking-establishment when and at which he reminded me of his immi-grant-acquaintance Frank, remembered to me his roles or his role which was, were, always as a Nazi,

which was, were, always acted in a voice that was less a parody of the voice — accent, not language — of his youth than a parody of the parody of Doctor Strangelove,

and when this Frank he died how — leukemia, Schneider-mann thought the telegram, the letter that he'd received had said — they whoever they were who they were sent over to his house in Bel-Air by his agent they found in his, in this Frank's wardrobe they found all the uniforms according to his agent whom he found only Schneidermann's address to contact in case of emergency, and why? sad,

he told Schneidermann who he told me, that the agent this Frank's he'd found all those Nazi, all those morbid, moribund, insignified SS uniforms that this Frank he kept from Wardrobe after doing all those roles, all those movies,

told me all about how this survivor-actor, this actor-survivor, how he indeed had found work in America, in L.A., but

had

had found only work in playing the very same people who they had tried to kill him and had indeed succeeded in killing his entire family, who it only now seems had tried to kill him for the sole purpose or the sole purposes of the American film industry and how Schneidermann he said that this was funny, yes,

admitted this to me at that nonsmoking, coffee-drinking-establishment at which Schneidermann he reminded me of this Frank,

how Schneidermann he admitted to himself as much as to me that, yes, this was funny but not as funny as it was wrong, false,

that indeed everything now it was false, that everything in and of itself (all the

*ding an sich*s of this world as Schneidermann he put it) — no, it was that this German-vague-Everything that it wasn't false, that it was just the time that this German-vague-Everything existed in according to Schneidermann, that existed in it and through it that was false,

which rendered it false and like what for example? I asked when I wanted an example (how I always wanted Schneidermann's philosophy to take form, greater structure amid triumphant, quadruple winds and do you hear me now? this?),

and how Schneidermann he said that for instance, example, there's the ozone-threat, it's false, and African-American judges just as African-American rapists and murderers (I apologize, Schneidermann he always said *shvartze*), how they're false now too,

all the movie-tropes following: last-minute love-deaths, false since before I was born Schneidermann he said,

misunderstood mafiosos, false, rappers killing people for their fans, false, so that their fans don't have to, false Schneidermann he said once you understood their pose,

the redux of the 1980s, false, use of the word *redux*, false,

suburban angst, false, playing angst-ridden punk in the garage with the minivan parked in the driveway, false, popstars using heroin so that their fans they don't have to, false (might as well sell the drugs with the album, Schneidermann he suggested),

all technology, false, the guitar, false,

DJs, false, overdubbed string sweetening, false, sampled and superadded harmonies, false,

music in the workplace to increase efficiency, false,
shopping music, surely false,
records, false, recording, false,
public performance, false,
and, in the end, music itself, false and so what's left?
where's a line drawn? and if it's drawn (anywhere!) —
Schneidermann he once asked at the intersection of Help &
Amsterdam Avenue — then is it authorized by the Picasso estate?
and laughed, as if Picasso he didn't do it to himself, Schneidermann he added (said that when he met Picasso that Picasso he
struck him as the worst kind of genius, the kind of genius that
never grows up, a prodigy to the end),

as if Picasso he didn't pre-Warhol Warhol, out-Warhol
Warhol, shoved art into a Warhole, stuffed it in a Warhole (Schneidermann he once said *Warhölle*),

told me that Rilke he saw it all coming and recommended
instant oatmeal to at least one of his correspondents Schneidermann did, told me that Mozart he saw it coming all along, having
to write mechanical organ pieces for Constanze and rent,

and that all these fractures, that they're also false:
this Lesbian/Jew art, this Actor/Recording Artist and just
wait until he writes his memoirs into the heap, this Terrorist/
Movie Star idea that Schneidermann he'd had, that it'd occurred to
him once on the corner of Why & Columbus Avenue,

this White/Anglo/Saxon/Protestant aesthetic that Schneidermann he hated — but what are they still protesting? he asked,
then asked for two tickets to a movie about them (produced by
Jews, GEFFEN KATZENBERG, DREAMWORKS, tickets paid
for by me),

said that the end of last century must mark the end of all
argument, told even me to give it up, to leave it lie, told me to stop
all this German-speaking German-language with him, that we
should just visit in the language — non-language — of America,

then told me to recede to the minority, the fringe, periph-
ery, the *edge* Schneidermann he said if that sounds good to you —
and to remake yourself, me, and we went in, (I) bought concessions and sat.

Schneidermann to me: remake yourself (but he never
talked at the movies).

Schneidermann

Schneidermann to me: pay me to play me.

Schneidermann to me: pay me with your application.

Schneidermann to me: make up words to my music to aid your memory.

Schneidermann to me: to help you interpret.

Schneidermann to me: to guide you in your interpretation.

Schneidermann to me: but the words they can't be American.

Schneidermann to me: will you teach me grammatically correct American?

Schneidermann to me: I haven't heard a bird in 20 years (outside of music, of course).

Schneidermann to me: what do I do for a living?

Schneidermann to me: what do I do?

Schneidermann to me: help.

Schneidermann to me: you think this picture's any good?

Schneidermann to me: what did he say?

He said (I'm summarizing): *I can't help you, Herr Schindler,*
(interpreting) *you're on your own, Herr Schindler,*
don't look at me, Herr Schindler,

and how you stood up when the matinee Holocaust movie it began after the ads for COCA-COLA CLASSIC

and the previews for those boy-meets-girl-meets-boy-meets-girl-meets-death matinee movies — how after all of that Schneidermann he just stood up and shouted into the empty theater as much as to me (that was the sign I should have noticed, his own illuminated EXIT), you shouted:

What's the problem with the quality of the picture?
Black & White, who ever heard?
What's wrong with the color?
I paid 10 bucks for this ticket and I expect my color!
all the colors! (which wasn't true, I always paid),
you trying to rip me off?
Jew me out of my movie experience?
Is the projectionist dead or asleep? and how I — who never knew if you were joking or not — tried to shush you, explained that that was how it was intended by SPIELBERG, all about how black & white, or the lack-of-color, all about how that was supposed to be

like you know artistic,

a high-browjob, was supposed to make you, us, take it the matinee Holocaust movie more seriously, as an artwork, as a work-of-art,

how that it was supposed to make the quote unquote true historical events darker (and darker, as if they could be any darker!),

or maybe just maybe to subconsciously comfort us by maybe saying (whispering into an ear, me into Schneidermann's):

don't worry, Sascha
all this stuff it happened in the past, Sascha
it won't happen now, Shanya, not ever again (I only called him Shanya when everything else it seemed less familiar than him),
see Shanya, it's black & white which means all this stuff it happened a long long time ago Shanya, and in a galaxy far far away,
like you-who-you-are-now, he wasn't even born — like what I often said to my own children:

you, no, don't help me, no hints, starts-with-a-D, Deborah, yes, Dina, like when you were born the world it was already in color,

like my second son Noah you don't know what it was like to be born into a black & white world,

God! how you youth-of-today (that's how Schneidermann he talked),

how you take your spectrum for granted, ungrateful for the rainbow, your covenant with colors, the flood of all those typhus-yellows, and neckwound reds that Schneidermann he insisted on never remembering to me (whenever I asked him about the camps Schneidermann he'd grab my bow and with it bow at his neck, lips pressed tight together he'd fiddle his scar and make these strange high squeaks in his mouth that),

like Schneidermann to me: the basic form of life is the passacaglia. Schneidermann to me: the passacaglia is basically not a form. Schneidermann to me: not a form at all — it's a lazy man's device as you explained it again and again and again as Schneidermann and I we exited the matinee Or Other movie in which an animated woman, girl, she struck me as sexually mature in the extreme,

told

told me that Shostakovich he loved it Schneidermann he
did, the passacaglia the form, non-form that repeats and repeats
and that Stalin did too because he could understand it.

Schneidermann to me: ever read any Walter Pater? (He was
trying to read an essay on the art of the Renaissance at the matinee
movies by the glow of the screen.)

Schneidermann to me: I don't recommend him (as sheer
light it shot across the role).

Schneidermann to me: tickets are getting expensive (they
were), but I always paid — Schneidermann he was always sitting
one seat away from me, one-over, astray-estray, always sitting as I
always sat next to our jackets (my fur-lined down and his jizzum-
rag),

our Mount of Olives jackets in that animated matinee
movie in which an animated woman — girl, mermaiden — she
struck Schneidermann too as exceedingly sexually-ripe, even
arousing and was that a totem in your pocket or were you just
happy to see me? or is that question taboo?

and yes, I know that I should have all the answers, after all
I am to Schneidermann what Horace, not Greeley, said of Orpheus,
said that he was the *sacer interpresque deorum*,

the sacred interpreter of the Gods in your own translation
and as such I address you directly,

as Orpheus, as the man almost God who dies trying —
ever hear that spiel before? as Schneidermann himself would often,
rhetorically, ask,

but Orpheus he wasn't too much Jesus who he or He
wasn't much of a singer,

was more of a talker (so says an exwife),

more a mamele's boy according to Schneidermann, less a
sainted castrato like Haydn who in his youth he was bribed with
cherries — loss-of-innocence — to sing trills,

was almost castrated to preserve his youth too (like
Florida, the last resort, I'm willing Doc),

as opposed to Orpheus: who he hated humanity and loved
instead what he could never have: a woman who the deeper she sank
like the basses into hell became less and less a woman to him than
his idea of a woman, of women, or more accurately his idea of a
love, of love in and of itself like this girl who,

a friend of my daughters' who,

actually of a sacrifice, THE sacrifice for this the first of the world's singers according to Jean-Jacques Lefranc, marquis de Pompignan if you know him in poems that at least according to Schneidermann were indeed earlier if not greater than Homer's and how I wish O I wish that Schneidermann he were here tonight! now!

how he, Schneidermann, how he'd explain it all to you even if he'd opt for silence, his presence it would be all that would be necessary, to explain himself, and his times, all about his work and his life, about a life of work and how he managed what even the greatest of philosophers they didn't (not even Spinoza, not even Pascal according to Schneidermann),

all about how his life it was his greatest work: surviving death and its trends, ultimately surviving survival, adapting, mutating,

morphing is the newest nomenclature under seven names on nine passports with six degrees on 10 diplomas and all the while staying true (until America),

true to himself (until America),

to his purpose (until America),

the urge to get through (everything except America),

to approach and to say (in American),

O how he'd explain it All! just by just being alive again, by working again, how he'd embody it All! and, well — let's summon him up, shall we? an Upper West Side séance of sorts, let's rap the tables of the enormous diamonds set in all your waist-sized gold rings, sound good?

and see, no hear what he's up to? what Schneidermann he's been doing with himself lately?

what's the latest news from the underworld most real? or maybe a timpani roll for this on the tympanum? but no:

because how I'd hear it during all those seasons when I was on tour — and for years, and every night, after every gig and after every seduction — was through the magnificent invention of distanced speech, a sort of mundanified extra-sensory-perception by which I of course, obviously, mean to invoke the telephone:

O how I touch myself to the moist as heavy sound of the dialtone, and the all-knowing as young, machine-operated and so

lonely

lonely operator!

and so now let us praise the telephone's inventors: Philipp
Reis, Antonio Meucci, Elisha Gray and not to forget Mister
Alexander the Great Nevsky, gram for gram the greatest man of his
time and on anyone's dime while his, Schneidermann's it was an
early century model or just seemed like it, might as well have been
and yet still in work, still at work, let's say that at least it served
his purposes, or lack thereof — while we're not quite talking
Siemens & Halske, it was old enough, obviously rotary, and the
funny thing (*ding*) about it was, well, it wasn't as much funny as it
was a fact that you just couldn't hear through it:

in another word Schneidermann he could only *talk*, at
someone as someone but who besides me? called him up and
Schneidermann he and always after seven rings picked it up and no
more and no less (who knew or had the time for an explanation of
this sevenfold significance?), had to guess who it was, or not, or
just not care that it was always me and so Schneidermann he'd just
start talking, or just begin the continuation of his talking-to-
himself from before the phone's seven rings no less and no more
and Schneidermann he'd pick up, have no way of knowing who it
was, had no idea of who it was besides me and so Schneidermann
he'd just go on and on, again and again and again:

talking, eulogizing, monologuing, ranting, sermonizing to
the desert rabble of my rubbled soul, and then sometimes he'd end
or start the day lonely — angry, yes, even him — and so then he'd
call someone,

me or,

but only when I paid his outstanding in more than one
sense phonebills so that still he had service — who did he know in
Trebišov? who still alive in Michalovce?

AT&T ANYHOUR INTERNATIONAL ADVANTAGE
PLAN, person-to-Slovakia, $0.26 per minute of air,

and sometimes he couldn't even remember who by the
time the other party they picked up (who could guarantee seven
rings? a memory of seven rings' duration?), and so Schneidermann
he'd just start going off again, but of course he couldn't hear a
gottesdamned ding

(in his own Kissinger parody of a parody of the accent
that Schneidermann he still had, worked on into every mirror)

anyone if there even ever was anyone on the other side was saying
and so if and when they hung up, dialtone, then Schneidermann he
hung up too and so if I ever got lonely, found myself angry, and
let's just say that I wanted, needed to hear then I called him up so
that he could give me my piece of his mind, his peace of his mind
— Schneidermann, among so much else he never fully, mentally,
grasped homonyms in this language that he anyway spoke so
fluently, fluidly (American whiskey) — and then when I had had
enough I hung up, and then I guess at least that Schneidermann he
did, too:

easy enough, didn't want to trouble his own house (apartment), you know?

Schneidermann he never called women — if he even knew
any — thinking the telephone too crude to use to call on women,
that it was for the exclusive use of men to discuss absurd, weighty
things,

what we know of now as *issues,* you know? or else
oftentimes he'd hum (kazoo?), or sing in his terrible worthless
voice that it always seemed an nth degreed parody of a parody of a
parody of itself and its others, or sometimes Schneidermann he'd
read his translations of Shakespeare into a language he invented
and so only he understood, so who knew if they actually were
translations and not just pure mock? or else he'd rest the receiver
down on the piano's lid and he'd play:

O God how he'd play! (sniff, lick) that old synaesthesic
Scriabin, who Schneidermann he was smart enough to admire and
obviously that great, venerable composer of the mid-19th century
Late van Beethoven,

only the latest sonatas of his, *Opus 111* and all that jazz
obviously but also his, Schneidermann's, own keyboard versions,
self-made, one-handed arrangements of Beethoven or van
Beethoven's symphonies, a one-finger arrangement of the *5th,*

dumb, dumb, dumb, DUMB,

numb, numb, numb, NUMB,

a no-finger arrangement of the *9th* and, but only if your
ring it rang and seven times late-late at night into the aspirin wisps
of morning, lefthanded whorehouse piano in the latest style,

I'm talking four-five ante meridian with period performance practice meaning dead drunk, JIM BEAM whiskey mixed

1:2 with COCA-COLA CLASSIC

and thank *you* for keeping *your* telephones off or at home,
phones which they ring only in the key of SEE when you arrived at
this whorehouse *this* evening — or else Schneidermann he'd also
improvise a Requiem for a polka, a mass for the Jewish Godless
God or maybe he'd pull a fugue, a death-fugue out of his tush as
Schneidermann he always said, FUG as in fleeing from his own
forehead that he'd hold against the keys and then slam the keys' lid
against, down, smack! on his neck like a guillotine when Schneidermann he let's say got stuck for an academic Mahler screw-you-
Apollonian-bros. stretto or for a further development modulating
to any one of the O so many other unto infinite manifestations of
the world's worthlessness,

unredeemable phenomena,

things that made him smash his throat with the lid of the
keys: Asians, Asians, Angst-ridden Homosexuals, Asians Who
They Lifted Weights, Single Old Women Who They Owned More
Than One and Sometimes, Depending, Only One Cat, Jews, Jews,
Jews, Women Who They Spoke The American Language, Women
Who They Used Deodorant, Women, Students Of Philosophy,
Sexually-fulfilled Paraplegics, Young Men, Young Men, Young Men
Who They Wore Jeans, Men Who They Were Younger Than
Himself Not Always Excluding Me, Poets In Languages No One
Speaks but

and, truth be told in this language, if that's even possible,
Schneidermann he envied them the poets and that that
was, the envy, the source of this hatred, yes all this hatred, anger
(loneliness),

rage against anyone and everything unprovoked, and
smashing because,

yes,

this is what I wanted to get at all along,

from the beginning,

the roots, the tendrils if you will, pubic — this is how,
where and when everything it went wrong, the needle to this
Schneidermann's thread,

the seed,

the key if you will:

because his nine aunts, his nine quote unquote musical

aunts who they raised him they also murdered their nephew, they
pretty much, might as well have murdered and with malicious
intent Schneidermann's brother, Schneidermann's only brother a
twin too and only by moving his, Schneidermann's, piano, by
pushing his grand like my hotel, unlike what Schneidermann he had
or could ever afford over here (an upright),

pushing it, the grand (this the essential event in
Schneidermann's longest life, the key to the keyless all),

or maybe, okay, by pushing the babygrand across the room,
the MUSICROOM,

to have better, dappled — eastern, Ukrainian, Asian —
light for the young prodigy's now early morning practice and study
as prescribed by the aunts themselves, and so what did they do?

or what was it that was done through them?

nine musical aunts pushing, they pushed with too much
energy, strength, dedication, excitation, they *pushed too far*

and the piano it went right out the large nearly floor-to-
ceiling-window, taking much of the rotten, wet-soaked wall with it
from their house's topfloor, right through the window and the wall
coasting on casters that they seemed dipped in schmaltz lugged off
the Oriental rug and sliding onto the slippery probably just-
mopped with gribnes parquet and so across the room they referred
to as the MUSICROOM

and out the windows and the wall, through the glass and
the sodden plaster, shattering the mullions and out of the topfloor,
third floor I think it was as Schneidermann he told it though only
once,

dorfer with the extra key it was, a new model — this was
in Pest, on a street that still exists though the house it doesn't
anymore (I've checked map-in-hand, Schneidermann he never went
back, money and will),

or a house now in hiding under an assumed name, anyway
the piano it shattered out of it and fell up to six stories in another
version that Schneidermann he often told, as the survivor-Schnei-
dermann he often told it though only to me and when drunk on
JOHNNIE WALKER 1:2 mixed with PEPSI,

when drunk on talent, his, or that it was pushed, the piano
(but not its bench), and that it fell to crush and kill his,
Schneidermann's, younger and only brother,

his

his only brother younger by a minute, also his twin, a
totally unmusical personality who he was named Rudy even though
he was of the same gene pool and religion as,

and killing him forever — clearing out sinuses dancing to
its tune, tunelessness the late spring hora behind his unglassesed
eyes (this was a week after the termination of Passover as Schnei-
dermann-the-living-and-now-possibly-not, spring-seasonal-allergy-
season he often told it),

all the pedals like gold or at least gilded teeth: una corda,
sostenuto, the disappeared-Schneidermann's favorite pedal the
damper and the unfortunate kid's school-stockinged feet stuck out
from underneath the whole tumorous heap like in what's it called?
that movie with girl who? and the tornado and the dog? Oz, fell
like losing pitch to that which is Most High, a string constantly
tuned higher and higher until it snaps to the sidewalk with a sound
that it was like the atom bomb, which was only a handful of years
later, actually 25/5ths of a handful later and that he, Schneider-
mann-alive-and-now-disappeared, this Rudy's three-minute-older-
brother, he claimed it ruined his hearing and for forever after —
and so that might be the answer to your telephone questions right
there,

and to the persistent tinnitus that Schneidermann he
would often attribute to the very same gnat that so afflicted that
great friend of the Jews his name it was Titus,

not to mention the issues that Schneidermann he had —
of form, structure — with Late van Beethoven all resolved easy
enough,

neat and simple like the dominant to the tonic, the Also
Sprach Zarathustrian V to the I above the shrill tinnitustinabu-
lation of the glowing-as-if-blister-burning pedals,

buzzing like those of the bicycle that young Rudy he
would ride as unfettered physically as his soul it was free,
superadjusted this healthy youth,

and simple, almost sacred-idiotic as Schneidermann he
often told it with a tear in his tear-shaped eye,

all happy and civil-service-competence as Schneidermann
he often said and remembered: the one half of the twins alive —
for a while at least — while the other half, our Schneidermann, he
was the one who was dead, who was always dead to Rudy, indeed

always dead to the world, already, Schneidermann who while his Rudy he made the most of his few as young years he Schneidermann instead stayed alone, paled and inside and

practicized and didn't play well with the other children, indeed didn't play at all with them but instead Schneidermann he *played with himself,*

with white men long dead — the other children, the neighborhood children from in and around Kálvin tér they didn't even know that he, that Schneidermann, that he even existed yet, that the much-loved-and-appreciated Rudy he even had a brother let alone a twin, and maybe they didn't even know after,

after *what happened*

and *half* was that Rudy he denied Schneidermann out of spite,

the other *half* it was some still immature and so possibly unrecognized embarrassment about not his Schneidermann but *my* Schneidermann who he was one whole minute older than Rudy and in that minute how Schneidermann he came to know, how he came to know and to perfectly understand, to perfectly know this huge as it is imperfect world in which things just happen like nine musical aunts, in which they're trying, they're really truly just trying to do some good instead end up exacting the exact opposite, indeed end up killing one of their two nephews (though the disposable nephew),

one of the duet of sons of their one dead and only brother, the boys' musical father — though it must be said, it must be put on record, related that at least according to Schneidermann that they the aunts loved Rudy much less than they loved him, Schneidermann ours and mine (or that they just thought they could earn their retirements off Schneidermann, off his talent),

that at least they demonstrated less affection to Rudy who he anyway seemed to need almost none, that at least it seemed to anyone who'd enter, be admitted into that Kálvin tér house that if one of them had to be, that if one of them must be, then indeed it was Rudy who was the disposable one (in utility and so in affection),

that indeed it was Rudy who was the disposable nephew, the liquidatable nephew, that it was Rudy who could be done without, who his brother's brilliant career (hoped-for),

future

future greatness (please),
   genius — yes — would have killed him slowly anyway:
   so there *was* maybe something unconscious at work, but
you have to understand that this it's the testimony of the one
Schneidermann who he didn't die, that this is, was the account of
the one Schneidermann who he survived, survived survival, lived
long enough to suggest to me one summermost afternoon in the
Park that there was maybe something sub or unconscious in the
works here but who knows for sure? Schneidermann he added,
       because by the time that Schneidermann he'd found out,
       or dreamed out,
       or un or derepressed,
       precisely what had happened Freud he was at the other
polar end of the Continent and his students, well, most of them,
       some of them Schneidermann's later friends or just
moneylenders according to Schneidermann, they would have
forsaken him, Freud, by then, for something much less fantastic,
something much more mature, sophisticated but — Schneidermann he was at a harmony lesson that morning at the Music
Academy, was told that afternoon that the piano it had fallen, that
Rudy himself he had indeed pushed it out the window and its wall
and all with some amorphous inexplicable malicious intent and so
was and immediately sent far and away to a home for delinquent
piano-pushers, was exiled to the end of the world and there to its
home for delinquent music-haters, its home for incorrigible art-
enemies that early Sunday morning that the piano it umpteen-five
stories fell:
       Rudy squashed, huge strings umbilical-severed, loosened
keys not tumbling head over heels like lovers or angels or arch-
angels they fall but falling hard with eclipse, darkness pure,
straight-down — indeed it was a virtuoso fall (the only art Rudy
did right, according to Schneidermann, it was art done to him), a
true plummet, its sound the sound of an anthropomorphized pluck
of an infinitely-tuned string strung up to a heavenly sphere (at
least according to the living Schneidermann):
       yes, it almost pulled the dead sun down with it at least as
Schneidermann he once told me in the dusk of the summermost
Park, and the mammoth snap! an infinite gliss up and down,
sounded like an infinite glissando infinitely up and infinitely down

an infinite piano keyboard played infinitely upon by infinite hands
bearing the infinite fingers of all Bach's relations, you know them?
Schneidermann he asked me, Schneidermann he told me with
Jewish tears in his Asian eyes that his relation, his Rudy, that
according to Schneidermann Rudy he was just riding his bicycle
around and around, in fat circles of circles happy and, yes, why
not? I indulged him, it was his life after all — eating a banana
according to Schneidermann, bananas that Rudy he kept in the
pockets of his shortpants, peels on the sidewalk at least according
to Schneidermann a man on the street how he saw it fall, pointed
to it, forefinger, on the corner he cried out, his trenchcoat draped
over a puddle for his ladyfriend (then you had ladyfriends Schneidermann he remarked that day in the Park where),

   and O God it hit!

            did it hit! Schneidermann he screamed
murder and thanks in the Park,

                              hit!

            hit!

      hit!

   hit! — the legs they buckled, pedals stuck out from under
like feet,

      an accordion squash, dead squeezebox and but I wasn't
there to see it,

      to witness,

      to see the sides split, hear the tensions exploding off
tuning pegs,

      lids bucking, and how the women they wept freely into
their — Moravian — lace handkerchiefs as their gallant husbands
they held them by their junk necklaces around their thick necks
and looked,

      still pointing,

      forefingering to every new arrival on the scene, then
ducking fresh haircuts and shaves to glance at their watches as
you're doing now,

      how the nine musical aunts they just stood there floors up
above the open according to Schneidermann according to his
dream, according to his dreams, to his recurring nightmare(s),

      peering down over their partyshoes, or their homeslippers
dream-depending deep into the anus mundi, the dark pianistic

terminus

terminus potholing their sidewalk and thinking just thinking all
about how much this whole thing it will cost them in fees, repairs,
hush-ups, Landsmannschaft-cemetery-upkeep-burial expenses,
would bankrupt them with the oldest of them, the oldest musical
aunt of the nine musical aunts in Schneidermann's often-had and
more-often-recounted-to-me-nightmare,

       she just taps her toe according to Schneidermann (his
nightmare)

       somewhere in the vicinity of Largo or Larghetto, slow, and
this is not, the dream, in an apartment overlooking Pest but in an
apartment overlooking the Park West that the nightmare it had
usurped and explain that! Schneidermann he insisted — impatient
for the final chord, for the resolution of the cadence, the dominant
to the tonic, the Zarathustrian V to the I and then we'll turn it
over to the audience,

       the curtain's cheap velveteen, applause as cheap if not
cheaper,

           curtain,

           bow,

           curtain to dark, pitch:

       the sharps and flats of enharmonic night, the black-black-
black-keys, night falling with that piano until the Continent entire
it was dead, gone according to Schneidermann standing at the N/
NE intersection of Null & Void,

       like in the circus I played at once, one summer when I
taught an acrobat to play a — secondhand — violin in midair:

       they fired him from a cannon to play the ten notes the
acrobat he knew in midair, at the apex of his flight,

       a Heifetz he's not went the joke high up in front of the
Hungarian moon and how once, the last once how he landed but
past the net and into the grandstands, to manic applause and how
he his name I've forgotten never stood or spoke again I told
Schneidermann that I didn't dream about it,

       not-my-fault,

       but the piano! said Schneidermann, in my life and in my
dream — nightmare — of life, God! how it *bit!*

       and the noise Schneidermann he said it filled mouths,
filled history,

       inflated the past with sound we can hear even now, only if

we listen:

hear the sublimated urge to arrest, to express, to remake the world in your own image, making the world outside yourself in the image of the world inside yourself as Herr Doktor Göbbels always recommended, propagandized, said if he heard the word *culture*

he reached for his gun,

bang! boom! (keep yours in your holsters for now!)

but only if we listen,

if we hear,

if we listen to Bach (and his debt to Buxtehude),

if we listen to Mozart and that genius friend of his who he really wrote his *Requiem*, if we listen to Ludwig and his twin brother Late van Beethoven riding astride each other, sabers drawn, brass choir fanfare as they invade Poland where,

according to Schneidermann if we would only listen to the speeches of the great and surely immortal Adolf Hitler,

if we listen to Nietzsche,

if we listen to Schopenhauer who he argued and loudly that noise it is the revenge or just the weapon of the underprivileged, the mass, the mob, that these lumpen proles are or were according to Schneidermann according to Schopenhauer: "the beasts of burden among mankind; by all means let them be treated justly, fairly, indulgently and with forethought; but they must not be permitted to stand in the way of the higher endeavors of humanity by wantonly making a noise,"

but the problem, Herr Doktor Professor Schopenhauer as Schneidermann he would say to a waiter who he might have looked like him (Schopenhauer, the same facial hair traits at least),

or should I say the reversal, transference is what Schneidermann he said, the odd inversion in our time Schneidermann he would say, is that now it's not the lower classes, that indeed now it's the upper classes across the great divide, the GAP who they make all the noise, and it's not that they're uncultured or even unculturable, no — it's that noise is what they do best and get paid for, what we pay them for, that noise is their calling, their duty to the stockholders,

taxpayers:

to whip us with wirelessness, the absence of continuity, its

charged

charged ghost — and so noise it no longer disrupts thought as
Schneidermann he thought (could barely),

it aids thought, is necessary to thought, actually *is* thought
or what passes for thought, as thought passes:

example being made of Jimmy backstage, him always with
his transistor radio and listening to the Yankees or is it the Mets?
in-season while I saw away:

No offense, Mister Laster, he says, *just never miss a game — you
know how it is?*

and no, I don't, but if it was an example you wanted, an
example of outer noise drawn in, internalized according to Schneidermann, or of the drawing of our in out according to Schneidermann — drawing more like intellectually doodling on the napkin
of his time, blank and crumpled — it would have to be:

well, after we left this matinee movie about a boy who was
a clone who he was also a boy Schneidermann (but only after he'd
rescored the matinee movie's titular music in his own head, for his
own head),

Schneidermann he just wouldn't stop talking, wouldn't
stop going on and on his way down Broadway all about all this
craziness, all about cloning, about clones, about the future that is
already our present Schneidermann he told me:

all shiny, all wrapped up because haven't the Asians, haven't
they already, in our time, perfected human cloning? asked Schneidermann, reached the apex of droning, and by merely existing? by
only engendering?

but even so everyone's as scared as they're supposed to be
according to Schneidermann,

as the millennium it embarrassed them of I added
(Schneidermann he ignored),

wary of the futureless future or was but no, but they won't
admit it anymore like Schneidermann who he'd kept hidden
throughout all those years, throughout all those concerts, throughout all those concentration camps and Schneidermann he was in all
of them a lock of Rudy's hair in a locket with a photograph, a
faded daguerreotype of his mother that he'd stashed in a subterra-
nean storageroom of the Music Academy (in a piano),

and then retrieved upon Liberation, once up his tush as
Schneidermann he always put it — through Immigration, the

locket it was gold, his mother's — and now around his neck never
hocked despite all, the locket and the lock redeemed from the ninth
aunt's third dresser drawer that night when he, when Schneidermann knew that his brother Rudy he wouldn't ever be coming back
and how Schneidermann he wanted to bring him back anyway and
as we were walking down Broadway (Schneidermann he always said
Broadvay),

indeed to bring him back now and on Broadway (like Rudy
he'd walk right now out the petri of a Midtown subway stop),

to recreate Rudy from his own hair and how I had to tell
him, to let him down easy, let him know that not only would this
twin of a twin of a Rudy be in point of fact a different Rudy than
the Rudy that Schneidermann, hardly, knew (wouldn't speak
German or Yiddish, Hungarian, Romanian or Russian unless you
taught him, example, might even be musical),

but what's more grave is that that technology it hasn't yet
been perfected and indeed might not ever be at all, how it's still
only in the movies as I told Schneidermann, it's only in the
matinee movies and that that science fiction that it hasn't yet
become science fact and so we,

Schneidermann and I were actually walking out of a
matinee movie, in doing so forsaking its CREDITS for coffee on
West 72nd Street to talk about the matinee Cloning movie that
we'd just subjected ourselves to and forsook, indeed cloning or
recloning the movie itself in our own heads and to each other for
free as

and so we, us, here, now, there, then and for at least the
foreknowable futureless future we can only imagine, can only
dream of a futureful future in which men they will be redundant I
said (as if we aren't already and always have been at least according
to an exwife of mine who she's since converted to the Church of
Lesbianism),

of a futureful future in which women and all on their
liberated ownsome they'll split their own ovaries/eggs in the hopes
of having a prodigy was what I suggested to Schneidermann,

in the hope of hopes of having a prodigy to end all
prodigies or — if that seems too much work, or too expensive I
equivocated — then of engendering at least a totally unique,

different (unequally unique, unequally different according

to *Schneidermannus interruptus*),

    designer child, which is a desire at least as fruitless as any male desire,

    because as Schneidermann he then countered over his over-frothed cappuccino to my more sophisticated triple espresso the fact is is that no one person is totally unique, that no one human is, truly, different and that designer it just means that you're paying for the name (Adam, I joked and he didn't laugh)

    and that, anyway, according to Schneidermann who he then poured sugar from the singularly unsanitary bowl into plastic ZIPLOC baggies that he'd brought to bring home with him full: all clones they would be like prodigies, indeed would be prodigies:

    that according to Schneidermann these genriched virtuosos if you will that they'll never accept their own mistakes, ever, indeed will attribute them to their mothers, to the father of Science, further that they'll never find the genius to accept their own mistakes, that they'll never find the recourse to exploit them, mistakes inevitable in a world as mistaken as ours, into something fresh,

    new,

    some future's idea that everyone's going to laugh at as every age does at their own when I tell you that cloning's the answer,

    Schneidermann he spooned his froth and went on, a dollop of fluff nested like a white Hitlerian moustache in the declivity between nose and lips (the nasal septum, *Gray's* globular processes) — that cloning it's the only answer to the ageless question of sex according to Schneidermann, that cloning's in fact the end of and to sexuality or so Schneidermann he'd so ardently insist:

    that the idea or more accurately the psychology of heterosexuality is that you want what people call the Other and overcharge on whereas the idea or,

    better, the psychology of homosexuality as Schneidermann he put it is approximately 6billion times more narcissistic, approximately 6billion times more self-involved,

    is that as a homosexual you essentially want yourself — so we can imagine, can't we? Schneidermann asked, the day dawning when these faggots (Schneidermann he didn't use the term, Schneidermann he always said *queens* or *queers*, sometimes *faygeles*, for Schneidermann *Fagott*, which with his accent it always sounded the same as, it was always German for the *bassoon*),

and so we can imagine, can't we? Schneidermann asked, the day dawning when these homosexuals they can clone themselves at let's say 30 (and homosexuals they're among the few who can afford such a procedure, according to Schneidermann),

and that by the time they're 46 to be safe they can go and molest themselves in their own 16-year-old anuses — but Schneidermann he asked me as I flirted with the, female, waitress and proceeded to take care of the check, as I always did, as was my half of our relationship, Schneidermann he and in all seriousness asked but why wait that long?

why not just fuck (Schneidermann he said *congress*),

why not just fuck the infant inside you? in rhythm to his primal screams (and so I'll never return to that café again)?

which anyway makes you think, doesn't it? Schneidermann he thought and out loud on our, my, embarrassed way out the door and onto the street (the jang-jingling of the steely, tubular entry/exit chimes it always scared him, surprised the conversation right out of the Schneidermann),

made at least him think all about the wet smacking of our atoms,

of our subatomic particles that produce what music? Schneidermann he often asked, our electrons kissing past each other rub what vibration? Schneidermann he always wanted to know, sympathetic or rather no? music just pathetic enough for our cloned prodigy — Schneidermann he answered, non-answered, himself when the chimes they faded from his most memorious ear — our cloned prodigy bowing away at his helixes perfectly strung and yet still,

when time asserts itself, Schneidermann he asserted,

and yet still eventually quieting, giving way, mortal as all else, Schneidermann he insisted, mortal as music itself it is not, able to produce at his farewell gala maybe in this very hall only noise, geriatric flailing, past-his-peak-thrashing:

the noise of his innards, once-perfected and now just wheezing away to his death, to their death, its, finally to silence and Schneidermann he silenced himself — until I got the phonecall at 3 a.m. that evening or was it morning already? from

St.

St. Luke's emergency room that Schneidermann he was there, and
was raving,

    Schneidermann who he filled out all my information on
the requisite form,

        that my friend, my only friend (the doctor he said *brother*),

    and so that my brother Schneidermann he was there and
almost violently demanding that the young, yarmulked doctor still
doing his Residency take the hair from the locket of our, his,
mother and go ahead and clone Rudy his, our, brother his twin and,

    that Schneidermann he'll be by tomorrow around noon to
pick him up, so that the two of them they could ride bicycles
together again in the Park (for the first time together anywhere I
believe),

    and to charge the cloning fee to yours truly who I apolo-
gized over the phone to the too-respectful-to-laugh-at-this-doctor,

    sped my way Uptown and picked up my Schneidermann,
redeemed him my brother in Apollo let's say from all the AIDS
whores and METHADONE pushers and let him sleep himself to
sanity however temporary on the three-pillowed ashen loveseat at
my penthouse at the Grand.

    Harmonious, the description of the all within the all was
what Schneidermann he said when he finally said something again,

    after a medium-sized-eternity, 10 minutes of silence
earlier that afternoon on 7th Avenue or that next morning I forget
which after his first coffee and cigarette on me.

    Beauty, the long last gasp longless lastless of recognizance,
Schneidermann he said I think as he worked himself up again as he
walked on down the street (West 72nd) — in that silence probably resenting my naysaying of his Rudy-plot, probably plotting
the escapade at St. Luke's later that evening into morning (the
doctor at St. Luke's and the doctor in the matinee Cloning movie
they even looked alike if you could ignore the yarmulke, the
professionalism of the former).

    Because we have scored the genome and will play it.

    Because we will sing our own praises to the vault:

    as much new and improved vox humana as we're capable of
but something it will still be missing Schneidermann he thought
the next morning over roomservice and daze and I agreed (what else
could I do?),

agreed with Schneidermann when he insisted that something it will still remain missing, always remain missing, must —
and, yes, I know that I'm old-fashioned, Schneidermann he knew
that too, we both knew that we were, outdated, outmoded, that we
were fashioned from old stuff, a Jewish seed to its Jewish egg and
so that it was time to move on, is, to move over,
          give-it-up,
          at least recede,
          know that I'm being phased-out, being made obsolete and
soon to become even more so but that doesn't change the fact that
I have IT,
          what he'll never have, our prodigy, that I am IT, what our
clone he'll never be:
          IT, that I have and what's more important have night after
night earned the Birthright (with my ears lentil-shaped),
          that I have IT in my blood, that it might be yesterday's
news but that tomorrow it will still need to know it and won't was
what Schneidermann he feared and I, I know that tomorrow it
won't, will not, and not even if you try to warn like a prophet,
          because the life of a true musician it's too difficult for the
future,
          because the future is indeed futureless for a true artist, and
that prophecy it's never paid well either — that the future it might
be bloodless for us but that it will also lack the passion (according
to Schneidermann, who he lived, survived it all and with all his
naivete still intact),
          that the future it will lack the — death-vomiting — of
who,
          of I (*Ich*),
          of who I am, the-who-that-I-am — the insides of my rot,
the diseased love, the transcendent need, that's right,
          need: that to be born to something, into a way, is not to
need it for your very survival,
          that there's still work to be done, life to work on, work to
live on and that to deny talent, ability even, even predilection,
means another life:
          of more ease but of less joy and that to deny need,
          to deny an inheritance of need as Schneidermann he once put it,
in favor of embracing an engineered model means to deny the one

and

and only melody,
        the lifeline according to Schneidermann,
        melody, the umbilical cord according to Schneidermann,
        a ladder of no rungs and of one leg, itself, in a dream that
Schneidermann he often had and even more often recounted to me,
        an arrow too large for any bow, this was another dream
that Schneidermann he had and refused to interpret (interpretation,
that's your job, Schneidermann he always said),
        a room made from an arrow, hollowed out of its head,
        point set against any door which would open in as Schnei-
dermann he recounted it to me one pre-matinee movie conversation
over coffee-flavored cigarettes and coin-flavored DIET PEPSI,
        a poisoned point, Schneidermann he remembered,
        the arrow of Eros entombed or on permanent exhibition in
the highest and only room of an ivory tower, it seemed to Schneidermann (who he once asked me if I believed what the Talmud it
said, that a certain proportion of dream it is prophecy, a given
percentage and I, well, I answered 99.9% what Schneidermann he
wanted to hear),
        lonely as high above the archives, Schneidermann this he
remembered too,
        the basement repository, Schneidermann he told it once,
        the records room, same dream another night — and what
will ultimately save us now, as Schneidermann he often insisted, is
annihilation and only annihilation:
        as what will be left on the — ice ash — plain is that
vision of his, that prophetic vision of his deep at night,
        possibly Schneidermann's most frightening, sheet-wetting
dream: a dream of one piano key (Schneidermann he told me but
only once and quietly),
        one lone piano key and so who knows which note it once
sounded? Schneidermann he once asked me as if I had the answer,
which note whether pitched heaven or hellwards it once was fated
to, which note it was burdened with, condemned to? Schneidermann he wanted to know, told me that once up at his apartment,
room, about this dream (Schneidermann and I we were standing
because he had no chairs),
        almost one year ago exactly about this one disembodied
ivory tower of a key that it's standing high and upright in a pile of

bone chips, ice and ash, an idol with no worshippers Schneidermann he offered to my interpretation or,

rather, Schneidermann he prophesized:

our death, all death was, is the worship of this God rising
only then, after, now — an Auschwitz/Lubyanka death that Schneidermann he often mentioned to me as a solution, a Schopen-
hauerian the-door-is-always-open-fantasia (Schneidermann to me:
the best doctor is suicide, sometimes it's best to just begin all over
again):

a violin string wrapped thrice and tied twice around my,
his, erect penis, tugging bloodied strings to bulge, a G violin string
tied around my, his, penis and tied to the other end to the
chandelier's glowing hang and a man,

him,

me, I'll be standing head high on a block of ice slowly
melting down to room temperature, the melt and seep and string
and the taut ripping off my endowment bloody and me then
bleeding to death on the floor of my penthouse suite, ice-block
obtained, bribed up from a puzzled roomservice

who they indeed constitute the lower-class, oppressed to
the point of calling you the police in response to my howling,
writhing noise above it was a daydream I once had — the prole-
tariat so oppressed by the noise of people like you and me that
when and if they finally get enough money to afford a weekend of
noise just for themselves they end up just falling asleep in front of
the teevee,

showing anything we want to show those benign but still
worrisome lumps so sanctimoniously descried and accused by the
sexless, artless Schopenhauer

who he also believed that a chord with a wide gap between
the soprano and the bass registers it gratifies our sensibilities
because the spacing of the notes it represents somehow,

don't ask Schneidermann he often asked me or of me,

the gap between the animate and the inanimate worlds
according to Schneidermann for whom reading it was just another
form of memorization (like hearing, like existing),

of remembering,

of imagining for instance a Marxist music in which each
class it is assigned a voice, a range, a class of pitches to sing to the

vault

vault their degree of economic/spiritual impoverishment — an imagination of Schneidermann's (though never realized, met the same fate as the operas, the sonatas, thought-out-in-full and yet never realized on-paper)

　　that could go on and on as worthlessly well as all imaginations if it wasn't for that line that I was trying to remember (with no one to prompt me tonight),

　　it was Schneidermann's favorite passage of Schopenhauer I think it goes: "philosophy, like the overture to *Don Juan*, starts with a minor chord,"

　　from his *Vorstellung*, an untranslatable word whether *representation* or *idea*,

　　Vorstellung, which Schneidermann he once joked should be translated as *Schneidermann* — as opposed to Leibniz who according to Schneidermann at least thought that music it was an "exercitium arithmeticae occultum nescientis se numerare anumi"

　　I think it went, or as Schneidermann he once translated it for me: "an unconscious exercise in arithmetic in which the mind does not know it is counting,"

　　and then we have — at a Downtown diner over bagels and bacon, Schneidermann quoting German philosophy to a 20-year-old waiter with 19th century facial hair and an ambition to become a filmmaker, no, *to be recognized* as a filmmaker as Schneidermann he was told after he'd flirted, a filmmaker specializing in music videos he the waiter then had to explain all about to an over-caffeinated Schneidermann whose teevee it never worked let alone MTV,

　　and then we have Schneidermann quoting to a waiter with artistic ambitions in lieu of a tip Schopenhauer's last words on music that according to Schneidermann say that "music, since it passes over the Ideas, is also quite independent of the phenomenal world

　　(such as film, filmmaking, ambition Schneidermann he added),

　　positively ignores it, and, to a certain extent, could still exist even if there were no world at all," and so there you have it, ladies and gentlemen,

　　thought-police of all ages, or there you don't have it and direct from the mouths of one of the first, Leibniz, and one of the last, Schopenhauer, German philosophers — or else if you like

Schneidermann he'd abandon his reason,

    his memory and its always fluffed quodlibet and instead
just refer you, me, to Heidegger who he thought, knew, that
thinking that it was the mortal enemy of understanding,
Heidegger who he once told that Jew Husserl to go to hell or to
Auschwitz

    and though with whom, Heidegger, Schneidermann he
anyway often agreed — yes, why not? Schneidermann he would say:
thinking is wrong and understanding is right, sure, I agree,
Heidegger he thought pretty much the same thing that Louis
Armstrong he did about music, or was it Duke Ellington? who he
said that good music is music and that everything else it just isn't,

    that you just know it, feel it and no matter how untoward
that sounds,

    Schneidermann who he neither thought nor understood,
just remembered,

    Schneidermann who he was oftentimes as difficult to
understand in thought, and in music, as Heidegger he was,

    especially Heidegger as interpreted, understood, by
Schneidermann and his American mouth,

    Schneidermann the last musician or just the last philoso-
pher among the musicians the last while I, Laster, I'm just sifting
through the ruins as that proverb goes:

    the tumuli of notes, seeking some proportion, some
harmony or at least some overtones of meaning:

    is music just math? is the bass the mineral world, the
tenor the plant, alto animal and soprano just a man shrieking atop?
and if so is he castrated, or has he just been Rudy-flattened by a
piano?

    O the fundament of questions! as Schneidermann he often
put it when he wasn't bitter or constipated:

    did a piano just fall on my testicles? should you ever fall
in love with anyone who doesn't think death-by-falling-piano to be
funny (I asked my last wife)?

    what is the nature of fate? of free will? are you out there
paying attention to serve and to protect? so many law-enforcement
personnel and medics, EMTs and fire in this hall now, at least it
seems like all of you and if so then who's minding the city?

    your badges glinting back at me,

my

my harpist gone home to tune maybe the veins of her
anus,
        forsaken even by my timpanist shocked and unsure,
        done with his moment in the sun (the only entity accord-
ing to Goethe according to Schneidermann that has a right to its
spots),
        and so I'm left with only a smattering of lay members
(don't take this lying down!),
        a minyan of high-rollers let's say and among them one of
this hall's prime supporters, yes, Mister Rothstein you're still here,
        thanks,
        each to his own I guess and so, fates:
        they tie things up, loose ends, strings wound in string and
so: mugged and shot dead? gang-raped and executed with a shotgun
12-gauge? hit by a subway on the 1 or 9 line? Schneidermann?
        Do you know, Mister Rothstein? He seems to know
everything, Misses Rothstein.
        No, no piano, no suicide: after the matinee Holocaust
movie that Schneidermann he just disappeared from, Schneidermann he just disappeared — insane you might say, you might
think, insane maybe as all artists are, me included and instead of
who knows what wouldn't it have been better after all for him just
to have pushed *my* Steinway? my grand at the Grand? push it to
drop out of my penthouse, its patio and railing urge-high? Stein &
Sons every time I move in for a six-month stay they haul it all the
way up (in the service-elevator and not on a rope),
        and in the end that then it would have been the end of the
end wouldn't that have been better? more dignified? more fitting
for this Schneidermann? for me just to go, have gone to the
matinee movies and alone one day, one afternoon just leave him
alone in the suite, in my penthouse, the elevator's P,
        Schneidermann he had the motive (life), just give him the
opportunity, let him push it off? then just sit in the matinee
movietheater while Schneidermann he'd limp his fall down the
floors 90-plus, take the express elevator with its gilded filigree all
the way down to the street? or why implicate myself? why be an
accessory? why shouldn't he have pushed *his* upright out of *his*
room? his own right through the thin wall and its thinner plaster
thinnest? then run his fall down the six floors of his apartment

building (without an elevator and so over drunks highstepping, slipsliding on their most intimate fluids)?

of the black joke of the brownstone that Schneidermann he so deserved?

and Braunstein, where is he now? wasn't he? dead too and gagged with armbands,

to catch it on the bald of his head?

Push the piano out the window, Schneidermann he'd have to think,

then run downstairs and out the door, hoping it's remained unlocked since it was last shut, he'd have to think,

then find and stand on the exact spot where the piano I pushed it would hit (probably, windspeed and direction dependent), he'd have to think,

and then the easiest part — just stand there (eyes open, eyes shut)

and get hit! and he wouldn't have to think anymore — maybe a test before with an X marks the spot and dot dot dot? but this is ridiculous!

No.

What rumors have I heard?

I hope the reporters out there are getting this down, this drama, this preparation for a Wagnerian liebestod, my own,

a lovey-wovey-deathy-weath — this a wife's friendspeak, a Long Island native so you just have to relate, her Jane and me me in one of Schneidermann's favorite matinee movies,

Schneidermann who if he would've been born earlier as he always reminded me he would've been born an ape, but a great ape,

or a Romantic, or a Roman earlier: an offspring of some Greek God and a mortal Jewish washerwoman,

an offspring straight from the stone forehead, some true Greco-Romance and so — as Schneidermann he would always remind me — born to a world of harmony, of proportion,

of *art,*

of *time,*

of *philosophy* Mister Rothstein our resident multimillionaire who if he would've been born earlier he would've been born a poor wretch in Czernowitz near Sadagora like Mister Rothstein Sr. his father was, like your father was, like I was,

only

only to be shot dead let's only hope like my relatives were
at the river of no names of a thousand names in Krasnopolka,

but instead you're here, a well-tailored, well-fed, well-
financed New York son still responding — or at least with your
wallet — to *gesture,*

to *hope,*

to *struggle*:

Mister Rothstein (a *sustaining member* of this institution!),
have you been listening to anything I've been saying? Because you
have to understand that Schneidermann he had to think, that for
the sake of symmetry and everything Classical that Schneidermann
he had to think that everything in the world it is or at least was
completed, dialectic-fulfilled, by its opposite (Es muss Sein!
Schneidermann he would carp to a categorical imperative less
German-stoic than it was actually Jew-whiny),

and whether they know it or not, whether they like it or
not like as Schneidermann he once offered: Male/Female, Alive/
Dead, Sound/Silence, absolutes possible yet not always evident
Schneidermann he allowed and then said almost all, yes, almost all
except poverty, extreme abject poverty, yes, that it has no opposite,
it's perfectly oppositeless and so listen Schneidermann he said:

you can have a man totally poor, without a dollar, nothing
to spare with nothing, indeed wholly impoverished say like myself,
and he has no opposite, no duality, that that man say like myself
he has no opposite who's infinitely rich, so infinitely rich that he
has or would afford all, everything, the sum total wants of every
other,

that there's no one, not even Billiam Gates or the Sultan
of Brunei (both of whom I've met, and played for),

with the means to satisfy, fulfill, all possible desires
Schneidermann he once said,

whereas this one man say like myself he has nothing,
absolutely nothing, the non-means to procure not even nothing,
that this one man he does not even have the ability to procure for
himself everything he *needs,*

understand, Mister Rothstein? a one and a zero Schneidermann he said, and that zero that it has no opposite in life because
show me infinity Schneidermann he'd often say and I'll show you a
scam,

or an advertising or political campaign,

like a plentitude and a nothing Schneidermann he offered,
like no kings he knew of and just ascetics everywhere:

outside on the streetcorners, in the alleys leading to and
around this hall, that there are plenty of incarnations of pure
nothingness Schneidermann he often noted, pure nothingers
Schneidermann he would say — and that not even you Mister
Rothstein are their opposite, their true mirror, not even you can
reflect or,

and so fulfill them,

like has America mislaid its brain Schneidermann he often
asked himself as much as me?

left it at the matinee movies?

like paging Lost & Found! Schneidermann he often asked,
left its mental apparatus in its other suitpants? when you Mister
Rothstein as a prominent Board Member when you voted with the
others to refuse our composer, our Schneidermann, a commission
that it might have saved him (if Schneidermann he wouldn't have
doubted or refused it like Peter or Thomas),

when you Mister Rothstein when you decided against
lobbying for his appointment as I urged you almost bribed you for
Composer-in-Residence of this worthless concerthall, how could
you?

and all in favor of some flavor-of-shit-of-the-month,

in favor of some popmusic musical idiot who you thought
he would appeal to the younger generation, appeal to the younger
demographic, to the younger Wall Street money and the
Westchester County/White Plains set, some retired pop musician
who after his popband it went pop, bust! in the late 1990s what
did he do? he turned to quote unquote serious composition, who
now he makes his primary living off of scoring for the movies, off
film scores and only descends to the orchestra every third picture
or so just to prove to his bros. in Apollo that he still has it or that
he ever had it at all, hasn't lost the touch, still can move like a
Midas between pop power ballads and symphonic bombast with
relative ease, indeed can set six sonnets of Shakespeare to some
unwieldy overarching string melody that he, 10 interns and their
20 assistants and at the last-minute pieced together with ejaculate,
theirs, from the remnants of Brahms or Schubert,

or

or that madman Hugo Wolf with his lover the tenor
deepthroating the work to wild though one-night-only applause
and acclaim while Schneidermann he was sitting at home, in room,
and to his detriment he was reading, which for him it was memorizing or remembering, his Walter Pater:

 quoting whom I have to insist that Schneidermann's *life* it
constantly aspired to the condition of music, in that it was
unfixed, free, irrelative amongst the mechanics — this Pater quote
it's from *The School of Giorgione*, anyone hungry?

 published in the year of Schneidermann's father's birth,

 1873 at least Schneidermann he once told me, year amid
another Renaissance for our people, for us Jews flung loose from
our ghettos, allowed into all the capitals and their Kapital, into
world!

 for us Schneidermanns born out of date and unborn of
date (like Mahler, his time will come, and again),

 stillborn in too fastening a time, quicksilver as these
fingers,

 as these fingers that are my entire life or just its justification,

 these four fingers applied to four strings — wood and
some metal like the materials for the gallows for the death of their
God, of the man who thought he was God, the God who thought
He was a man,

 and of course, yes, obviously some bow-work,

 some of the old righthand-sawing, masturbation —
because I want you to understand that speed I have, yes, but an old
form of speed, analog before analog, outdated, outmoded,

 because understand that this, this is courted speed,
gestured-for speed, gestured-at speed, gestured-to speed,

 understand that this speed, that my most virtuosic speed,
is only a glissando adumbrating the possible presence — if you're
so indulgent, Mister Rothstein — of infinite pitches within
pitches, but it's not fast, not fast enough anymore:

 it's on a human scale as the old saw goes,

 it's that all our speed is too slow, now.

 But how fast — some argue, is the question — can the ear
really hear, Mister Rothstein? Some Schneidermann he once asked
me as much as he asked himself, Mister Rothstein, how fast can

your ear hear? just sitting out there in the one, two, three, four, FIFTH row and hello there! you listening? and don't bother to answer is it funny or appropriate, Mister Rothstein, media mogul, that now speed, all speed, is measured in units of convenience? and don't think that there's not a science to this as Schneidermann he thought, understood.

You've wasted hours of my time, Mister Rothstein. With your matinee movies.

You're wasting your own time, Mister Rothstein. With your life.

Doesn't *haste make waste*, Mister Rothstein? and wasn't that Benjamin Franklin, whom we all have to thank for the electricity running through our veins?

and but is a speed not conceivable, Mister Rothstein, that's so fast as to render it grossly inconvenient?

which was Schneidermann's idea: a speed that was for all practical intents and purposes worthless, Mister Rothstein of the nine mergers before brunch and I want to know,

and that that's where the human use of it Schneidermann he would add, the human taking to it, the human attempt to adapt to this speed it must end according to Schneidermann,

and so you can understand, Mister Rothstein, that our limitations they still bound the illimitable, according to Schneidermann,

the Limen of a speed so fast, so speedy, as to make it, to leave it, to render it useless, seeming the same to us as slow, mentally *ungrippable, ungraspable*:

manual terms, metaphors as all words are metaphors, as metaphor is itself a metaphor,

transferences-of-temperament applied to this cord of power:

this umbilical and yet invisible cable live-wiring our lives without actually being a wire (need we address your telecom interests, Mister Rothstein, your satellite dividends?),

this live-wiring wireless wire living our lives, our own lives, for us,

and so fast that we discover ourselves dead already before we're even born into the stream, according to Schneidermann.

Or don't you like my metaphors, Mister Rothstein?

Don't

Don't like them, Misses Rothstein, as mixed as your drinks?

and so you'll understand that we must ask, Mister Rothstein, must descend to the most impoverished in-our-day, idiotic-in-our-day underworld of infinite underworlds, the underworld of philosophy, of metaphysics which was Schneidermann's true home, HUDlike, HUD-dled welfare apartment, and ask, as Schneidermann he often asked me:

when does speed become too much itself? Schneidermann he always wanted to know, when does it galaxy-collapse-in? telescope back in on itself so as to render it its intended opposite, useless, or, more dangerous, worse according to Schneidermann: unperceivably worthless to us?

Well, Mister Rothstein of your two television networks, when?

At our limit, I answered Schneidermann.

And where's our limit? Schneidermann he asked like he was Socrates in a secondhand wig. Which it was.

Understand that it's different, Mister Rothstein of your three film production outfits, that it's different for every individual, for each of us according to Schneidermann — could you, Mister Rothstein of your season's subscription, could you ever hope to play this priceless violin worth a damn? ever hope to carry hours of sound around on your shoulders?

and in your future according to Schneidermann, our children they will surely extend that limit, Mister Rothstein, always, count on them to continue Schneidermann God how he hated to admit it! Schneidermann he actually hated them (anyone younger),

always one foot forward even if they are just babysteps Schneidermann he always said, leave it to them, Mister Rothstein whose three sons now they pretty much run all the cellularphone, mobile technology companies in Eastern Europe — yes, leave it to tomorrow, to those relentless, tireless, eternally young because eternally born bastards:

limitless extension, sure, the longest wireless wire was Schneidermann's image that I have usurped (the longest wireless wire if we don't strangle ourselves by then was what Schneidermann he added as he struggled his wig back into bloom), but limitless extension in increments is what Schneidermann he always insisted upon, in generational increments, Mister Rothstein,

and I'll tell you why that's not progress, why Schneidermann he didn't think that that was progress: it's not progress, Mister Rothstein, because each older generation, each death-generation — me and you, Mister Rothstein, me before you — each will perceive the limit, their limit, the limit of their own birth-generation, in the same proportion as we perceive *our own* limit to *our own* ability,

our own possibilities, Mister Rothstein, mine and yours, Mister Rothstein, according to Schneidermann — and so perception is all and proportions they never budge, cede an inch according to Schneidermann, a damn centimeter,

all being relative with Einstein long dead — call it a sliding scale and the backstage unions, Jimmy who just loved your new fall lineup among them, will know what you mean

but isn't this *proportion*, you don't ask Mister Rothstein, isn't this whole proportion-thing just a little too Apollonian of an idea? well, isn't it? I asked Schneidermann:

this whole birth-generation to death-generation spiel, what's with it? I wanted to know, these bookends of an era, these ears to a head and what's in the middle? I demanded,

the *undefined* middle as defined by all too many of those Uptown professors who they thought it prudent to flee here and early (perhaps hoping to get an early start tomorrow on their eulogies for my sanity? my talent?),

and come again? Mister Rothstein on the board of every think tank worth your while: don't sink down in your seat springing around, Mister Rothstein!

I need something undead for my voice to echo off — and it's old news, isn't it? Mister Rothstein, let me bounce a few ideas off you, run a few ideas up your spine's barren flagpole:

that the instant it's not really instant, false advertising and so who do I sue? Schneidermann he often asked, that according to Schneidermann there's no such thing as *instant*, as *instantaneous*, *instantly* and so on,

that an instant it's merely a question asked of patience, of forgiveness, a question begged of cost/effect ratio, a finagling with

the

the powers of perception up on high, that instant is, in the end (of the instant),

whatever we're willing to wait on, and let go

of all these memories that fail us, that fail themselves when they're remembered and fail to become real, that instantly fail to become instantly real, fail to become life now

like I, Schneidermann said to me once after a matinee Teenage movie, I will only have use for technology when it (whatever IT is Schneidermann he added gumming his stub)

will be able to take the most abstract, unformed idea direct from the deepest recess of my unknowing head and then realize it, fully, totally, immediately, instantly Schneidermann he said. For me. In the world.

Absolute, and immediate, same-thinking, thinking-with, thinking-along transference is what I'm after was what Schneidermann he was after.

Nothing less Schneidermann he asserted spitting out wads of his stub gummed.

Fundamentally, Schneidermann once said, I am seeking the obsolescence, or the elimination, of my mind.

As for the world, Schneidermann he added nodding to a gaggle of queuing 12 year olds, as for the world it can't seem to wait — and the reason that I'm addressing specifically you, Mister Rothstein (besides that your wealth it's one of the most reprehensible wealths around),

the reason I'm picking on you,

why I'm pushing-you-around,

beating-you-up, bullying specifically you, Mister Rothstein, is because of your father, is because your father, Mister Rothstein, because your sainted father he is no longer alive, is with us no more.

Allow me to remind you of your inheritance.

Allow me to remember to you your father and of his folly that I won't ever allow even you to forget.

Allow me to remind you all of Mister Samuel Rothstein, and not his folly, his dream:

of all the boatloads of money he made right off the boat, right off Ellis Island, right out of Yiddishfied German, penury and quarantine, of all that money that your father he then poured right back into Kultur — because he sought only the perfect conditions, Mister Rothstein, your father did, because he sought only the perfect surroundings, the most perfect set of most perfect particulars and arduous exacting specifications all for the making of violins. And that after the age of 50, Mister Rothstein, the age you are now I'd guess, what did he do? your father he dedicated his life solely to this admirable pursuit. And that slowly the shoe-manufacturing, impresario-related radio and recording interests they receded like the Reed Sea,

dropped away,

had other people for that, middle-managertypes, paid them well, and that then only this one thing it existed for him, only this violin-mania, only this violin-obsession, this violin-perfection, this life-of-violins existed for your father, Mister Rothstein — and so land in the forbidden continent it was purchased, in Cremona, fascist soil, indeed your father he needed the soil, his mania required it,

the Italian water too (*aqua musicalis*),

and maple trees they were planted thereupon,

acer pseudoplatanus I think it was, Mister Rothstein, they were and, yes, there's much pseudo, though heart-intentioned, about this: being based solely on your father Mister Rothstein's research, Mister Rothstein, this whole operation, this whole private obsession (but at least he bled for something, as least your father he *felt*),

the wood, the trees being newly-planted because who and even if they could afford it could get his hands even then, even in the 1950s on some serious quantities of old-growth-forest? he, Mister Rothstein, let them be watered by Italian water, by violin water, let them to grow in violin soil, waited for them to Italian-grow, to violin-grow under the Italianate sun, and then what did he do? your father he sawed them all down,

all their shades,

with a saw like a bow Mister Rothstein, your father he experimented with quarter-sawn-jointed two-piece backs for his fiddles (Mister Rothstein, he always referred to them as *violins*),

quarter-sawn one-piece, even slab-sawn one-piece backs — and then your father he went ahead and planted spruce for the table of the devil's instrument in this the devil's obsession, Lucifer's

luthiery

luthiery and found that he had yet another decision to make:
should he make it *picea abies, picea excelsa* or *picea alba*? because spruce
it isn't just spruce if you get deep into taxonomy, into Linnaeus
and all those *nomina trivialia*, you understand? but whichever I don't
remember with exceptionally even, fine grain (your father he'd
hoped, were the criteria),

then invested further unto pearwood and poplar, rosewood
and ebony and boxwood he chopped, and just think! Mister
Rothstein who I know you just want to forget your father who and
his mania that he and it they forgot you, are indeed in your mind
as in mine inseparable your father and his mania, Mister Rothstein,
just think of the 10 long years of his longest life that he spent,
though you'd say he wasted on varnishes alone! oils and resins,
walnut or linseed of the best-of-the-best old Eyetalian school as he
liked to say:

redless reds like an engorged vulva or a split sea,
jaundice-yellow to GOLDEN BROWN the official color
of Cremona: home too to the Amatis and O so many other great
luthiers: Andrea Amati and the four generations that issued from
him, Antonius and Hieronymus, then Nicolò, Hieronymus' son
and the greatest of them all until what do you know? the Plague it
hit Cremona in 1630,

330 years before your father he ever got there, Mister
Rothstein, three centuries and change before your father he ever
introduced his own Plague there (*Peste!*),

when Nicolò, with no sons of his own, Mister Rothstein,
he took on apprentices: one Rugeri and one Rogeri, and then, of
course, Nicolò's greatest disciple, a wop named Antonio Stradivari
whose work I played for you earlier this evening, Mister Rothstein,

though no Messiah of 1716, the Strad I have, that has me,
that's on permanent loan until now from a corporation that you
I'm sure have connections with it's assuredly a good vintage,

and so verily Cremona it begat also the Guarneri family:
Andrea, Giuseppe, Pietro and Giuseppe known to all or just to me
as del Gesù whose archings they did much to inspire the later work
of Carlo Bergonzi if you're interested and then,

skipping a few generations, governments, regimes, the
fields of Cremona lying fallow, all the work moving to Brescia or
Venice — and then we have the Rothsteins, Mister Rothstein, your

father who he bought outright and out of left field a plot of land actually smack dab halfway between Brescia and Cremona (or was it Mantua?),

Brescia the home of da Saló and Giovanni Paolo Maggini and then,

of course, not to forget the Rothsteins or ROTHSTEIN — and you I'm telling you his son to never forget ever that *passion!*

the purity of your father, Mister Rothstein! who you might hold it against him that he left you behind, at home, a victim to the moods, the degenerative schizophrenia of your mother — a shikse steel heiress your father he impregnated too soon if I may remind what's left of the audience, an anti-Semite too with family ties to Henry Ford and,

while he your father he flew back and forth and back and forth to and from Italy, to and from and to again the continent he once fled and now hated but still regarded as necessary, as necessary to art,

to and from Italy, the penis of the continent, the boot of the Continent that it kicked him out not two decades earlier and there not to drink vino, to sun, tour the Classics and enjoy but to *work!*

to make violins! and then flying *me* out and gifting me two of his finest, the ripest fruits of the trees of his most manic obsession and how they played terribly, worthlessly, ten times a thousand times worse than even these 18th century Neapolitan jobs that orchestras they rely upon for that arch-familiar swell (that's if they weren't sold fakes like),

but these fiddles, Mister Rothstein, your father's fiddles (and your father he'd spasm when I'd say that word, *fiddle*),

ROTHSTEIN fiddles they were, quite simply Mister Rothstein, against all thought, intention and work they were absolutely, totally, wholly horrendous, shit, dreck as I told your father (we always spoke Yiddish together)

and found myself apologizing for the truth or just the fearlessness, recklessness, that I had to tell it like it was and still is, will always be,

useless except for firewood was what I told your father who — instead of responding to my most dispassionate evaluation, or to my most passionate apology — your father who he

merely

merely explained it all to me and all over again:

all about the joys of taking a pine tree, taking out a
section of trunk, removing a wedge was how your father he explained it to me and then resawing it, opening the wedge your
father he gestured by opening his palms and then (shaking his
stumplike, Jew hands)

rejoining it along the outermost edge and there! your
father he exclaimed, there you have your table (and rapped our
table wobbly, our marble-topped trattoria spanse),

explained on and unstoppable unshutupable on all about
pine which is of course a softwood (as is spruce, without a breath),

as compared of course to maple which is obviously a
hardwood, Balkan maple (whose trees they provide sanctuary for
the most obliging of nymphs as I observed in Venice, Mister
Rothstein, I am sorry to say one of your father's foreign mistresses
who,

Io, che d'alti sospir vaga e die pianti is how I feel about it,
Mister Rothstein, from Jacopo Peri who, you'll excuse my voice
this *Spars' or di doglia, hor di minaccie il volto*), Balkan maple your father
he insisted being ideal for backs and so his expense-account trips
to Yugoslavia-the-former — maple being denser and harder than
spruce, your father he offered me to punch him in the gut as he
discoursed on and on on all the ins and the outs, an involved
structure of interlocking cells (like a honeycomb, he offered)

vs. the spruce's *light rigidity*, a sum of long hollow tubes like
arms your father he offered transmitting vibrations across the
grain, about the varnish being all-important your father he insisted
as bad varnish, Mister Rothstein son of Mister Rothstein —
shellac-infused, alcohol-infused — it will stifle the natural sound
while all I wanted to do throughout all this at that Venice trattoria
off the Ghetto Nuovo was to stifle *his* natural sound! (but I didn't,
because I loved him, loved him even when he insisted we take a
gondola ride together and insisted on pointing out to me and his
Yugoslavian mistress, later mine, the similarities between the shape
of the gondola and the shape of the violin, the similarities between
the construction of the gondola and the construction of the violin,
saying over and over and for no reason I'll ever understand the
word *Phoenician*)

yes, Mister Rothstein, your father he went through this

whole gauntlet of insanity, survived, all this research and work soaking up all his time, all these acquisitions and international flights soaking up all his disposable money (and there was much to dispose of),

and for what? and for nothing: his ROTHSTEIN violins they sounded like reliable shit but like shit nonetheless, especially when played — even by me — with the bows the man also made:

ROTHSTEIN bows strung with white horsehair handplucked by his staff of peasants from the shit-stained asses of his own fleet of horses that your father he kept liveried in who knows where Siberia? Mister Rothstein, 180 butthairs for each bow, Mister Rothstein, with homemade homegrown pinetree resin for rosin for all these outwardly gorgeous fiddles (violins)

(but you just wait until someone came along and played them!), for all these outwardly dare I say it even perfect fiddles:

unadorned, reserved, nothing kitschified, Jew-fancy or Jew-tacky, just noble, elegant, nothing inlaid or jeweled to get in the way — your father, Mister Rothstein, checking, comparing, contrasting, consulting almost daily with Sacconi of Rome, at Wurlitzer's of New York, with Charles Beare in London, comparing measurements in on-loan rare documents your father he took out insane insurance policies on, handled with nuclear gloves and had to learn or at least gloss Latin, Ventian dialect, *Venesiàn* and 18th century Italian to decipher:

355 mm. back length as your father he told me bending over to pick his GUCCI glasses up off the marble-topped table, 130 mm. length of neck your father he told me with irisated, sleepless eyes leaking themselves from their sockets, 270 mm. length of fingerboard your father he demonstrated by grabbing my forearm and tight, 41 mm. height of bridge with thumb and forefinger spread just-so apart in the heavy air between us at that trattoria in Venice off the Ghetto Nuovo, the old iron-foundry turned first ghetto in the world where your father when he was in town — though only without his, our, Yugoslavian nymph — he liked to walk, recite the Shylock's lines from his favorite Shakespearean play and sip espresso after espresso after doppio, triplo espresso after 20-plus-years essentially, wonderfully, wasted on violins, Mister Rothstein, on bows of rare pernambuco (*echinata caesalpina*, your father he once clarified for me),

and

and on the horses he kept first who knows where in Siberia
but then when they began dying of worms and their peasant —
Nenet — handlers they ate them and died too your father he kept a
herd in China and fed them only with the most premium, grade-A,
artistic, music-inducing oats,

it became a mania, it became sad but gloriously sad,
Mister Rothstein, enormous and beautiful too because you can't
set conditions,

you can't have total control,

oversight,

hindsight, Mister Rothstein of your inheritance — your
father calling me transatlantic in the middle of my night and
babbling on and on all about the Cramer bow,

about Tononi of Venice, Louis Tourte, Jacques Lafleur,
Edward Dodd and his son John,

François Tourte (Louis' son), all these secret-sharers,
adepts of his mania, of your father's manic-obsession, bebabbled
through the static (before the advent of the satellites you own,
Mister Rothstein)

of the makers of Mirecourt from his newly-found
Mittenwald, long-distance from his newly-wrought
Markneukirchen, his newly-defunct if not just always, perpetually
failed Schönbach: all about Vuillaume and his self-hairing bows
that were so typical of technology's early artistic hope, your father
lecturing me on hollow steel and interrupting me hollowing out
one of my particularly untalented, Asian, students, an Asian
studentess untalented only musically though whose name it was
nothing like those coming over the ocean and down the line, wet
(your father he might have been drunk):

named nothing like Kittel, not named Bausch or
Nürnberger, those German bowmakers of the 19th century who
they became above all and beyond everyone else including your
mother and yourself his only son and heir the loves of your father,
Mister Rothstein — your father, Mister Rothstein, who he took his
dream of a new violin-making Renaissance (by Americans, by Jews)

to his violin-shaped grave

(he suffered from gout, and diabetes), and you, Mister
Rothstein, you as his only son and heir you quickly divested
yourself, didn't you?

of your father's all-too-embarrassing preoccupation, of all your father's wasteful though true musical interests, of all his passion and great intentions? ensuring only one generation of ROTHSTEIN violins with your by-then totally crazy mother too relieved or is it stricken-with-grief to even notice or is it care?

while you today support the orchestra still and why (your donation squaring the *Conductor's Circle*)?

only as a gesture, because you think it's the classy thing to do, because you think it's wholly appropriate to your class, your economic and so to your social standing — but I'd take your father any day, his urge over your lack, his obsessive mania from which you saved the world, Mister Rothstein, or any of the world that cares, can be bothered with music, art, saved it from mediocrity, from shitty ROTHSTEIN violins that your father he gave away anyway, and for free! or at least for the merest glint of recognition from artists like myself whom he held so pedestal-high:

I myself have 10 of them, own 10 ROTHSTEIN fiddles or 10 ROTHSTEIN violins and though I'll never play any one of them even when drunk as an amateur they're undoubtedly the most precious things that I own (in my divorces I wouldn't let any of my wives touch them, any of their lawyers and their quote unquote experts assess them),

and he made strings too, your father did, wrapped and unwrapped, the total package, one-stop shopping in gut or steel, gut and steel, keeping kennels stocked with cats with papers for this very purpose — also using iron cores, wound or unwound, unwound and wound, rope-twist revived to overspun as your father he explained it to me that day in Venice in a tourist-trap violinworthy gondola that your father he insisted on taking down the Rio dei Greci and playing, breathless, capsizing-nervous, with his hair the entire trip (or what hair he had left)

out of embarrassment for his obsession, his mania for silver and aluminum wound, his unrepentant penchant for synthetic astronaut string theories considered all the while,

as he was manically as obsessively occupied with comparing Chladni patterns, free-plate tuning results on his fiddles, violins, via holographic interferometry (and still I don't know how he pronounced it),

your

your father fiddling like God with rib structure! this man who he never played the violin in his life but if he could have made violinists themselves don't think that your father he wouldn't have, and all for what?

all to be thought of as a joke, as a sad joke, pitiful, an absolute failure in art though an absolute success in business, to be regarded as a fool, to be pitied for having so much interest in worthless violins but to have so little unto no interest in his lucrative impresario-interests, his radio and recording ventures that your father he all but abandoned the day-to-day operations of years ago,

years prior and all for what this early you would say too-early retirement? to be scorned even by his own and only ignorant son whom he himself scorned or just art did,

by you, Mister Rothstein, and your ideas of ascension, of assimilation, of moderation, of prep-school status quo and its expectations, the responsibilities of wealth, which to you I'm sure must include a responsibility to your sanity (unlike your beloved mother his beloved wife who she was born to it, monied craziness),

a responsibility to the middle, to mediocrity and so as an idiot you scorned him who he couldn't help but scorn you (his mania did, his obsession too)

and even more in return, you who spurned him to never forgive him and all for what? for depleting even a small unto miniscule portion of your inheritance,

your need I say wholly undeserved inheritance,

of your inheritance as an only son and heir which you've managed since his death to septuple if not moreuple with an absolute minimum of exertion and absolutely zero passion whatsoever

(so unlike poor Luigi Tarisio, a hero to your father, a famous violin collector such as Walter Benjamin he would've liked to get his hands on who died in 1854 in total irrevocable poverty much like Schneidermann did that's if he's dead, but Tarisio with another way out, another door open: with 24 Stradivari hidden away in his Milan attic — including 1716's Messiah, which was named as such according to Schneidermann according to Alard, son-in-law of Vuillaume, as the public they always waited for it, to see it, to hear it, but it never appeared, Tarisio would never let it

out of his sight, out of his hearing, out of his mind), which just
leads me to ask, Mister Rothstein anyone but you:

    what's with obsession? what's the obsession with
obsession?

    why — in life as at the matinee movies — are artists
always obsessed or at least portrayed as obsessed? Schneidermann
he often asked me as if I knew, a question with which Schneidermann himself was obsessed, or a question with which Schneidermann he attempted to seem maniacally obsessed, and why?

    it's art imitating life imitating art much like opera with all
its worthless plots and dialogue is much like life but the music of
all operas, of our opera of life it's from God and so again you have
art that's imitating life that's imitating art according to Schneidermann, that's mimicking life that's mimicking art and so where
does it all end? Schneidermann he often asked me as much as
himself, as if I had any answers, as if I would be the one among the
two of us to mention death,

    like when does it all get interrupted? Schneidermann he
interrupted me and my answer, still wanted to know, or doesn't it?
Schneidermann his suspicions they interrupted his ask, was afraid:

    with imagination aping thought just as improvisation,

    Mister Rothstein you've had your due,

    just as improvisation it should mimic the fixed, just as a
cadenza it should mimic the concerto that serves to excuse it, just
as singers in the 18th century they were expected to mimic violin
figurations in their performances — and it's thanks in part to
Corelli, and no thanks in part (second-fiddle)

    to Vivaldi that before long you had gentlemen playing the
violin that the ladies they were then expected to imitate in song,
ladies and gentlemen, with Monteverdi's *L'Orfeo* first produced in
Mantua in 1607 featuring a violin duet, indeed featuring the first
virtuoso passage in the repertoire, this one a duo designed to
imitate Orpheus' technical accomplishment on the lyre as if it was
his only accomplishment

    as it was Corelli's, the first virtuoso, a man of many
embellishments and filigrees musical as much as personal whose
death it might as well mark the birth, the date of the knowing
development of the virtuoso personality such as one Francesco
Maria Veracini, a student of Corelli's who he once found the

testicles

testicles to declare that "there is but one God, and one Veracini"

to which we have to agree as much as to Gaetano Pugnani's utterance that "with a violin in my hand I am Caesar" without specifying further as to which one he was, or thought he was as Schneidermann he often joked.

Understand that from there, then, we have the birth of the violin concerto, the composer's conscious integration of instrumental impurities into his purest, purist music as soon enough Geminiani he introduced dynamic markings into his publications, his 1715 treatise explaining everything you need to know but probably don't and don't want to about the tenets of refined ornamentation — I owned the manuscript, an exwife does now — for so long that his influence it's suddenly interrupted with the appearance of Tartini, his apparition, that dream and the famous *Devil's Trill*,

I figure as long as the press are here I might provide the public with a rudimentary education (please, no flash photography):

and surely his Tartini's most famous student it was this Nardini his name it was like a third-rate magician or a guy in a $200 suit who insists that you owe him some money,

about whom the German critic C.K.D. Schubart with an *a* wrote: "ice-cold princes and ladies were seen to cry when he performed an Adagio; often his own tears would fall on the violin as he played and each note seemed like a drop of blood flowing from his tender soul,"

to be absorbed into the pages of the 1806 Viennese primer *Ideen zu einer Ästhetik der Tonkunst* which Schneidermann he kept a blurred monograph of in the toilet he shared with his entire loose-bowelled floor,

whereas we have Vivaldi 89 years earlier being censured in the Republic of Venice by the venerable likes of J.F.A von Uffenbach with a *u* who relates that: "he added a cadenza that really frightened me, but I cannot say that it delighted me, for it was more skillfully executed than it was pleasant to hear"

which should remind you of something else, something nearer, something nower

which *I* should remind is anyway necessary — unlike Lolli was, who he was just an outstanding technician who like Schneider-

mann he barely lived into the 19th century just from the other end,
the other way around,
head-up-his-ass Lolli who was the basis for Paganini's
devil image, the evil Faustian P.R. despite the pointed fact that he
was an impostor Lolli was,
a stunted finger's God as much as Paganini was,
like a stuntman without a movie like those old Technicolor
CinemaScope DeLuxe musicals when the great José Iturbi he stops
the classical selection he's playing to give out a barrelhouse/
boogiewoogie piano riff — indeed that kind of nascent
postmodernism it was the soundtrack of the 1950s:
the era of recording, the decade I came to this country
from London from Amsterdam from Hungary, the decade that
Schneidermann he came to this country from London from
Amsterdam from Auschwitz from Hungary, from Olympus for all I
know,
the decade of stereo, the decade of homesoundtechnology,
the decade it all fell apart, died, ended,
IT meaning *everything*:
10 years of pilgrimages to the Theatah,
10 years of the office-manager dipping his nib into the
secretarial pool without fear of reprisal, lawsuit,
what a virtuoso! what a ladies' man! yes, that's when we
laugh (laugh-track repurposed from radio to teevee, autumn of
1950),
nod to one another (tamp pipes, snift scotch),
wink knowingly because we're all old friends here, aren't
we?
fellow speculators who might with six degrees behind
them and a vaguely Marxist bent opine that everything it fell apart
not after the War or with the War itself but instead way before,
with the death of patronage, of the aristocracy:
as these Italian virtuosos they became international
virtuosi or virtuosos, became town-to-town virtuosos, bribed or
coaxed out of their hometowns and that whole network of artistic
associations to travel and tour and so becoming totally reliant on
public support, the public's taste or its lack, its whim, popular
fashion, subject to trends and to politics: the example being Viotti
who he fled Paris in 1792 to London, fled his association with

Marie

Marie Antoinette only to be deported from England six years later
under suspicion of being a Jacobin activist,

and others, too many others and earlier who left, got
drafted and traded, who forsook their courts for tours, for courting
the public's taste or its lack and so inadvertently courting the anger
of their patrons: example here being Händel and King George, the
German who he woke up one morning and found himself in
England, and monarch, in the popular territory of his old court
composer,

or else you have overtures sent out, into the world to test
your opportunities from the security of your pensioned position,
such as Leopold Mozart (the father who my father most idolized,
my real father's true father maybe and not the thrice-bearded
rabbi)

with his 1756 *Versuch einer gründlichen Violinschule*, the most
total violin treatise of its age instructing among a thousand-
thousand hopeful others Haydn, Dittersdorf, Mozart the Son and
the quartet-making Vanhal playing for some vaunted high-society
party in popular legend like the one of the Romantic, the itinerant
virtuoso:

the most debilitating institution in the history of all art,
responsible at once for the heights of rapture and the absolute
defacement, total debasement of the instrumental tradition,

the trend Viotti birthed, created the trend I can't kill even
for the life of me and it's amazing, isn't it?

that you're still here Jacob, amazing that I've neglected you
for so long, until now, my cue, God! I'd forgotten I'd comped you
— ladies and gentlemen, Maestro Jacob Levine I'm embarrassing
myself in front of, Maestro Jacob Levine our greatest living violinist, after me, of course, Jacob, after me who I anyway salute you
because you and possibly only you understand of what I'm talking
(now that Schneidermann he's dead or missing or both),

you who befriended me and not falsely, not like Salieri,
not in a rivalry but you Jacob you truly befriended me when I
arrived with my dying father from Hungary to Amsterdam to
London to Here and in the 1950s, you who helped me find money,
a plot and a stone a month after we'd arrived and my true father
but not my true Schneidermann he died (heart),

you who introduced me to a cousin of yours who she

became my wife though it's not your fault that it didn't work out, that she and all too soon became my exwife, helped me with immigration and naturalization issues and formalities and lawyers and lawyers and lawyers (even the one who did that divorce),

you who gifted me as a housewarming present two-dozen oranges and an orange-squeezer and gave me non-degrading instructions as to its use,

you who indeed put me up at the ungrand Ansonia before you found me that first Riverside Drive apartment and set me up with your booking agent: your impresario Mister Rothstein father of Mister Rothstein who he handled both of us for years and for millions!

you Jacob who you had me out to the new suburbs back then, me and your cousin my wife and now ex over for a Memorial Day weekend to your house out among that Levitt insanity,

you who guided me through the breezeway that was the American 1950s and all because why? because we were both Jewish? both spoke Yiddish? both were immigrants? both were violinists? both spoke music? you who were selfless incarnate if that's possible,

you who loved America, who just jumped right into it, jumped up and down in it, took to it almost immediately (or so it seemed to me, then),

you who asked me more like ordered me to just imagine all the possibilities! you who extolled, were maniacally obsessed with such 1950s modernity as radios in automobiles, dinnertime variety-show teevee and Technicolor matinee movies, Jesus! you the leisuretime oenologist who you knew from all the vintages telling me all about the sturdy California Napa Valley grapevine stock, all about how it was used to resurrect the weakened vineyards of Bordeaux after all those decades of uninterrupted harvesting and the ravages of phylloxera I think it was,

how that as you Jacob you insisted how that was what America's responsibility it was to every domain of depleted Europe, how that's what America it had to do now, our duty you said *our*, Jacob,

to lead the world, to graft ourselves everywhere, to strangle the world entire in our strongest Westernmost vines is that what you wanted, Jacob? (and so should the half of the world that now

hates

hates us darken your doorstop next Friday night, all those Arabs
and naked black boys in fezes, yes, should all those Frenchtalian
philosophers with teaspoons or busts of Pallas Athena up their
asses stop in to stay to Shabbos dinner and thank you?)

you who even — though you never programmed him —
once when you met him on the street lent Schneidermann five
dollars, which was a huge sum in those days for a meal at that
automat on West 57th Street if you remember,

you who once in — drunken, Beaujolais then-Nouveau-
now-Postveau — post-concert conversation at the Baroness'
Uptown, remember her? praised me for my intense interest in what
you referred to as "modern music" which was really just my *intense
interest* in modern Schneidermann,

Jacob, you ever get the feeling that no one cares (and that
only the strange ones do)?

that you're just a showhorse or showpony to be trotted
out of the stable nightly, to be praised and pampered like those
geldings that you keep for yourself out in Bucks County? like that
eternally young and eternally gorgeous one woman you've stayed
married and I guess faithful to for going on 25 years now (I tried,
unlike me and your niece),

it's amazing, amazing to think that we still care, that we
still practice (though I only play scales along with the WEATHER
CHANNEL),

that we still perform, that we still think we're doing
something worthwhile,

supporting the arts you know if only for the free totebag
or umbrella,

that we still believe in this, in ourselves, in empirical value,
posterity, tomorrow and all — that, Jacob, Yakov, Israel, that you
still were able to make even me most-skeptical believe and just last
month when I caught you (though I wasn't comped)

playing Mozart now decomposing at the Uptown YMHA
and why? why did I go? why did I bother when I usually almost
always never bother? indeed when I can never afford — not
moneywise, which I always tried to give my charity to Schneidermann, but egowise — can never afford to hear my competition?
but Jacob you must know that I always go, that the only concerts I
ever go to as an audience of one they have Mozart on the program,

always have K. not as in Kafka (who he had no love of any music
from without according to Schneidermann according to their friend
Max Brod who knew them both, who he knew everyone it profited
him to know)

but as in Köchel number 563, rather the only performances I ever attend offstage are those featuring Mozart's divine or
divineless *Divertimento in E♭ Major*,

a work that's really a symphony for a string trio of you,
Jacob, and those two Asians that I don't know how you play with
them,

in E♭ major,
the *Magic Flute* key,
the trinity-of-flats, trinity-mad Masonic key — the
appropriate handshake going out to lodge-brother Michael
Puchberg for commissioning the work as a response to Mozart's
penury, his abject poverty which is a gesture that I extended more
than 10 times to Schneidermann but which he only refused some
50 times and more with the response, question, that how could he
compose a work on demand? a composition for money?

might as well orchestrate the jingling of three dimes was
what Schneidermann he offered me as an indication of either how
pure or how puerile he really was,

and as I am: me, with my Mozart rule, with my string trio
rule, with my *Divertimento* rule,

me with my 563-fixation for which I skim all the major
newspapers in the tri-state region in order to drive out anywhere,
and at any time, to hear this divine or divineless piece and this
piece only — no soloists for me, Jacob, only this instance of
chamber music as it's not called outside of its chamber (gas),

its ghetto,
only this pinnacle of the pinnacle named Mozart for which
I wait in the lobby,

it's usually the first work on the other, second, flipside of
the program, so dictate the programming Nazis as Schneidermann
he called everyone in the business of music,

to herd in with everyone else after intermission for the
Mozart you sung if not played so perfectly, Jacob,

so gorgeously, Jacob: played like a heaven I then left
immediately after the Mozart, I always leave immediately after the

Mozart

Mozart, immediately after the last E♭,

I always leave immediately after the last E♭, no more and no less, not one note more and not one note less, only that divine or that divineless work for me, Jacob, just that diverted string trio that I've of course and possibly unconsciously assimilated,

studied,

gotten-under-my-fingers but have never performed in public and never will, Jacob, because unlike you I'll never descend to their underworld,

unlike you, Jacob, I never play ensemble, you must know that I'll never defile or degrade myself with others, won't ever trust them, won't give them the privilege of being responsible for me because Jacob you must know that unlike you I am only and forever a soloist,

a true soloist like any true artist is a soloist only, like a composer like Schneidermann he was also a soloist, a great soloist and isn't that, I ask, asking all too much of two hands and one head already?

that it's enough just enough just to be a soloist, only a soloist that it takes it all out of you if you do it totally which you must, and that all the mass, the ensemble-players out there that they're just sublimating,

repressing,

just denying the obvious that deepdeepdown we're all of us soloists,

or that at least we all want to be soloists, on our own and that once you admit it to yourself, discover yourself, the truth, that once a soloist you're always a soloist and that's it, that you'll never regress, devolve, never return to what I never even was and so obviously am not, wasn't ever intended to be.

You were wonderful, Jacob. You should've gone, Mister Rothstein.

Pure melody, Jacob.

Pure melody, Mister Rothstein if you're listening but, Jacob, did anyone else? does anyone else — besides maybe you and Schneidermann who he hated to love this piece too, anyway took it as the model for his own string trio efforts — know it more purely, more total, than I do? this string trio? this most divine or divineless work of the divine or divineless Theophilius Mozart?

I who even though I never play ensemble, always play solo, by myself, with myself I'll admit that, yes, that I still play this piece and often — and you have to know each and every part, equally which is what I hate: the violin, fine, the viola also that it was Mozart's most-loved-instrument, the cello too God I know all of them!

play the violin line while I sing the cello, and make my mind hear the viola walking between the door of the Grand and the door of the cockroachlike cab,

the door of the cab and the door of the monstrously elegant Grand:

a one-man-band, Mister Rothstein, a divertimento, Jacob, and you can consider me diverted but not enough you can understand I hope to change essentially who I am, what I am, not diverted enough to descend to Friday night company (when my exwife whichever she'd call me downstairs),

to descend to the public, to its taste or its lack which will earn you a fortune but not me who I still can't afford to be anything but a soloist (again, it's not money, I'm speaking merely of ego, Freud's mistranslated *Ich*):

that there's a dialectic here, that there's only me and the people who are, simply, not me, that I'm always alone, that I was fated this way, that indeed I've willed it this way — that trust it has been invested in me to interpret: Schneidermann's trust, your trust too but don't worry,

others will play this *Concerto* in full (maybe even you, Jacob),

maybe, if there are even any concerts after tonight, after this, if this cadenza it serves as an effective enough PR stunt that'll guarantee media on and so possibly programming of this work too-long-neglected (neglected too long even by its own composer),

which will earn all zero of Schneidermann's descendants an enormous fortune to be forwarded to his — posthumous — publisher, his recordlabel, moguls who they make more money off television and matinee movies but still stay involved with art as a soul-ennobling sideline much like Mister Rothstein here, who don't worry,

don't worry because as I've maybe calculated or just intuited, prophesized that others that they'll play this *Concerto* in

full

full (but I hope with better cadenzas),

they just won't play it as well, or don't worry because no
one ever again will play this *Concerto* either in part or in full
because, well, now it's cursed,

a specter now darkens like white around the notes, unto
the pitch of tomorrow:

when nothing's immortal anymore it was Schneidermann's
idea, or, rather, what with our technological memory as Schneidermann he always said, what with our recording of everything, that
everything's immortal but the problem is according to Schneidermann, the problem will be, that everything's equally immortal
according to Schneidermann:

the other work that I love your early more than your late
recording of, Jacob, the *Partita No. 2 in D Minor*, BWV not a car
make 1004 it's Bach's *Chaconne* now as immortal as everything else:

as all advertising,

slogans, pitches and catchphrases,

as lubricants like music is,

like a nonoxynol that it actually feeds on latex, as we feed
on the false emotions that music it slathers us in (all for our
protection, I'm sure),

as you and me, Jacob Levine,

as Paganini he's just another name on the list, on the
enclosed instruction sheet still, and forever, unfurling over our ears,

as Grumiaux he's still dead, worms feeding on his fingers
— *that* technology, to bring him back, it hasn't been invented, yet
— but at least I still like to think that his Berlin recordings of
Bach if you know them that they'll live forever but only as a
replacement for not playing Bach yourself,

for not going out, getting a violin, getting a teacher or not
and just studying,

practicing (yes, children, that was what art used to require!),

only as a replacement, in lieu of my never having heard
him Grumiaux live, of my never having heard him and Bach
together ever but that they,

the recordings, are still not as much a testimony to the
composer's achievement as is the memory,

or the memory-building,

memory-erecting,

memory-preserving and passing-on that Jacob and I do,
right, Jacob? because our lore is stronger, because raw data is not
understanding, no, because information is not understanding, no,
because as I promised your father, Mister Rothstein, the Bach bow
that would enable all the techniques in the master's solo violin
music is useless now, yes, because Bach, yes, the technical innovation to actually realize the intended unrealizable, no, because Bach,
yes, because Biber, Walther, Westhoff, no,

because four-part-fugues and for a one-line-at-a-time-
instrument they are supposed to be impossible if not just sound
impossible, the technique required commands the command of the
performance if you will, because balance, but inner balance,

tightrope walking like at the Hungarian circus I played a
summer for with the black brass troupe from America, the first
shvartzes as Schneidermann would say I ever met,

those July days of fiddler-on-the-roofing like in that
matinee Anatevka movie that Schneidermann and I hated is anyway
what's required, what it takes, to be a soloist — and then of course
you have that Jew Mendelssohn preparing safe, harmonious piano
accompaniments to Bach's solo violin pieces despite orders,
instructions indicating a wish to the contrary stated direct from
Johann Sebastian's very grave,

indeed writ large on the manuscript's title page defying the
Jew Mendelssohn who he anyway revivified Bach across the centuries, tempting the Jew Mendelssohn's will-to-transgress, the will to
present if not popularize,

to showbiz-it-up,

to tinker,

to introduce is what it takes, is what's required to be a
soloist and so forget Tartini, forget Paganini:

the devil, He's with all of us, his name is — it's just that
a handful of us realize it or have IT realized for them,

like the voice in the wilderness deep in my vibrato, you
know what I'm getting at, Jacob?

the touch of the true artist, the imprint of the truly
playing mind, of the true mind at play, of the true mind at true
play (*ludus*, Schneidermann he always said),

my sound if not my technique the same tonight as it was

and

and has been every other night of my life, I like to think, I need to believe,

    live in Hungary as it was living in Amsterdam, in London, in every nowhere town I ever played in Switzerland: in Berne, Biel, Olten, Aarau, Winterthur during that epidemic of Spanish influenza when,

    what I learned from Schneidermann, the intelligence he possessed and represented so well, that passion-in-bounds, that passion-under-control is the only thing that can get us out of this computer sound (with COMPUTER such a last season word, as Schneidermann he once remarked only after he'd had the Information Revolution explained to him),

    this *digitizedsoundworld* or whatever Germanisch monster that it haunts our music today,

    this impersonal lushness that we hear all around us,

    Heifetz's canned corporate warble and that, truth be told, sacrilege, that's my final answer, judgment, the only verdict I can have on Heifetz, who he should have lived to hear me now!

    you should have heard me on a hissing, sparkling 78! because I want you to understand that too often the idea is the beauty and intensity of the violin rather than the expressive flesh of the music,

    the meeting of touch and your touched heads,

    swirled thumbprint of God on your heart you then wring out outside into the gutters, Westside:

    God! that's the touch that we're talking about, the touch that it interprets the music as well and as much as it interprets its listeners, its you:

    this touch Schneidermann he had,

    not least in his *Violin Concerto* I've been interpreting for you without interpreting,

    more like invoking, and in so doing invoking his life, his legacy, his secret, his meaning, invoking a ghost in the wings,

    in the dark wings of a hall hosting not a musical performance but a play on the stage of another play,

    one stage of evolution giving way to our more accomplished, happier, more memorious,

    not-invoking-a-tradition-as-much-as-living-within-a-tradition,

enabling-a-tradition ancestors no longer around to take a
bow,
to meet a curtain's call — as I once took a bow, I admit:
some Baroness she lent it to me, never returned it after the
London tour, then the War,
what happened happened,
it prevented me from,
it suited me,
the bow — never asked for it back because she the Baroness she didn't want to disturb the natural order of things, because
the rich they preserve dignity, no matter however false and rotten it
might be, right Mister Rothstein? who else do you think pays my
rent? my roomservice tab? my alimony? my legal fees? my sexual-
harassment suit pay-offs? Parkside-narcotics dead-drops? who else
do you think keeps my traveling healing show, well-snake-oiled, on
the road? I took because there was no other road, because it was the
road that my — true if false — father he paved for me with all his
stones of dream,
because it was less a road than a stairwell,
less a stairwell than Jacob's ladder,
the angelic ladder in the wilderness,
the artistic, intellectual as much as everything-else wilderness because Schneidermann and I, well, we might have been born
— artistically, intellectually — poor but we took and quickly to
ascension, elevation, loft: me following my father who he was only
following the only road left open to poor eastern Jews like us:
the road of Kreisler and Flesch, yes, but more like the road
of Elman and Heifetz, Huberman and Menuhin and now me, the
only one I'll allow leftover — I won't say survived — from those
days as a father's dream, as a marketable prodigy in a white alpaca
sailorsuit with shorts so short that when I sat down my putz it
would almost stick out the left leg that in the Jewish Kabbalah as
you all must know you're such experts is known as Hod and
represents the attribute of majesty I undoubtedly didn't display
that day when I stood and played for the famous virtuoso whose
studio I forsook soon enough and against all judgment, advice and
reason for the single spare room of my Schneidermann at the
Royal Academy,
or if you want the Ferencz or — Modernized, then

Germanized

Germanized — Ferenc or Franz Liszt Academy of Music (which only two handfuls of years earlier was the stopover for my early model and later friend, Jacob's teacher Jacob's Schneidermann Joseph Szigeti who he had to wait for Berlin and his tutelage under Busoni for similar enlightenment),

Schneidermann to me who he taught me *music*,

who wrote me *music*,

who was *music*,

who he took me from the flash (in the pan we usually ate dinner out of, Frau Schneidermann she couldn't have found the kitchen even if you'd hidden gold bars and chocolate cakes in the oven)

of the typical display pieces, the creamy crumbly salon numbers, the typical schlocky prodigy repertoire, the little ambitious Jewish violinist's stock-in-trade and traded it in to life in unequal measure for the relentless rewards of art,

for the rewards of maturity,

of understanding,

of deathlessness,

taught me, Schneidermann did that the violin is for the violinists and that the music is for the musicians, raised me, enlightened me to the point at which my faults they weren't my faults but the faults of and in the world and so my remedying them, my healing of them, was, is, indeed perfecting or at least seeking to perfect this imperfect as it is imperfectable universe,

not that anyone, any of you out there deserve it, these efforts, mine, his, because Schneidermann he also taught me much about them, about you too, because Schneidermann he taught, told me all about your indifference, because Schneidermann he told me all about your indecisiveness when you weren't indifferent, insecure, in-everything,

all about your hate and your rages, your stupidity and your immaculate forgetfulness,

your insistence and then your withdrawal,

your acclaim and then your damnation,

your will and then your idea of yourself because you need to understand that we, that most virtuosos they spend as much time practicing and learning, memorizing and getting their fingers around the once-improvised cadenza as they spend on its concerto, and but don't think that *this* cadenza it gives any indication as to the (style, tone of the)

music of the *Concerto* it has interrupted, this *Concerto* it has ruined, has destroyed — you need to understand also, no,

you need to mourn and then question why is it that cadenzas they're so codified as to be as lasting as the concerto that they incarnate? as the true through-composed work? and yet at the same timeless time cadenzas they have no form, no harmony, structure,

no physiognomy but ego,

un or subconscious memory,

masturbation,

memory-masturbation,

ego-masturbation and so rendering it the perfect form, non-form, for our time:

because a cadenza's a form that isn't a form according to Schneidermann, cadenza, a non-form that's also a form (which is life according to Schneidermann in the all of no words that Schneidermann he ever spoke to me about my cadenza for his *Concerto*,

this),

cadenza, a painstakingly constructed ruin, cadenza, calcu-lated abandon, cadenza, planned recklessness, cadenza, calculated recklessness, cadenza, planned abandon,

cadenza cadenza cadenza

cadenza cadenza

cade

THE CHILDREN'S CHORUS

and so it seems that they've schlepped in my kinder, thought it
out, thought it was a workable plan, a play, a ploy, a scherzo if you
will to implore my sentiment if not my sensibilities you've
subwayed all if not just the most telegenic of them in to Midtown
— how many of you have been here before? fixed the place up nice,
didn't they?

  yes, if not all of my children then you've rounded up most
of them I believe, I have as many as Bach, I think: there was
Wilhelm F. and C.P.E. and Johann G.B. and by Anna Magdalena we
have Elisabeth and Johann C.F. and Johann just plain C., all
grandchildren of old Hans Bach who he had a son, no joke, hand to
God Schneidermann he once told me he was named Lips, who died
all of 1620 — but mine, all they do is *give lip*

  hahaha, yes, hello there! yes, sure I hear you, Amiel and
Ariel or — what's your name? no, don't tell me, Lena and
Nathaniel and with Akira Queen of the Night now, what's your
new last name? your new husband's? what? repeat it for me, slow
with the accent you still have, always will, it's Akira Goldberg,
God!

  once you go Jewish you never go,

  never go back to being Asian again I guess, can't be content
with anything Asian ever again, can you, Akira Gold?

  in my alphabet, in music's alphabet wherein the G of Gold
it's followed by the *A* of Akira, the *A* of Asia and America with the
enharmonic note, the G♯/A♭ stuck in the middle, bringing about in
Schneidermann at least a synasthaesic phenomenon of light blue, a
cerulean-coral sounded by that note that Schneidermann he
claimed came to him every evening invariably between six and seven
p.m. (over liquid and smoke after a matinee movie),

  a light blue of the eyes of Lena, also of my daughter Dina,
G♯/A♭ eyes they have except now when they're blurred, the whites
beclouded in red — but why are you crying (you're even more
dramatic than your old man)?

  How have you all been? how has life been treating you?
and no, I know why you're here, I know what you're here for, no, I
won't come to my senses, no, I won't *come down*

and *be reasonable!* — I must have raised you all, or your
mothers have, too politely, too mundane.

How's the new gig, Nat? treating you well? and the wife? I
hear through to-remain-anonymous socialites of the Upper
Eastside species that you have three children now of your own, and
so I'm still reproducing, even as a grandparent — but how far do
you reasonably expect my love to spread?

like creamed cheese over warmed pumpernickel and O how
I need a nickel! would always pluck one from the freezing street
and for Schneidermann, a dime spared, a Jew needs anything he
could want as Schneidermann he always said, hahaha

the nerve, the nerve to have so many wives, the nerve to
have so many divorces, the nerve to have so many children, to
weigh down this world with evermore replicas, drones, ever lessen-
ing imitations of a love that it doesn't even touch down to my new
shoes anymore — patent leather with a bow atop and black as my
father's, mother's later cancer shoes that I stood in in that studio
in the Music Academy in Budapest in another century, indeed in
another world and to play one of my handful of show-off,

stock-in-trade-your-soul-for-flash,

for quick applause prodigy selections at my audience, at
my audition, at my first and only presentation of myself to my
Schneidermann who he then gave me the advice that I now give to
you, advice more like a divine decree from Schneidermann to me
and now to my children though it might be too late, probably is, to
myself as to you:

that you must be man enough to realize your own mistakes! but it sounds so much better in the original (German,
Yiddish),

or at least from the mouth of the original Schneidermann:
that you must be genius enough to claim, to believe, indeed to
know as you know nothing else that your mistakes they are better
than what you do correctly! than anything you do correctly! the
faith-leap of all the great soloists: Hitler, Stalin, Caesar, Alexander,
Moses even and so on all according to Schneidermann, let the
future or the rediscovered past fill in more names here and that
this, that this quality that it's the essential evolution, metamor-
phosis if you like, from Prodigy (which you all were, which was all
you were)

to Man, from Prodigy which I or your mothers made all of
you to Human, from monkeys to true intelligences, to individuals,
to responsible intelligent individuals, which I wasn't then, yet,

which I wasn't that once when I told my father — my true
father and not my true Schneidermann — that it was my sister
who she broke Bubbe's dish even though I didn't even have a sister
(she'd died in infancy),

even though I was an only child with a concert to think
about in three hours for rich patrons that my father he wanted to
know better, rich patrons who my second father, my Schneidermann, he couldn't have cared less about, my second and I have to
say greater father Schneidermann who he had to insist that mistakes,

once you're talented enough to make them real,

they make it all better, all the more correct if you'd just
accept them (I began having children at a relatively late age),

my second and greater father — I hope you've all found
one for yourselves — who instead of taskmastering me as my
interim virtuoso violinist teacher he did over scales and fingerings,
which I knew I'd figure out on my own anyway, Schneidermann he
instead and leisurely, with a recognizable measure of irony dueting
with scorn, set up for me the dialectic:

that Ysaÿe he parted the waters of Joachim (expression),
and de Sarasate (technique), how in parting them he miraculously
— with irony and scorn — united them and how according to
Schneidermann according to Flesch at least (*my* flesh was dead, or
not yet born)

he Ysaÿe did so by instituting vibrato,

that shake of Adam's appletree as Schneidermann would
often say,

as an essential component of style — vibrato, that artful
inaccuracy that Kreisler he explored further, engaging it even in fast
passage work until now, well, what's left?

with my arms and my hands and my fingers and my wives
and my exwives and even my prospective wives and my children all
giving me problems, this carpal tunnel vision that I have and even
an arthritic putz requiring pills to stand up and still for any
reasonable length of hurt and spurt, with my arms hurting and my
wrists and my hands and my thumb, my index, my FUCK YOU

finger and my overtimes-ringed ring and pinkie fingers and all their
joints, knuckles and pads they just ache!

can't even be a violinist anymore soon enough,

can't even be a musician,

a husband, a father, can't even be a monkey anymore, a
prize-winning pig and so I have to remove myself from the Zoo
(where Schneidermann he gifted me this *Concerto*)

before all the bars fall,

before all the bad reviews they begin flowing in,

before my chordophone as they say is taken away from me,
repoed, impounded by the trustees of the Carnegie Corporation, I
can take a stand!

from the 1st violin section most probably,

O will you just shut up, Nina! I've always loved/hated you
because you sound and you look so or too much like your mother,

but without the cymbals of breasts (aren't those her
triangle earrings?),

and what a tailpiece on her too! when she was young,

when we were young and she'd stay up until dawn as I
slept off a concerto just to iron my handkerchiefs in some far
Eastern Intercontinental Hotel that it tried to seem like Vienna
where,

not like my Frieda who she just slept all day — this was
my first woman who she cleaned Schneidermann's house in the
days of his wife and his daughters and his opera-money and his
peace, or who was supposed to clean it but she never did, no, all
she did was sleep, yes, she just slept, slept and drank huge cups,
cup after cup of steaming, scalding-hot tea, teacups after teacup so
huge and day after day that eventually, because no one did the
cleaning, not her nor Schneidermann's then-wife or then-daughters,
they just piled up, eventually they hid her face, nested one within
the other like faceless glowing matrioshki, Russian dolls and so
huge that you weren't able, after a month of the lung illness that
killed her, that you weren't even able to get into her quarters, her
room, was as if the huge handleless teacup of teacups was so huge
like immense, hulking that it was blocking all my and the doctor's
ingress, and so her egress if she could even get up out of bed,
impeding progress and allowing only regress, and the heat!

she had an important job in the Schneidermann household

which

(which she never did in health as in death)

and yes, Nat! I know that I've Scheherazaded this story a
thousand times and one time previous (that night in Paris where
we bonded like proteins!),

but, well, it's important in that she this Frieda she was
supposed to be able to differentiate (and after only one lesson with
the Master)

between butcherpaper which was to be thrown out and
away and butcherpaper, kosher, that it had useful musical sketches
sketched across its incarnadine seep in Schneidermann's always
wild and yet hermetic, innerly-meticulous hand and — God, think
of the loss! — she must have thrown out the equivalent of 16
finished and unfinished piano sonatas and I don't know why, not
sure why I pick that number except that that was their ages and
maybe their age combined for all I know,

the Friedas',

but *ppp*,

because the heel of the bow, right here if you'll look and
for no reason that I know of (or that Schneidermann he provided
that sounded plausible and not just one of his many evasions or
jokes),

is called by those in and out of the know the *frog* and that,
that's what she called me and her sister after her that's what they
called me, *the frog* and I still don't know why either but it's maybe
because I tongued her so well before I betrayed her (O! such
sounds we made! Straussian!)

(betrayed, or do they still say *cuckolded*?) for her maybe
younger or she just kissed that way sister who she was hired more
like sold into white slavery when she, Frieda, catarrh-croupy
got sick, to replace her older or she just sucked that way sister, to
clean Schneidermann's house that her maybe older sister she never
cleaned in sickness or in death or maybe her,

the maybe-younger-sister, the one with the shoulder-to-
pelvis TB operation scar I would rim with my tongue,

yes, maybe *she* was the one named Frieda (but who remembers at this remove?),

anyway, she which whoever drank great steaming cup after
cup after cup after cups of this dark tea imported and at great
expense, nearly all her salary spent on this dark tea from Turkey

that she loved, was addicted to — you first had to heat the grinds
in a pan before steeping, to release the aroma and taste maybe that
was as salty as the deadest sea among the stiffest hair is how she
tasted, which was wet as the deadest sea of tea among the reeds,
which was hot too, so hot the cups after cups were that you'd never
touch them,

    arrayed around her bed (every cup in that cupful
cupboardful house she had there, all the sets so that the then-
Misses Schneidermann she had to buy more that they didn't
match)

    when you came in to *clean for her*, this girl whoever she was
who he,

    who Schneidermann actually the first one he overpaid all
too much for cleaning or actually not cleaning and, I admit, whom
I also paid and always too much for my first sexual experiences
with — children, do you like to hear that? but later when in ill-
health with all practices and positions already old I just cleaned her
room in exchange for any, miscellaneous, favors she felt well
enough to grant, by the end just a quick toothsome suck because
in truth I'm lazy and who likes to work?

    especially at pleasure?

    as little as she did with her instructions to clean the whole
entire Schneidermann household — the then-Misses Schneidermann and her daughters were lazy, good-for-not-much and weren't
even awed by Schneidermann and his

    ethic — with her instruction to clean the whole thing top
to bottom of which she only ever fulfilled the *but*,

    the but never, ever, never — and this was Schneidermann's
own instruction, the only words he ever addressed to the Friedas
whom I did mit Holz if you will, to:

    never, ever, ever, never dust the piano or its bench that, the bench
Schneidermann he custom designed and carpentered himself, often
during late nights, during early mornings doubled as his, as
Schneidermann's toilet,

    and sick! the both of them sick unto death! ministered to
by tea and their teacups huge, piled high to obscure their
groundfloor windows (their rooms were in the cellar, the cellar was
their shared room, damp, wet as them with me, TB-inducing to the
Davos they only dreamed of when sleeping, which was always, as all

European girls they all slept too much, all the time,
        Rilke who,
        and they were also always so sick if it wasn't a chronic cold
it was flu, sick and asleep their natural state or unnatural states)
— what gigs these girls had! like the scam that Schneidermann's
neighbor he was working,
        a man who he was cheating on his wife with *his* charwoman
then/cleaninglady now, the man who he was a civil servant of some
sort, who knows? (he probably didn't either)
        like the Asians or the African-Americans we men are all the
same, he told his wife that he was interested in you know taking up
the piano, to improve himself (in a soul-ennobling way),
        to impress others, also undoubtedly to move up in social
and business circles (which a musical education it could do for
you, then)
        and so on and that since they were fortunate or was it
unfortunate enough?
        enough to live next to a great piano virtuoso it would make
perfect or at least perfectible sense just to enroll nextdoor (in
those days no one knew of Schneidermann as a composer as much
as they knew of him as an opera composer or as an operetta
composer, as a pianist and above all as a madman and a Jew),
        that since the nextdoor piano virtuoso Schneidermann he
was a very occupied, with himself, man the only lesson slot available — but the man he meant another slot — it was late-late at
night and so his excuse to be out and at that hour or more for
intensive hours of fingerwork was that he was taking late-at-night-
into-early-morning piano (and theory, for good measure)
        lessons from and with their nextdoor Schneidermann at
something like two-three in the morning,
        soontime and time in another dimension, the past with
this man actually paying Schneidermann to keep up his front, his
cover, actually supporting Schneidermann's then-excessive gambling
habit between commissions, which they rarely if ever came as they
never were accepted anyway while Schneidermann he accepted this
man's money as all he had to do was to do nothing whatsoever at
all, just keep on living, perpetuate his own existence (which is
more difficult than any of us realize Schneidermann he soon
realized),

or rather all Schneidermann he had to do was to play the piano late, which he did anyway but now it never annoyed, bothered his neighbors, the man's wife, because she as stupid as all women at all times always are just thought that it was just her husband taking his lesson(s), plunking weirdly as inept, atonally away (shows what she knew, what you would know too) — and Schneidermann even, though the man he didn't ask him to, to entertain himself as much as to ensure his evening's practice Schneidermann he would say to the man's wife (always in Hungary Schneidermann he would speak German to everyone, it always annoyed, thought it was sophisticated Schneidermann did, artistic, as imperialist then as speaking American to everyone abroad now,

   which of course I do anyway but),

   Schneidermann even though he didn't have to, wasn't obligated to he would say to the unfortunate woman when he happened upon her — shopping, for hats and for lovers (hat-salesmen) — in the street (Práter utca):

   You know, Frau Whatsoever, your husband's really coming along. His Verbinski Sonata is quite accomplished, taking into account how long he's been playing.

   which is funny one because obviously it's not true and two because there never even was a composer by the name of Verbinski, Schneidermann he made it up, composed it, or at least no famous composer known to me as Verbinski or maybe Verbinsky with a *y* and I would know, I would think,

   hope, and so no *Sonata* by him or not by him, not even one numbered Opus Zero — which is thirdly funny because there was at least once,

   the man he told Schneidermann and Schneidermann he told me that the man had told him that he and his wife they were once out at some society party when the wife of the host, the Hostess her name was she went and asked this man's wife to ask her husband to please please please entertain them on the grand that it sat there the other 364 days of the year unplayed (though to be sure it was regularly dusted and tuned),

   and so of course and with all the formalities a wife then serviced when in society she asked her husband who he had to say

to her, to tell her the excuse that he later repeated to Schneidermann the next Wednesday I think it was always Wednesday afternoon when the man he paid him and they played chess, which
Schneidermann he always won even when he handicapped himself
without one of the rook's pawns, an excuse then repeated again to
me on Thursday, yes, it was always my Thursday long-lesson,
Thursday was always *the long-lesson-day*
     at which Schneidermann — who never played white — he
told me that the man he told his wife and then, rising through the
chain-of-command, told Hostess:

     I'm sorry, but my teacher, Herr Schneidermann, he has forbidden me
from playing in public until such time as he feels that I am adequately prepared
or something like that,
     and, you know I'm so eager but Teacher, he must be respected

and they: *Well, he* must *know what's right!*

     and the man and Schneidermann — and I, I was permitted
— laughed dark, while the wife and the hostess, Hostess, they were
disappointed, apparently said as much to the man, to this most
probably tone-deaf, stone-deaf man:

     What a disappointment!

     as Schneidermann's reputation as an eccentric it was only
given new life, rumor, heightened and of course this man he went
on shtupping as Schneidermann he always said his cleaninglady,
not María, whom I do at our hotel where, Marta I think her name
was who the man he did at his charwoman's blind grandmother's
house until and as if he couldn't hear or see it coming he con-
tracted syphilis (without first consulting a lawyer),
     which it put an end to his affair,
     his life,
     and so his arrangement with Schneidermann,
     his party-going with his wife too to parties that Schneider-
mann he was never asked to, invited to anyway because once he was
caught at one early in his career — his opera days — doing
something he never exactly specified, to me, what went on

in the whitest linen-closet at an after-opera-party thrown
loose-fisted if you can believe it by a real live from the grim fairy
tales Princess — also there were the rumors going around then
(like syph, spirochetes like corkscrews to bad wine)
about his toilet habits,
his idea of *shit*,
of artistic excess and his, Schneidermann's assiduous
personal if not musical embodiment of that ideal, non-ideal, giving
rise to rumors about his piano throne with the built-in custom
toilet so that Schneidermann he'd never have to stop composing,
so that Schneidermann he'd never have to stop playing,
yes, playing!
playing being the ultimate thought, thinking which is after
all what you do on the toilet,
which is what you're supposed to do with the roll that
Schneidermann he'd always had prepared inside the piano, those
old thin waxy sheets we used to use if we were too sensitive to use
the evening newspaper just resting on the strings around C4,
explosive!
(didn't I tell you that I was a terrorist?)
and then not to mention, to forget that other (all-too-)drunk
evening when — on some *absinthe, mère des bonheurs* some minor
poet or another (came-out-of-the-closet, wormed his way out of
the wormwood-work), had managed to smuggle in and aflame —
that evening-evening at one party or another, they're all the same
this one hosted by some duchess who she was still seeking her
duke,
holding auditions in her bedchamber and blindfolded,
at which Schneidermann who I don't think he was even,
formally, invited he anyway entertained — mortally shocked — all
present by climbing up onto the ass-bone-white-grand-piano,
undoing his astronomical belt,
dropping his pants around his shins into a squat Schneidermann he, yes, actually and indeed took a shit *in* a piano, right
onto the soundboard, shoeless sockless feet on the keyboard with
his toes tapping out a polished accompaniment to the Beethoven's
9th he was — making an overture to — singing:
Dumb, dumb dumb, numb numbnumb numbnumb,
the European melody par excellence as the Germans say,

the

the fraternal muzak of Beethoven's *9th* and first and only
sell-out,

his, Schneidermann's to be sure, turds just vibrating hot
and sympathetically the shat-upon strings with everyone just
mortally shocked (except the servants) — but this is not what an
artist does, Schneidermann he told me after telling me this,
swearing to me that this is not at all what an artist does — that if
he does, he's a fake — but indeed actually insisting that this is
what *art itself* does:

though this isn't an apology, not for him neither for me,

not a repentance, an atonement, not an admission that
neither he nor I nor any of us we could control our outbursts but
rather that our outbursts they couldn't control us — but this isn't
for polite company as that proverb goes,

such as my Leah here who besides having a weak constitution (she seems to get mono, visits with Epstein-Barr/Chronic
Fatigue like she gets her period),

a weak stomach (no dairy, a lactard, no fruit either she's
fructose-intolerant),

a weak most everything except a weak Will she just above
all and everything else could not stand Schneidermann, didn't like
my, our, Schneidermann, outright hated the man who I tried to
have her address as Onkel who she wouldn't even address at all,
wouldn't even acknowledge his existence, ignored if not defied all
his overtures:

didn't listen to his

old-man-memories as she called them, like when Schneidermann or Uncle Schneidermann he told her or tried to tell her all
about his grandfather who was from Ukraine and how he used to
wear a wooden coat with hinged lapels (birch),

You, Leah, thought he was ridiculous. And me by association.

didn't laugh that afternoon he was up at the house when I
lived there with your mother and I was telling you over and over
again that despite all the money in the world (which was mine and
not yours)

it would be good for you in every way that's good to get
up off your Levi-Strauss and get yourself a summer job, Leah, and
how you just argued your adolescence out until Schneidermann or

Uncle Schneidermann he told you or tried to tell you that a store up near him on Mt. Morris Park they might have an opening for a mannequin,

　　didn't laugh even when Schneidermann he was up at the penthouse at the Grand and when he left he mistook the doorbell for a mezuzah (and so kissed, kissed at the ring),

　　didn't understand his

　　old-man-ways as you put it on another afternoon that last summer of living together when our air-conditioning it — thankfully — died and you just screamed and shrieked all about Jew-pit-sweat and frizzed Jew-hair for an hour until Schneidermann or Uncle Schneidermann he offered or tried to offer that on a hot day there was no better place to get yourself cool than inside a place-of-worship.

　　You, Leah, that's what you thought that he was ridiculous, strange and me by association whereas you, Dina, you went even further, Dina,

　　thought that Schneidermann he was an excuse,

　　my excuse,

　　a recourse, my recourse, Dina you thought that Schneidermann he was my out, my exit or at least my preferred method of disengagement,

　　of distance, of distancing me from you from me, of putting him between you and me and you with him in-between but I want to tell you that,

　　to promise, to swear to you Dina my girl that Schneidermann (and so that *art*)

　　he — it — was and emphatically *not* an excuse,

　　not a recourse,

　　that invoking and/or honoring a prior engagement with Schneidermann (and so missing your school assemblies, spellingbees, wet-T-shirt carwash fundraisers and pre-prom rituals as elaborate as any church's or cult's)

　　it was not an illuminated exit from a theater on fire, it was not an escape-hatch from the sinking ship of the mundane, an out or a pass from the demands of the mundane,

　　God, all those accusations! like sewage spewed from your Mund! as Schneidermann he would say and but,

　　from day-to-day responsibilities, not at all, emphatically

not

not, not as Dina you claimed one young night as I put you to bed,

      sang or tried to sing you to sleep with the half-remem-
bered liturgy of the Day of Atonement and you interrupted, Dina,

      claimed that Schneidermann that he was just my imaginary
friend just like you had an imaginary friend whose name I am sorry
to say that I have forgotten,

      if he's here tonight, Happy I think it was,

      or Slappy maybe, Nappy?

      that Schneidermann he was an imaginary friend that I your
father I visited at a whim, on a whim and who — by virtue of his
nonexistence — could never be inconvenienced because our imagination, I want to tell you, Dina,

      that our imagination it is never *that* accommodating,

      never *that* convenient to our need, even to our need most
vital:

      in fact, forget now that Schneidermann he's dead or
disappeared from me and under the most embarrassing of conditions (non-conditions),

      I want you to know that even when he was around and alive
Schneidermann he was often indisposed (to me),

      always at work, always at play, unable to stop, couldn't
stop or at least wouldn't,

      always cranking out the hits,

      the parade,

      never stymied, never at an artistic impasse as the Europe-
ans say, at an American dead-end — indeed his days they were
everything like the days of *my* childhood, Dina, my childhood days
of a routine imposed,

      of a regime that I couldn't control (destroy),

      didn't understand and probably wouldn't have wanted to,

      those prodigy days of the early violin and afternoon play
(my only joy), with the toy soldiers — his days, Dina, they were
everything like the tin toy soldiers, black, I used to line up,
marching even now and still in step back to the Old World:

      each identical to its predecessor in ranks and yet each
individually open to loss, indeed predisposed to loss in degrees
varying in relation to my placement, to its position within the
whole rank and file,

      or just to absurdity, pure chance, coincidence mating with

the soundless unknown (their faces they didn't even have mouths
or ears painted on):

each tin toy soldier available to go falling under the sofa,
or behind the damask loveseat, the warped Empire furniture that
my dead mother she had inherited, behind my father's favorite
Biedermeier chair (seemingly upholstered in skin, his, bought from
his brother on the cheap as it lacked its matching footstool),

and for good, never to be found again:

and so the general impression of order it was never
disturbed, only, if inspected closely, the amount, the quantity of
order,

over the years,

growing up,

it became gradually reduced — and I, Dina, I your father I
was all too often his, was Schneidermann's lost soldier, depleting
the ranks of his life,

unknowingly (to both, to either of us),

and yet I could also blend, once found, rediscovered in a
rare idle moment, once retrieved from the secret of oblivion I could
blend into a triumphant pageant that spoke for if not trumpeted
the fullness of Schneidermann's mind,

the overabundance of his effort — but as they were toy
soldiers, tin, enamel-painted and peeling,

his ultimately childlike effort,

his outdated and yet postdated effort,

in that old time,

in our old time of soldiers and marching,

of losing and finding,

of chance and luck and coincidence and
youth I want you all to know

that Schneidermann that he raised me, brought me
up when no one else could and

that I was unable,

in our time when the consolation of childhood it
wasn't enough, when it itself needed to be consoled, Schneidermann for me he was that greater consolation, and, yes, that often
for him I was the consolation of the child,

innocence, youth and but,

sometimes,

unfortunately

unfortunately Dina,
I was merely the child.

THE CHILDREN'S CHORUS

yes, I'm sure you remember my sins, Leah, my dear, you were at just the perfect age to know and to understand, to perfectly know and to perfectly understand all that was going on with, all that was happening to me your father old enough to be your grandfather, even your great: all my lies, the dodges and evasions performed only with my tongue unaccompanied and in SEE SHARP MINOR,

all my affairs, the late-night telephone silences unmarked adagio that we shared and greedily like starving Ukrainians when I would call your mother, or when I would try to call your mother up late at night and instead you'd answer because you'd be awake and she wouldn't be (that eyemask she wore like she was robbing a bank when all she was robbing was safeless, uninsured me),

you'd be awake because you were waiting, because you were always waiting for a telephone call from a boy, a man, from this boy, from that man it changed by the week (that night-sweating pimple with the head of a penis),

and instead you picked up, you answered and instead of an adolescent Don Giovanni with a dago-moustache and a voice fit for a Mozartina soprano on the line it was your father on the other end who he, who I just wanted to know one whether your mother was awake and two who and how you were and how you answered, or how you didn't answer, with just silence, quietude, mute as you aren't now just screaming your porcelain head off for me to come down, for me to calm down and but remember how it used to be reversed (like that VCR button I've only lately found the courage to press it, our camcorder home-movies, how to make doublearrowed time spend itself speeding in the other direction)?

the opposite, how I used to scream, to yell minted mouth-wash and Hungarian dentistry at you?

to eat your veal when we thought you were anorexic, to go to your sessions of homeotherapy or whatever that bitch she billed me a fortune for when we knew you were anorexic (your mother she had done her library research),

when at the age of 13 you wore that intestinal-white mesh shirt that it also showed your navel too-hairy,

when

when at the age of 12 you wore your mother's expensive imported makeup that I got for her on a stopover at the Frankfurt Airport in the DUTY-FREE because I felt terrible about a certain position I'd just attempted with a Dutch journalist I think she was from Spinoza's hometown?

too much makeup as always — the drip-drop-running of a temporary tragedy mask,

will someone get her some cold-cream? and always with your gold, your gold it's glaring my eyes out,

but Shayna! Shayna, it took another generation but you, you are the true prodigy,

you the only one of my descendants with a future beyond your braid-stage: a flautist to silence all flautists, a fluteplayer nobler even than Fredrick the Great her fellow instrumentalist — and but girl prodigies sell! I'll tell you, I'm telling you,

my granddaughter,

my daughter's daughter she's Leah's one and only,

who's now, Leah is, an admitted, resigned, failure who she raises funds for what or for whom? for my burial costs, I hope, for the burial expenses this me will incur,

who I remember all those nights when I put you to bed (Leah your mother I think it was who she always favored the American *beddy-bye*),

put you to sleep Leah, laid you down and sang that German lullaby to you do you remember how it went?

Rucke di guck, rucke di guck

Blut ist im Schuck and so on,

laid you down deep in the grave perfection of childhood, Leah, the perfect innocence of childhood — and maturation is improvisation,

Shayna, if you're listening, growing up into a woman, into breasts and consciousness, remember that it takes a man or a woman like a man, you know what I'm saying anyway to know his mistakes, to love them — those are my true wives, Deborah and Rachel, your true mothers and I've evidently paid my alimony, must make a note, which one? to thank my manager, but no time now, not for me,

not the half-hour that Schneidermann in his youngest youth he had to be paid, to be bribed with to practice the upright piano before the babygrand that,

paid by his aunt of one of his nine musical aunts two — overinflated due to the war they called Great — crowns the hour and what he'd buy with this windfall:

his two-octave handful of morello cherries, a piece of krumpli cukor (a potato sweet that an uncle of mine he always said resembled the shape of my head),

an ice like you Akira Goldsomething, as frigid, when licked as melting — how's husband # he seems one thousand and nine treating you? flat daughters, a sharp mother and he's here too, isn't he?

yes, he has to be, this husband numbered late opuswise, almost posthumous, slinking out the rear like an extra in a matinee Thriller movie,

disappearing toward the back of the house unguarded because who would ever attack art?

or through the illuminated fire exits,

house lights on, off, on, or just the spot on me, in my house,

it's my house, you understand?

this hall is, the only house you wives out there you won't ever take away from me,

you spoiled Jews! and half-Jews! and quarter-Jews! you ingrates and purebred Philistines! let's ask him, get his opinion of this mess I've made, this husband, yes, why not?

Okay, Doctor Goldblatt or berg, Goldenthal how have you been feeling? and have you been feeling, lately?

Might I borrow your prescription pad for a moment? a rest or two? I'd promise I'll return it,

but you adopted my daughter — no! you, shhhhhhhhhhhh! *pppppppppppppp*,

hear the dynamic markings! quite snobby, oboe-high-nosed she's become, this Judith or Judy of yours, no? of mine too, but is she in possession of any talent whatsoever?

No, I wasn't around long enough to find out. And there are no encores.

Listen, listen, listen,

I almost fell. No! no help! you just stay!

Children, I'm going to die. I want to die. Free and alone.

And

And you all will surely want something to remember me
by. A word without artificial sweetener. A memory of New Jersey
ocean frolic that never existed.

But there's no money left. No more fame. No more
privilege. There's nothing.

Here's my handkerchief. Can you catch? like a dove, Noah
in his ark, watching golf on the screen as wide as the wingspans of
a million ravens — what a disappointment! You all are.

I am too.

I should've been a European as my mother she wanted. I
should have stayed in Europe and died or survived but stayed there
in Europe in any form alive or dead so that at least I wouldn't have
had to witness

this, I've often thought in weaker thoughts. The death of
my people while they're still alive. This America so alive and so

deadly.

What about getting reparations from Germany? I once
asked Schneidermann as Schneidermann he and with a hand
extended leagues beyond me to posterity perpetually refused a loan
perpetually on offer, once and once only I asked him straight-out,
as if man-to-mann and

No, Schneidermann he answered and meant it. Adamant as
Adam. As-if.

Guilt gelt. Wiedergutmachung.

An artist, Schneidermann he said, always has to worry
about his reputation.

Yes, jeer and heckle you few remaining

adherents! boo! crumple up those lies passing for pro-
grams and throw them at me — I'm a good catch for those long
days of short centerfield,

that day that Schneidermann and I we went to the Yankees
game, or was it the Mets?

but instead, I apply pressure to allow sounds, fingers on
the tightrope like that summer I worked the circus,

the circuit,

the Hungarian summer theater troupe with whom — then
I had TB, had to spend some Swiss-watch-time taking the cure,

and now we have the disease of people like my friend Jacob
Levine, those other old Jews and even young Asians or maybe, I

don't know, don't even listen anymore, my landsmen and so, working the circus and circuit gigs there wasn't that false ascension to forsake my development:

instead there was a seamless uninterruption between my prodigy and, well, my adult careers — you understand that like unlike Jascha, Mischa, Sascha, that I never appeared as an adult under my prodigy name? my diminutive but always and don't you forget it as me,

like as if which Schneidermann and I we picked up at the matinee Adolescent Sex movies,

that knowing Schneidermann, a modern composer whatever that is after the Second Viennese and their War they liquidated everything, bit of the infant terrible to him, that all of that it made me hate that prodigy aesthetic, discontent with standard repertoire, the pander, the pose and so on and so forth into middling America — because the idea's to and intuitively get at the heart of the piece Schneidermann he once told me rapping the shallow swell of his arching aorta, the heart of the heart of the heart was how Schneidermann he went on:

a passage, a goddamned note, as no one else, and that you always need to be open, to be able to circus-it-up, need to be open to improvising, experiment, to always approach afresh, anew, with fresh new unorthodox fingerings like me and Schneidermann's which then-daughter or wife?

because Flesch he had warned and whole generations ago of the monotony obtaining in thoughtless application to all musics of an exaggerated vibrato, improper, nauseous stuff as Flesch he said the "sensuous, artificially inflated rather than naturally matured, spirit of our times,"

as Schneidermann he once said while sitting on his El-Al-blanketed boxed stereo-coffeetable,

or as Szell he once put it that:

"any subtle function of the wrist and fingers of the righthand is practically unknown to them (the new violinists of his generation)".

I'm full of rage, true. I'm genius and worthless, true. I'm an interpreter as much as a memorizer, true.

Unorthodox bowings heighten expression, true.

As Schneidermann's admirer Artur Schnabel always said:

Safety

"Safety last!"

and maybe (though Schnabel he never programmed him, *Alex, vy do you always make it zo difficult?*) — God! why am I even holding this ridiculous log? for the fire, this beacon, this crutch?

this piece of junk-jewelry?

RETURN TO PROP DEPT. RETURN TO PROP DEPT. RETURN TO PROP DEPT., like that once I played Vegas when that guy who he was a gaming mogul as much as that's a mafioso he — after returning from an in-hiding vacation to La Scala that he enjoyed perhaps all too much (on the lam from Russian diamond-mine-owners from Israel who) — returned to the middle of the desert and as if in thanks to his old Roman Gods for delivering him from the gun-toting hands of the Russians (Israelis) and their Kazakhs (Israelis) the don he went and erected that world's largest amphitheater inside a structure the shape of the world's largest violin:

ribs as high as the heart of the sun, the don who he asked me and personally to play it, said he loved my playing, needed it out in Vegas to mediate between a revival of CATS and a Folies Bergere-update Siegfried & Roy-style latent homosexual liger-taming spectacular to bring in the intellectual set, the Los Angeles elites the don he pleaded, made me an offer I

wouldn't refuse (I myself offered to fly Schneidermann out, eager to show him Vegas as if America it was mine, the desert, Vegas' Egypt and Athens and Rome,

Babylon too and but Schneidermann he accepted the ticket, couldn't make the flight, told me over the telephone that I couldn't respond through that he'd again lost and somewhere his shoes, couldn't find Idlewild on any map either Schneidermann he said though it had been called JFK for years,

ever since the Reds and the Mafia down in Dallas they shot a purse full of lead into the head of the American Dream),

and I, with my credit-lines, with the loans I could line up, with my influence and pull among various universities and private wealth, now I could just about afford this,

this violin, but then I'd be broke, the Baroque chapter numbered eleventh, all I own,

and then I could just wander around with it, stand on roofs, fiddling away for the insomniacs, lowering myself from artist to the condition popularly known as *New York-street-crazy*,

     raving for what you'd spare in the subway, maybe on the tracks of the 1 or 9 train that it trains-in the rolling-stock from the blast-radius,

     general-vicinity of Schneidermann's apartment (which I'll have to deal with soon enough, if ever)

     up-Uptown and down to 66th Street, Lincoln's center, the music-district, the music-quarter or let's say sixth-borough of this the most musicless city, home to the Conservatory too at which I teach, taught and was finally fired from for seducing if not just paying off just one Asian female student too many, one Asian studentess too many that the deans they couldn't control, couldn't hush up because she had to talk, because she knew, just knew that she was a failure already and so how could I have hoped to help her? just one failure among the many millions of failures in this borough alone, just one musical failure among the many millions of musical failures at this Conservatory alone (which three of my daughters they also attended),

     these millions of violinists who are forced — by themselves, the world — to become instead failed violinists better known as violists,

     and there are hundreds of millions of them — but there's an absolution in failure, isn't there? a strange success, a metaphysical redemption, just ask Judas,

     and as violists they should also give it up, should stop even listening to the stuff, should grow earlids,

     détaché yourselves, *non legato* — because who likes it anyway? who finds this art enjoyable?

     No one, let's admit it, at least you should, come clean, face the fingerpoint of fact: that no one actually likes this stuff, all this European pretense, that it's just an excuse for a discipline,

     a snobbery,

     a reason (an excuse),

     a pretension, a put-on,

     to let ideas know that you're rich and you're fabulous, to drink jeroboams of bubbly, vintage Cliquot Veuve at the Reception afterwards amid information misrepresented as intellect, mistook for intellect, to gossip really and so here's a choice snatch, a snippet:

that

that I play better and better the less and less that I have to lose. The closer and closer I am,

to death.

I don't even own a plot. I had two, sold them, settlements, divorces — and what's involved in obtaining a divorce from one's self? ask one of my lawyers out there, tell him to begin billing, in his box,

among his season tickets — you have a mitt? because if you did, I'd pitch my head on out, a curveball, let a child run home with me to his mantle,

that he'll remember this to his grandkids, all cough-syrup/ medicine-breathed in a punta d'arco/á la pointe/an der Spitze voice,

the opposite being at-the-frog (al tallone/au talon/am Frosch,

an hausse or),

me, on a Lili which was my mother's performing name (Leah): the piano teacher of my uncle and,

children, have I ever told you that my sister she was conceived at a music lesson? just after? that my father's younger brother he was my mother's pupil? the pupil of my mother-to-be?

all about how father he came to pick Uncle Paul up (Paul who he was making no progress, couldn't concentrate that's how round-thighed your grandmother was, after lessons allowed students who practiced to pick a treat from a jar of sweets she would hold tight between her nine legs),

and then the quick wedding, no spread to speak of and no,

no music, with a disgraced rabbi officiating like he wasn't even getting paid (disgraced for playing Pope with the local priest's daughter I'd heard),

and not that music it wasn't allowed, it's that it just didn't seem appropriate — as per the same rabbi's opinion — in this instance, with a quite obviously pregnant bride, a bride knocked up, knocked up with my sister that is, my parent's only daughter who she died in infancy, their only daughter only three months on and thrashing like nine already at the musicless wedding,

musicless because music it must not attend on guilt, shame, not musicless for the old reasons that Schneidermann he knew so well, that Schneidermann he often told me about at our regular post-matinee-movie screenings of Western Humanism,

at which over coffee and coffeecake, an appetizing redun-
dancy as Schneidermann he often quoted Brecht to me who
Schneidermann he said still owed him 100 marks for a tab Schneidermann covered at the Café Canard:

erst kommt das Fressen,

dann kommt die Moral it went: first comes the eating and then
comes the moral (which, as I told Schneidermann, is after all a
decent description of weddings if not marriages themselves),

Schneidermann he often told me about the historically
heavy taxation of Jewish musicians, for example Schneidermann he
offered after sending the six-handed waitress back with the milk
cold and demanding that it return hot:

did you know — and no I didn't — that in that nation
you might remember it as Germany, this was after the 1500s, a bit
before your time you understand that no Jew was allowed to
perform his musical art as a profession without a permit from the
local government and since,

Mister Rothstein if you're interested Schneidermann he
said that such governments they were as many as there were cities,
towns, villages, dorfs in Germany, that many Jewish musicians they
were rendered unemployed unemployable Jewish musicians, that
some just starved to death Schneidermann he said with a lump of
coffee and cake soaking to formless dispersion in his throat and so
we have the huge-German-S System once again enabling the
stereotype of yet another huge-German-S Suffering and so it's
their fault, not ours though Schneidermann he didn't believe this
as much as he did,

as further restrictions they followed like pursed sip after
sip after miserly sip of chemical-flavored chemical-infused $4.99
coffee (MOCHANUTTA, HAZELOTTAFUDGE and so on)

that it was just killing our bowels and brains according to
Schneidermann: restrictions issued as to the days on which the
Jews they were permitted to make music even in their family now
you say lifecycle celebrations, events for example Schneidermann he
offered:

weddings not unlike my parents' after which the bride, my
mother, she went to her house and the bridegroom my father to
his, and why? well, because my father's father who he was a rabbi
too, a scholar himself who he wouldn't perform the ceremony, he

also

also and restrictions heaped upon restrictions wouldn't allow a
knocked up, thoroughly disgraced daughter-in-law in his house —
in fact, Mister Rothstein, we hear already in the 1400s of in-
stances in which the Jews they were punished for having made
music at weddings on days prohibited to them as many Jews they
were compelled to celebrate their weddings in other districts where
these prohibitions were not effective, with according to Schneidermann at least there was this Rabbi Jacob Mölin, the Maharil (not
to be confused Schneidermann he added with the similar-
acronymed but more famous Maharal of Prague, he of the dumb
and deaf Golem),

        who he the Maharil thought instrumental music most
essential at weddings, even ordering such temporary relocations,
change-of-venues, in cases of local restrictions — but Schneidermann he added while spooning some sugar then dumping it back
in the bowl and spooning again and again with reptilian swift licks
in between that even at times and in places when and where music
it was permissible, Mister Rothstein if you're still following me,
some governments they set limits, quotas as to the number of
musicians that might be employed, and for quite other reasons,
Misses Rothstein hold it in, you'll pish when I'm finished, Jewish
authorities themselves restricted the size of the orchestra, seeking
to erect a fence, a wall against hilarity,

        out of respect for the ever-remembered destruction,
        just doing it to themselves like Schneidermann he always
said, just like it was the converted Jews who they came up with the
Spanish Inquisition,

        the marranos who they discovered the Americas — and
after every new disaster and each new persecution, the rabbis
whoever the rabbis were they would reinforce interdictions against
music-making at least according to Schneidermann:

        in Worms, in Brest-Litovsk, Selz and other places, com-
munities, music, even at weddings, it was forbidden on account of
calamities,

        for example in Brisk in 1623 Schneidermann he offered
me as an example that no cantor was allowed to sing more than
three musical selections per Sabbath (Schneidermann he wetted a
finger with tablewater and attempted to rim his saucer to what
effect?),

and on special Sabbaths no more than four were allowed, how in Selz according to Schneidermann after the persecutions of 1650 it was agreed that in no Jewish home should there be heard music, except at weddings, how in Metz (like the team whose hat Schneidermann he was wearing over the wig over the skull),

only three musicians were allowed to play together at once, a quartet for weddings, how in Frankfurt, a quartet it was permitted but the musicians they had no permission to play after midnight like now,

how in Fürth, only three *instruments* were allowed, not to say three *musicians* — and that that was in the comparative west, all-things-considered, while my parents they were deep in the east, where things they were always worse:

like take Shklow for example, Schneidermann he said where he had cousins by marriage, not exactly right nextdoor to my parents in Bukovina but close enough, closer than Germany anyway or the Vienna of my dreams,

birthplace also Schneidermann he reminded me of Michael Guzikow:

born there in Shklow in 1806, Guzikow a totally forgotten virtuoso, now, but my grandfather (whose house it wasn't open to his knocked-up daughter-in-law)

he would often remember to me when I returned home from a tour for a visit how his, Guzikow's, bad bum lungs had made him, thankfully, quit the flute for the Hackbrett, what you would maybe know, Maestro Jacob Levine have you ever heard of him? as the dulcimer, and it's out of this instrument that Guzikow he invented another, the so-called straw-fiddle (*Strohfiedel*),

then left home and toured Russia, on foot — 1836 Guzikow he played Leipzig (my grandfather he wasn't there, rather heard Guzikow in Warsaw early in life),

to an audience that included that other Jew Mendelssohn (in Paris Guzikow's Hasidic hair became all the rage, *Coiffure Gusikov* it was called, women grew sidelocks that season), Mendelssohn quite possibly the greatest genius of all music to whom?

and to whose great enthusiasm Guzikow he played Jewish themes and famous, well-known secular themes, often improvising between the two and (according to my grandfather the rabbi, then

studying

studying-to-be-a-rabbi in Warsaw),

but my grandfather the rabbi neither Guzikow they never
answered the question (as no one else did either, neither even
Schneidermann)

that when Jews they play so-called secular music, do they,
by default of course, make it Jewish? impart what? and forget
music:

in all the arts, if practiced by a Jew (like Mendelssohn in
music, Felix Mendelssohn the musical great grandson of the
philosopher Moses and son of the nobody Abraham, Felix
Mendelssohn whose genius it was stifled by ideas of the bourgeois,
of assimilation, like don't make any noise, don't rock the ship
already sinking),

like in all the disciplines of art a Jew has ever attempted, is
his art then Jewish? is any? perhaps unconsciously?

and like don't expect me to have an answer, Schneidermann
he said with a mouthful of cake felled and shipped from the Black
Forest, like what did God Himself say? or what was He supposed
to have said in the matter? using his blackest buttonless sleeve for
a napkin worn Schneidermann he said I am that I am He said,
right? Schneidermann he said, I do what I do,

like didn't Wagner, though only when he needed their
support of his mania, declare Jews Meyerbeer and Mendelssohn the
greatest and purest of German composers? Wagner who also
though attempted to convert the great Hermann Levi, son of a
rabbi and conductor of Munich and *Parsifal?*

Schneidermann he often reminded me of Wagner, who
when the Nazis they invaded Prague and went to the Rudolfinum,
Schneidermann he once told me, to the old parliament and later
new concerthall there they ordered that the statue of that Jew
Mendelssohn it should be removed and so the workers there they
removed the statue of Wagner instead, quiet, artistic dissent you
know?

and but the Nazis they didn't know the difference, like
what were they looking for? Schneidermann he once asked fisting
his wig straight like Mozart reprimanded by the Archduke more
like Schneidermann reprimanded by his own sense of propriety,
maybe the statue with the largest nose? the statue with the most
sickening talent? Schneidermann he once asked me reaffixing and

rereaffixing his dangling chinbandage stained with seep,

told me that already in the 1400s it was customary for Jews to employ Christian musicians to play music for them on the Sabbath and festivals, asked me if I thought that the music it was sacred or secular? and whose sacred?

as I then — motioning for the bill, the check, Schneidermann he was getting too loud, attracting impatient if maternal stares and tsks — remembered to him my old cantor in Czernowitz:

a wheezy orchestra of bones, arthritic joints and sloshing, lukewarm washwater for blood it seemed who he dragged everything out, was over-pyrotechnical (though the synagogue it burnt only later),

who he used to dash through the other prayers so fast but then he'd spend an hour per Psalm just dragging it out, like don't tell me his ego was ego for the sake of the sacred, Mister Rothstein, quite the opposite, Misses Rothstein who she probably doesn't know of Abba Areka who he recommends to us that an ear that listens to secular music it should be torn out, or Raba who he warned a generation later that music in a house must bring that house to destruction (like Jericho, mind-the-walls),

forsaking, Schneidermann who he told me these rulings, imparted to me these traditions Schneidermann he, once, said that we had forsaken the Temple music, the Levitical music, the cymbal and the drums

and but he Schneidermann he once asked one afternoon over two or 10 of those strangely-named cocktails that he hated to love like a SINGAPORE SLING or a SEX-ON-THE-ROCKS

or something like that, asked me after all isn't word the instruction and music the inspiration? mentioning Kierkegaard and Schopenhauer, the Idea as the Will in itself, the immediate stages of the musical erotic, through his favorite pinkest loop-de-loop straw Schneidermann he was quoting and misquoting and quoting again and again, dicting and contradicting, glossing and summing in truths half and one-and-a-half (Karl Kraus, a great musical mind),

adumbrating the phenomenon of rabbinic decrees as regards art, and God! how Schneidermann he was shouting in this lounge as sleek and dark as an Ethiopian, populated with invest-

investment

ment advisors and their ex-stripper girlfriends Schneidermann he'd
dragged me into because he needed to use the toilet and now!
(Schneidermann, his bladder control it was always less than
refined)

     lamenting Schneidermann was over the techno music or
non-music on his return from the toilet that there never was such a
decree issued to shoot the cantors! Schneidermann he said, to kill
all the cantors!

     as to eradicate all those totally un-Jewish if not actually
anti-Jewish overtures to the sublime, to let the Jews sing for
themselves! Schneidermann he almost screamed as I led him
through an Amazon of neon thongs to the door, each for their own
supper! some foie gras or maybe a phalanx of lightly-mustachioed
minorities manning a filet-mignon carving station, as I remembered
to Schneidermann once outside, down the street and reseated at an
establishment more appropriate to our reputations, non-reputa-
tions, and emotional impotence:

     an American wedding I once attended (Jewish), the bride,
daughter of a senator she had her cantor from when she was young,
the groom the son of a homeshopping-magnate he had his, the
groom's cousin who he lived in Cleveland was a cantor and the
bride's uncle from Milwaukee, by way of Baton Rouge, yes, he too
was a cantor and so what did they all do? they had four cantors all
cantoring and at once like one side of a Middle East peace-negotia-
tion I told Schneidermann,

     going at each other's throats as the wedding it went on and
on:

     singing longer and longer and louder and louder each than
the cantor previous, and late, until you could bounce a quarter off
the gelatin congealed atop the turning gefilte fish, or gefülte —
your choice, Mister Rothstein, your choice as the regional, mediocre string-quartet in the Long Island synagogue's social hall, Far
Rockaway maybe they played over and over again some Ludwig van
Beethoven,

     amid the waiters like sentries at their stations of stir-fry,

     waitresses goosestepping with platters piled high with
miniaturized maize in a sweet & sour glaze — they played over and
over again some Beethoven quartet (an Opus 59 I remember it was,
forget which one exactly),

and they begged me to sit-in, almost groveled once I was
introduced to them by the host's brother-in-law, said it would be
an honor, to play with them but I refused,

they asked, I refused like a wife with a migraine,

they insisted and so why not (I was already drunk, had a
gut full of whiskey)? I took the 1st violinist's violin, asked them
what they wanted to do,

what they knew (nothing),

got out the sheet music,

arranged it on the stand (which it was strange for me, I
very rarely read music anymore, it's all memorized or at least most
of it is),

then joined them then in Beethoven's Quartet in C#
Minor, Op. 131, just the 6th movement though, the *Adagio quasi un
poco andante* — the first five measures of which Schneidermann he
was obsessed with, the quartet entire composed all of 1826 and a
year before Beethoven's death:

the *Kol Nidre* quartet somewhat depressing, somber, for a
wedding I must admit but it wasn't my choice, the *Kol Nidre* quartet
if it must have a nickname in addition to a key and two numbers
because in the previous year, 1825 it was as Schneidermann he
once told it, me over a fresh-squeezed 100% tropical juice and a
hotdog the size of the spaceship that exploded in the mouth of
Ronald Reagan,

in 1825 it was that Beethoven he was commissioned by
the Israelite Community in Vienna to compose a cantata on the
occasion of the dedication of their new temple,

but Beethoven, brooding probably too much over everything as per popular imagination, matinee-movieness,

the Master he took too long to think it over and so a Jew
named Drechsler, don't know him but heard from Schneidermann
that he was relatively famous in his day, instead he did the job,
last-minute and purportedly acquitted himself well — Beethoven
however, or so the legend goes that Schneidermann my source for
all this trivia or inspiration he once told me with more sauerkraut
on his face than in his stomach olive-sized,

Beethoven in that mulling-time, in that thinking-it-over
time that Beethoven he occupied himself with the melodies of the
synagogue liturgy, with synagogue-melos so as to become ac-

acquainted

quainted with any — false, nonexistent — sense of style (though
it doesn't sound much like him to do something like that, according to Schneidermann tonguing each dewdrop of pulp from his
plastic, pulp Schneidermann he always loved pulp, *Fruchtfleisch*
Schneidermann he never had enough),

all this coming a long nearly 50 years after he Beethoven
fell in love with a certain Rachel Löwenstein, whose religion —
mine and yours — prevented her acceptance of Beethoven's offer of
marriage,

yes, Beethoven the great genius he was refused and
Beethoven, as we all know, only matters as he relates to the Jews as
Schneidermann he once joked after he told me this once,

or only half-joked over leftovers that I'd smuggled out to
him from the Five Towns, Hewlett-Woodmere-lawn-tent-encamp-
ment-wedding-reception I'd escaped from to meet him and feed
him (wrapped weenies and miniature kabobs so small that they
must have had a glandular disorder),

first the eating and then the moral, Schneidermann he
always said (then reminded me that Brecht he still owed him
money for a tab at the Café Dunkelspiel):

because all things Schneidermann he always said they must
relate to Jews, to the Jews, have to, a prerequisite to my interest
said Schneidermann, indeed to the world's interest:

and so the *Kol Nidre* melody from the service of the Eve of
the Day of Atonement — when all Jews we disavow ourselves of
any false promises we'll make during the year — appears in this
string quartet, though you can always cling to the interpretation of
coincidence:

that Beethoven he got the suspected-Jewish 6th movement
theme from experimenting,

that according to Schneidermann if you wanted to deny
the Jewish element you could always attribute the melody or
motive to a technical development, to Beethoven's mania for
motivic expansion, his fooling-around with the 1st movement's
fugue, his obsession with thematic development according to
Schneidermann that would be a logical argument — Beethoven, a
man according to Schneidermann who lacked the ability to create,
to invent, instead becoming the great mechanic, the great technician
as Schneidermann once he once told me when I told him and told

him again (always feeling like one of his stories it deserved at least
three of mine)

all about my childhood in Czernowitz,

and the neighborhood's great eccentric,

mad-scientist,

mechanic and general progressive personality in the
kingdom of technology — told me about Beethoven and his
technique Schneidermann he did only after I'd remembered to him
(while Schneidermann he was gorging on wedding leftovers,

the sugar pressurized and preserved into rose garlands
they'd have enough to festoon the divorce party)

a man who I am sure that my parents they knew his full
and true name (because he was wealthy, his house it was adorned
with baronial thrusts that rivaled even the hopes of the Episcopal
Seminary)

but who I and my friends — I had none, just those around
my same age, the Children — knew only as Otto as in

let's go to Otto's house and see what he's up to,

or if and when there was a big-boom explosion-sound we
would all ask each other with no concern and yes just curiosity,
what has Otto done now?

because while you historians and musicologists out there
might think that the first time that music it was available inside an
automobile it was with the introduction of the 1948 Cadillac, just
in time for the suburbs all American pump and thrust with tailfins
and a radio console you would be mistaken, because indeed this
man Otto of Czernowitz, Bukovina, he was indeed the earliest, the
first inventor of a — primitive — system that allowed you, him,
to listen to music in your automobile as I told Schneidermann,

I remembered, I reminisced over life-wasting, time-wasting
cigarettes and coffee in an outdoor café near the Park where — this
wealthy man Otto, a technological pioneer who he was of the most
minor nobility he, yes, was the first to place a radio inside of an
automobile I believe, in the passenger seat but he didn't stop with
that innovation:

no, as I told Schneidermann that this Otto that he was
fond of tying, with a length of rope as long as a small intestine,
wrapped thrice around the chassis and tied, a phonograph onto the
hood of his MAYBACH MERCEDES I believe it was and then

driving

driving, and very slow, around and around the grounds of his
ramshackle, Eastern estate to the accompaniment of us children all
clapping, yes, but also to the strained tinny music of Mozart's
Haffner symphony,

the *Haffner* symphony I remember it was and almost always
the *Haffner* symphony,

blaring (as much as the VICTROLA VV-50 suitcase
model it could),

even blasting (metallic),

indeed, I told Schneidermann, that it seemed as if nothing,
not even this Otto's gorgeous though always-sick-always-sleeping
wife made him happier

as this most minor-noble inventor or just monied neighborhood eccentric he drove around and around and around his
estate, and slowly, and when the phonograph it died he would get
out of his automobile idling, run to the hood, crank up the
portable VICTROLA again (obtained from America for this very
purpose)

and get back into his automobile, right back into his
MAYBACH MERCEDES W-3 one of 300 or so of that model
and obtained directly from the MAYBACH-MOTORENBAU
GmbH and drive around and around and around his estate — mud
— again and again as we children we clapped and when his
cabriolet cream-colored dung-dappled automobile it would die of
heatstroke then this Otto he'd get out,

run to the hood,

cool it down with some water from the well that it was
shaped like a star — on nights of full moons the water gave a
reflection that,

he would circle and circle and circle and stop,

then get back in to circle and circle and circle again, and
drive, and often singing though tunelessly along as I told Schneidermann as we walked from Parkside and south by southwest to
the matinee movies,

as I always did when I drove my own MERCEDES M-
CLASS down from Maine to New York, listening to the radio and
that man he's named Schaap and his jazz program,

WSOMETHINGSOMETHINGSOMETHING FM
swinging all the way down 100 mph from Maine to Manhattan

(Bartók's celesta was a siren, second violins swell a cop pulling me over) — that once I got into that accident, rear-ended and yet still I managed to make the last piece that you Dina that you played at your debut recital,

the last work on the first program and the encore too, Dina, the encore that you played, that was demanded of you at 8 years of age and what a recital it was! a resounding success (as it was duly noted in 300 words, PAGE X12)!

with you Dina stretching your smallest fingers all over that Schumann who he himself ruined his — virtuoso — life trying to stretch his already longest fingers with a mechanism that it was designed to do just that, to lengthen your fingers and so your talent,

Dina you were divine! though I heard only your last piece (and the prodigy encore as fast as a life, as blurred — by the pedals — as a hangover),

I was drinking, BLACK LABEL but not too much to drive and,

your final selection, that Schumann that you had practiced to me like an x-million times and all over the telephone and here I was a, minor, accident — dents in my dings, rear-ended on the George Washington, I sued and I won — later to hear it in person, among your siblings, your mother, the Conservatory deans and the critics, always the critics who they treated you so well (because you were you Dina and not because you were my daughter, as you cried to me all over your new purpling dress fluffing fake cleavage,

air-pockets,

false-advertising I called them),

and then afterwards how your mother she took you out but not me,

Shayna, how I wasn't invited to go out to meet your new Jewish-American bestfriends or boyfriends

BEN & JERRY for black cherry ice-cream, a wishniak treat later and instead how I just kissed you, hugged you, kissed you again and spat patrimony at your mother, my daughter, went back to the garage, got back into my rental car (a MERCEDES M-CLASS, always a MERCEDES M-CLASS)

and drove Downtown and alone, fueled-up with what liquor I had left in me to the Village Vanguard to hear some jazz

music

music as I had promised a lover that I would as I had lately —
since the minor accident of six-seven hours previous, the recital and
my exclusion from my offspring's success and jimmie-sprinkled-
pistachio — resolved to keep all promises made to whatever extent
that was possible,

down to the Village Vanguard (impossible to find parking)
to hear some American music you might know it as jazz, the
absolute pinnacle of America's musical achievement I once told
Schneidermann who he was always too brilliant, cynical to agree —
when Schneidermann he told me that even our out-of-proportion is
out-of-proportion,

that what Beethoven or his century would have known as
snap rhythms, that dotted quarter notes becoming in our century
swing, the triplet beyond the triplet that that has been America's
only contribution to world musical culture (and that it still isn't
much, according to Schneidermann),

that this swing and these timbres, these bent or blue notes
too, that these are the only musical advances that America it has
ever given to the world is what I told him, and Schneidermann he
agreed if just to shut-me-up so that he could listen — and it's all
thanks to the shvartzes! Schneidermann he said (and God! I told
him a trillion times not to use that word!),

that white Americans of European descent they have given
nothing whatsoever, at all, to the universal language of music was
what Schneidermann he often said and I agreed if just to shut-him-
up from ranting about art and race in public,

excepting me, Schneidermann he said, that is if I am an
American Schneidermann he added as we entered, drunk, into the
Vanguard, into the vestibule and down the red as my thrombosed
external hemorrhoids

stairwell of tongue,

that night that we first heard an Orpheus, another
Orpheus, a true shvartze Orpheus according to Schneidermann and
as if that made or makes any difference,

that night that Schneidermann he'd ducked the turnstile to
subway Downtown to meet me (it was a Thursday, our old long-
lesson-day)

to hear a man that I had been hearing much about from a
lover and had to admit that I was skeptical (the lover she had ears

but not like she had thighs),

here I was the musical mind that I was and I am perhaps not as transcendent as Mozart but certainly as parasitic as any Händel or Michael Jackson and taking listening-tips from a good pair of tits I told Schneidermann who he had agreed to meet me to mitigate the expected aural disaster as this lover she was off,

out in the state of Lincoln for a Memorial Day Weekend, in Illinois visiting relatives (Chicago, she was related to an aunt who the glimmer of her existence was that she had slept and only once with Saul Bellow),

Schneidermann and I we were there to hear and on her advice an under-appreciated saxophonist, and aren't most of them?

a tenor saxophonist who he was indeed great (though less than genius, especially with the mirrored sunglasses he wore and),

this young man who he still had much time for growth, some potential only if, practice practice practice (while between sets Schneidermann he began telling me all about a dinner that he was once at in Paris, a fête he said hosted by the Conservatoire at which Schneidermann he was seated next to one Adolphe-Edward Sax, the son of the instrument's inventor who he had recently sold his patent to SELMER and was — according to Schneidermann — occupied with the refinement of a never-finished or just never-perfected model of nose-flute, a sinuphone or at least Sax he told Schneidermann who he told me over whiskey-and-carbonated-cavities adding that at that time his French it wasn't that great and so),

a young man of much talent who he regularly went down into the subway tunnels to blow his brains out to the vaulted acoustics and was instead about six months after I, we, had heard him cover and two-drink-minimum at the Vanguard guarding what? he was flattened and at midnight by the F or was it the D train I had read in the paper? heard on the radio?

the fate of this Pied Piper not of Hamelin, Lower Saxony, but of swinging Manhattan, N.Y. — but here the water's too dirty for even the rats, and so they just scurry the underground tracks for mile after mile in corrupted circles much like the manic,

Hosannahfied worship of us Jews around yet another member of the animal kingdom:

this one a bird I remember well, one of the highlights of

my

my musical life I often told Schneidermann who he took no
offense,

or seemed not to: this was the Bird, whom I played with
the once or twice that I've ever deigned to play with others, to be
accompanied, indeed to accompany, when I first — and unfortunately last — played with, more accurately I'll even admit played
for, this Bird *Charlius parkerus*

who it was named Charlie Parker it was in the golden,
gilded summer of 1950 and I was a new immigrant, was the
greenest horn on the head of the year, here in New York, it was a
session issued on 10"-LP as *Charlie Parker with Strings*

also known as *The Greatest African-American Musician Who Ever
Lived Plays Some Incredible and Mind-Numbing Alto Saxophone to the
Accompaniment of Old Fat Jewish Men in Stilted and Stifling Arrangements
Arranged by Even Older and Fatter and Inconceivably More Jewish Men,*

specifically Mercury MG 35010, I played on some David
Raskin-Johnny Mercer tune and don't consult your liner notes
because I wasn't billed (*I* billed *them*),

I asked in my best British accent not to be listed as on the
session for professional reasons (on the recommendation of your
father, Mister Rothstein, who he also got me the gig),

instead I was a ringer there alongside my landsmen Sammy
and Howie, Harry and Sammy who he was Sam to his friends, and
don't forget Zelly Smirnoff in the violin section playing second-
fiddle — actually third — to the sounds that Parker he made, and
what sounds!

of a Bird pecking, squawking gorgeous his way out of this
egg-on-your-face world, through the sky's shell like when Parker he
played this hall — dead Manny Albam or was it Manny Fiddler? or
maybe just the drummer Shelley Manne he once told me — all of
1947 while I was still trying to get out of London (we all have our
own shells, some larger and harder than others),

and the tune three years later it was *Laura* — a standard to
set all standards like the real-life Laura who she would sing (but
Laura it wasn't her real name, I just think of her whenever I hear
the song and I don't know why, probably has to do with Bird's way
with the blues, with Charlie's genius and I say Charlie because he
winked at me once between takes and she),

she loved to sing:

would sing all day in a voice that was less a voice and more the whining of a menstruating showdog (her Galician aunt's new assimilated pleasure, a poodle her daughter named *Yenta*),

she was white, needless to say Jewish and, to tell the truth the only feature I can still recall of her face is her teeth,

they were perfect, pearls yes and each perfectly proportioned,

shaped as if they were after-dinner mints that God He'd mass-produced and expressly for the sweetening of her own tongue — her father he was one of the very few name orthodontists in the world, you'd be lucky to get an appointment next millennium if the world it still exists (I was always trying to get Schneidermann in for an appointment, to get him fitted for dentures, whenever I had secured one Schneidermann he always went and lost his shoes),

and then there was her brother-in-law, a plastic surgeon,

then equally renowned as the father-orthodontist, he did all the porn industry starlets,

big-money circuit-strippers in from Melville, New York and but I'm getting ahead of myself because there's Charlie Parker who's dead just five years later, 1955 in the Uptown apartment of a Rothschild Baroness, patroness Pannonica de Koenigswarter no umlaut for her with whom Bird he was just relaxing, watching some primetime, varietyshow teevee as insipid as

and this girl then that I was remembering, talking about — though not a Rothschild, not even a Warburg — she in some sense hated culture too, hated it like Göbbels did who he said (or was it Ronald Reagan?)

that when he heard the word *culture*

he reached for his gun, but it wasn't a gun that killed her — she hated culture in the way that cultured people they always hate culture, the way that cultured people they deride that which they merely reference, always, must (as if they could do more, as if she was responsible for her culture, as if it wasn't her parents, the immigrants):

with her it was fiddling with a barrette while gnawing a lower lip as I serenaded her nude,

her scratching too at the tattoo new to the inside of her thigh that only itched at her mind (it had been her aunt's first

husband's

husband's Treblinka number, she'd told the Puerto-Dominican
parlor owner it was still),

yes, that's how her end it begins, and if I had a whole
string section at my disposal anymore I'd swell it for you now just
as swollen as:

but she wouldn't listen to my music, to what she called *my
music*, by which she meant so-called *classical music*,

as if the canon it was mine to do with it what I will with
no balances neither checks,

as if I owned the last hundreds of years of the West, kept
it under lock and key in my navel — as if it was my fault, as if all
those hundreds of years and their geniuses (or aural mutants, or
just syphilitics),

that they were mine and only mine to apologize for and,
well, instead she'd only listen to popmusic,

to what she called *popmusic*, indeed to all popmusic and for
hours on end and on almost every technology imaginable from
almost every decade of the American Century her family — both
sides, all — knew only 50 years of,

she being at the time 25, playing and singing along to her
popmusic for hours upon hours and at huge volumes,

and she'd sing along in the shower too: in the blue and
white tiled shower she sang if not the blues then the whites on that
day,

singing along to popmusic in the shower, and soaping her
new breasts — what rolling, luscious globes! cancer-hard worlds of
tit! hulking implants just implanted by her brother-in-law, a plastic
surgeon,

the plastic surgeon if you'd asked around,

and implanted for nothing, on courtesy, the family-plan:

they were silicone back in the silicone-days, scars still ill-
hidden before methods of enhancement they became perfectible,

tucked under the booming, secreted beneath and in,

scars in a strictly supporting role, holding up the swell and
but who got their hands on the settlement money afterwards?

her only next of kin that's who, her sister older, less
attractive, I never and of course her brother-in-law, the man who
he'd installed the new breasts to begin with,

singing along in the shower she was soaping and one of

the implants it began to leak (the right one, playing opposite the heart),

or maybe it had been leaking for awhile, who knew? was it over-vigorous soaping that brought it on?

and the silicone it seeped into her blood,

through her bloodstream, poisoning, and there — singing along to popmusic mid-soap, mild raspberry and Dead Sea salt soap — in the shower, this girl she had herself an aneurysm, silicone streamed to the brain, a clot and, well, she collapsed against the shower's tile,

skull cracked open against the soapdish,

red-highlighted-hairline chipped and then the coma for eight weeks,

life-support for 10,

before the sister — and, again, the surgeon-in-law — they decided to pull the plug, and she died,

and of course the sister she soon entered — initiated — a mass tort, class-action lawsuit whatever vs. the implant manufacturer,

the maker of those sternum jellyfishes washed up on her palest shore (that weekend we did the Taj Mahal! the one they have down the Garden State Parkway),

and of course she won, the lawyer he was an uncle, money into the plastic-in-law's pocket and but I was there visiting her in the hospital Uptown, after she was dead but before the funeralhome and the grave, having just returned from a South American tour to a message left on my service I went to the hospital immediately, like taxi! taxi! like in the matinee movies but real, violincase still with me, and but no one had told me (this was 10 weeks later, after the shower),

she hadn't told anyone about me, evidently was embarrassed, of me over three times her age just stalking the ICU's halls like a girlscout,

a Pole candy-striping,

an earnest-idiot mailman-letch,

just searching room after room after room, pedophile! all for this great-titted girl almost one-quarter my age who she would remain that age and forever, was dead.

I sat shiva alone and with my Schneidermann, at a café of

habit

habit and drinking brewed polymers for the practice,

   showed up at the funeral because I had nothing else to do that morning, then decided to go to buy a new suit because the one I was wearing, had worn to the funeral it was defiled, now it was tainted, ritually unclean and so I and with an hour to waste or waste me until Schneidermann,

   our matinee-movie-appointment (non-appointment),

   went to MACYS, MACY'S tried one on and bought it,

   AMEX card cleared (the third one I tried),

   the one, actually the suitlike, shroudlike tuxtype one that I'm wearing right now, tonight,

   then went to my tailor, an old Jewish Schneider who due to his German ancestry was in point of fact really a Schneider as opposed to Schneidermann who due to his Hungarian life would more accurately be called a szabó,

   went to my own old Jewish tailor for 10 years (and everyone should have one),

   a great tailor his hands they're still relatively intact (nine fingers),

   and steady but eight years he has already with Alzheimer's, a Schneider born actually in Herr Doktor Professor Alois Alzheimer's city, in Pforzheim at least the tailor he once told me that he remembered it, near Tiefenbrunn he once said to me who he knew, should have known but who the last few-five years he forgot — a Schneidermann himself and so maybe that's why I felt significantly comfortable then in confiding to him my feelings, my thoughts all about this girl, her enhancements and so on and so forth as he stared at me kind if absent, then a refocus this Schneidermann he just stared at me deep as a wrinkle and I and finally just asked him like what?

   and Sol the Tailor he said that he knew me, that I was famous,

   I said great, because I don't know myself, like who am I?

   and Sol the Tailor he said, well, aren't you that actor? in that movie with that girl? haven't seen you in anything for a while, my daughter she doesn't take me that much anymore, since that one that you did when you played that private detective,

   or secretmost agent or,

what have you been doing all these years? and I laughed,
how couldn't I thank him with money in advance as my answer,
asked could I have cuffs on these? and then went to tell Schneidermann the real Schneidermann all about it but only after Schneidermann and I we had watched our matinee movie, which that funeral-
day (Schneidermann's *Trauermarsch* for 35 flutes and piccolo solo!)
it was to be a selection from the horror genre, was a matinee
Horror movie all about that popular phenomenon that they're
known as zombies, a matinee Horror movie in which people, the
actors, they and incredibly enough rose from the dead, indeed rose
from the dead and only to take revenge on all those who might
have wronged them,

were unbelievably stupid or ill-cast enough to have slighted
them in life, which Schneidermann he said (afterwards over coffee
and crêpes at this Uptown coffee-and-crêperie with an address as
high as its price, Schneidermann he always loved that word *couvert*),

which revenge-fantasy Schneidermann he said would entail
for him first getting his bones up out of the ground,

the humus Schneidermann he said wherever American and
then buying a, oneway, ticket on an airplane — windowseat, if
possible (Schneidermann he'd never flown before, ever) — direct
to that landmass formerly-known as Europe, then upon arrival
taking his unspecified revenge on for example the Director of
Budapest's Music Academy, his then-wife dead in Birkenau, a
violinist in some Viennese schraml ensemble who had told him
that his music it was the most worthless he had ever heard in all of
his 65 musical years, Hitler *1889 †1945, said all this all the
while squirming, shifting awkwardly like a worm with legs in his
seat (on his stool),

and so I asked him what was wrong, naturally! *natürlich*,
Schneidermann he said that he had gone to the toilet this morning,
that morning of the funeral and having no toiletpaper (only foil
from candy and chip wrappers, Schneidermann he had had horrid
experiences with them previous),

and having no toiletpaper neither money to purchase more
and how could he have?

gone to the drugstore while he was still in the bathroom
he shared with his entire floor (Schneidermann he like all Europeans said not *bathroom* but *toilet*)?

Schneidermann

Schneidermann he instead walked pants tied around his
ankles with his shoelaces to his room, took one of his innumerable
musical manuscripts, walked back to the shared-with-the-entire-
floor bathroom and wiped himself with a musical manuscript, ink
smeared with fecal scrape and seep and that since then his anus it
was ripped and ripped hard, tract torn, seeping blood and burn and
I instead asked — my true apprehension — what musical manuscript it was (later when he couldn't find it, flushed clogged
flushed, Schneidermann he said it was the first draft finale of
this),

and but Schneidermann he instead asked (a refusal for a
refusal like his last real tooth for my own stained-authentic
dentures),

You really need another suit?

Do you want money for toiletries? I asked him and
Schneidermann he ignored, instead asked me all about Sol my suit-
tailor,

asked me about my other Schneidermann and all about his
Alzheimer's disease from Alzheimer's hometown Sol he no longer
remembers but always anyway describes, asked specifically what
actor did he mean?

when Sol the Suit-Tailor (Schneidermann he solfeggioed
my *Solschneider*), when he said that you were that actor he meant
which actor? which movie? and then screwed himself like a nail
with legs up in his seat (on his stool),

and I told him that I didn't know, didn't ask, never found
out and asked him what do you think? well, who? and Schneidermann he said John Wayne with a yarmulke,

I said thanks but no thanks and Schneidermann as he
poured always more and never enough béchamel sauce on his crêpes
he said that that's what technology does,

that that's primarily what technological progress it does as
Schneidermann he insisted (Schneidermann he thought that after
only one and truncated at that explanation of the http://www.
Internet and so on that he knew it all):

that it links you up in the minds of others, in the world,
with those who look somewhat like you, those who might sound
somewhat like you do,

or what technology did, for a while, Schneidermann he

added,

as half-educated people who they read the newspapers, who they watch the public teevee when it's not on mute, how they talk!

all about artistic DNA, how they talk about the genes of a style, about art evolving genetically and all,

and then according to Schneidermann just airing his gums in earnest playing the role of parody, God!

how they wait it out until sabbatical, take their minds over to Europe for a semester, to research their own excess — that that's how they talk Schneidermann he said, ridiculous! over dinner, with the university paying, or on the company expense account but it's all wrong! Schneidermann he once told me on another occasion (Schneidermann and I we were at the Museum of Modern Art):

IT being the idea of an artistic code, an aesthetic genome, a helix shaped like a syphilis spirochete double-doubling in on itself,

spinning out Klee or maybe you like Franz Kline-lines through space, way past the reach of the Museum's seismographs, shattering through the fourth walls of lucite, God all this security! Schneidermann he said at the Museum, all this admission-fee and surveillance mishegas that Schneidermann he noticed at the Museum, and to see all these paintings by all these painters who they barely lived long enough to not starve to death (Schneidermann at 90 he still awaited his discovery, expected his true love the goddess Fama at every moment, kept the kettle on),

forgot to tell you that Schneidermann, that you would think to ask how besides the infrequently offered because even less-frequently accepted loans from me, to ask how Schneidermann how he managed to survive at all in New York and its economy and I should tell you that, to reveal his secret that Schneidermann he loved but that it always shamed him to think about, to talk about it (but to who except me?),

which Schneidermann he anyway didn't but I should, tell you that Schneidermann he often moonlit off-the-books (Schneidermann he never read while he played), untaxed and for only $100 a night at a dive, well, at a luxury hotel, well — at the Grand but for him every place it was below his stature 30 short,

and there Schneidermann he was engaged to perform and in America only there, it was his gig, steady, this playing piano,

playing

playing in his own words: whorehouse-don't-shoot-the-piano-
player-piano-playing,

as Schneidermann he often reminded me much like
Brahms himself did in the early, hard years before the Hungarian
firebrand as Schneidermann he described him Remenyi saved him
and how Brahms he thanked him by forsaking him after Remenyi
he introduced him to Joseph Joachim who played the hell as the
proverb goes out of Brahms' *Concerto*,

and, yes, this was nothing new to Schneidermann who he
often played to, serenaded whores over there, filling-in for one
Rezso Seress in Pest up near the Nyugati tér train station in his
spare time, in his spare insomnia with the express to Romania
pumping and thrusting at all hours of night and surely he slept
with them for free, the whores, a house perk as Schneidermann he
said, often for miscellaneous favors including but not limited to
the purchasing of junk jewelry and molar-rotting sweets, and how
in doing so, yes, by his own admission Schneidermann he was
unfaithful to art by being faithful to his roof and to his stomach
— in later years and established (meaning having been prolific for
years but with little to no success after the opera-fiasco, and none
whatsoever in America),

there I was going to hear him three nights a week (Friday,
Saturday and Sunday 9 p.m. to whenever his alcoholic tab it
exceeded his musical take)

playing the most filthy, gorgeous, uproarious, genius but
still so-called cocktail piano imaginable at the bar or as the
Management insists the Lounge of the Grand, whose owner is
needless to say a huge fan of so-called classical or serious music
and is probably, are you still? out there, here, tonight?

Schneidermann he was there in the Lounge three nights a
week 9 to Whiskey playing all the American-Jewish songbook, the
American-Jewish liturgy, all the standards from the 20s, 30s and
40s, the classics you love to remember if not remember to love, all
the showtunes, moviethemes, World War II lovesongs, X-mas
songs in-season like now only if Schneidermann he was still
around or alive by all the Jews and all the songwriters who they
should have been Jews:

all the Gershwins, Richard Rodgers, Hammerstein, Berlin
who he was really and earlier Israel Baline and Cahn, like *Cohen owes*

me however many dollars and so on, and playing them all not heartfelt, sentimental or anything like that but with pure irony, total sarcasm, with absolute holy enmity was how Schneidermann he played them and played down to them in the lobby-bar of the Uptown Grand,

the Lounge, and Tony or just Ton or Tone with an *e* as it's pronounced, that yes, he was the one who told me about this, the lobby-bartender there at the Grand's lobby-bar (but not here tonight, not that he hates music but that after 20-plus years of working at the Grand he's developed a hatred for the rich and so when off the job he tries to avoid them, lives like a King on his own in Queens),

Tony or Ton or Tone who he still anyway likes me or pretends to, talks to me and listens to me or pretends to, who he anyway keeps me supplied with my

VICODIN, my XANAX, my PERCOCET, ADDERALL too when my expoolboy he runs dry, keeps the medicinechest in my forehead stocked with my quite necessary painkilling, attention-getting medication far exceeding any of my prescriptions from upwards of 10 doctors now, sorry and but — once Tone he once told me that a nosegay of tipsy divorcées he thought that they were from Asbestosville, Iowa maybe who they were there, were staying in New York at the Grand on a splurge and how they just waltzed-in from the Lobby to the lobby-bar and in the wrong time-signature,

drunk and staying upstairs on their entire monthly salaries, here in New York on a Broadway junket, and how they all asked Schneidermann who he was playing in the lobby-bar, all beechwood with a slight 3 a.m. stain,

a bar like a vivisected violin — how they all and in unison asked Schneidermann to pleasepleaseplease play for their pleasure a song that you might know it's entitled

Somewhere Over the Rainbow and then at least according to Tone who I have no reason to doubt him he said that they laid three $20s on him, on Schneidermann — understand that three of Andrew Jackson equals one of Judy Garland in at least some economy — and Schneidermann said Tone, like Jesus, what did he do? he just returned their money, fished the three $20s out of his fluted frosted glass tipjar, Grecian urn then asked Tone like he was

doing

244   *Joshua Cohen*

doing sports play-by-play he asked, what did he do?

    he, like Schneidermann he proceeded to play,

    to play his *3rd Piano Sonata* for them, no subtitle, one of
nine piano sonatas that Schneidermann he ever acknowledged,
would acknowledge I think but I'm not quite sure (have to sort out
Schneidermann's apartment, his whiskey bottles and their canon),

    played it and played it for them, and straight through —
according to Tone they were enraptured, their first orgasms in
decades he said when Tone he called me up in Maine from the
lobby-bar's telephone and held it up, aloft, a disembodied ear for
me to listen through and, God! at 11 p.m. sitting on a heap of
decaying gilded wicker my, an exwife she'd found at an antique
market up in Maine and there! and still! there it was again like I
hadn't heard him Schneidermann in years: that great breaking,

    crashing-around

    dish sound,

    his gut-wide tremolos,

    the silent gaping hells of his subtle, nuanced hesitations,
and the volume! the sheer Old Testament power! a sonata that
Schneidermann he later rededicated to president Harry Truman
who's on no bills because why not? after all, he was almost nobility, with him killing all of those would-be violinists, decimating
what must have been hundreds of thousands if not millions of
would-be Asian violinists that qualifies him at least for landed-
gentry if not for sainthood I once told Schneidermann,

    but then again saints they don't get dedications, do they?
Schneidermann he added, not that they don't merit them, but —
especially not on what academics as various as they might be
obscure would label,

    would feed the pigeonhole,

    would wrap for the refuse pile known as history as an
atonal piano sonata of some serious complexity, some considerable
technical difficulty (not that that makes it good, but):

    a more than worthy heir to the miniaturized efforts of
Webern, not to mention Barraqué's and Boulez's best as Schneidermann he once told me without a hint of modesty one evening as I
was treating as always at a fancy Frenchtalian restaurant that (I
always treated, Schneidermann he always insisted that he was the
treat),

a piece in my opinion leaving even the sonatas of van Beethoven,

even the whole entire output of that genius named Beethoven to the wiles of the Boston Pops and whichever homosexual's conducting them this season, having signed his, her, contract with a fresh load of healthy sperm,

dotting the line with certified undiseased sperm now that the treatments they're so affordable, right?

signing with the X of unfettered happiness and optimism — because as Schneidermann he said as the quite obviously homosexual waiter he brought us our entrees at that fancy Frenchtalian restaurant,

because not even homosexuals are worth knowing as Schneidermann he said,

because not even organ transplant donors are worth knowing, according to Schneidermann, because no one is interesting! because no one is different!

or rather how Schneidermann he said that everyone is equal in their differences

and how the waiter he just then fell into a Dead Sea of tears on his way back to the kitchen, but Schneidermann said, but he might be an actor, they all are — because you have to understand that Schneidermann, and I want you to understand that I'm making no excuses, that he and despite surviving all and surviving survival was a militant racist, you understand:

hating everyone as they so deeply wanted, no, needed to be hated, and so everyone they were happy, Schneidermann and everyone else,

that that was Schneidermann's function in-the-world (Welt), his practical-utility (I forget the word *auf Deutsch*) — that according to Schneidermann all America it shouldn't be a pleasant honey coloration like this $18 caramelized escargot appetizer that we'd had,

no meltingpot with too many onions according to Schneidermann,

added that the chef in this particular metaphor (like what's multiculturalism, global-integration doing to our stomachs? sushi one night and deli the next? how are we becoming less like ourselves? or what, who, we should be? knew? Schneidermann he

wanted

wanted to know, like why aren't my bowel-movements the same in
consistency and color as the bowel-movements of my forefathers?),

that the chef at this particular Frenchtalian-restaurant-of-
the-mind, well, it was one Francis Galton who was of interest, the
founder of the science, non-science, of Eugenics, no, not a man
named Eugene who he set forth the future's trash-heap, sewer war
of natural children against the gene-enriched, genriched children
about which Schneidermann he wanted to do an opera but never
did,

like an update of *West Side Story*, María — normals vs. the
genrich was his idea, Schneidermann's, pipeline fantasies of
genriched children leaving the naturals, the normals in the dust to
be unfounded according to Schneidermann, who he was writing the
libretto himself, Ticonderoga pencil on his four plastered walls:

these children confounding everyone in their failure to
succeed in the way that they were made, disappointing everyone,
especially their grandfather:

a scientist, non-scientist, named Francis Galton, founder
of the science, non-science, of Eugenics, 1822–1911 he was the
first modern proponent of sterilization, of eliminating the unfit
and having the elite propagate with each other, an endogamy of the
rich and famous, an endogamy of the gorgeous and genius,

class incest his recipe,

Galton the direct precursor of the Nazi's 1933 Eugenic
Sterilization Law that was unpopularly though necessarily repealed
by genocide just in time for this old idea to seem American enough
to be implemented, possibly even and subtly legislated:

to have the elites breed with the lower classes,

the minions not in the Jewish sense at all,

to make them all unto the middle — which proposal
according to Schneidermann it seemed to be a fixture of all too
many utopias, dystopias if they exist, democracies and so on,

like what's the alternative? would anyone want to rouse the
dozing ghost of Charles Fourier? of his Perfect Harmony? of the
Third Reich? of Stalinism? I didn't ask — and but speaking of
entities no longer extant or just always of-the-mind, it was rather
Verbinsky or Verbinski with an *i* that one of our quote unquote
better music critics he was harping on to me about at a party given
recently by some old fat widow of a real-estate magnate who her

head it just seems like a mole on her neck,

open for development (her husband dead he did strip malls as long as her waist it was wide),

some old as fat widow with none of her own money who she calls me her friend, who she calls herself my friend because for years she just wanted me to, well, let's say perform her and hello out there!

we (me and this critic, remaining nameless but he's probably here too, reviewing me, this, just following orders, doing his job like he was that night when),

when whether as a joke or because he was drunk (home-made unicum a Hungarian cellist-conductor-friend had flown in, undrinkable despite its ideational VSOP),

we were both drunk and I, I was harping on and on all about Schneidermann as I usually do to people, non-people, like that,

you,

to make unto them an example and instead this critic he said:

ridiculous! your Schneidermann is at best a minor composer, my friend (I wasn't his friend),

the critic he said: never leave it to the performers, the interpreters to hand-out greatness, that Schneidermann he's at most a footnote and a footnote only whether sharp or else flat (I then protested with zeal),

trivia,

and I don't care what you say! this critic he said, I'm the safeguarder — his own drunk nomenklatur — of posterity! and I'll tell you, me, that there are many more worthy and terribly overlooked composers out there, many more terribly underheard composers who are or they were equally if not more sad, tragic and genius!

why, take Verbinski! (he spit out 1850–1907 as if dates are enough justification),

take Verbinski for instance who he was born in 1850 into poverty and who died in 1907 in even greater poverty (which I would have to assume would make him the greatest genius),

a genius if I've ever heard one and do you think that anyone plays him anymore? played him ever? I ask you, me, and I

told

told him, drunk, that yes, that I'd once heard of a Verbinski, that a
Verbinski yes he comes to mind, is somehow familiar but that I
can't quite place him, from who or from where (and you, Zeit, you
probably thought that I was calling your bluff, or just playing
along),

      don't know where I had heard him or of him and maybe
even from Schneidermann himself but that no I answered him the
critic, no way, that he couldn't be greater than Schneidermann, than
my Schneidermann, it's just not possible, I mean what about the
piano sonatas? the nine string trios that they represent the height
of that instrumentation ever, since K. 563, since the efforts of
Webern and Schönberg at least (Schneidermann to me: string trios
are string quartets that wrestle with angels, lose a limb, hobbled-
quartets he once said, lamed-quartets)?

      the spring cassation music for seven horns in F, solo
trumpet and baritone voice?

      that chorus for 12 children on that poem of Paul Celan's,
or Ancel's as Schneidermann he often said, though not as much as
he said Antschel,

> *Die beiden Türen der Welt*
> *stehen offen:*
> *geöfnnet von dir*
> *in der Zwienacht*

      but he the once a critic for a major metropolitan newspa-
per and always a critic (drunk),

      how he just insisted: VERBINSKI, VERBINSKI,
VERBINSKI as if the name it was a product the critic he was
selling and on commission ear-to-ear, and so the next hangover
what did I do? I went to the library, nothing (I wouldn't ask
Schneidermann, pride his and mine),

      then asked the most knowledgeable musicologist known to
me in the world, an older homosexual gentleman but that shouldn't
matter in Basel and, well, they both told me:

      that no, that sorry, that this Verbinski he never existed, no
way, sorry again, no mention of him whatsoever anywhere or when
and so even if he ever was then who could he be?

      that posterity or the history of posterity if you will that

it's just never that negligent, that sorry, and that your friend (non-friend),

this critic who he was drunk on just two glasses the second his ashtray that he was just using a made-up man to make his point,

was trying to elicit feelings all about a man pulled out of the hottest air of his ass,

out of any intellectual thinness, Verbinski a man who historically didn't, who at least probably never even existed,

like why should I care to cry about an invention? or has the world spun to the point where a symbol of artistic strife, failure, dedication, failure — ultimately — has to be conjured up, lied-about? like is the only way to embody the injustice of the world in a figure that isn't, was never, *in* the world? *of-the-world?*

a figure thought up and fleshed out — and under-the-influence — on the spot?

and when we have the real thing, the true deal named Schneidermann who he's just right around the corner, cinematically dimly-lit? Or was.

A decent try, Zeit. A decent deception, my friend, my non-friend, good work, Z., critics they are most certainly forever,

but and according to Schneidermann we can all take comfort from the future's promise, the future's assurance, the future's guarantee of the greatest eradication of them all:

being according to Schneidermann at least the eradication of lies, of lying, and eventually — because their purposes can no longer be served — of liars themselves, of me included and God knows certainly of Schneidermann too if he's not been eradicated or self-eradicated already:

because according to Schneidermann and his late-acquired knowledge of everything technical, technological, in the future lying it cannot and will not exist: because once the Internet and the worldwideweb it, they, was, were, explained to him then Schneidermann he realized that all the world's facts and figures, that all individual facts and individual figures are already or will be at least at our fingertips and instantly (like the piano and its notes)!

and so that every statement (Schneidermann he gouged an eye with a hangnail),

every proposition (Schneidermann he swiped a hangnail

down

down the whitest scar on his neck, the tissue it was the sovereign
territory of Poland),

it is or at least will be instantly verifiable — meaning how
long we're willing to wait for something to be proven true, infal-
lible, a future that Schneidermann he predicted in which even our
most subtle impressions, inklings they can and will be put out on
the market for confirmation appropriately-priced,

and so according to Schneidermann leading me as if on a
shortest leash up up up and into his neighborhood your tastes they
won't live another generation,

neither your preferences,

neither your likes, neither your dislikes,

your turnons nor your turnoffs,

neither your incomprehensions (which they have to be
worth something to be proven honest as Schneidermann he once
said to me),

and neither your most valued, lifelong understandings.

Whatever (which Schneidermann he always said like
Vassefer).

Schneidermann to me: as far as truth is concerned, it is
with death.

Schneidermann to me: just when you think you know
someone, they know you.

Schneidermann to me: most people get on my nerves, but
not in my veins,

Like for example as Schneidermann he once offered over a
churro or three from a stand up in his neighborhood (as always my
treat),

like for example Schneidermann said like I am a Jew,

and how is that verifiable? how can that be proven?
Schneidermann that mortal enemy of all one-sided existence as
Hölderlin put it he asked: well, some might think that I look like a
Jew, that I talk like a Jew, that I smell like a Jew, that when I hear
them it is a Jew's hearing,

Jewhearing,

that when I touch them, pound their flesh and all that
Shylock-stuff, well,

that they might think that my thinking it is the thinking
of a Jew, that my philosophy it is the philosophy of a Jew, but

these are all impressions, and so what or which is verifiable? is
provable? and how? that, yes, I say, that yes I admit that I am a Jew
and maybe even apologize for it to the world as to myself but
perhaps I am in error (or am inconceivably lying, Schneidermann
he added popping the cap off his cerveza on the curb),

that my parents they were or might have been in error too,
and that their parents and so on and so forth, that no genetic tests
that would prove this Jewishness yet exist or will ever Schneidermann he flaunted his new knowledge of technology as received at
the matinee movies (and that if they the tests would ever exist,
Judaism by that time it would be long dead),

and so, again, I will state stated Schneidermann I will state
that being a Jew, that the state of being a Jew that it might be the
last unverifiable state out there, possible, but then,

can it always be said of me that I am a Jew? Schneidermann he asked almost choking on his 12 inches of over-
cinammoned churro, cough cough cough is it possible that I am a
Jew for only one or two or maybe three days a year (the High Holy
Days)?

could it be true to say that I am a Jew for only five
minutes per day? that some days, though, I am a Jew for a whole
eight minutes, sometimes even a half-hour (which takes much
concentration, Schneidermann he added)?

but for no longer?

but of course Schneidermann he went on with a
parkingmeter wedged in his tush we must insist, we must understand that to be a Jew, a true 100% Jew, for any length, shortness,
of time that it requires that our entire mind, our entire body,
indeed our entire being for that period, non-period, of time it is
focused and wholly on the state of the Jew, on the Jewish state as
Schneidermann he said to me once over a churro and a cerveza or
seven from a cart up up up in his neighborhood,

and I — who paid, as always — offered then that if that is
the case, indeed that if those are the criteria, then once I was a Jew
for an entire day, actually for a whole week as I remembered it to
him as I remember it now at my then inlaws' house out on Long
Island,

or at the five-floored house of one set of five-paired inlaws
now ex, my then-lawful now-ex-inlaws out in one of the Five Towns

maybe

(maybe Lawrence, a 20% shot),

and that God it almost killed me! as I exclaimed into the summering waste as Schneidermann he empathized (because I had paid, as always)

but anyway doubted because Schneidermann he had integrity, saying that it's difficult, this even being a Jew for 30 seconds, 10 seconds, three,

like try it some time,

and so I said okay, fine, I understand the idea of total focus on a state to subsume such state into a total identity, alright, I understand it all well enough — after all I'm a musician, an artist, a virtuoso in one discipline and so a virtuoso in all but let's focus now on the state of that focus: let's answer the question that I then and already half-drunk asked Schneidermann, asked him what exactly is your definition of a Jew?

and Schneidermann he answered and soberly but with an expired parkingmeter wedged up the seam of his tush that if you needed an answer, if you truly required a definition, then I will say to you that a Jew, a Jew is a man who serves — and that to serve someone other than yourself for more than a fraction of a second of a thought it's unthinkable, am I right? wholly out of the question, no? which is itself unappealably verboten Schneidermann he added while rubbing wishes at his Solomonaic temples,

and then Schneidermann he took off his hat, then his wig held around his head with a chinstrap fashioned,

almost but not quite Rube Goldbergized,

from a string threaded through an elaborate pulley-system that worked how? and sewn among the darkest hairs of that partihued wig the ultimate in fustian that Schneidermann he found in a dumpster Uptown, stuffed the wig into a denuded jacket pocket with the string dangling out to flapping in trashalley winds gusted from the diaphragm of the damned, his chinstrap of string tied in one worried noose of seven worried slipknots over a generic-make chin-bandage over a wound incurred from shaving despite the fact that Schneidermann he no longer needed to shave, was hairless and alone Schneidermann he answered in his quietest voice,

like molto serioso: listen — Schneidermann he said grappling with the register shift like an adolescent or an unformed mezzo — there is no reason for music, like for music there is no explanation (Schneidermann's mind it was always on music),

just like there is no reason for the Jews, for the Jew, for Jewishness there is no explanation of or for our mind and our existence,

that just as there is no use for music, there is no use for the Jews, for the Jew, for Jewishness, that music and the Jews they are both totally worthless, almost perfectly worthless, equally, and that that's why they've both been almost totally, perfectly,

eradicated,

exterminated, because Schneidermann he said in his smallest still voice like a third of a decibel above pure obmutescence Schneidermann he said, because music it is the Jew of art,

because the Jew he is the music of humanity: there and there only, serving no purpose at all, none whatsoever, but still there and so I — though only a silent 10 minutes later on that sweltering Uptown intersection of absolute nowheres & Americas — I then answered Schneidermann what I thought it was that he was working toward (staggering):

that most people who say they are Jews are in point of fact not Jews, mistaken or lying and why? and Schneidermann he disagreed and I asked why (it was my turn to ask as it was always my turn to pay)?

and Schneidermann he said that to agree with me it would be disastrous for him, for his sense-of-self,

for his art and his work, asked why should I gratify you in agreeing with you? why should I serve an idea of yours that it was always and originally mine? that it was indeed all I had ever? was indeed and all me, myself? and so I asked him — I had to — then would you instead disagree with me? and Schneidermann he answered also no, that disagreeing with me it was exactly what I wanted now, wasn't it? and I admitted that,

yes — it was always like we were actors in some play, some tragedy on the stage of world,

and then a trapdoor it opens in the floor of our Weltanschauung, we all fall through into void and but — asked him are you an Apollonian or a Dionysian?

and Schneidermann he answered on the way to the subway Downtown to the matinee movietheater for our matinee movie that day a matinee Vietnam movie, Schneidermann he answered that he

has

has always been above all idiomatic,

or that he has above all always strived to be idiomatic and in all situations,

that that and only that it was, is, the key to survival and the survival of survival, is indeed actually survival itself and indeed at all times: that when Schneidermann he wakes up — according to Schneidermann — he attempts to wake up idiomatically, that when he falls asleep he attempts to fall asleep wholly idiomatically,

that his waking it is, was, as idiomatic as his sleeping, that when Schneidermann he plays music,

according to Schneidermann who he waited for me to swipe my metropass to hand it off to him for his use as if we were training for the underground relay as Schneidermann he always said, the Olympics, Schneidermann his mind it was always summering in Greece,

Schneidermann he said that when he plays music, he attempts to play all music in a totally idiomatic fashion according to Schneidermann almost a ghost already through the turnstile,

almost intensely idiomatic as Schneidermann he once told me,

just like Schneidermann he died or disappeared in the way that Schneidermann he disappeared or died — but doesn't that approach, that existence, doesn't it too intensely deny the self? is what I asked, as those two tones they heralded the subway doors shutting (in this train the mechanism it must have warped: they were two half-tones, off-tones, intervals strange like the death throes of two mating goats),

and that when Schneidermann he used to have sex, which it seemed so long ago now, an ash-hard life ago Schneidermann he interrupted, said that when he used to have sex and he used to have much (in early life, yes, Schneidermann he was a Sybarite, an Epicurean (an *apikoros* Schneidermann he'd insist), Sardanapalus Schneidermann if you want, Heliogabalus who,

and maybe just maybe it was just now that he was atoning, paying-the-piper's-price),

that Schneidermann he attempted to have sex in the most intensely idiomatic way possible — Schneidermann he added that because I am a Classicist I have always insisted on performing the oral act on women first, that because I am a Romanticist if you will I always have insisted on having recourse to the anus,

that because I am a Classicist I always enjoyed rimming
women's aureoles with my tongue, that because I am a Romanticist
I always enjoyed having my anus rimmed first,

Schneidermann after our second matinee movie which was
of the erotic-thriller genre or genres in which an American woman
— an Asian actress who she had previously done only teeveemovies-
of-the-week — she falls in love and has virtual sex or else virtually
has sex with the masculine consciousness entombed Pharaonic in
an enormous pyramidal military computer after which Schneidermann he insisted that Classicism it is the tongue, and that Romanticism it is the penis,

that Classicism is the vagina, that Romanticism is the
anus,

that Classicism is knowing where the clitoris is, that
Romanticism is knowing what to do with the clitoris,

that a Classicist is a virgin (mother), that a Romantic is a
whore (mother),

that a Classicist he or she expects to be bought dinner
first and that a Romantic she brings dessert, and her or himself,
over and up to your wrecked Uptown apartment at 3:45 a.m. in the
morning,

that a Classicist or is it a Classic he or she practices
foreplay, that a Romantic has had his or her orgasm and is already
asleep,

insisted that making love to your sister, and in the process
deflowering her, is eminently Classical, whereas engaging your
sister in her unlubricated anus is generally regarded as Romantic,

that to climax inside someone is unmistakably the Classical approach, that to climax all over someone's face, on and in their
eyes, that there is no approach more Romantic,

that smothering your lover to death with a, goosefeather,
pillow in the heat of passion and then — in tears,

I fear, *and in rhyme* — admitting your guilt to your cousin
the Police Commissioner it will always be Classical, that
sodomizing your lover with a telephonepole, hacking him or her to
limbs and a torso with an axe of rust and then burying each morsel
in a different grave in your father's cornfield it will always be
considered Romantic,

that

that a lover who calls him or herself a Classicist is really a Romantic just as a lover who calls him or herself a Romantic is really just a Classic — because at least according to Schneidermann as we parted on the afternoon street outside the post-matinee-movie-coffee-and-cake-café, because it has always been that simple,

because people are, genuinely, the diametric, exact opposite of who they say and who think they are and that often what they say and what they think (about anything, whether they know it or not)

are themselves at odds,

according to Schneidermann's image flitting into our ears and enacting love-deaths in the gray middle:

and so it's war within wars within wars within wars, private aggressions, police actions of thought and deed, idea and word, Laster to you and, as not last as I am least, Laster to myself — the man I am, a Classicist, and the man I am not, a Romantic,

the man I was and will be, a Romantic, and the man I am for the I hope it won't be infinite present:

a Classicist appalled at my own appetites and abilities, that's one,

and disgusted by my own standards, my own-imposed proportions: me with nautilus ears and a torso that resembles nothing like that of Apollo,

a Classicist applying obsolete criteria to purposeful realities, dead requirements to living embodiments of just a new standard that I'm not too old to understand but that I understand well enough, and, yet, refuse to accept, and that's not just the opposition in me, the naysaying,

a real true No and not a Jewish No,

the thumbing of the nose or the biting of the thumb up the nose held high in the air, not my airs, not my putting on of anything except the skin that I was birthed into, and it's too late, way too late, to apologize for that.

You might take it up with my mother. But she's dead.

And the dead they do not have to answer for those that they've left behind. Just as I don't have to answer for you after tonight.

Instead, I am attempting to give you the questions: are you

a man or a machine? a liver or a dier? a liver or a spleen (yes, with all their Kabbalistic implications intact)?

a Classicist or a Romantic? or just Independent? forever Undecided? a blue principle or a white? stripes or solids? boxers or briefs?

would you like fries with that? and all those banal catechisms of upselling? like large or supersized at the matinee movietheater at which the carbonated beverages they come in only two sizes:

LARGE and/or SUPERSIZED, which Schneidermann he always referred to peering down into the cylindrical void as the CIRCUMSIZED (with his voice echoing huge),

those two sizes and only those two sizes: you can have either the LARGE (by default the SMALL)

or the SUPERSIZED AKA the extralarge (by default just the plain old LARGE, or UNSMALL),

and nothing else:

no *true* SMALL, no *true* MEDIUM and no *true* LARGE — options they have been eliminated from the moment you've entered the lobby if not world itself:

that there can be no middle ground, no judicious medium, no compromise except with — between — absolutes, void of yes and no

(and a No is not a void, a void is an absence of choice according to Schneidermann at the concessions counter, a No therefore is a definite according to Schneidermann ordering the drink and no ice,

a real true No and not a Jewish no and ice it's a scam, at least according to Schneidermann), that a void it's an absence of intersection according to Schneidermann as I paid for it the soda like liquefied asphalt:

or else a single crossroads as Schneidermann he always said like Poland this way and Life that,

that these concessions they offer you an either/or which it resembles life according to Schneidermann, or death according to Schneidermann, depending if your particular sodacup and no matter the size if it's half empty or half full and with either soda or — boot-crushed — ice,

(or rock-shaved) that what you have here is the opposite of the future, of adaptability, and so of survival itself according to

Schneidermann

Schneidermann, like where's that transcendent American multitude
that I've heard so much about? that protean aspect that it's supposed to save us all? the panoply of sizing options that they flatter
your dollar whether honest or not? each size adequate to a specific
need, a measured thirst, but instead we play-it-safe as which of my
exwives you always said? and cater, actually cater, offer concessions
to the eliminative need (or rather impulse):

    not satiation but stuffing, not quenching but drowning in
tiny caramel bubbles with larger and larger and larger sizes made
more and more fundamental to your most modest whim according
to Schneidermann who he always packed his own pinkmost
gummed-white loop-de-loop straw that Schneidermann he once got
in a HAPPYMEAL from MCDONALD'S (I won! Schneidermann
he screamed, I won!),

    and no options extant except those permitted by conces-
sions in more ways than one as Schneidermann he added stuffing
napkins in the pockets of his DICKIES: there's more ice melting
up valuable liquid space and so maybe the sizes they're smaller
after all, smaller and smaller and smaller unto just a thought, a
notion, an urge,

    modesty clothed in immodesty just like Schneidermann
who he'd bring his own cup too smuggled in in his loud panther-
print rag of a jacket and me, I'd order a SUPERSIZEd (what
else?),

    pour out half of its contents into his cup (an old card-
board cup from the old matinee movie days that Schneidermann he
always insisted on recycling, reusing, rinsing out after every
emergency urination, an old cardboard cup before plastic and so
lamentably lacking in structural integrity),

    and Schneidermann and I we'd top both cups off with
JOHNNIE WALKER RED LABEL WHISKY,

    or JACK DANIEL'S, or else JIM BEAM, which it was
always an interest of Schneidermann's, this quite evident if di-
rected-from-the-corporate-boardroom whiskey-feud,

    this whiskey-war,

    like a shotgun scrimmage in the teevee-lit livingroom of
America it was his concern for the aggression obtaining between
the whiskey-producing states of Kentucky and Tennessee, the
conflicts obtaining between the whiskies of Kentucky and the

whiskies of Tennessee,

this choice that it often caught him unaware: which to support, Kentucky or Tennessee (Schneidermann he'd never step a shoe in either)?

like Daniel Boone the Injun Killer or Davy Crockett the Establishment Senator seemed to be the choice that Schneidermann he drank it down to, didn't want to play favorites and so Schneidermann he just drank them both, all — or else sometimes Schneidermann he just went with OLD GRANDAD, whenever JIM BEAM it wasn't available or out of his, my, on-loan price-range, either genuine Kentucky or Tennessee essence mixed with sodawater and artificial flavoring, sugar and HIGH FRUCTOSE with

džen-ů-eyn as Schneidermann he would say it when he talked in his Dracula voice, all with gen-u-ine effervescent toothdecay as Schneidermann he said to me once in his Vlad-the-Impaler-Dracula-Lugosi voice when we were out parading Greenwich Village and on Halloween,

down where even the streets they have AIDS, where you could get AIDS just by walking the streets, pedicural transmission as Schneidermann he always insisted (asked me to keep an eye on his shoes),

to which I asked him who he was dressed up as this year to trick-or-treat my largesse to which Schneidermann he answered, sidestepping a float: I'm Jack Daniels, Johnnie Walker and I laughed, I'm dressed up as Jim Beam and I laughed or just, I'm just an Old Grandad and Schneidermann he began to cry, rattled a finger in his mouth, among his gums like an uprooted suppurating graveyard — yes, I remember, that Schneidermann he did that once, after a matinee I don't know what movie which, when a tooth it fell out, Schneidermann he just put it in his coke cup, leftovers, to save it because Schneidermann he saved everything (himself, me, teeth),

upon my returning him home to his apartment, room, Schneidermann he absentmindedly if he ever did anything absentmindedly he just placed the cup on the lid of his piano in his place I have to sort out before the lawyers,

and went to retrieve it a month or so later, Schneidermann did, he told me, the cup, to drink from it, what was left, when Schneidermann he was thirsty and had nothing else to drink

neither

neither money to purchase anything else to drink and so remembered it and it, the tooth that it had been loosened on a candybar
(Schneidermann he always began a matinee movie with the candy
he disliked, then the candy he hated after the previews, and saved
for the feature presentation the candy that it would induce vomiting in him and so on, all on my generosity),

 the tooth it had caught in his throat to be coughed up at
the matinee movie and then placed in the coke cup to be placed
once back at his place on the lid of his — upright — piano,

 and a month later or so Schneidermann he insisted that
the tooth it had decayed to near-nothingness, the tooth it was ½ or
maybe even ¼ its original size, no larger than the head of a nail we
used to kill their God with as Schneidermann he often told me,

 often showed it to me if indeed it even was a tooth and
not a,

 Schneidermann he'd schlep it the eroded corroded cavitied
tooth in his pocket (one of his pockets),

 until it fell out of a hole (which hole? as each and every
one of his pockets it had a hole),

 and so, no longer in possession of the sugared-away tooth,
and so unable to bandy it about as he always, usually, did, Schneidermann he merely smiled at you and the conspicuous gap (I do
not say *hole*)

 in his smile it communicated everything that Schneidermann he both *wanted* and *intended* to communicate: a canine tooth
missing, to the left, setting him always slightly off-kilter, though
his somewhat higher, raised right ear (higher, more raised than his
left, which it resembled the ear of an ermine),

 served to compensate to some degree, to an allowable
degree, but then you still didn't know, ever, if and when to take him
seriously or not if ever,

 which, though, in the end, was ultimately his problem and
not yours, mine — though I often responded to my doubt(s) as if
it, they, were my problem, my very personal problem,

 my exactly exuberantly totally wholly ineluctably ineffably
personal problem, though I had no one to blame but him (because
how could I hope to ever blame myself, to accept blame on my
head, on my shoulders already with the stoop of a five-floor
walkup in Queens),

with this image I have to maintain, with this level of talent I have to gift, and to prove, with this height of stardom I have, somehow — against my mother's will but cleaving to my father's — I have however and in whichever way attained, which level, I might add, I am not responsible for, which level I don't in any way have to answer for because answering for it

(for me, myself) would be in point of fact answering for Schneidermann, would, ultimately, indeed be answering for God, something, I might add, I have no right to do,

something, though, I have the daily, evening-long privilege of actually doing, or hoping to do, pretending to do, playing-at doing (Huizinga who), here, now, for you,

as if you have the right to judge my performance, even an indulgence given over in a moment of extreme laxity on my part — no, never, impossible to surrender this pulpit,

this perch,

this soapbox,

boxcar,

lilypad,

unthinkable, uninspiring — idea that can't even be chalked up to inspiration that circular curse, that curse coming in circles that it's called inspiration:

this cyclical pox of generations upon generations all vomiting renewal, revival — old artists revived into new artists, suddenly relevant, suddenly arrived and with a coin on each eye,

an old Schneidermann renewed as a new Schneidermann, old Schneidermanns renewed, they used to say rehabilitated into new Schneidermanns like the new line or model of artist, yesterday's Schneidermanns rediscovered as, yes, today's Schneidermann's, the-Schneiderman-for-the-new-millennium $29.99 plus shipping & handling,

decomposers resurrected into composers, old Masters retired into worthlessness, works Joseph-hoarded into the granaries and storehouses of the moment's Ramses,

into obsolescence, into irrelevance in favor of, to be replaced by — clean out our cages for the young lions already with matted, pilling coats and ragged manes, starving for their day to loll lust in the sun,

their heavenly due,

their

their New World discovery,

their lion's share at the Zoo at which Schneidermann he
gifted to me the manuscript of this his *Concerto*,

the painstakingly written-with-arthritis-and-etrog-sized-
knuckles manuscript of this *Concerto* at the Zoo so Uptown as to
not be Uptown anymore and to be merely the Bronx,

up near Einstein and Heine their schools and their statues
where,

off the goddamned map,

white as white as a void:

gifting to me his *Concerto* manuscript, his work, his genius
at that it-should-be condemned municipal Zoo barely serviced
anymore by even the most extreme measures of mass-transit that
white people of European descent we would ever think of to take,

visited only by the children of minorities — majorities —
and don't forget me (limping along with)

and a nearly 100-year-old Hungarian-Jewish composer, a
Zoo populated only by me, his almost 80-year-old monkey among
all these showponies and studs trotted out,

all these showstuds and geldings groomed into glue,

all these pets that they should just be put-down,

out-of-their-misery,

to death, (not that I haven't been responsible for it, for
this phenomenon, for them these prodigies, these phenoms and
their phenomenon, their prodigy-phenomenon but, then again, I am
never responsible, can't ever be held responsible, never, by dint of
my destiny, my destiny-dint wholly unencumbered),

my (illusions of) inevitability,

my (great faith in my) greatness,

my (dreamed-for-and-of) purity,

my (dreamed-about) definitiveness:

an awkward thing among things in any eye's pocket, among
me and Schneidermann, among Schneidermann and his selves,
Schneidermann's selves and Schneidermann's selves' selves, and
Schneidermann's selves' selves' selves unto all made whole again
(Schneidermann he was sure)

(Schneidermann he knew)

(and why not?) — do you have any better ideas? of how
to survive? how-to-get-through-it-All? I ask rhetorically, because all

I ask is rhetoric, because all I do is rhetoric, all I am is rhetoric, rhetoric head to ten rhetorical toes (I haven't seen them in years, it's the lower lumbar spine stenosis my chiropractors all ten of them sent me for Asian acupuncture for when all I needed was a baseball bat and someone with a good swing,

a solid follow-through),

all I am is a scribbled score of arguments and counter-arguments, writ across my face, countenance all these ideas and counter-ideas just carved mad with a stylus on my eyes, just these negations and negations of negations and negations of negations of negations that are, again, just negations of the original question no longer even cared-about let alone remembered, to the asker or even to itself, bent on death, hell and bent bouncing on the squat dot, its own mark, the mark's mark down the street and clad in a 50-plus-year-old it seemed it had to have been pantherskin trenchcoat (all holes in the pockets of all hole),

and an NYFD baseballcap as if all firefighters they play short-centerfield anymore,

scooping up popped up to flying burning babies, not in their mitts — no, you're playing to a packed house, you understand? — but with what? with the very hats off their heads! in a Willie Mays scoop:

a save, a great save! and the crowd goes wild as that proverb goes

as the baby it's dunked in the cooler and all is, and finally, right with the world — for the simple reason that you've got your money's worth.

Like my first wife did. Like my second wife she did. And much like my third, fourth, and maybe even my fifth wives they did. And you're all welcome to it, six times over — the finger I admittedly don't have, the finger in the middle of my middlefinger, growing out from the tip and really and totally meaning exactly, perfectly, what you all think it means,

like 12 notes to 10 fingers Schneidermann he never understood it, wanted to know why the octave it wasn't divided into tenths? ten-thousandths? 12 it was arbitrary enough (Schneidermann he never liked anything well-tempered),

as arbitrary as 10 at least, and at least with 10 notes to an octave a pianist he could play every note at once, one with each of

his

his fingers, all with and in one thrust like Schneidermann he could,

like Schneidermann he often played all 12 notes in the octave and at once, managed 12 tones with 10 digits Schneidermann did who he used also his — hairless — palms, wrists, forearms, his head even too when Schneidermann he smacked it against the keys out of despair, for more sound, for more art, for more world (cloning his brother his twin? dreams were downsized, at the end Schneidermann he wanted only to clone his hands),

there are those who perform Schneidermann he said to me at the Zoo pointing among butterflylike birds like lepidopterists' wives Schneidermann he interrupted himself,

and them in their cages, and then there are those who they live Schneidermann he said to me at the Zoo forefingering among the dens of lions lamb-tongued,

there are those who do Schneidermann he said to me at the matinee movies mentioning a famous actor who he shattered his spine doing his own stunts (fell off a horse),

and then there are those who *are* DO, like some teevee advertisement that Schneidermann he insisted he insourced himself,

JUST DO IT,

like when you hear a performer Schneidermann he often said you should hear only a composer, like when you hear a performance Schneidermann he often insisted while you should hear the music Schneidermann he often said, there are the virtuosos — or the virtuosas — Schneidermann he often said and then there are the virtuous, the interpreter Schneidermann he often said and then there's the interpreted, the interpretations Schneidermann he said and then the interpreted Schneidermann he insisted out of the left side of his mouth as Schneidermann and I as we sat in the bleachers at the baseballgame up at the ballpark in the Bronx as he spit from the right side of his mouth, this once

(it was a doubleheader, 9-7 in extra-innings against an infield flown in from Havana) spitting out a tooth,

after which Schneidermann he had only three left, in the rear, three wisdom teeth, three teeth most wise like the Fillings that they visited the Manger (one cavitied black), the right top and bottom and the left bottom like the Father the Son and the Ghost of a Molar — spitting out yet another tooth this one into the cup of beer of the man sitting in front of us who he probably didn't notice, this obese man of Italian descent who he most definitely didn't notice and so drank it down,

a fellow major-league-alcoholic, Schneidermann he joked if he ever — but it was impossible to know for sure because the lard he was so fat that sitting behind him I we you could barely see in front of him, only hear the plash of the tooth to the plastic of the cup and the foam of the watered-down beer,

hear the plash of Schneidermann's tooth and the urgent nervous tugging of Schneidermann on an apple-lobed ear (like a thirdbase coach with the d.t.'s),

mad-urgent rummaging in his pockets, in Schneidermann's pockets' holes, that which fell out of Schneidermann's pockets' holes, those who found that which fell out of Schneidermann's pockets' holes, those who loved those who found that which fell out of Schneidermann's pockets' holes:

a cola'd tooth that Schneidermann he never found again, an advertisement found in the CLASSIFIEDS section of a major metropolitan newspaper,

an ad CLASSIFIED as if an embarrassing, KGB-type state-secret that its advertiser he was just seeking a gig, teaching or playing or God anything you would give! (Schneidermann he thought that the young man he was possibly a recent Russian émigré and okay):

A young, virtuous pianist seeks work it said, yes, *virtuous* and God bless him! Schneidermann who he never subscribed to God he once commanded, this kid he breaks my hard heart! Hire him to play a wedding and let him shtup a bridesmaid! Schneidermann he once insisted when he telephoned me to share, God let him shtup the bride! *jus primae noctis* invoked for such yearning! such need! Schneidermann he once insisted to me over the telephone as if I as if Schneidermann he could ever hear my answer to,

as if Schneidermann's unit it ever granted me the voice to agree — once but not now, no more now that Schneidermann he was gone, poof! just vanished like the opus of János Kohn and I was standing outside and then inside and then outside again of the matinee movietheater just going through his pockets,

rushed-saneless rummaging like the homeless man that

I

I am,

just burrowing like a worm in heat — in doing so in my
defense to justify just trying to find some idea of where Schneidermann he was going to, where Schneidermann he had gone to, for
how long if not for forever and maybe why:

an employment wanted advertisement for a *virtuous pianist*
was all that I found, and a staple, also an old 33¢ stamp with a
famous — dead, o.d.'d — jazz musician on it, not to forget to
introduce into Evidence a two-year-old application for an absentee
ballot all of which indicative of

meaning nothing the junk I found upon leaving the
matinee movietheater from the matinee Holocaust movie in the
pockets upon pockets upon pockets of the jacket (pestilent
dilacerated rag)

that Schneidermann he left behind when he left the world
behind, this one, when Schneidermann he left the matinee Holocaust movie to go to either go to the bathroom or to concessions,
or to concessions and to the bathroom in that order knees and
elbows all smeared in Paleolithic swirlies of pink-powdered soap I
went into every stall, bent down, bowed thrice and crawled to check
for him but no, then into the lobby I always say foyer Schneidermann he always said *Empfangshalle* (as if a hotel, where he lived) of
the matinee movietheater where I asked the ushers, the ticket-taker,
the concession and box-office wageslaves but also no no no no and
no,

not Jewish No's but real true no-no's:

like sorry I can't help you, wish I could help but the
answer is no and firm as a goy and so exited out the matinee
movietheater to the street where I stood like a pillar of salted ice,
went back in to ask the manager, another and real no again, then
went with him the pigtailed and I think stoned-off-his-glass-house
day-manager into every other theater in that matinee movie multiplex in order to ascertain whether he, whether Schneidermann he
had left our matinee Holocaust movie to attend another matinee
Miscellaneous Whatever movie showing on another screen — of
10, rather 9 — in that matinee movie theaterplex, or else maybe to
sit alone and read (though Schneidermann he'd left his book
behind, in another Platonic pocket),

and if not then to maybe just sit alone in an empty

movietheater (but which?)

      showing nothing and just staring at screen all the while
ogling,

      staring seductively at,

      staring slyly at posterity from the periphery of his third
eye, the other two just staring dead ahead at the silverscreen God
ARS GRATIA ARTIS MGM M.akes G.reat M.ovies!

      just like that dream that Schneidermann he once had! just
like that dream Schneidermann he once recounted to me! just
waiting for me at a post-matinee-movie eatery of his choice which
was so unlike him (Schneidermann he was always as broke as your
Bubbe's best dish),

      or just in another screen another theater (of 10, rather 9),

      or in another screen in, of another matinee movietheater
altogether (of possible hundreds that I knew),

      and there meditating on nothingness and the absence of
nothingness which is — are — the same thing or thingless, like in
that dream that Schneidermann he once had! like in that dream
that Schneidermann he once recounted to me that afternoon
Uptown at the Park's darkest edge up near his place (non-place),

      in whichever theater in whichever screen — Schneidermann
he always said *hall*,

      not as much as Schneidermann he said *Saal* — just
meditating in silence, in inner-music which was very much like him
but not,

      and so I and again and this time finally left the matinee
movietheater, exited in toto, leaving my personal and other extrane-
ous information (name and telephone numbers, NAME@
email.fax, the name of my agent and his information, the number
of his roaming telephone and a greenish piece of paper with a
portrait on it of Lincoln the Great Emancipator who he was shot
dead in a theater just like this, a greenish piece of paper IN GOD
WE TRUST that's probably not worth anything anymore and a
description of Schneidermann was what I left)

      with the squiggly-pigtailed and John Lennon-glasses-
wearing day-manager to again and totally in toto exit the matinee
movietheater and never to return,

      ever,

      to the thousand-throated street and still holding his jacket

jerkrag

(jerkrag, jizzrag and his leatherbound book on the death of
Socrates,

and poetry that sacred, winged, fickle thing) — then sitting on
a bench on Prospero's traffic-island between Broadway & Broadway
(*Brot-way*, Schneidermann he often said),

to an undeserted traffic-island between the Uptown (Schneidermann's, poverty's)

and Downtown (mine, wealth's)

cardinal directionals of Broadway to just sit on a bench there
and aside a sleeping or just dead homeless gentleman with a
midnight o'clock shadow and a psychedelic, tie-dyed fisherman's
cap to go through the pockets of Schneidermann's jacket (jizzrag,
pocket-poker-rag)

that Schneidermann he left behind on the seat between us, to
find some information, some indication of what, of where, of
when, why and how,

of Schneidermann and an explanation of his disappearance,

of his exiting of the matinee Holocaust movie or maybe I did
it, went through the pockets of his rag just because I was curious
(though if I would have asked him for permission to be curious, to
be curious in that way, it's not like Schneidermann he would have
denied me the satisfaction, or the dissatisfaction:

all our visits if he was there or not they indeed were *dynamic visits*)
— enough to find a two-year-old application for an absentee ballot,
an ashtray from a café that Schneidermann and I we had visited after a
matinee Action movie the week previous and don't ask,

a handful of warm applesauce,

and a XEROX of a decade-old movie review of the decade-old
matinee Holocaust movie that we had just left (at different times),

that Schneidermann he must have obtained at the Countee
Cullen West 136th Street public library, which read,

and how after all the ads for the COCA-COLA CLASSIC and
the BMWs and the MERCEDES sitting two up front two in the
back and six-million in the ashtray,

and after all the previews for the I-meet-you-you-meet-me-
and-we-get-married-matinee-movies, all the I-stole-money-from-
you-who-you-stole-it-from-me-who-I-stole-it-from-you-first-
matinee-movies,

how after all of them Schneidermann he just stood up

and shouted into that eave-packed theater as much as to me (yes,
that was the sign that it should have tipped-me-off, his own EXIT
in which the bulbs they hadn't been replaced in a generation or
more),

God! how you shouted:

The picture quality's unacceptable!
There's no color! It's colorless! Thieves!
I want a refund! I demand a full refund! (of my money),

and how when everyone they rightly shushed him down
with gaudy lisps Schneidermann he just turned around and shouted
at them in jeremiad-voice, Prophet-mode:

you're going to put up with this?
what's your problem?
you want Holocaust?
Holocaust I've got! I survived!
who needs a matinee movie?
who wants to meet a real survivor?
who wants to pay 10 bucks to meet a real survivor?
give me 10 bucks and I'll give you the Holocaust!
I'll even throw in the color for free!

Schneidermann he shouted to more heckling and jeckling
and less rightly shushing lisps until I — who, again, never knew if
Schneidermann he was joking or not — I quieted him down with
an embarrassed overacted sigh (I was always embarrassed whereas
Schneidermann he was never embarrassed, Schneidermann he was
always embarrassing which, as I was always embarrassed, it like
everything else with him it was always more my problem than it
was his),

with a paw placed lightly hard on his thinnest — book —
shelf of shoulder,

anyway I sat him down again, explained that that was how
SPIELBERG he intended it, how black & white, or the lack-of-
color as Schneidermann he put it to the entire matinee movietheater,
all about how that was supposed to be artistic — and so on and so
forth all into his most peerless ear, went on translating the script,

the

the lines from American to American until Schneidermann he just
got up and he left,

in the middle of the 300-minute-travesty

and so on and so forth I waited nervous and occupied
(with my Schneidermann as much as with the matinee Holocaust
movie)

until the matinee Holocaust movie it ended,

thinking that Schneidermann he would think to return,
would indeed return and not just in my dreams but physically, 3D
presencewise in all his American 5'2" and 100 or so pounds —
because that's what we Jews do we return,

but Schneidermann he didn't by the time the matinee
Holocaust movie it had ended and after almost 300 minutes of
something that it took a millennium to finally happen, occur
(Holocaust-as-the-death-of-the-West and so on, you're all so smart
with scholarships already to Heaven I'm sure you know all the
arguments for and against),

after which I — and against all advice, all warnings, all
judgments — provided the police with the same description of
Schneidermann that I had provided to the matinee movietheater's
incense-stick-necked day-manager previous:

told him that Schneidermann, he had Beethoven's hair, that
Schneidermann he had the nose of the Jews, the nose of Moses
Mendelssohn as much as the nose of his grandson Felix (and
financial acumen in inverse proportion to that of the intermediary
Mendelssohn, Abraham),

the eyes of the Asians or the Eskimos or the Hawaiians if
you know what I mean:

Mongol eyes, Siberian eyes, the median Mongoloid lid
more like slits more like those flaps on the wings of 747 airplanes
that peer down insensate over the world unknown and but,

that Schneidermann he looked like Scheidemann if you
knew him, the first Prime Minister of the first and only and soon-
dying Weimar Republic which Schneidermann he hated to love and
so loved to hate (the dream it was the worst of it according to
Schneidermann, the excess the most laudable),

that Schneidermann he looked like T.G. Masaryk too in
later life if you're familiar, the first and only president of the first
and only Czechoslovakian Republic if you remember (and you can

just forget all about both of their moustaches, Schneidermann he always insisted that a stork in Poland it had stolen his favorite pince-nez),

that Schneidermann he had three rotted teeth left, that Schneidermann he had three rotten wisdom teeth left, that Schneidermann he had Mozart's ears but that one of them it was higher than the other or that that other of them it was lower than, that Schneidermann he had America's lips like the Rolling Stones who they were British but that they only spoke the truth as I did when I told the matinee movietheater's incense-stick-dicked day-manager as I told the sketch-artist who he had the knuckles of a Klee or maybe Kandinsky as I told the Head Detective in Missing Persons that Schneidermann (whose case it should have anyway been delegated to the department of Missing Geniuses),

that Schneidermann he was once mistaken on Times Square Midtown for Gandhi, that Schneidermann he was once mistaken on Verdi Square Uptown for the actor Ben Kingsley in-character who I also told him the Detective starred (though only in a supporting role)

in that matinee movie that Schneidermann and I we attended (though the Detective he never asked which movie it actually was, and but I never thought to tell him, enlighten him and why?),

and so that unidentified matinee movie, that matinee Unidentified movie from which Schneidermann he disappeared and then and instead asked him had he, the Head Detective, and in his whole longlonglong experience had much success in finding these missing persons such as Schneidermann? in magically turning missing persons into just persons alone? in recovering lost people such as my genius Schneidermann?

to which the Detective he answered, or rather asserted

You were saying that this Schneider man he's shaved, do I have that right?

to which I answered that no, that yes that Schneidermann he once was shaved in a town it was called Oświęcim but that you might know it as Auschwitz — *Oshpitzin* in Yiddish, whatever, Schneidermann he never named it a name — to which the Detec-

Detective

tive he answered, or rather asserted

I was born in the Bronx but it was more like Jamaica,

and then

*I just want to know if this musicman of yours, if he's bald is all,
don't need to hear you talk about what happened in Germany.*

In Poland, I said to which the turkey-gobblers-under-his-
eyes Detective he answered, or rather asserted

I thought you said that this Schneider man he was Hungary,

to which I answered when the pubic-haired Detective he
asked me just after if there were any other distinguishing marks I
should or would remember, if Schneidermann he had any other
distinguishing marks (other than an NYFD hat and an AWOL
wig),
        I then found that I remembered his number, that I remem-
bered my Schneidermann's number, his Auschwitz number as
tattooed on his left forearm and so I gave it to him, the Detective
who he then wrote three words on the paper of the Report that it
seemed pulped out of lukewarm dregs and nicotine stains:
        BALD, TATTOO (LFOREARM) which could describe
anyone I thought and I think, at least it could describe almost
anyone and regardless of sex race religion prison-record in New
York,
        indeed among these 8 million-plus almost anyone but
Schneidermann who I then went on to tell him the Detective and
his three chins coming in and going out like the tide down the
Shore (as I just then also remembered)
        that he, that Schneidermann he had had a previous arrest-
record:
        once for smoking a whore's cigarette in a public building
(the Unemployment Office),
        that once when Schneidermann he was mistaken for a John
soliciting a prostitute for directions to a new multiplex on 10th
Avenue, that Schneidermann he was never mistaken but I can't say

that the horn-nosed Detective he believed me — when I told him
also that Schneidermann, he prevented me from becoming a creator
(our history, our mutual history it poured out,

anything relevant the Detective had said),

that Schneidermann he had frustrated my own composing,
my own compositions I insisted to him the Detective (our lives
streaming across the desktop like skin-black coffee spilled to
stain),

indeed any output and above all any input I had and
offered whatsoever about his own art was what Schneidermann he
frustrated, nullified and so that Schneidermann, that he forced me
into becoming an interpreter (the Detective he gave me his card,
said *be in touch*),

and that I want you to know that Schneidermann he
offered me no solace for this determination, Schneidermann he
offered me no succor for his insistence, his quiet insistence, his in
truth silent insistence, his example I want to insist:

Schneidermann he offered me no hope, no escape, no hope
of escape and no escape from hope I always told my students when
I had to have students or studentesses to satisfy the salary the
Conservatory it paid me, because I — my wives present and ex —
needed still I need the salary the Conservatory it paid me I had to
satisfy them but not necessarily the few students or predominantly
studentesses I had who,

the minimum of studentesses I had to have (salarywise
and sexually),

because anxiety it is the optimal state of the interpreter as
Schneidermann he always insisted as he embodied it, I told them
(my studentesses of necessity, and remarkable sexual fortitude)

that nervousness it is the optimal state of he-who-inter-
prets,

that the edge it is the only address that understanding
arrives at, the precipice the only city, the only capital, the only
destination to which I'll allow my thoughts to wander I have often
told my children, you, the only and last stop of my train of
thought I have often told my wives present and ex, you, the final
resting-place, the grave, the iron grave in which I can leave my ideas
knowing that I couldn't have raised them in any other way, for any
other fate,

I

I think,

I dream — much like Schneidermann he dreamt, in all
those 50 years of an eternity, those 50 years of matinee movies
you should know that Schneidermann he dreamt and dreamt much
(underactive life-life, overactive dream-life Schneidermann he often
said,

though matinee movies you think would usurp dream,
would render dream superfluous), and recounted to me more:

a dream of his that it was less a dream than an existence of
sleep was what I was after,

another mode much as Spinoza he,

one way to pass the world between wakings,

a dream as much as a manifested and manifesting fear-of-
dream,

as much as an image for the private lexicon of his

silence while on the subject of interpretation (*Traumdeutung*
it was now the property of the matinee movies was what Schneidermann he concluded only after much conclusioning),

when faced with the how and the personal and all that
who-dreck that it gets in the way of the work as Schneidermann he
always said Schneidermann he was silent like the oldest and
greatest of movies (like Harpo Marx Schneidermann was, at least a
priest of the luftmensch's namesake, Harpocrates the Greek god of
silence and secrecy, guardian of the rose of Eros).

Schneidermann he slept and it began, the dream that it was
always the same until it ended it always began with him waking up
and not in his whitewashed plaster paradise on the upper-upper-
Upper Westside but on the Eastside:

in Poland, actually, in Auschwitz, Schneidermann in dream
he would wake up in a barracks bed he said he remembered,
dreamed, more from the matinee movies than from the reality (ice,
ash, the matinee movies),

waking up in bed (alone!),

to an empty barracks,

how the dream it began, Schneidermann he began when he
first told me this as we walked the upper extremis of Park up in his
neighborhood,

Schneidermann he said that it began as he woke up from a
dream unremembered and left his, an, old barracks building in

Auschwitz,
  that it was empty, the whole camp it was empty,
  like now and even of American and Israeli tourists (I had
been back despite never having been there THEN,
  Schneidermann he never went back, I returned despite
never arriving,
  Jews we always return, Schneidermann despite being a Jew
or despite trying to be a Jew himself he could never bring himself
to return),
  walked through the empty to the gates as Schneidermann
and I we walked the uppermost lip of gaping Park, was saluted by a
lone faceless guard, Schneidermann he said that his damp rotted
crotch it was licked and twice by the lone faceless guard's three-
headed dog,
  like Cerberus-of-the-Humane-Society
  as we walked the Park past drug-deals and love-affairs,
theologians and terminals and their interns Schneidermann he said
that he just walked shoeless, unshod, up from the empty
Auschwitz underworld through the mud and — razor-tipped —
lashes of grass and right up to the guardrail,
  which it lifted for him (and Schneidermann he lifted his
right forearm like the horizon sieg-heiling),
  like ADMIT ONE Schneidermann he said as he recounted
it to me as we walked the uppermost vaginal lip of the gaping hell
of Uptown Park (Schneidermann he once sketched a *Sextet for Winds
and G-String* in the key of Labia Minora was what he labeled it,
unplayed),
  Schneidermann he said that afternoon's descent into
evening that he opened the gates with his hands, his own hands and
such hands! and that the gates they opened — yes, *as if in a movie!*
Schneidermann he said,
  and opened into a movietheater, a room with a screen and
don't ask Schneidermann he asked a passing drunk and his personal assistant, don't ask me they just did Schneidermann he told
me, asked me or just world what's to expect? you waste your day
living junk and you think you'll dream deep? you want me to
apologize for sleeping?
  Nothing, No and No I answered as Schneidermann he
said: *just like a movie the gates they opened and opened into a movietheater,*

a *Saal* Schneidermann he said that — in his dream — the
gates they then swung shut behind him,
> *rustily* swung,
> locked on their own,
> dark like
> don't ask,
> said as we rimmed the squared zero of Park with our feet,
> middle's edge,
> that the lobby-of-his-dreams it was empty, as empty as
Auschwitz, as the Park this far Uptown formless and void except
for a teenager who she seemed like she needed an abortion or just a
hug, and an autistic Jew in a plaid yarmulke strumming some strain
of G major over and over again on a guitar swaddled in leather —
like you wouldn't believe how disappointing Schneidermann he
said it was to leave the huge open of Auschwitz, to be liberated! to
liberate myself! and into a small,
> cramped,
> claustrophobic,
> unlit movietheater — Schneidermann he said that in,
dream, Auschwitz he was wearing his camp uniform but now in the
lobby of the, dream, movietheater it had and suddenly! lit itself
into an usher's outfit:
> monarch butterfly tied though still alive to flap around his
neck (that's how thin his neck was, Schneidermann's, I remember
that day that we circumnavigated the Park like Magellans in
Schneidermann's shoes as large as boats),
> pants starched to sails and the shoes in the dream they
were polished to young moons, fit perfectly as if cobbled from his
own bone,
> the white of his shirt Schneidermann he said like you
wouldn't believe how deloused it was! went Schneidermann's voice-
over:
> like to go from the space, the delimitation if you will of
Auschwitz to just a tiny, delimiting-like movietheater (*Kino*, in the
camp they screened cartoons and propaganda for the guards,
Monday and Thursday nights according to Schneiderman if they
weren't showing Westerns):
> like anti-life into life that's just not all that amazing
enough to offer any opposition against,

to deserve all my fight (but after all that might be interpretation Schneidermann he dismissed it as interpretation, the
lowliest discipline after history, like how I defray my tabs at the
Grand),

Schneidermann he walked down the center aisle and all was
empty,

sat down anywhere according to Schneidermann according
to his dream,

hummed some theme-music deaf to himself,

and no picture it was starting though the lights they began
to dim at the moment that Schneidermann he entered this, dream,
theater,

dimmed to pitch from the Polish-polished sun by the time
that Schneidermann he had sat down anywhere but still nothing
started, a life unbegun,

all this according to Schneidermann according to dream, in
which Schneidermann he got up and walked up the aisle to the
door, gates,

back out but it was locked, they were, tried again, locked,
again and it was locked totally, Schneidermann he was locked in,
locked in inside this one-screen fall-apart theater that he couldn't
see or at all sense (no smell of mold, no taste of fungus, the seat a
whisper up his tush, his hearing it was always a hearing-within),

except for the delousement of the screen in the pitch of
his dream, locked in too to this dream and dreams, locked in to the
movietheather as Schneidermann he was locked into his own head,

Schneidermann he said that — in his dream, dreams — he
was in there, imprisoned there for it seemed like months, an entire
winter of this dream, years even, decades! wintry ages! that in there
Schneidermann he couldn't sleep and so he couldn't dream within
dream, couldn't dream his way out, a dream against a dream it
wasn't happening, no way, couldn't sleep or even rest Schneidermann he was sleepless and restless in sleep and rest in this darkness as Schneidermann he said as we performed a two-man geriatric hora around the uppermost reservoir of Park

(Schneidermann and I we were philosophical-strolling like
we were in the Olympics, would have won the gold for the slow-
ness of our thought, Schneidermann he hated the spirit of the
Games, loved its pomp:

the

the five rings and sacred torch of 1936, of Diem and
Hitler, and Riefenstahl, God! Schneidermann he once said, what a
movie-sense that woman had!)

the dark (the sun it was getting knifed by the darkest
horizon),

the dark Schneidermann he enjoyed the way it seemed to
fill all the spaces inside of me Schneidermann he said,

and that there seemed much space, room even for the Fire
Marshall whoever he is this term the same as the last — it wasn't a
nightmare, wasn't a dream actually either, that it was somewhere
between the two that Schneidermann he would call Ishmael,

just another existence as unpredictable as this one, a
second life, and to be most precise awake in that — dream —
theater for one night that it felt like a lifetime of lifetimes Schneidermann he didn't want to sleep in his sleep, mentally resisted the
physical urge:

according to Schneidermann he felt that to sleep there it
would be too

empty, the theater it was an enormous mouth according to
Schneidermann,

Schneidermann the last tooth according to Schneidermann,

sleepless to avoid getting swallowed himself as Schneidermann he said, all — the theater it was empty more like my head,
spent the life (dream)

(dreams) just sitting in darkness like,

as if the movietheater it was the dull glassy gray arc inside
his own skull according to Schneidermann whose spirit-of-inter-
pretation,

whose desire-for-interpretation no philosophizing-against
it would ever dull,

like sense-freezing-night,

nights, or were they days upon days upon days of dream?
Schneidermann he would ask answerless me as much as himself,

wrapped shroud in filthy sheets,

old movie posters (worn-thin and stained),

and, well, stared at the empty rectangle of eyes and of eye
— movietheater's walls unknowable as if the limits of his very
mind, untested, unassured,

as the foundations they settled like studio laughter
and the seats they would squeak (twin-bed),
　　synapses unsynapsed (springs springing stuffing) — life
lost in perpetual shadow according to Schneidermann the
movietheater it had a balcony
　　of bird's wings (what birds don't ask, we were Jews who
lived in the city),
　　far,
　　distant, denying caryatids gracing its haunches,
　　and soon — after those many nights of one of this dream
— the theater itself it just disappeared,
　　walls and seats and even the dark,
　　faded like elegance, well, to pure vanishment:
　　Schneidermann himself finally, always finally, just Schneidermann in the vacant theater-of-dream-and-of-dreams
　　in which Schneidermann, well, he just attuned himself let's
say to the empty screen,
　　and thought of
　　thoughts — according to Schneidermann that late night in
the head of the Park, this is, was, where and when Schneidermann
he thought in dream in the theater-of-dream,
　　thoughts that were his or were as much his as they were
anyone's, which was enough even for Schneidermann and at-the-end
(Whitman, Emerson, the Neoplatonists and so on) — having a
dialogue with himself and his selves,
　　I/Thou-stuff,
　　and so on,
　　but in the spring, last spring and in waking life, Schneidermann he said that the dream or the dreams they, it, just ended,
stopped, and as suddenly as they, it, began:
　　CREDITS and thank you very much for your patronage
— that the last dream it was the last of the dreams that it had
happened last night,
　　that last night, the first day of spring it was and we were
walking again, doing our most thought-provoking paces in a
seminary's park, parklet up in Morningside Heights,
　　near the seminaries and the university that it nearly killed
Bartók,
　　up near Mozart's librettist Lorenzo da Ponte when he

moved

moved to the States fleeing a pedophile rap and opened an Italian
grocery there,

up around where Gershwin the George one he once lived
— it was spring, young as Schneidermann he was old and he told
me this dream,

this last dream:

sirens! Schneidermann he said, there were sirens!

honks, horns and sirens!

whispering muttering — O mutter! my mamele! — in a
to-himself stutter all about

WORKERS-OF-THE-WORLD UNTIE (Schneider-
mann he knew all the movements, was the king of the propaganda,
the flyer and pamphlet, Head Librarian of waste Schneidermann he
always took anything given-away-and-for-free),

Die deutsche Frau raucht nicht! dead slogans that Schneidermann he'd set to music out of habit, nervous, and now repeated
and repeated and repeated as if less a mania than a test of his
retention,

"Democracy means the opportunity to be everyone's slave"
(Kraus who) — old aphorisms the more singable the better
(Schneidermann he then said at nearly 100 years of age that he
just now was growing into his ear),

Schneidermann he was losing it but what if ever even was
the *it*? and *why*?

(the city it had just gotten around to demolishing the
building next to Schneidermann's, a luxury crackhouse and so
maybe)

muttering all about acts, parts and roles assumed in
adolescence if not earlier and without any understanding let alone
acknowledgment of an essential purpose being skipped,

a justification maybe implied, okay hinted-at or alluded-to
but not worked-out-and-through (don't ask, I didn't understand
and Schneidermann he),

that the noise it came — to him, for him — first, from
the outside and shattering in, as if the theater-of-his-dream it
indeed was nested in the dull sugar-gray arc of his skull (the shrink
I referred him to she went unvisited, Schneidermann he missed his
appointment, I was still billed an hour for 45 minutes that they
were never put to his betterment),

Schneidermann he said that the windows (the windows of
what? to what? Schneidermann he had only one window in his
apartment, his room facing rust and shaft and so what windows,
goddamn it?),

that all the windows they were being shuttered with
sheetrock and wood,

nails driven through layers of soft insulation, muscle, deep
into his pupils to hard flame — the emergency exit yet to be
opened at the rear of his mind,

as Schneidermann he put it that day when were walking
through the smog-hatched light of Morningside Heights in a
seminary's garden, primrose gardenlet in a walking-talking theo-
logical mood — like in each of my eyes, Schneidermann he said,
there's this countdown, you understand?

I didn't, Schneidermann he said like it's clocked, that old
Fritz Lang litany as unsubtle and so artless as everything else in his
filmmaking:

10-9-8 usw., why? but in one eye the numbers they go up,
and in the other eye the numbers they go down,

and it's not 0 to 10 or 10 to 0 (Schneidermann's zeroes
they were always Øs, always struck through with a line):

Laster Schneidermann he said to me (and Schneidermann
he hardly ever used my last name),

they're numbers I've never known before! like infinity and
in either direction Schneidermann he said, in every direction
though always opposite, and they're less numbers than they are,

God, Schneidermann he said I'm *acting* this for you!

I can't help it! but I lived it, or dreamed it or,

I'm *acting*! (Schneidermann he said *acting* like you'd say *rape
an aborted fetus*

or *genocide* or)

I woke up Schneidermann he told me as if all the tenants
who had ever lived in my building, in all the buildings on my
block, in all of the world it was as if they all and at once took up
hammers more like their distended forearms,

frozen to iron,

and to my own head: nailing wood and sheetrock over my
ears — they were all dressed in overalls, khaki and

I woke up and my landlord resplendent in inexpensive

denim

denim he was standing glaring hate like a mother at me in the
doorway, screaming at me and in Polish for my rent,

like three months overdue,

Do you want money? I asked as we dodged two — female
— students probably of gender playing neon frisbee with a scholar-
ship dog,

I got up and went to my piano Schneidermann he said,

on top of it was an envelope, my envelope I keep any
money I have in, you know (I did, it was the envelope that he had
received permission to emigrate — immigrate — in, along with a
letter signed by the Ambassador in a hand guided by the fame of
yours truly)?

it the envelope it was empty of course but I Schneidermann he said I just stared at it as Neugebauer (that was his
slumlord, who that day he was deinstalling hotwater heaters)

he was screaming at me in this language (whatever-
language-this-is),

I swear I was awake, and Schneidermann he never swore,
but as I stared at my — dirtied-with-life — envelope,

this — near, off — white rectangle as I stared at it a movie
it started playing on it, a picture began and as if I was projecting it
the picture and from my very own eyes,

and What movie was it? I asked in obbligato the question
most obvious (as opposed to Where should I have you committed?
Do you want to stop at your apartment before we entrain to the
asylum?),

I'm not going to live much longer was what Schneidermann he answered,

I'm going to die (half-lucid and half-mad like any artistic
masterpiece Schneidermann he always was),

No you won't, I said because I believed it like I believed in
nothing else, then,

And then what? Schneidermann asked.

And then silence.

Schneidermann to me: your playing gives my work life.

Schneidermann to me: you give me life.

Schneidermann to me: when you begin to play, my work
ends.

Schneidermann to me: you are the death of me.

Schneidermann to me: but what is more tragic is that I am your life.

Schneidermann to me: but you too will die and I will find another.

But will he? and what made him so certain?

as but I am so certain that that was the utterance of a man grossly unfamiliar with the time in which he lived, of a man who indeed did not wish to be familiar with the gross time in which he lived,

or that possibly our time it was unfamiliar with him, willingly unfamiliar (there's too much on teevee):

the way a mirror does not recognize another mirror (like the mirrors in the elevator of the Grand),

does not recognize, that is, without an object between them (me between the walls of the mirrors on the walls of the elevator of the Grand),

or the way in which a mirror does not recognize what's behind it, its reverse,

a mirror, a limitless limited, an illimitable Limen, a finite infinite like the huge wall-length one in my penthouse at the Grand, a walk-in closet's door of a mirror into which when Schneidermann he visited he gazed hourly, breath steaming up his Asian eyes, my enormous mirror into which when he visited Schneidermann he made mouths by the second:

his Beethoven hair — a secondhand wig he often wore like the wig of Beethoven's youth, underneath which he was bald, all skull as I told the Detective — told the Detective all about his Mozart ears though one it was larger if not higher than the other which it was lower if not smaller that Schneidermann he though only toward the end said he was and finally about to grow into,

described his Bach chin, even though the Detective he didn't ask I described, told him all about his Mendelssohnian penis, if Mendelssohn he was ever circumcised and I doubt we know Schneidermann he once said and doubted, doubt we'll ever know Schneidermann he once doubted and said.

Schneidermann to me: Europe is blue, America is white.

Schneidermann to me: no, reverse that.

Schneidermann to me: Europe is over here and America is over there.

Schneidermann

Schneidermann to me: no, reverse that.

Schneidermann to me: Europe is as far away from America
as America is from Europe,

and that this is what I know, that this is all I'll ever know
according to Schneidermann.

Schneidermann to me: but of course America is everywhere.

Schneidermann to me: but of course Europe is everywhere
too,

because when it comes down to it, everything is Europe's
fault, isn't it? because America is Europe's fault, isn't it?

and so today Europe is America's fault his, Schneidermann's, thinking went:

and so today the world can only breathe between America's
farts (and Schneidermann he farted, on my pianobench, on the
pianobench of the piano I rented and rent no more, insured it to
have it elevated to the penthouse of my hotel at which Schneidermann he farted,

poofed), and so today the world can only sense between
America's movies, between the exports of America's film industry
was his, Schneidermann's, thinking,

and so today the world it can only exist as long as I exist
his thinking went, because I am the last European, because I am
the last of the last Europeans (because no one who was born in
Europe after the War is a European Schneidermann he actually
believed),

because I survived the Holocaust Schneidermann he said
and Schneidermann did, because everyone who survived the Holocaust will be dead within the next 20 years (and that after that all
we have is the American film industry),

because I survived the Holocaust (Schneidermann he said
to me as much as to himself, to assert, to believe),

because I intend to be the last survivor of the Holocaust
left alive Schneidermann he said and actually believed, the last
living artist as well as the last living survivor of the Holocaust that
is what I intend to become Schneidermann he said still becoming,

but once and he meant it — but Europe is of course
responsible his thinking went on (it always went on, until),

that of course Europe it is responsible for America, for

the Holocaust,

and so for the American film industry and so obviously
for America itself, that everything it is Europe's responsibility,
because Europe is of course at fault,

it's all about getting to the root of it all, his thinking went.
To the roots.
To the root,

and if Europe today is America's fault and America today
is Europe's fault, then what faulted Europe prior? To the origin,
the genesis,

because the Jews they are responsible for Europe, his
thinking went that Europe it was the fault of the Jews,

and so America and Europe today they have the Jews to
thank for everything, have the Jews to fault for everything —
because there is no Europe and there is no America without the
Jews, because there never was any Europe and there never was any
America without the Jews, without the Jews according to Schneidermann Europe is inconceivable, that without the Jews according
to Schneidermann America it wouldn't exist,

and whose fault is it for the Jews? Schneidermann he once
asked I think me as much as himself on our way down in the
mirrored quaternal elevator from my penthouse to the lobby (L) I
said foyer he said Latin's *Introitus* of the Grand from the P of the
penthouse, to escape the mirror,

the rotten-lemon/roasted-almond smell of his fart —
and not that I hate the Jews, it's not that I hate being a Jew, no, it's
not that I hate myself but that this is the essential question was
what Schneidermann he said and he asked, indeed the question you
have to ask to determine who is ultimately responsible for the
world, its people and so its art Schneidermann he said and then
asked:

and whose fault is it for the Jews? I asked Schneidermann
you mean who is responsible or who are responsible for the Jews?
and Schneidermann he asked, the Jews are the fault of whom?

through the lobby I said and foyer he said of the Grand,
through the revolvingdoors both of us Schneidermann and I we
pressed 10-tight together into one revolving cubicle revolving
around twice Schneidermann he asked diffuse in the revolverous
Doppler and echo:

whose

whose fault is it for the Jews?

Our own. Once we were out on the street graven in spring, Schneidermann he said Ours.

Mine, Schneidermann would say.

Yours, I would say as he said.

Mine as a maker and yours as a remaker, Schneidermann he would say, mine as a maker (remaker)

and yours as a remaker — maker — Schneidermann he would say.

Ours, Schneidermann he would say while making the post-matinee movie argument he loved the most over mandelbrot and wild fruit tea,

over RED LABEL or BLACK LABEL WHISKY and COCA-COLA CLASSIC at the matinee movies: at the matinee movie with the archaeologist in which he finds the Ark of the Covenant, in which he finds the Holy Grail of that great Jew Jesus H. Christ, and his or His blood,

at that matinee movie with the great white shark in which it just goes wild and jaws everyone's genitals off,

at that matinee movie with the vaginal-pink triceratops in which it just let's say disburthens huge turds in the Park,

at the matinee movie with that alien on the bicycle with the glowing middlefinger it will let you sniff if you just give it enough quarters for a telephone call home,

at that matinee movie with that boy who he's really a robot who he just wants to be a boy but he can't because he's a robot,

at that matinee movie about genocide during which he, Schneidermann, remained perfectly silent and attentive,

attention the soul's natural prayer except (according to Schneidermann so said Antschel in the name of Malebranche),

the only movie we'd ever gone to during which silence it — mostly — prevailed,

Schneidermann and I we'd been kicked-out a lot, ushered-away,

at least through the first hour and 18 minutes of the *thing*

after which Schneidermann he merely got up, hiked up his pants, kneeless DICKIES, excused himself past me to the aisle, leaning almost into me with a faceless face and quite simply as my testimony would reflect disappeared, and never to be found again: not him alive and not him dead, not him ever again and, yes, I'm ruling out anything in the dimmest future:

because even if Schneidermann he *is* still alive, once disappeared he'll never return, he can't, because his return, any return, it could be as much mystical, triumphant even — Moses coming down from the mountain — as it could be embarrassing (Charlton Heston coming down from the mountain):

if Schneidermann he has nothing to show for it, no new revelations and just more time lost, no new insights and just more life wasted, more life gone, more life dead as if alive — and found, undisappeared — Schneidermann he wasn't dead already, as if Schneidermann he wasn't already and for over 50 years living without really living:

because being alive without living in a culture is actually being dead, Schneidermann he once told me that he had been dead for over 50 years, that his life it had actually been (roughly, approximately, I'm just saying that Schneidermann he said),

that his life it had been lived between 1650 and 1950:

because his music it was 1650 to 1950, because his art — and I'm not defending, taking sides, just saying what Schneidermann he said — was indeed 1650 to 1950, Schneidermann, born 1650, Schneidermann, dead 1950, Schneidermann, the 300-year-old and yet ageless man.

Schneidermann, born with Bach, dead with Schönberg. Schneidermann, born in Leipzig, dead in Los Angeles. Schneidermann, born in Europe, dead in America. Schneidermann, born a Jew. Schneidermann, dead a Jew.

Laster, born a Jew in Europe, to die a Jew in America. Maybe here. Soon.

Schneidermann's first and only wife, born in Nagyszentmiklós, Hungary, now Sînnicolau Mare, Romania, which was then actually Austro-Hungary k. u. k., dead in Birkenau, which wasn't its name in Poland (which was Brzezinka).

Schneidermann's daughters, born in Budapest (all in Pest), dead in Birkenau. My daughters, born in New York and Maine, Florida and, Florida, yes — as Schneidermann he was born in Europe but he never returned to Europe because of

what happened, because of

what

what had happened (and because Schneidermann he was as
broke as the Liberty Bell),
     as I who was born in Europe have returned there and many
times because I have to, because Europe it appreciates culture,
music, art or because it once did and it hasn't yet dropped all the
pretense (because it earns too much money off it from my fellow
— naive — Americans),
     and because the ensembles of Europe they pay as well as
they play, because the concerthalls of Europe they pay well as well,
promoters they put you up in the most luxurious hotels, showers
with soapdishes of it seems Herodian stone
     and in the toilet a little ruby sliver of button you are
welcome to press if you should ever need immediate assistance in
the bathroom (though they charge you extra based on the services
you might require, fellatio, a slip-and-fall accident I know now the
way I shouldn't),
     and all because they respect you, me — I have returned
there many times, almost too many but it wasn't Europe rather it
was Florida, yes, the Florida where Deborah, or was it Dina?
     where she was born but which she only returned to that
once: that week that the then-Misses Laster now Misses
Somethingstein or the present-Misses Somethingthal,
     Misses Somethingberg, Misses Somethingblatt anyway the
week that she persuaded — ordered — me,
     because I loved her (which I didn't),
     on threat of divorce (which happened),
     on threat of kitchen-knifing-off my endowment she
persuaded — in the imperative — me to drop all engagements
both personal (adultery)
     and professional (art)
     and, and with my money, to take her and the children, our
children and for a week, down to Florida:
     the only time that Deborah or Dina, do either of you
remember which? returned there, was back in the land (state)
     (penis) of her or their birth was when we all went there as
a family, as a nuclear-unit, as an atomized agglomeration of
humans who we shared either love (or hate, me and my then-wife)
     or DNA was when we immigrated to Disney World,
     was when we became naturalized into Disney World

(*Dizney Welt* Schneidermann he would have said),

from which I forged him, Schneidermann, an obscene postcard I signed MINNIE MOUSE (because Schneidermann he once, after a matinee Animated movie about a rabbit with rabbit-problems — it was a matinee Half-Animated, Half-Acted movie with images licensed from Steamboat Willie to Now — Schneidermann he told me that he had a weakness for female rodents in polkadots),

from Disney World from which I exported for him some headgear, imported to the quote unquote greater world outside of Disney World and expressly for Schneidermann a mousehat with ears that Schneidermann he refused to remove from his head except when it — the head, his — was otherwise sheltered.

Because he had what is known as a *thing*, and for hats. Because, and maybe it was his quote unquote observant upbringing (beards for breakfast, prayers three times a day while under his grandfather's roof),

but Schneidermann he always kept his head covered when not otherwise covered (hat on the wig on the bald amidst the wig's pulleys rusted to *vanitas vanitatum*,

or in the spring and summer of his thought just hat on the bald on the head), when outside, outdoors, except when Schneidermann he was indoors, otherwise covered, inside, otherwise sheltered by metropolitan overhangs, scaffolding, outcroppings, girders, struts and truss, stone pigeons flying overhead, hijacked airplanes, satellites, a star in conjunction — and it became his obsession, this coverage, the idea of keeping his head covered and at all times:

Schneidermann he'd enter a building (his, the Grand or a matinee movietheater)

and take off his hat, he'd exit a building (a matinee movietheater, a pre-or-post-matinee-movie-eatery)

and put on his hat, and walk — limp — down the street but if Schneidermann he walked (minced)

under a scaffold or an umbrella, he'd take off his hat, then, when out in the open again, Schneidermann he'd put his hat back on — and, soon, after the mousehat with ears it was gifted, all his time it was occupied with taking off and putting on his hat, this hat, this mousehat with ears, with placing and replacing his hat,

this

this hat, under a hijacked airplane, or a star or a planet that Schneidermann he felt (knew)

was directly above him,

like you know that astronomical phenomenon when two
stars they come into conjunction while each it still maintains its
separate identity, what's the word again?

syzygy it is, which it might as well be Hungarian or some
off-Slavic, might as well have applied to Schneidermann and I and
our own ruinous stars — and off it came again, and then, when it
the phenomenon or they the phenomena passed, on it went again,
the mousehat with ears that I'd bought with my money and
brought him from Disney World while we-the-extended-family we
were there on an extended-family-vacation, on our nuclear-unit-trip,
on that atomized-agglomeration-of-in-some-way-related-humans-
outing I was persuaded (forced)

by my wife (now exwife)

to enjoy, to undergo, to appreciate, to endure, to finance,
to survive,

the mousehat with ears that they soon wilted, got rained
and snowed on to undermine the integrity of the plastic and soon
they fell off and the hat it was discarded (without ears, Schneidermann he said, it's all worthless),

in favor of,

all his time occupied in this putting on and taking off, all
this puttingon-time and takingoff-time, all this puttingoning and
takingoffing taking up all his time and putting off all the other
and so many of them projects (operas, piano sonatas, string trios,
vocal music, matinee movies, sloth, waste and so on, O)!

the mousehat once with ears and now with no ears that it
was discarded in favor of (I showed him the album later, photographs of us all posed in front of Cinderella Castle, which was
erected in the style of the Château d'Ussé of the Magic Kingdom
of Indre-et-Loire, along with another postcard I bought but never
sent of Sleeping Beauty Castle of Anaheim, Disneyland, knowing
that Schneidermann had been out there before, back when it was
known as Neuschwanstein, refuge of Ludwig II, the Mad King of
Bavaria),

or the European fedora it was 50 years out of fashion if it
ever truly was in,

or else the beret Schneidermann he claimed that Stravinsky
he stole from him,

or the plumed turban Schneidermann he claimed that
Rembrandt he stole from him,

or maybe the baseballcap: the brim that Schneidermann he
when nervous, always, could never bend enough of the Mets hat or
was it Yankees (I forget, a sacrilege)?

that Schneidermann he maintained — and felt betrayed,
crestfallen — his favorite matinee moviemaker STEVEN
SPIELBERG he stole from him:

a hat a homeless man he maintained that Schneidermann
he stole from him and so Schneidermann he gave it to him (the
Mets or the Yankees),

the homeless man and for free and then went and borrowed some money from me, Schneidermann did (just this once!
when it came to his head no cost could be spared!), borrowed $10
from me to buy a NEW YORK FIRE DEPARTMENT hat or cap
like everyone else they were wearing in the aftermaths of that
tragedy that was and that tragedy that wasn't, in the spans of the
war that was and the war that wasn't, in the glow of the defining
event that it defined itself or else just nothing, in the end.

When the planes they hit the metal phalluses, when the
towers they were hit with, well,

you remember, and I should apologize to the police and
firemen out there, swear my respect as much as I respect anyone
but I have to tell you that, well — because when those two towers
they went down (way down-island from Schneidermann who he
hadn't heard about it any of it until a month or so after if you can
believe, his mute teevee it was dying of apathy and Schneidermann
he just bought the hat that he'd seen walking around),

yes, when those twins they went down they went down
alone.

Yes, because America is a baby as Schneidermann he always
believed, because America it is a spoiled baby, believed that
America is a spoiled baby thrown out a window,

the bathwater too Schneidermann he would joke if he ever,

from the topfloor of the towers when they were hit with
the,

well, you're either dead, remember it from surviving, or

remember

remember it from the always memorious image of the, well,

you remember, as I do — as Schneidermann he asked in
response to my asking had he heard about it? seen about it? does
he know about it? the only IT of that year in retrospect and
Schneidermann he just asked,

and asked deep into the months after,

deep during the year and two-three months after the event
that Schneidermann he was still he, undisappeared Schneidermann
he occupied his undisappearance by asking that one question that
he asked though as many questions because in the end any one
question it would not have sufficed, satisfied, was impossible to
ask alone,

asked if Dresden, does it seek revenge? Schneidermann did,
does Hiroshima? and worse, Schneidermann he asked, does
Nagasaki?

do the homeless right here at home and yet not at-home?
do the otherwise marginal? the artists? seek revenge on those
seemingly intent on their destruction? America's response much
like Germany's eventual response Schneidermann he once remarked
in a lucid moment, then-rare, much like the Nazi's response only a
few short years after that insanity at Versailles, that Schandfrieden,
that Schmachfrieden Schneidermann he said that humiliating peace
that it was 10 — trillion — times more damaging to the soul-of-
the-nation,

the Volk,

than the well-you-remember well it was to us — like do
citizens who they're suffering from diseases government-spon-
sored, do they have such recourse? those retributive options?

and what about the otherwise utility-irrelevant? like
myself, Schneidermann he asked, the terminals? like myself,
Schneidermann he wanted to know: people in unsubsidized
potholes?

those in mortal need of brandjobs? Schneidermann he got
that word *brandjob* from me who I got it from a grandson in
advertising,

Madison Avenue Schneidermann he didn't even know
where that was, is, what about those fetuses with needle problems?

men who they dye their hair the same shade as their pills?
and Schneidermann he tore at the wig under his hat the wig above

his skull, the wig on pulleys like a hairy *deus ex machina*,

enough anxiety swelling to mass-grave proportions in just-daily-life

that the two towers they seemed like, well — because America it believes in its own Constitution, because America it believes its own publicity (propaganda), in its own might according to Schneidermann who he thought, to think what other nations they have suffered and then what they've done with that suffering, to think what other nations they have survived and survived for what else, to think,

enough, enough to say, to assert that the only if not objective then action that that event and America's response to that event that they ever accomplished was in selling a 90-year-old Hungarian-Jewish immigrant a hat,

was indeed selling this 90-year-old Hungarian-Jewish immigrant a hat,

which I paid for: an overpriced FDNY hat made in Taiwan, or China, and sold by Arabs in New York.

Because the president's, because capitalist-democracy's one and only success was in the field of haberdashery,

and that verily that success it begat other successes: people they grinned when they saw Schneidermann Baedekering the street in his hat (I've never known something so retarded, so truly autistic even Schneidermann he noticed),

they full out grinned acid-white like the teeth of that mouse that it's named M-I-C, K-E-Y, mentally-impaired like fit for the gas they were inspired by a 90-year-old wearing a two-week old hat, took heart and verily people who wore the hat they formed a society of sorts, indeed a middleclass of headwear-consumers, an entire strata of society:

your dentists, your doctors and lawyers, Afghans, Pakistanis, Slonimer Hasids, trashmen from Queens and a 90-year old Hungarian-Jewish but, well, assimilated composer — assimilated *from assimilation*, Schneidermann he'd insist — who he'd once played for the Kaiser all wearing the same hat, all united in hatwearing, all bound up in hatness, in hatitude but when I told him about the towers,

I called to ask how he was holding up with the shock or was it the aftershock?

a

a month late, and from Jerusalem which I suspect that it
secretly loved the gasoline jeremiad, the strike preemptive, ap-
plauded the spectacle like Purim their Fourth of July

and Schneidermann he asked why,

and after he understood, Schneidermann he gave the hat
away to the mailman on his appointed rounds who refused it
because he the mailman he had two of his own back at home
wherever the mailman he lives:

one knock-off the mailman who he never had any mail for
Schneidermann except thin AI envelopes sheltering rejection he
told Schneidermann who he told me and, when he the mailman felt
guilty, one exactly the same, twice as expensive the second one he
bought but approved by the FDNY.

Because you out there don't only fight fires and exude raw
sexuality, you also approve hats, you license your public trust to
hats, to headwear, headgear — with the money going to the
families of the invested victims who they're now millionaires
multi-plus,

even richer than they were before the flights as if that
money it could somehow stop flight, arrest flight, the real redeye,

the televised flights, and the flight of memories into a past
— seemingly — untainted by hate,

a past (seemingly) untainted

by (seemingly) immediate threat,

into a past that — seemingly — never existed according to
Schneidermann,

because it's a flight, it's a fight as old as time itself and
older even older and oldest,

because it's a crusade as old as old:

it's the Dark Ages and the Enlightenment, the Church
against the State, my virtuoso teacher and Schneidermann my
Master who,

robots versus humans, man and then there's machine,
those who are willing to die and those who are willing to live, and
Schneidermann he was which?

and me? I'd jump on a grenade for Shakespeare, would take
a bullet for Beethoven, I'd die for Schneidermann if Schneidermann
he was still around to live or die for — and all this in reflex,
without a second thought nor even a first,

and I'd expect you to die for me if it ever came down to it, if — I'd even die for myself.

Because and according to Schneidermann all humanity it is ultimately a hierarchy of sacrifice:

your life for mine, my life for Schneidermann's — this Schneidermann he knew from the camps, from every camp and Schneidermann he was in all the camps (Schneidermann he would practice the piano, its fingerings on the withered wick of forearm of his Auschwitz barracks' bunkmate until),

Because all humanity it is a scale measuring the weight, the worth, of your soul — but who will die for you?

and that's why Jesus he or He was in the wrong, according to Schneidermann if you're interested, sorely mistaken as Schneidermann he insisted last winter as we walked around the Rockefellers' World Trade X-mas tree proud against the laden terror of Midtown wind,

as if the evergreen it was being fellated and roughly by the sky's gaping mouth moist with dark — because He got it back-wards according to Schneidermann:

the whole world it should have died for Him and not the other way around, because Jesus he or He should have been the only person to walk it the earth until the full eternity of His days according to Schneidermann walking (noctambulating)

into a semblance of eternity but instead he or He got it opposite, was mistaken in the exact inverse proportion as Schneidermann he insisted (that I buy him a candycane),

and that the span between his or His mistake and its eventual rectification with the end of this world has been what we understand as the West,

or so went Schneidermann's thought who he never be-lieved,

as what we understand as us, me and you — and but you need to understand that my awareness of this it earns me no reprieve, no exception,

no exemption from suffering its existence, my existence, me — Schneidermann, who he never prayed at all (not even in the camps, and Schneidermann he was in all of them:

was in Buchenwald, in Auschwitz, Washington Heights).

Me, who only prays when I want something I can afford

though

though shouldn't buy.

My daughter, the female rabbi who she presumably prays every day.

Schneidermann's grandfather, the — lay — rabbi who he presumably prayed three times a day for a Messiah who would never arrive,

for a Messiah who had already arrived and, 33 years after his or His arrival, had made the greatest mistake possible at least according to Schneidermann,

and yet if *Schneidermann's grandfather* the — lay — rabbi had made a mistake, the smallest, most insignificant infraction (in his prayers, in his observance),

it was just *more* praying and *more* observance (also open to mistakes, to infractions and those mistakes and infractions to microcosmic mistakes and infractions more unto),

it was fasting until sundown for a month just like the Muslims who they hate us and at all times,

not just during Ramadan, their month of prayer now fasting on the winter of ours, year of their Lord 1423 — the Muslims who they keep their heads covered, the Jews who keep their heads covered, the 90-year-old Hungarian-Jewish composer who he'd once composed a piece in the style of Chopin that fooled even the likes of Rubinstein, who he'd once and early on distinguished himself by losing the Anton Rubinstein Composers' Contest (with a piece he'd entered written by Chopin), and who'd once worn and worn well an FDNY hat until he realized that all of New York they stole it from him and he tried to foist it off on the mailman (who he never had any mail for him, save professional regrets),

but couldn't and so Schneidermann he just used it as an ashtray.

Schneidermann who for the last year of his life here at least he didn't smoke anymore but who anyway provided no less than 10 — stolen-from-various-post-matinee-movie-spots — ashtrays in his excuse for an apartment for the sole use of yours truly.

Schneidermann who for the last 10 years of his life here at least he didn't

engage in sexual intimacy as Schneidermann he would put it anymore

      but who still provided me with a set of keys to his apartment — room — to use at any time for various amorous assignations,

      who he didn't even

      defecate as Schneidermann he would put it much anymore

      but who still kept his shared bathroom stocked with all the classics of German philosophy in case I felt the urge to sit while visiting.

      Schneidermann who he didn't even

      play-the-piano much anymore as he would put it — the last month or three of his life here where — and who also didn't want to disturb his sexually-industrious,

      dios-mio-invoking,

      Sunday-night-liquorious,

      three-a.m.-five-fisted-spousal-abusing

      Spanglish neighbors downstairs and so who ripped all the strings right out of his upright piano, less a pianoforte than a piano, less a piano than a pianino and less a pianino than a pianette, whatever Schneidermann he ripped all the strings out of it so that he could still play it but now only silently, in silence, fingering the keys and just hearing the result, the work-product, the music in his own head like when Schneidermann he kept dexterous, limber and in-practice in Auschwitz running scales on his barracks' bunkmate's forearm (left, thin-as-an-eyelash),

      and after that millennium — non-millennium — and the world it didn't end,

      after that plane/tower event (non-event)

      and the world it didn't end, Schneidermann he'd often when I could bring myself to actually enter his room (mess, disaster-area, oblast-of-insanity),

      Schneidermann he would often play me some of his new or old or just pieces of his by playing them on his stringless upright piano, his unstrung upright piano and then ask me what I thought, and I had to answer.

      Schneidermann to me: you hear that?

      Schneidermann to me: shhh! this is the best part!

      Schneidermann to me: hear the transition? Oy papi! Masterful.

Schneidermann

Schneidermann to me: the señorita downstairs just had a
baby and so I have to play like this. Or not play like this.
Schneidermann to me: you're not the father, are you?
Schneidermann to me: hear the inversion?
Schneidermann to me: so what do you think?
but you wouldn't know, would you?
because you, you need stars like the Trinity that Nicene
mishegas as Schneidermann he often said,
four stars, five like a bright wealth seeking constellation
(LIVE LIKE THE STARS! And then fall.),
two enthusiastic opposable thumbs up,
Zagat guides like Phlegyas the ferryman taking you across
East 68th Street to,
like you're to eat the praise with your money as garnish,
a limo, factory-wrapped in necklaces,
a girl with a pearl, no — an obolus perched on her neck
for a head
(all's fare in love and war!), a son with diamonds for eyes
who he tells me that my music it's worthless, that my Schneidermann he's worthless or was, Noah, that in the end, of the now that
art that it's worthless, don't you?
and he's right, but you aren't right in the way you think
you are, Noah — because you need to sin to repent,
because you need to die to live (and isn't that a shame?
Schneidermann he'd say a *Schande*),
because you need to have been there, though I wasn't, at
that most European soirée, on that night most European when
Schneidermann — who was a spine with some skin on it, even
through the soprano-fat opera-years of banquets and tribute
feasting when and where he ate like Fort,
Dionysus — like that night in Berlin, in Europe
1930something I forget as I wasn't there, 1930something it was
when Schneidermann he told it, when Schneidermann he and by his
own account and accounts was at the Baron's who'd joined the
Party not three days prior, the Baron who he liked Schneidermann,
indeed loved him because he thought though erroneously that he
was the Baron in and from *The Goat*,
which the Baron he undoubtedly was if he wanted to
support me, Schneidermann he once remarked,

let the Baron think that he was the Baron on whom the
Baron in the opera was based, the Baron of Schneidermann's one
and only opera *The Goat,*

the most minor noble he was immensely flattered and
why? and so often invited and less often had its composer over for
dinner at which, the last dinner, Schneidermann he exclaimed like a
schoolgirl or a homosexual public school music teacher over that
new lapel pin of his! Schneidermann he asked him the Baron where
he got it from? that interesting four-pronged, was it Indian-with-a-
dot or was it Indian-with-a-feather design?

and where could I get something like that? Schneidermann
he asked, or is it a custom-job?

and who knew how to answer? how seriously to take
anything in those days?

Schneidermann to me: the dinner it was perfect, all their
dinners they were perfect,

as Schneidermann he said to me one night at another
dinner, my treat as always at a fancy Frenchtalian restaurant of
some international repute (chef a past winner of the MICHELIN
BIBENDUM drizzled in infanticide saliva and presented raw on a
ragout of shredded VISAs and MASTERCARDs accompanied by a
most agreeable 1954 Chateau Latour).

Schneidermann to me: what were those mushrooms that
the Baroness she served as *Vorspeisen?*

Schneidermann to me: God who remembers, shiitake?

Schneidermann to me: no, they were ceps.

Schneidermann to me: no, not ceps, but definitely not
shiitake.

Schneidermann to me: they were really, truly delicious,
maybe boletus (and the waiter as attentive as a graduate student he
asked me if my father he needed some water,

no, not water, EVIAN).

Schneidermann to me: no, on second thought they must
have been trompettes — shaped like the instrument, like Gabriel's,
like Buddy Bolden's or was that a cornet?

like Louis Armstrong's, Dizzy's, Miles' though,

like the Baroness sneezing all night through her two fluted
nostrils all stuffed up with seasonal sinus problems, which it
wasn't necessarily a tragedy (and maybe the Baroness she was just

allergic

allergic to Jews according to Schneidermann),

because even in those days Schneidermann he smelled terrible, seating one seat away from him at the matinee Holocaust movie you'd think that you were sitting next to a goat,

and how Schneidermann he ate and drank! a soundtrack unto itself! because you need to have personally played an all-Mozart recital for an audience including one Oskar Schindler in 1933 or 1934 in Berlin before you can walk out of his matinee movie in America later on in the century,

as Schneidermann he did (and remembered the man, then an entrepreneur fresh off failure, from newspaper photographs reprinted, appearing just after the matinee Holocaust movie it was initially released,

would never forget it was that same face, opera-fat, that same satisfaction),

yes,

as Schneidermann the pianist he did, Schneidermann the virtuoso pianist, as Schneidermann the genius musician and genius artist and genius matinee moviegoer he did: once met that *Schinder* meaning *slavedriver*,

taskmaster and,

at an all-Mozart recital that Schneidermann he once maintained he played in Berlin in Schöneberg at the Baron's villa in the musicroom packed like a Jew's deportation luggage amid the opera and the fame as Schneidermann he once told me when the matinee Holocaust movie it first was released 10 years previous to his disappearance when I asked him to go, not to disappear on his own but to disappear with me, accompanied by me and our disappearance into the matinee Holocaust movie to which Schneidermann he refused and (again, his shoes),

because you need to have witnessed, personally, him Schindler all suspicious elegance in borrowed, collaborative tux-and-tails fingering his date's vaginal orifice dripping empoisoned milk-and-honey (not his wife, a redhaired, paprika-freckled Hungarian girl actually it was according to Schneidermann),

Schindler's silver like a swan's lake watch on a wrist metronome-ticking second by second its way up her skirt while you, Schneidermann, you're just trying your hardest to *interpret*,

because you need to have, personally, heard him Schindler

yawn to have any opinion,

 Schneidermann in the *Sonata No. 8*, K. 310 in A minor in the opening of the *Allegro maestoso*

 as Schindler's mouth it opened wide as God to swallow the moon (smoke-stained chandelier),

 because you need to have seen him Schindler fall asleep in his chair in the style once known as Empire an arm or a bow's length away from you before you can pass any judgment,

 because you need to have heard his lightest, most intellectual applause,

 like a hummingbird masturbating — after his date he was cheating on too she woke him up with a Wolf's Lair whistle in his ear (left) — to know,

 and so when your history as a member of a race, a religion, or just as an individual is dictated to you and by the American film industry at the end of the most diseased century ever or just the beginning of the next-most-diseased-century-ever, you understand: that Schindler he didn't respond to that music either (don't worry, you're not alone),

 that it registered nothing with him — it was showing only in that matinee movietheater in the West 60s of Manhattan and for only that 10th-anniversary week,

 a resurrection of only five days total or maybe seven if they held it over over the weekend (though I don't remember and),

 of an entire history and its loss the greatest in — recorded — history though I've myself audienced the thing,

 the travesty,

 moving-picture-abortion, if I have to admit, and I must as if this isn't a recital or concert but a 12-step-meeting at which (doctors-orders, lawyers-orders, judges-orders, the pills and the whiskey and),

 something like 6 — million — times since on various Asiatic technologies up at my penthouse at the Grand and on-the-road in,

 and yes, okay, sure there are problems with the artwork just like there're problems with any with every work-of-art as Schneidermann he'd be the first to admit, that nothing's perfect and that that's why it's great, what makes it great, indeed that art that it's nothing but an artifice,

even

even if especially if you've invented a system however
elaborate to defend it and all its propositions as well (like the
Nazis they did Schneidermann he'd always remind me),
    that everything in moving-pictures, it just has to move
quick enough that you'll never notice, that I'll never:
    like those trains chug-chug steaming through Poland on
tracks just under the American scopes as Schneidermann he'd
always remind me,
    yes, that there are always those weirdnesses in an artwork
like this one, those little irreconcilables of the work-of-art, absur-
dities of production, deadlines and rushed schedules seemingly
negligible though not with what memory is nowadays,
    that there are always those on-set-strangenesses I've found
out upon audiencing and reaudiencing this one matinee Holocaust
movie up at the Grand in my penthouse the P,
    like connectivity if you will or continuity problems like
for example, yes, they're always the result of shoddy editing,
    poor composition attempting to coalesce pure invention as
Schneidermann he always explained it to me, his process or non-
process and
    that, yes, what with all those reels and all that cutting,
editing it ends up sometimes the matinee movie does and its flow
or lack-of-flow
    with something that almost resembles the multiple
exposures,
    flip-style of early photography, even now in the modern
Schneidermann he once noted upon our exiting a matinee Age-of-
Enlightenment movie full of dukes and duchesses, filched pearl
necklaces and,
    like for example, since I've audienced and reaudienced it
and rereaudienced it privately again and again and again and all in
search of some idea,
    some inkling,
    something to go on Schneidermannwise — for example if
you're interested, and you should be I've noticed that in
SCHINDLER for one the placement of that actor, of Kingsley-
Stern's arm around a one-armed worker as essential as everyone else
at the D.E.F., well, it's inconsistent from shot-to-shot, inconstant,
there around his shoulders one moment and around his waist in

another just for example,

just strange that scene of fellowship however fleeting on
the saving floor of the DEUTSCHE EMAILWAREN FABRIK,

also I've noted errors of a factual nature they appear like
that Irish or Scot, that anyway vaguely Hyperborean his name it's
Liam Neeson as Schindler and his wearing and proudly of his
Golden Nazi Party badge or pin it was that he could have sold it to
save more Jews but he didn't but, in truth, point-of-factually he the
real Schindler he was never awarded that pin ever as I've — since
— been told by a friend an acquaintance,

and anyway only a few of those badges they were ever made
of gold-plated brass (the Nazis they were sometimes as cheap as
the Jews if not cheaper),

and anyway Neeson-Schindler in the matinee Holocaust
movie I've noticed through the accommodating offices of PAUSE
that he's in point of fact wearing the larger military version of that
Goldenes Parteiabzeichen and not the smaller civilian version that
he would have worn had he been awarded it to begin with which
again he wasn't and,

other examples of poor connectivity or continuity if you
will they abound,

as Schneidermann would say, *mushrooms after the rain* — like
when Neeson-Schindler he goes to kiss the Jewish girl who she's
up in his office to thank him on the behalf of the formless Jewish
God it might seem, and he Neeson-Schindler he puts his hands on
her cheeks but in the next shot pulls his hands away from her
shoulders like with him Neeson-Schindler you have to ask where
were those hands in the meantime? the non-meantime? I asked
roomservice at the Grand but they didn't know,

tipped the young man a palmful of lint and sent him on
his way — like when that boy whoever he is I forget because I
always fall asleep on the floor of my penthouse, wrapped in the
monogrammed — G — house robe before the CREDITS they
roll,

anyway, when he the boy is caught by the Nazis as boys
who are forgotten they always are he drops his suitcase next to his
feet but when we cut back to him a moment later the bag it's like
ten feet away,

for example I've noticed too late at night at the Grand

with

with the REWIND rewinding and presenting again,
  like PLAY and there's world,
  one arrow nearer to death,
  screwups for example like when Neeson-Schindler he's
negotiating with potential Jewish investors in their car and the
camera and its cameraman they are and clearly reflected in the
passenger window of the car that they're negotiating in, visible,
  yes, I hit REWIND and REWIND and REWIND again
and again and again,
  the two arrows giving you life you've already lived but it
might be worth it when, if you know the alternative (death),
  yes, over and over again that image in reverse:
  indeed it's SPIELBERG himself who's reflected, and in a
hat or — baseball — cap or whatever, its legend CLASS OF 61
like the one that Schneidermann he wore but only later FDNY
2001 that's reflected in that passenger, side, window in that car in
Kraków in it's supposed to be the 40s when,
  yes, it's SPIELBERG showing real class
  in issues of connectivity or continuity like Judaism itself
it's supposed to address,
  like when Neeson-Schindler he's reprimanded by an SS
officer I think his name it was Schermer like some music publisher,
  reprimanded for giving that kiss to that Jewish girl who
she was up to the office, the SS officer who I think his name it was
Scherner played by some Pole or another they're all the same he
picks up his coffee cup twice in the same line but which line I
forget,
  little things, bare negligibles, yes, but together all-falsifying,
  like at some trainstation or another, who knows? destination death and departure now, at some trainstation, yes, where
Neeson-Schindler he arrives and just in time to save Kingsley-
Stern from deportation as an officer, who knows who he is?
  I'm asleep by the CREDITS, he's seen flipping through
his roster, through pages upon pages of names, of dead names on
his own lesser list but all the pages upon pages upon pages they're
all exactly the same, like Xeroxed and by some college intern as I've
noticed with my thumb aching numb in the prison of PAUSE,
  like when Neeson-Schindler he's in bed with his wife

Emilie-Caroline Goodall like the woman who she talked to the apes,
    like Schindler who he's talking to her as his head it's resting on her his wife Emilie who'd outlive him, yes, but in the next shot when she leans up and turns over to talk to him Schindler he's a lot further away than he was previous,
    and like why? like when they the Schindlerjuden at the end, before the CREDITS when they sing that song that it's called *Jerusalem of Gold*
    like it wasn't composed by that woman Naomi like a judge I forget her last name until years upon years after the War,
    like the gold then it wasn't in Jerusalem, God! the gold it was in their very mouths!
    like when some office lackey in the DEUTSCHE EMAILWAREN FABRIK, like when he like the intern he is is first seen painting the word DIREKTOR onto the door to Schindler's office, Neeson's trailer it's originally in a serif font if you've noticed but in a subsequent shot the word DIREKTOR it's shown in a sans-serif,
    a font like a stencil like the man Schindler he really was,
    like when Ralph Fiennes-Goeth he's originally introduced to us in TITLES it's as a 2nd Lieutenant, an Untersturmführer if you'll say it with me, but on his uniform he has the rank insignia of an Obersturmführer, a 1st Lieutenant if you didn't know on the leftmost collar of his uniform and that of a Hauptscharführer — or Sturmscharführer in the Waffen-SS — if you're following, which indeed was what he was (was a Captain, as indicated on his epaulets with two silver pips and two scars of stripe),
    like also I've found out from an acquaintance who he cashed a whole lot of money to consult on the film,
    a fellow Schindler-Jew and old American friends with the Auschwitz survivor and one of the matinee Holocaust movie's producers who got him the gig,
    the man's name it's Lustig who he also played the maitre d' in the matinee Holocaust movie's opening sequence, well, I've heard it from him who he's an old acquaintance of mine who he once sold me a yacht that an exwife she's since sunk first into disrepair and then into Sag Harbor
    that no, that Hauptscharführer, Hauptsturmführer Fiennes-Goeth that in point of fact Fiennes-Göth that he didn't

shoot

shoot random prisoners from the balcony of his house in the camp
then at Płaszów, indeed that his house it still stands, and that the
location of the camp indeed it's still known and so we don't need
SPIELBERG's revisionist history however visionary,

revisionary and (Špilberk, Schneidermann he once mentioned, that castle in Moravia that imprisoned all those conscien-
tious objectors to Austro-Hungary from the First World War,
Spielberg Castle in Brno, which was Brünn, Schneidermann he once
reminded himself, which the Nazis later rebuilt, reconstructed into
a fortification worthy of any matinee movie),

indeed, according to my acquaintance who he was also and
for longer this Lustig's good friend, the camp it's on the other side
of a hill the house faced and still faces and so Fiennes-Goeth he
couldn't have seen any prisoners from his balcony, couldn't then
have taken aim and shot,

and so killed them,

however my old friend the Schindler-survivor his name it's
Lipkin or Lipschitz I forget which he said that Fiennes-Goeth that
he did indeed shoot prisoners and at random from the top of the
hill, its summit, and that he did indeed parade around his balcony
and with a rifle, was indeed a schmuck but a schmuck as he was
and not as he was portrayed by an actor who you just knew he was
giving a performance,

just earning his bread,

5-minute-breaking bread and then you're back on the set,
in costume and character just like the Nazis they were, Take 6 —
million — and Action!

like when Neeson-Schindler he's talking all about sending
these gifts, like thank-yous, these sacrificial offerings, all these
personalized amenity baskets for the corporate-death-set,

to Nazis higher-up Nazis — did he send a card too? sign
it himself?

all those bribes bought to buy the bribed and all with
Jewish-money, always,

like when Neeson-Schindler he ticks off that list that was
his tongue:

not Hudes or Kohn, Neeson-Schindler he's not naming
names, instead he's listing all these delicacies, rarities, specialties-
of-the-West,

like boxed teas are good enough for them Neeson-
Schindler he says, and coffee, pate, um, kielbasa sausage, cheeses
and caviar,

and of course who could live without German cigarettes?
Neeson-Schindler he says, asks, well, I think I know someone,
6million-whos (Schneidermann he thought Auschwitz it would
help him stop smoking but),

and some fresh fruit, they're real rarities according to
Schindler according to Neeson:

oranges, lemons, pineapples, yes, I need several boxes of
German cigars, the best Neeson-Schindler he says again and again
(REWIND after REWIND after),

and dark, sweetened chocolate, yes Neeson-Schindler he
says: we're going to need lots of cognac, only the best Neeson-
Schindler he says, HENNESSY,

DOM PERIGNON champagne,

get L'ESPADON sardines and, O, yes, he Neeson-
Schindler remembers, try to find nylon stockings,

like yes, Neeson-Schindler yes he actually says
HENNESSY,

names names after all, Neeson-Schindler he's not afraid,
then goes ahead and stacks bottles of the cognac behind him but not
the original bottle that it was taller and with a different label but the
new shape, released on the American market only in the 1990s,

new-bottle-old-cognac, right?

like the Holocaust and product-placement, product-
positioning, together-at-last and why not?

like how much did they the producers make? how much
did HENNESSY pay? did they cater the wrap party?
SPIELBERG's son's bar-mitzvah?

baffling continuity issues like the position I've also noticed
embedded (what Schneidermann he would say were he in bed),

propped up on my elbows and grinding my hardness
among the sheets and the pillows while,

baffling connectivity issues like the positioning of one of
Fiennes-Goeth's arms as he delivers his lines to Helen Hirsch the
maid in Fiennes-Goeth's house at the camp then at Płaszów,

the maid who Fiennes-Goeth he saved from Selektion,
Helen Hirsch, Embeth Jean Davidtz is her real name, the actress'

it sounds like a Jewish name but she's not,

just her name is it seems, Davidtz, the name that I'm not allowed to forget,

that I can't, that I'm court-ordered in-absentia and just last week to remember

and to differentiate,

you-from-you, the actress from the real in that basement in that house at that camp then at Płaszów, before Fiennes-Goeth he beats her, Davidtz, just out of the shower and drip-dripping with the wet of a Jew,

Jewish nipples pulsing like aroused Stars of David,

of Davidtz and, yes, Helen! that's who I want to remember to you, her name it was Helen Hirsch, it is, God! I should apologize in public, shouldn't I?

remember to you all out there how her husband, how her entertainment-lawyer-husband who he issues injunctions to get starlet pornography off the Internet and,

how he just wanted it all, to get all this hushed up and in a quote dignified fashion if that's ever possible, dealt with quickly and in a quote respectable, professional manner,

Helen, how I should apologize for all that embarrassment, should I at all?

just know that I didn't mean to,

that it was done for me as much as for Schneidermann,

an obsession I just had to exorcise, that it began when Schneidermann he ended, for me, and in enough innocence that,

all that telephoning it began as two weeks ago, yes, indeed it was innocent enough, I just wanted to do lunch, maybe dinner, but no, you refused or your agent did for you, didn't pick up the phone, return messages and why? then some light stalking, still it was relatively innocuous, the hiring of a private detective who since,

surveillance photographers who they'd done apprentice-ships at the studio of the great Luigi Paparazzi,

and that wire-tap which,

then last week or so ago I was out in L.A., doing an evening of Western Humanism with the Philharmonic to benefit geriatric AIDS (or were they FAS babies?),

surprising you, Helen-Embeth if I may, if you're watching, in that dressingroom of yours on the set for that film that I

think maybe it was SIMON MAGUS (don't worry, it'll get
decent reviews),

   or at least I felt like him, like Simon, in that I'd gone too far
too as my lawyer he said as his lawyers they said, well, didn't you?

   me having to bribe like a Schindler, having to buy my way
in to your trailer, pay-off Security, shaved-head-like-Auschwitz lot
heavies and just to get a peek at her in her trailer, a Gulfstream,

   to maybe have a chance to kiss your cheek like,

   no, to sniff at her undergarments — Helen, God! if you're
watching if you're listening if you're out there tonight:

   you were so good in that matinee Holocaust movie that I
admit that I watch it on video or on DVD, which is an acronym for
DIGITAL VIDEO DISC or whatever they have now at the Grand
in the P of the penthouse,

   whenever I have a chance I do it, I watch her as a matinee
but alone, without my Schneidermann and always too late,

   Helen that day I walked in I wanted to walk in on you, in
your trailer you were there, yes, if in the shower,

   then Security, the police, lawyers and,

   I had my whole speech prepared my whole spiel, my love
declared in sentences and sentiments familiar enough to most,

   not this but all those lines that they could have been
written by a Goeth, not some hack named Zaillian, the screenwriter
SPIELBERG hired — huge money — to punch up the extermina-
tion scenes and,

   O Helen, I came there to the set that day and to tell you
that you really are a wonderful cook is what Fiennes-Goeth said,
yes,

   I've memorized it all, and a well-trained servant I wanted
to add, and I mean it, Helen, like if you ever need a reference after
the War, well, I'd be happy to give you one,

   and know that that offer it still stands — like sometimes
it went we're both lonely,

   I thought as I sniffed and licked my way through her
drawers as you were showering in the shower in your trailer, a
Gulfstream,

   all that lace prim as a schoolmarm I rubbed and I sniffed
and I licked, yes,

   I mean, I would like so much if the script went to reach

out

out and touch you in your loneliness, like what would that be like?
asked the movie,

was what I wondered like a miscast Lieutenant as I went
through your purse: tampons and three cellphones (labeled pen-on-
tape HOME, SET and JASON),

tropical fruit chewing gum and a baby's sock, pink — I
mean what would be wrong with that? Fiennes-Goeth he asked you
as I wanted to ask you for me and for Schneidermann, Helen, as I
asked my lawyer to ask his lawyers as,

like Helen like Embeth (and is that short for Emma or
Emily or Elizabeth or Beth and Amber

or just embers?)

like Helen, like I know that she's the fake Helen Hirsch,
the actress acting, actressing as I told the judge through my lawyer
through his lawyers but that she's the only real Helen for me
(as she was showering and toweling I launched a thousand
ships out of my testicles and onto that dark Wardrobe skirt), that
she was Helen, is, indeed needs to be to vindicate not the matinee
Holocaust movie but just my belief in it, its justification for
Schneidermann and his disappearance,

yes, to me she's not the actress with that husband who he's
an entertainment lawyer too with the firm of Hansen, Jacobson,
Teller, Hoberman, Newman, Warren, Sloane that's him your
husband JASON and Richman Llp. yes, we've all been in touch,

indeed she needs to be Helen and not the actress who she
drives a Mercedes E320 (that cost me too much to find out, the
private eye or dick if you want he wiped his nose with my personal
check),

who she has two cats, named Sebastian and Sarah and a
dog, a bull terrier that he's named Frank that she got from her
exboyfriend that Jew he's an actor named Harvey Keitel if you
know him,

and a much more accomplished actor than that Fiennes-
Goeth who he said as I wished to say that I — we — realize that
you're not a person in the strictest sense of the word,

the word it was *person*,

I mean, when they compare you to vermin and to rodents
and to lice, I just,

and Fiennes-Goeth how he then strokes her hair, yes, I've

audienced it something like 6 — million — times just lying on my
bed, embedded in New York with my eyes vacationing in Poland,
    wintering in film,
    rehearsed it into my mirror I asked again and again as
Fiennes-Goeth he asked on perpetual REWIND, like is this the
face of a rat? Fiennes-Goeth he asks her, Helen, as much as the
screen, like are these the eyes of a rat? asked of the flat,
    like Helen Hirsch-Embeth Davidtz of a Venice more West
like Hath not a Jew eyes?
    then Fiennes-Goeth he puts a hand on her, on your starred
tit, like I feel for you, Helen,
    on a rehearsal break from the L.A. Philharmonic, we were
doing Beethoven two weeks ago and just as I launched all my seed,
    I had an hour until I had to be back at the hall and
suddenly — it's all these lawyers! these rulings and restraints!
orders and injunctions!
    like when they negotiate for you toward the end of the
matinee Holocaust movie: Goeth who he wants to take you away to
Vienna as his personal maid, a María, like the madman he was,
    Schindler who he wants to take you back with him to his
hometown of Brinnlitz, Czechoslovakia that it was on the border
with Poland and how they go and play cards for you (and how
Schneidermann had he stayed for that scene how he would have
loved that! that gaming and loving it's all a wager, all art, his habit
on my money and),
    and how everyone wins! how she survives! yes, you've
survived! not aging, no Helen, not at all,
    Helen, you're always that age, she's always young, perpetu-
ally shivering (maybe that's how she keeps so slim),
    forever vulnerable, yes, you're a Polish Jew and not some
hack actress 5 foot 8 inches born in 1966 a native of Lafayette,
Indiana not that I've been there (if my expensive surveillance is
Gospel),
    husband to JASON, attorney-hero of Troy, now pregnant I
think, and by who I wonder?
    and due any moment,
    60 years too late for who you were to me, who you are,
were supposed to be (*Hello, you've reached Jason and Embeth* your
machine it always picked up,

                                                              whispered

whispered failure into my ear and then BEEP),
        60 years later and Schindler's ears — interred in Israel —
they're just hearing the deep intestinal workings of enormous
antediluvian worms,
        annelid-writhing underneath the feet of survivors,
        marching over the Jerusalem hills paved in faux gold,
        all those feet in GUCCI,
        feet in PRADA,
        feet up the ass of the goddess NIKE,
        in KEDS even — Schneidermann's label — on the feet of
all these, yes, Schindler-enabled,
        dancing-on-the-grave,
        next-generation Jews:
        at their ritual-circumcisions, bar-mitzvahs, aufrufs,
firstborn-redemptions,
        lifecycle events is what they say now but only if they've taken
out appropriate
        celebration-insurance against videographer failure or a
        hired-dancer pulling a hamstring (not kosher) — Jews
RSVP'd as the Germans like to say to place stone-centerpieces on
the graved tables,
        to mourn a loss of identity as much as no seconds on the
brisket or chicken,
        weddings like a daughter's at which — and between a band
and a DJ set — a string-quartet they played that she a daughter
had hired on a friend-of-daughter's deaf recommendation and I
(still amazed that I was even invited)
        was there,
        well-tailored, groomed and perfumed as if for a Viewing
— my own — I was asked by the 2nd violinist to sit-in, to play
with the quartet and, well, I declined,
        wouldn't despite when my daughter she asked me and
then her mother, my exwife, one of my exwives she asked too (they
only invited me I suspect because they'd wanted me to come, my
talent too),
        told them that I'd never play ensemble, that I never play
with other people,
        ever but then another daughter's daughter, my grand-
daughter, one of my granddaughters this one her name's Shayna she

went up to me, at 5 years old she went up to the wrinkle of face on
my knee and asked through no teeth like my Schneidermann, well,

> *The men they play the viol?* and yes I said,
> *You play the viol like the men?* and I decided why not to say yes,
> *So you why don't you play the viol with the men?*

Shayna she asked and so I picked her up, took her out
from the party and across the parquet of the dancefloor,
    among the shattered tambourines,
    ruined maracas,
    party-favors and,
    the errant balloons blown up inside blown up balloons and
balancing her, Shayna my granddaughter on my shoulders I took her
out of the synagogue's socialhall, halls to the synagogue's lobby
    then out the synagogue's door and into the parking lot
where I put her on top of an Asianmade automobile,
    left her there on the hood and returned inside, into the
synagogue and to the rabbi's study where I had left locked my
violin and had the janitor open the door,
    with my violin I returned to the parking lot and my
Shayna sprawled out in her silverest dress on the hood of the
gilded Asianmade automobile,
    it was already late, not as late as now but enough and
especially for her — yes, Shayna, you were already asleep (and it's
way past your bedtime tonight!),
    suckling thumbs as I circled the car, playing my violin for
you:
    old lullabies set to words I didn't sing to remember them
which she'd, you'd anyway never understand (should I sing?),
    no, you wouldn't,
    circled the car as you slept light in your rubiest slippers,
    with my violin case
        like a grave
        open
        on the asphalt
        for any coins
            the sky
            it might have rained down.

THE CHILDREN'S CHORUS

Is the son coming up, which one? Everyone have cafeteria coffee on hand?

I'll bring the salt,

and Dina laughs, beautiful girl, *shayna punim* Schneidermann would say — it's all babble to you.

What can I do for you? Dina dear and if you weren't my daughter I'd be doing you after the show in my suite,

but that's not couth, no — I'd pluck you pizzicato, those nipples, I shouldn't.

Are you still dating that schmuck of a lawyer and if so, why? what do you see in him? Certainly not me.

You scream in such high and natural harmonics, I forgot.

No, daddy will not come down and hold you, though he wants to.

And why not a policeman for you, a fine husband? There are many here tonight, almost too many too young. No, not appropriate — with all the work I have to do, what do you think you, not you, pay me for? pay for me?

prostitution maybe — but I've never paid for sex just for love, not that I haven't had the opportunity but that I don't want to increase the surety that whores they must set in the patronage of artists (so said Schneidermann, who he bought them bouquets instead).

And then I made a mistake I won't ever let myself regret, I married.

And married and married and married again and again.

And had daughters. Daughters and divorces. Stuff money in their mouths and still they'll pant for more.

And then the psychologists family and private,

and I ended up having all too many, daughters and shrinks: in the 60s, in the 70s, even in the 80s and 90s, my 70s and 80s and,

in 70s fashions they looked sumptuous, in 80s fashions equally sumptuous, just updated for the 90s fashions in which and when they looked as sumptuous as ever and on into the newest millennium. In which my girls they are absolutely stunning — how

I'd tell them that and they never listened, you never did, understood, took it to heart:

it was always too fat — it had to be — too anorexic, bulimia-teeth, nose too long, ears too droopy, like what do they expect from their genes, most importantly why do they believe it? when all they have to do is to look in the mirror, the best mirror:

me, their father, who loves them as much as he can,

who loves you,

as much as I can, I've done my best do you hear me?

your father who sings through all the pained long-distance silences, person-to-person from all the great capitals of the world:

Antwerp, Buenos Aires, Cleveland, Dresden, Elmira, Frankfurt, Gettysburg where I once played the anthem at some teevee ceremony honoring Union and Confederate widows last-living, Hamburg, Ithaca, Jupiter, Kansas City, Leningrad no more, Montreal, New York, New York,

capital of the Ego, the jutting brain of a truly, and unfortunately, diseased body just floating in the Atlantic (the Dutch Schneidermann always said, how they used Manhattan, New Amsterdam only to warehouse, for trade, for money, and how nothing's changed!)

here where I take taxis everywhere I go because I'm a patron of the arts,

here in this stifling salon where the old dog on the recordlabel merely humps the dead gramophone like it's a job, dead-end, it needs in order to finance any higher aspirations.

Dreams, in the American sense of the word.

Which are, Mister Rothstein you're still here, needless to say, and Maestro Levine, unattainable.

Daughter Nina's higher aspiration: violinist, a soloist like her father, like me who when I told her in all honesty that she wouldn't make it she took it rather well, then wanted to be a violist, a soloist and then, realizing that that too was unattainable but on her own, just any ordinary violinist or violist in any ordinary orchestra and now: a professional Jewish fundraiser.

Daughter Dina's higher aspiration: to be the first female president of the U.S. of A. and now: a housewife and occasional freelance interior designer, landscaping queen.

Daughter Lena's higher aspiration and, yes, I listen to you:

Harvard

Harvard, then some sort of anthropology and now: attended NYU when Harvard they passed on her, soon moved to Provo, Utah, as a wife, mother of three who plays the organ at the church she converted to.

Son Amiel's higher aspiration, and this one is difficult for me:

painter, world-loved but not, he would add, world-understood and now:

paints signs-for-hire, like ARNIE'S DINER, DEAL LAUNDROMAT and HIRSCH, HIRSCH & HIRSCH, ATTORNEYS-AT-LAW.

Son Michael's higher aspiration, and this is the hardest: Michael, he wanted to be a poet, world-worshipped with lines like

Excavating
          the nose-church, something something something it goes
Meal
is the curb I remember one went

and

Wasp traffic I think
          (within the sphere of)
mental deficit

the partibirth of
forms thinned through and, well, I forget

or

motetropes in the
petri eye
high atop this tower of
heat

a disconnect among

and my favorite:

wake up!
a six-pointed hamburger falls
drip on your bald, step
your father's
seed into the rug, exit
the eye's vault
under the illuminated
wet.

    and now: Michael he went unpublished, dead of cancer, the liver, O God.
    But it's important to understand that I,
    that I had no aspirations, none ever, higher or otherwise, that I just was, well, already forehead-formed,
    dreamless,
    Athena with a putz as Schneidermann would say,
    perfect already — like all art is before interpretation,
    like all artists are before they have to create,
    like all religions are before anyone ever believes in them,
    Lena out in Provo with her Mormon wards and shortcake-baking, thrifty gleaning or whatever it is Americans do, her ten pregnancies to make up for the outlawed polygamy and the monthly pilgrimages to the Temple in Salt Lake (yes, *their* Temple it stands),
    or my daughter Elisa the female rabbi, giving seminars on Kabbalah and the G-spot,
    aromatherapy and the Godhead,
    yoga and Hillel,
    veganism and Shammai and whatever Moses he might have said about the marital sanctity of the genital wart,
    just like this pamphlet I'm just reminded of and its religion (non-religion),
    like this religious pamphlet that I'm thinking of (but that I never laid eyes neither hands on),
    and this other young man with aspirations who, himself sort of a son-figure — just like this religious pamphlet that Schneidermann he received one summer's day:

that

that day about one year or more ago on which this young
man representing some religion or another he just rings the bell of
Schneidermann's building, his apartment — room — Schneidermann he buzzes him up and why not?

the young man I guess he knocks at a number of the other
doors with nothing and no one behind them, then walks himself all
the way up to the topfloor (without an elevator),

the last apartment there and there he then knocks on this
his last door of this last building on this the last block canvassed
for the day and Schneidermann he opens the door that's anyway
unlocked (the lock it never worked, was never repaired since the
robbery, non-robbery),

invites the young man in and immediately without asking
as to the young man's justification begins at least by the young
man's subsequent — in his defense, tearful — account to me to
apologize for not having any refreshment to offer his unexpected
visitor,

who it is revealed in his subsequent introduction that he
the young man represents one church or cult, one religion or
another now proselytizing not only in the wake of *what happened* or

what had happened three months prior with the airplane and
the metal penises but also in the wake, or sleep, of the modern soul
as the young man he put it to me as he put it to Schneidermann
(who he might have been attracted and sexually to a man so young
and naive and),

a church or a cult or a to-some-degree organized religion
that they believed in the immortality of the soul,

alien-visitation-rights,

the impending Apocalypse, impending on some date or
another in the — distant-enough — future,

a personal relationship with a deity named SOMETHING
I forgot through the offices as obliging as they might have been
obscure of some ex-plumber from Staten Island his name it was
Gary or Harry or Gary with two r's (augmented chords, clarinet
solo),

or maybe just Harry with one r who he (they)
demanded (and for the greater good)

the scriptural 10% tithe of assets assessed annually and so
on (payable to guess yourself who),

Schneidermann he of course wasn't really all that interested but still he took a pamphlet to lighten the — eager, earnest — young man's soul as his daily canvassing quota and soon dismissed him (Schneidermann he had all the pamphlets, menus too, napkins, plasticine sporks, logo hats, shirts, ballpointpens and keychains, Schneidermann he'd accept, hoard, anything on-offer, anything free),

thanking him and showing him the door — too old for sexual intercourse, an intimation of lust it was enough, should have been — but Schneidermann, over the next six-seven-eight-nine-months, yes, Schneidermann he grew more and more interested in the pamphlet:

read it many times (hall's toilet),

memorized it in part then in whole, even quoted it to me (unlistenable phone),

and thought it a perfect example of either American naivete or else

a poem, a song text, a libretto or at least there was something interesting about it,

something there, something moldable, workable, suggestive,

something that was becoming to him more and more *something* (*zumding* as Schneidermann he too was becoming that other), an idea, germing, germinating until,

and but six-seven-eight-nine-months later there was another buzz-buzz-buzz, another knock and the young man he arrived again at Schneidermann's apartment — room — now not seeming so young anymore as Schneidermann he said afterward like he was telling me a Grimm, Grimmest fairytale that:

unshaven, tired, frantically-splotched the once-young man he explained that the church or cult, or the church of the cult and more specifically its leader whatever his name was he had decided to wed his, the once-young-man's, since-dad-until-now unwed mother and then to move with her (and all her assets, including dad's life insurance lump — cancerous colon)

to some address in Key Nowhere, Florida

that after he flew down there it didn't exist,

and so was truly nowhere,

that his inheritance it was gone, the little his father had

left plus insurance,

    that he the leader and now stepfather had earlier urged the once-young-man to hasten the Apocalypse — and so alien-redemption (Schneidermann was planning a phalanx of harps, first-contact bisbiglissando) — by killing another member of the church of the cult who had named the church of the cult in his will as sole beneficiary of his bad heart,

    and then that other member, the rich faithful and wouldn't you know it (a baritone-bass)? he went to a Swiss heart specialist who the Doc he helped him out, tinkered around in there, then gave him a bill and 10 more years and so the order to kill, to murder this member and so (and his mother-situation, mezzo-soprano),

    you might understand this once-young-man's tenor of disenchantment, disillusionment, dis-everything that was why every day after work (which was the setting up of pornographic websites the once-young-man he explained it to Schneidermann, which of course was disastrous as an explanation as it inevitably led to another explanation and yet another ad whateverum as Schneidermann he always said,

    to an explanation of the Internet, of the http://worldwideweb and in great detail to someone like Schneidermann who he had no idea,

    in addition to Schneidermann demanding that his return visitor — and prior to any explanation of the technology involved — provide him, Schneidermann, with his or at least a definition of pornography),

    which was why every day after work this once-young-man he returned to every building he was ever buzzed into in his missionary incarnation, attempted to return to every apartment he and his propaganda they were ever given quarter in, and there to warn anyone who they might have associated themselves with the cult of the church against it, to warn anyone also who inconceivably was still, almost nine months later, thinking about joining and tithing and so on, also — but this objective more moral than practical (how to dramatize that?) — he wanted to collect all the brochures (he once said *pamphlet* the way you or I might say *Torah*),

    to amass all the disseminated propaganda for the purposes of torching as a ritual absolution from the cult of the church — what a set-piece! furies and harpies dividing the strings! — in this

field upstate near Poughkeepsie that his friend that his friend's
father he owned (bass-baritone who):

planned to set up a stripmall there with a HOME DE-
POT there as the ANCHOR STORE, yes, that's the term,

and of course Schneidermann he understood as he understood all, only after inviting him in and understanding — or at
least trying to — the Internet and the worldwide dot web and the
once-young-generation's definition of pornography but,

I'm sorry, Schneidermann he said by this once-young-
man's account who he didn't truly remember as,

Schneidermann he added as is apparent my house — room
— is in a mess, Schneidermann he said that I don't know where
your pamphlet is, if it is at all because my memory,

memory,

but if you want to search for it,

hands and knees and all,

and so of course a once-young-man as determined as this
Once Young Man was according to Schneidermann, the bald fairy
behind this tale this libretto he searched:

through manuscripts finished and half-finished and all
wholly thought-out until,

and with luck in an hour or so he found what he'd returned to find — tutti! — the pamphlet and when Schneidermann
he found he discovered which pamphlet the once-young-man had
meant when he'd said *pamphlet,*

which one of who knows what he meant to retrieve, take,
then Schneidermann he said by this once-young man's account he
said

No! take any pamphlet here (Schneidermann he had many,
all: sales pamphlets, pharmaceutical leaflets, flyers, brochures,
takeout Oriental menus stained with dim sums, and O God!
everything else),

indeed take any piece of paper you want!

I have a manuscript of Stravinsky's that's all yours if you
want it, an autograph of Bela Bartók that's yours for the taking,

or one from the violinist Laster too (I think, or would like
to),

take almost anything you want but this pamphlet as I'm
thinking about doing an opera on the subject, on the libretto, the-

text-of-the-thing,
     and so I need it:
     it interests me too much! it's much too important to my
present or at least to my soon-to-be-present work to let go and like
this!
     but the once-young-man he pulled the pamphlet out of
Schneidermann's hands
     (later I told Schneidermann that his opera was here, that
his life was this libretto: an aging Jewish artist and a young
computer cultist and, well, Schneidermann he never listened,
Schneidermann he never finished his life or his work), and Schneidermann he attempted to pull in return, though too late, almost
jumped on the once-young-man
     (I said only later — bedside at the hospital, panting —
this is genius, Alex! score this for brass),
     attacked him like a starved German shepherd that answers
to Prinz,
     and the once-young-man he in fright, aspen shock, pushed
him Schneidermann off and away and there on his floor — pale-
of-settlement-mud — amid the freebies and the manuscripts and
but, yes, Schneidermann he had his first and his only attack-of-
the-heart, an infarct and,
     the once-young man he shouldered him down down down
the flights like a hock of ham (don't tell me how to compose and I
won't tell you how to breathe was what Schneidermann he said to
me when he said),
     put him in a gypsy cab (hearse-black, its medallion a
shrunken skull),
     the only taxis up there it took him to the minority
hospital where he refused everything musical but my cash,
     tried to dial what he thought was the telephone number
tattooed on Schneidermann's forearm, went through
Schneidermann's pockets and found sewn into the lining of his
jacket — my rag — my telephone number one of them once he the
Once Young Man discovered that Auschwitz it was disconnected
     and called me,
     told me in brief,
     I arrived to hear it in full and I,
     I dealt with the rest — and after that incident, which

Schneidermann he never talked about (like the opera),
>   never liked to (like the operas however ideational),
>   Schneidermann he quit smoking like a bird without wings,
>   ripped the strings out of his piano like a nose from a face,
>   life it slowed down like a drunk watch,
>   and Schneidermann he began to become obsessed with the
strangest:
>   told me that just hearing the American word — or words
— HIGHSCHOOL, HIGH SCHOOL was enough to give him an
unwanted, unintentional orgasm,
>   began to use the word TERRORIST to describe every
musician, as in I take it that you are familiar with the work of the
great TERRORIST Mozart? and invariably referred to the public
as *the hostages*
>   or *the hostage,*
>   told me also that day upon being discharged from the
minority hospital that he considered customer-service to be the
only art form or medium of the future (how Wagner how he would
have loved it!
>   like think of what Kafka he would have done with K. the
Konsultant! Schneidermann he said as he filled out the hospital's
questionnaire with my pen),
>   also thought it was the most subtle, ironic form or
medium of derision, indeed of pure insult, that our culture it has
thus far evolved, perhaps unconsciously produced,
>   like how do you like your pills?
>   bedpan comfy?
>   what could have been improved? health maybe? and so on,
>   like privacy! Schneidermann screamed,
>   call the nurse? I want a privacy button!
>   thought himself blessed by persecution, certainly, Schnei-
dermann did,
>   pitied only those — with great naivete upstaging scorn —
born into uninteresting times,
>   who they never rose to any challenge,
>   who you never had the honor of being persecuted except by
the forces that you yourself put into motion (Schneidermann he'd
say if he was),
>   the forces that you yourself set to spin above your

unknowing

unknowing
     and yet knowing
     and yet unknowing head, Mister Rothstein Schneidermann
with all those calls, all those quarters of mine, George Washington
he was talking or was trying to talk to you and, well, that's the
tragedy (all that the commission-mishegas),
     you who understand nothing!
     zero!
     zilch to *efes* (Schneidermann's Hebraic nihil)!
     nothing because the serpent it never bit you in the eye,
ever, wriggled in one ear out the other — Schneidermann he bled
for those born,
     those born into uninteresting times, those dead to the
possibility of History possibly enlightening you, numb to the
promise of Fate,
     there will be no genius death for you! my friend Maestro
Jacob Levine, nothing martyred, stump-high, like me you missed
out, emigrated (immigrated) — or History it's missed out on you,
out on us,
     on a Will ethical or practical — legal? — I hope against
hope to find amongst his manuscripts, Schneidermann's, his
toiletpaper one-ply:
     intact in all its particulars (what notes go to which
instruments, Schneidermann, in those works of yours you never
orchestrated? do want your string trios performed as a cycle, or not
at all?),
     because now only the particulars matter, actually have yet
to be sketched (dynamics, bow and breathmarks),
     the detailman cometh (forget about the what or how of his
music, Schneidermann he wanted to know only the why),
     the intricate interlocking of darkest measures in the
mechanism we know as the unknowable,
     as the waking sleep of America: no dreams except movies
(matinees),
     no more deathsweats,
     dreammares,
     no escape routes secretly planned through existences
silently (and more embarrassing: embarrassingly)
     hoped-for-and-against all at once:

Schneidermann he said that he knew well his sewer-system, had mapped out his getaway, said that if the Gestapo they ever returned the meetingpoint it was to be a specific grate in Perth Amboy,

all this life and work and work and life descending into the shadow's grave of the invented self, the self-invented self, the willed self sensing through willed senses, the willed self holding up the mirror,

getting tired,

tired,

tired — reflecting me as I was getting fitted that morning after that 9 a.m. funeral for a new undesecrated, untainted suit,

like of a red heifer's hide,

getting fitted for this: double-breasted-and-pants-with-cuffs-shroud, by a kind-in-his-forgetfulness-Schneider,

another — auxiliary — Schneidermann fitting me for naked clothes,

me staring into the ocean of mirror, the blue carpet reflected as the Atlantic's depths,

at sea like I was in steerage, and practicing fingerings on a length of rigging rope while Schneidermann he,

with whom I'd been touring and then the War — me living with my father in London, him dying as my father in Poland — and then the visa it came through for him after I pulled some strings (*G, D, A* and *E* to be precise),

the Leviathan's smokestacks steaming up the mirrored vault above, into New York, New York

and but yes, I'm all washed up, wet,

yes, I'm a Marinere, rime-stranded on Prospero's Island (well-trafficked all around), just trying to survive this soliloquy,

pacing and fretting my how long's it been? seven, eight hours now, it's almost, is it?

It's almost 4 a.m.?

I'm tired.

Music itself it stops time, according to Schneidermann who he shattered the casing of the Rolex I just gave him for one of his ten or more birthdays per year, shattered it and twisted its hands on the keys of my piano up at the Grand in the middle of demonstrating to me I forget what,

like

like Orpheus still singing even with his head hacked off,
or strumming music time suspended down in the Underworld
where,

or like the shofars or valveless ram trumpets or whatever
that tumbled the walls of Jericho that they propped up the sun that
Joshua he stilled out at Gibeon,

and time it is a way of enlisting two ideas in mutual
defense, dialectics (yes, I'm of German Extract, what Oma she
administered for a flu),

with this definition, utility of time we'll be able to divine
the proof for Schneidermann's idea that art and religion they never
flourish at the same time (post-the-events-of-September-the-12th),

that art and money they never flourish at the same time
(and that the Renaissance it wasn't art it was more like indentured
servitude),

no, think about it you in the front row, front lines, where
all you have is too much money and not enough time.

It's time I've wasted pulling the dialectic apart,

ritual rending of the intended victim, between on the one
gnarled, soon Parkinson's probably hand the enraged Maenads and
on the other, the Muses.

And which will María be? Depends if I ever intend on
returning to the Grand, if I'm even allowed to,

if I can get any work after this, if I can even get home
unassisted after this, if I'll ever get home and if home even exists.
Will any of you ferry me back? I've got cabfare.

Usher, you of winged Hermes, why do you flee fleet?

Sacred, winged, fickle things, why are you never tipped?

Here's some money for you — come and catch, or we'll
put it in escrow.

No, don't grab — it's for them. Get home safe.

O Shayna I want an aside, can you come to the stage, can I
speak to your ear alone?

No?

I'm talking to myself. Stage-directions.

Yes, home. Where? Onstage, apace and not fretting,
without violin, instead with my skull in my hand, kindled thoughts
— my skull, my father's skull, my Schneidermann's, everyone's, all
fractured, in fragments, all stuck together with spit.

Aside: To contemplate a bust of Homer, who Antiquity deliberately represented to us as blind, to emphasize the music of poetry over its written-down-form, according to Schneidermann according to whom? Orpheus, the union of poetry and music before the page tore it asunder — before recording it made music more about appreciation, more about passivity than about life, spirit, God I hate to say the word *harmony*!

Aside: Or to bust a contemplation of Homer, an interpretation of Homer! because all I am and ever was and will never be again is an interpreter:

a Romantic when Romance demands and a Classicist when it pays — that's who Orpheus was, the only Romantic among the Classicists, the one man who he stood up there high on Olympus and had the nerve to shatter the old idols,

their Gods,

the hubris to think: well, to hell with you Ecclesiastes! there *is* something new under your sun, Apollo's (the mistake of every soloist, the initial motif of the Cadenza of History, of which I'm only a germ),

because Orpheus he made art a religion and religion an art, and in doing so he did the greatest charity anyone could ever hope to do and that is to give the world something to live for,

something to die for (creative not destructive with the promise of heaven replaced by posterity, at least according to Schneidermann),

because Tchaikovsky he was a suicide, the pederast,

and Mozart he was short, pimpled, chronically constipated and depressive,

his ambition — Schneidermann's idea: with that talent, he wanted to know, why didn't he orchestrate the Rapture? — as inferior as Stravinsky was who he wanted to be Mozart but failed, as I'm failing Schneidermann now by not playing his unplayable *Concerto* to the press and police gathered here,

to the amazing, terrible and fanatic accuracy of ever improving recording equipment — hear a woman fart underwater in another hemisphere, in the Budapest baths,

in the Gellért where,

and the difficulty of achieving a consistent violin sound night from goddamned night after goddamned night, transfigured,

have

have together — recording, sound — encouraged a mode
of teaching I want to impart to you, only to warn you against, a
mode of teaching that it emphasizes an all-day-every-day-vibrato,
intense, dazzling lefthand fingerwork,

and uniform, even, powerful bowing — but who cares
about this anyway?

(not you!) too many privileges to understand — respect if
we must — how our dead they've earned them for us,

and but I've heard people back in Bukovina, in the early
past of last century God I've heard peasants play better than that!
faster too (the Zigeunerprimus who)!

but that this new as late style it wins laurels and makes
green money greener with envy for other money already made, wins
competitions and audiences and critical acclaim (or used to),

and so here, in this town, damned be the dead Ivan
Galamian and Dorothy DeLay the slut O the whore (poetic justice
too long delayed)!

teachers of too many of today's virtuosos, Asians, even
Jews! all-Americanized, with no explosion, no real immolation of
the soul and, so, okay, laugh at me,

fine, but I'm a soloist, a soloist only the only soloist,

never had a stand-partner, never played ensemble, not even
quartet to sit-in — guest-star — at a daughter's wedding and not
because I don't like people (I do and I don't),

or the ensemble literature (Beethoven! Bartók!
Shostakovich! even some young men and women who they think
they're Europeans who they don't exist anymore!),

but who cares for others if I can't care even for myself?
that I have only myself to worry about and who has life enough for
anyone else? because I'm a soloist, my part's always nailed,

to a Cross — especially now, in our day in which
everything's so much a drama that there's no drama left anymore
(even on Schneidermann's muted tube),

no tensions unresolvable,

no Poles,

under this proscenium arch,

this wedding canopy, this chuppah to the coreligionists
out there — what do you say, Akira? give me a second go at it? you
look great, and with Dina and all.

No Nat, leave her be: she's a mother of my children and
sad to say sort of my mother too — you do the math,

which has nothing to do with music: that's just the
intellectuals and the Classicists trying to out — eunuch — each
other,

instead to resolve or not to resolve is the question (outra-
geous fortune!),

and, well, everything else is worthless — dramaless drama
like those Russian Orthodox religious icons that,

because I assume that this is for broadcast,

the morning o'clock news,

because, yes, I see you out there recording this — reality
made less so through its presentation, its stage,

I see your microphones, the cameras you've allowed in and
maybe to embarrass me off but it hasn't worked and it won't,

those little red lights to squint away from, singeing
themselves into my eyes,

all this spectacle (non-spectacle),

turned into a non-spectacle (spectacle),

for the audience at home — shouldn't you kill the lights
before I kill myself? can't?

Okay, no, I understand, you've made yourself heard! Aren't
democracies great? excepting the orchestra, though I've always
preferred benevolent monarchies, but some positions are just so
hard to fill:

to attempt like the pestle position I'll never get to with
María tonight

that won't exist for me,

some sedatives, killers of pain please, and some padding
and maybe the straightest jacket the divine tailor he's ever cut,

and, Schneidermann, well, the pants he wore because his
musician father unlike my musician father (my true father and not
my true Schneidermann),

his musical father unlike my musical father, like his
musical fathers before him and unlike my musical father's
fathers before him, Schneidermann his musical father he died
and at a young age, in Schneidermann's youth and his nine
aunts, his nine musical aunts they had adopted him (Rudy too,
NEVER FORGET),

anyway

anyway his name it was Schneidermann and why?

because his family's name it was Schneidermann and so what could you do?

and his father's name it was Schneidermann which was also the name of his fathers before him, tailormademen all the way back unto a first tailor maybe, the first Schneider with the name of Schneidermann usurping, taking over his Jewish name, his Hebrew name, the son-of-a-Jewish-name of this tailoring forefather of this Schneidermann-name,

this Schneidermann dynasty that the War it soon ended and that Schneidermann's greater internal war it ended later, soon enough, this Schneidermann, my Schneidermann, well — like me he was a prodigy, the first and the last prodigy in his family (his father and his mother they were talented, yes, not amateurs at all but not geniuses, no,

in the measure that they weren't amateurs in the same measure were they not geniuses and Schneidermann himself, sure, he reproduced but they died in Birkenau, and anyway demonstrated no

proclivity), anyway Schneidermann he was a prodigy like the prodigies before him, before us and, well, his nine musical aunts who they adopted him after his father died (his mother she died in childbirth, on childbed, twins),

who they adopted him and Rudy (who absolutely wasn't a prodigy, who wasn't even talented),

they the aunts once and only once sought out some patron to sponsor his, Schneidermann's, early recitals,

Schneidermann's early presentations-to-the-public and, well, they agreed with a man, with actually another Schneider, in Hungarian it's a szabó,

a real tailor (his name it was Nadel, Schneidermann he once told me),

they agreed with a local Pest tailor named Nadel who he did up military uniforms, formal-wear for the aristocracy to sponsor these early recitals, these early exhibitions-to-the-public, and so made my, made our Schneidermann the prodigy — who would obviously grow out of it, everyone heard — into a living musical advertisement,

a playing musical advertisement,

Schneidermann's nine musical aunts they agreed with this
tailor and his scheme to make their prodigy-nephew into a living
physical advertisement for this Nadel, this tailor and his tailor-
scheme, this Nadel who he then made the young prodigy Schneidermann a — tailormade — pair of pants for his early recitals with
an advertisement writ large across the *tush* (Schneidermann he
always said),

the seat of the pants as Schneidermann he told me, an
advertisement sewn there and kept warm on the seat, a message for
when Schneidermann he got up from the pianobench to take his
bow to both sides of the house to manic applause and then turn
around to go back backstage into the wings after playing a prodigy
recital or an early concert of his,

across the tush in huge red stitching it said:

F. Nadel, Tailor
Quality Pants

or something like that and in Hungarian so that audiences
everywhere — in Buda and in Pest — they could understand it and
respond,

but forgive the man his eccentricities, his idiosyncrasies
and so on (money, the nonuplet of aunts they agreed, it had to be
made),

this Schneider the Tailormademan for agreeing to it but
what could he at 5 years old do?

with his tush barely large enough to encompass the
message — yes, this Schneidermann less a mann than a *Schneider*,

though more in the figurative sense such as, it's almost
untranslatable from the German, as in *frieren wie ein Schneider* — even
with these lights staring down,

or as in *aus dem Schneider sein*

and I (If I'm a Schneider Schneidermann would say, then
you you schmuck you're an Aufschneider too), well, I'm finding
my out, my way out — having quit most substances, even anaero-
bic sex I,

I try, try to put in 15–20 minutes on the exercycle in the
healthclub of the Grand in the mornings, sweating, shvitzing as
Schneidermann would say with that panther-printed rag of his

jacket

jacket like a worm's tallis draped over my shoulders,

the first tailor his (great-) great-grandfather according to
Schneidermann who he had heard it from the least musical one of
his nine musical aunts that he the great-grandfather he was
stooped, incredibly, and could have though not for sustenance
licked the spreads between his toes, that was the size of his hump!
but according to Schneidermann, or his aunt, you should've heard
him sing while he worked! sewed sewed and sewed, sure, but every
Friday! they'd heard from their parents who they'd heard it from
him or, and do you believe?

that I haven't even gotten to the most important memories
of Schneidermann, yet: the first days in America, the first months,
the first years,

his tongue licking another tongue:

learning the word NEON, learning — the hard way —
that NEON it wasn't edible (had to remind him once down in
New Jersey, it still isn't),

ASS-IM-A-LAY-SHUN Schneidermann he learned, TRA-
DISH-UN like they sing in that matinee Shtick movie, *Kitschenkino*
that Schneidermann needless to hate how he hated,

that you put a coin into a machine and — poof! — it
spits a piece of cherrypie (again, I won! I won!),

all about the first time — winter, 1955 — that Schneidermann and I we went to the matinee movies here (which I forget),
to get out of a snowstorm that it reminded him of Poland and,

but there's no time — I must modulate, would you like to
modulate with me? I'll be ever so gentle.

FYI as the Russians say, I also play the viola — not that I
thought I would fail, not that I even when knew from failure,

and that the piano too I play, though not as well as
(anyway, you always need something to fall back on as I was smart
enough to tell all my children falling to fail),

but to hear that's an extra charge, supplementary — you
didn't pay for that,

as if María she could care less, as if you could care less —
even though you all want to get your money's worth, though you
need to witness my failure,

need to destroy me by remaining silent now in your
sprung seats, in this hall where I'm reborn,

where you used to stay the same, never me,

but now where we both age: my audiences they're getting older, graying, fattening, sickening too (oxygen tanks, IVs in the hall, can you believe?),

as I'm paraded around to the halls of the world, the Auditorium Under the Sign of the Hourglass — that's where I'm reborn, these church and synagogue groups and colleges, associations elderly and rotary, university amphitheaters and later masterclassing in their lecture halls:

these amalgamations of glassed-in existences ingathering from the aesthetic diaspora as part of an annual subscription series, and me,

there, here I am and cranking out the same hits every time, over and over and over again, windup musicbox, mechanical bird like Pope Gregory's,

because I'm an interpretation machine,

a memory machine,

I'm Schneidermann's performing retarded masturbating monkey, a symbol with the cymbals,

because only one thing ever happened in my life: music,

early years listening to the town klezmers you say *klezmorim* I say as Schneidermann said,

then up late in Berlin and Paris, Amsterdam and London listening to older violinists on 78s and, yes, at first, admittedly, this can be a bit unpleasant, shocking,

because we've grown fond or at least expectant of that thick throb, the wall of sound between ear and violin, between us and music,

but once that's swept away, yes, once that's knocked down (walls are for knocking down, at least according to an exwife, a home-improvements-maven),

the violinist he seems naked, vulnerable, weak and maybe, yes, effete, impotent, ineffectual, light in the shoes, less of a man or a mann — but it's the still small voice!

Me? who I masturbated on trains, on planes, in my long life in limousines,

still it was just the same twelve tones over and over again — related to whom, Schönberg, your two beloved Nazis? — and nothing else,

on boats, ships, music it was me, even on the ship the
Leviathan was its name that it brought me and my father here
without my Schneidermann — vying for who gets what lifeboat
when and why? what merit? — and can I get the water I asked for?
(Leviathan the fish the sustenance of heaven — O to grow fat
upon your escape!)

or maybe not? almost three or four hours ago? is it? it's 5
a.m., already? an hour when usually I'd be all of passed out on the
floor of my hotelroom and with the heating full-on,

watching either SCHINDLER or a pornographic movie on
mute, reading Wagner and eating lo-fat/lactose intolerant vanilla
ice-cream to lose all this weight,

all this stomach vibrato that I've got to get rid of (health
and sex, health-as-sex and) — yes, I've put on a few pounds
(shylock it, a good idea, but to who?),

yes, you would've noticed: publicity-shot it's not quite up
to date, it's how I posed 25 years ago now as,

God! I want you to realize, to understand, no, to experience how much we've lost!

how Schneidermann he's been forgotten and who cares?

how the range of the violin it's been reduced, music's too
but who cares? your range as well and the irony is that in this day
and age, when you think that everything's open to you, and it's not,
openness only meaning less — is it hot in here or is it just me?

options just more to rail against as the cattlecars they
pass, rolling stock Downtown where,

and God! how Schneidermann he once took a shit in a
piano, yes, onto the soundboard, a bonewhite babygrand at some
party or another, they're all the same but this one it was thrown by
a duchess who she was still seeking her duke and holding auditions
blindfolded with garters behind an Oriental screen ricegrained,

that but Schneidermann he wasn't even — formally or
informally — invited but anyway he entertained if not mortally
shocked all present by climbing up onto the bonewhite babygrand
piano, undoing his belt, dropping his sails of pants around his
shins into a squat Schneidermann he, yes, actually and indeed did
take a shit in a piano (watery),

onto the soundboard, feet on the keyboard tapping out a
rough accompaniment to the Beethoven's 9th that Schneidermann

he was — making an overture to — singing:

the Schiller melody, the fraternal muzak, the first sell-out poptune that I know of according to Schneidermann that Schneidermann he knew of,

his steaming-hot — if somewhat milk-loose — turds among the watery stool vibrating strings in sympathy,

and everyone — mortally — shocked except the servants,

but according to Schneidermann this is not what an artist does, that if this is what an artist does then the person who did it is not an artist, is instead a fake, indeed according to Schneidermann this is what art itself does, that this — in-deed — is what art itself is and no,

yes, this is an apology, not for him but for me, because I've never done anything (except this, and this is a pity, is pitiful and),

never done anything real! huge! exploding and but — a grand Schneidermann he shit in over there and an upright he played over here, a grand Schneidermann he shit in over there and a grand Schneidermann he would have killed (himself, me)

for over here (though Schneidermann he wouldn't accept one from my wallet and I, it asked),

because grandpianos they were all that Schneidermann he played over there and mold-tuned fungus-actioned uprightpianos (and one with all its strings ripped out)

they were all that Schneidermann he played over here and why? well, because of money — though in his early years here, the 1950s, Schneidermann he went to occasional parties (cocktail, cock & tail), up near Columbia Gem of a University that it killed Schneidermann's countryman Bartók that is if Jews like Schneidermann they even have a country,

Uptown around Gershwin's and Mozart's grocer Schneidermann he was more feared, respected, than loved, respected,

none of which they pay the telephone or electricity or heating bills,

because it's Homer the professor who he gets all the medals and money and not Orpheus the artist:

it's the public intellectual half-raped into existence (that's the meat of the table-talk, Riverside Drive)

from a windblown seed renting out either the aither or the

ether

ether at what at least Schneidermann he couldn't, could never
afford — and but that's what they used, the ether, when Schneidermann he had his spleen out in Pest, a routine procedure as they say
(uninsured even then, out-of-my-prodigy-pocket),

his spleen removed, which Schneidermann he also couldn't
afford to and to not to or, letting me have a piece of it in repay-
ment, and I swallowed it (when it came to Schneidermann I always
swallowed, whatever the *it*),

and it leaves lesions on the mental apparatus like playing
or even listening to the goddamn A-whining oboe at 440 hertz per
moment however defined — the music of the Sirens, the music of
Orpheus the sailor lashed to mast,

like me on my ship, the Leviathan (my father getting
Jewsick below, my Schneidermann getting Jewdead in Poland),

the weakling artist with no sealegs under him,

because balance it's unnecessary for an artist,

because an artist he must be weightless, embodied-
disembodied,

sailing in your skull's vessel across the wide ocean, an
Argonaut to, and finally, silence the Sirens, to subdue them,

and so I myself have three tropes: Sirens and Muses and
Maenads, and which was which?

and which brother-in-law or overbearing father loosed his
snake unto my true Eurydice, whoever whichever she is (and if
you're coming for me tonight, please make it quick!),

name meaning *wide-ruling* as Schneidermann he once told
me, Eurydice does, translated it to my ignorance one matinee's day
— and do they ever rule wide! as the ocean, as my ego,

God! how even after all my divorces they still take me to
task and forever! *ewig, ewig*, like how did the women they get so
strong on this side of the ocean?

because it used to be our fathers we were afraid of, read
your K., okay? I'm sure you have, unfortunately (K. not as in
Mozart but),

trying to get at the heart of my own adopted father
Schneidermann while my real true father he was still alive if sick-
of-the-heart,

Schneidermann — an incredible taskmaster! phylactery
whips! — he was above all a religious artist, of incredible hours of

incredible discipline, all self-imposed (by him on me),

because I just couldn't be trusted with his then-wife and
then-daughters, could I?

because I told more lies than a husband all that was left
for me to do, actually more precisely all I could be trusted to do
was to run up and down my scales, scaling my scales: *do, re* and *me*
and singing

(hoarsing) along at something like quarter note equals
prestississississississississimmo,

and further ever furthest off the metronome's scale,

scaling always higher and faster always highest and fastest,
a warped mechanical metronome on the sill overlooking the garden,
herbarium that then-Schneidermann's-wife she shared with,

the metronome that in late humidmost summer it —
inevitably — slowed and so maybe that's how, when I became so
much of an interpreter (playing to pollinate the flowers just
outside the window),

as if Schneidermann he ever begrudged me his wife, but it
was his daughters who — yes, Chief, that's it, take a seat, finally,

will someone get him some coffee, two creams and two
sugars? but if you leave the hall, please, I beg and beseech you, save
your stubs.

Because outside is the descent into Hades, hell, with
Orpheus returning empty-handed,

with a shadow of a shade — the failure though being a late
addition, like the Florida Room Number Two,

an old-world-parlor, really, and as anti-life, anti-art as its
precursor the Salon Over There

my then-wife-now-ex she had added onto the house in
Miami where all the rooms they already were Florida Rooms, and
then she goes and Schneiderman he would say shtups the workmen
she'd hired and why? and all because I shtupped her sister, well,
listen,

mistakes were made, and made well and her sister, well, she
was her:

they looked the same in the dark which is why you can't
trust your eyes, especially my eyes, only your ears, your hearing,
though my ears they knew it wasn't her, my-then-wife-now-ex,

but rather someone else, maybe from the pitched moaning

or the cries and utterances and imprecations or maybe because she
actually moaned cried uttered and imprecated another man's name,
her husband's, who's a good man, into insurance,

> which is what I need right now like a hole in my head,

> which brings me back to my original point, my ur-request
(my Isaac to Schneidermann and his Abraham):

> that someone should seriously, or at least seriously
consider the possibility of,

> killing me,

> stabbing me,

> shooting me,

> not as in take-my-photograph,

> in my overburdened and overtaxed head: you know what I
pay in income, property taxes down there in Florida?

> No, it's the Alexandrians who came up with the failure
angle on Orpheus: they had that pathetic spirit, that *empfindsamkeit*
(Schneidermann he loved that word pitifully),

> yes, that's it, Charon or Sharon was her name, the pathetic
one, the sister getting older,

> new-aging to palmistry — a yoga-farter, O yes,

> yes, I've urinated in my pants again.

> Because I can't leave, can I?

> Diaper the diapason and allow me to remember to you
Aristaeus, Eurydice the Thracian nymph's or Dryad's undesired
lover according to Schneidermann who he would know:

> that man — because most of my wives they were as
unfaithful as husbands, as I was at least — he was my manager
(Mister Rothstein),

> my agent (yes, Adam),

> the neighborhood sophomore who he scoops the gorgeous
autumn out of an exwife's lap-pool leaf by sogged heavy leaf. Oak.
Poplar. Holly and Dogwood.

> But do you even know the names of trees? No, and so
they're not yours!

> Not mine either. I do stumps.

> Ornamented X-mas firs inclined to sweet music to help
them grow and then the animals they gathered and were subdued.

> Do I need to hold up a mirror? Surely some of you have
mirrors in your purses, maybe compact roundlings to reflect the

stagelights into my eyes so that I can't see anymore and only hear.

But I see that you've killed the overheads! and right on cue, bravo lighting maestro who he shtups his little — moisturized — hands up in the misted booth! yes, a masturbator, too!

But that's okay because Orpheus he too shunned the company of women for men or celibacy or music or death (the same things, the same *dings*, depending on Schneidermann's accounts).

And know that I'm there soon enough by the banks of the Strymon or the Styx, by the banks where all my accounts they've been frozen like my wives ex and present,

frozen like my now untended pool,

like the unsalted sidewalk outside HAMU in Prague, their Conservatory where I slipped and broke a hip three years ago,

and you don't want those doctors — you have to understand, that contrary to my doctor's recommendations (and they're only recommendations),

all you need is salt in the wounds of any ego, because that's what the Conservatories they offer:

that there's always someone better, faster, more talented, engineering you — not me — out-of-service.

But that was then — youth — and this is now — juvenescence Schneidermann once said — when most aspiring musicians or at least according to Schneidermann they have no ability to express anything musical on an instrument or with their voice, defective musical hearing, and some have, actually, actually unsurprisingly Schneidermann he added, no real interest in music as music qua,

because can you believe, Schneidermann he once asked me if I could believe that they can't sing a simple melody or improvise an accompaniment to a folktune,

or even reproduce a simple popsong (Schneidermann he had visited the Conservatory that I taught more like vaginally-engaged-Asians-at, and was, eventually, fired from and he, Schneidermann he went there and asked for a job there and they the personnel dept. they thought he meant janitor)?

but these students they talk! Schneidermann he said who he listened in the halls on his way out the door O how they talk! and all about the musical language of Beethoven as if his name it

wasn't

wasn't Ludwig but Late,

Late van Beethoven or all about aleatorics,

electronics, stochastics and that's because music it's no longer in their blood as Schneidermann he maintained, in our blood, in blood, and, Jesus! a goddamned Bach chorale it has forsaken us.

And atonality is dead according to Schneidermann.

And dodecaphonic music, 12-tone music, is dead according to Schneidermann.

And music is dead according to Schneidermann.

And the retards win — no disrespect intended to the wheelchairs who might be watching me at home.

Will you rise? I'm just joking — the metaphoric retards I mean, understand? you have to be peesee,

politically correct and incorrect in their own, respective and always respectful, seasons, have to be fair to each of J.J. Fux's five species of counterpoint,

polyphony,

rudiments of composition, which study — the *Gradus ad Parnassum* — it formed the basis of almost every great Classical composer's education,

like when that great composer Early van Beethoven's studies with Haydn's friend Albrechtsberger they were translated into French by the great musicologist Joseph-François Fétis in 1833 (six years after Early's early death), you wouldn't believe Schneidermann he promised whose names they showed up on the list of subscribers! everyone's:

Auber (married a Jewess),

Berlioz (friends with the Jews Halévy, Mendelssohn and Meyerbeer),

Chopin (wrote a Mazurka in A Minor subtitled *The Jew*),

Meyerbeer (Jew),

Moscheles (Jew),

Paganini (suspected Jew),

and what about Liszt? that famous anti-Semite, who he invented the idea of the solo piano recital according to Schneidermann but,

and on and on to some names long since decomposed on their own, without the — though appreciated — assistance of your, of everyone's, vast ignorance.

But now, deceptively according to Schneidermann, recordings they're supposed to teach, technologies teach — though
everyone quick to employ them are equally quick to admit that
nothing's an acceptable substitute for something they and equally
will never mention, nor themselves experience:

life! and not this updated Kappellmeisterism Version 2.0.
like in the music for the matinee movies (diegetic music inclusive,
I just heard that word this afternoon when,

diegetic music in a matinee movie it's music that it's moti-
vated by plot, occurs in the narrative, in which its source it's visible
up-on-screen,

like when they finally make the matinee movie version of
this, Mister Rothstein, of tonight,

and Schneidermann he gets his 15 minutes of play, a
quarter hour of air before me — quick! someone should resurrect
Thomashefsky!

get Dustin Hoffman on the phone! get him a fiddle! start
him on scales!),

like when Schneidermann he hauled himself 5000 subway
stops, all the way Downtown for him Uptown for most and to
apply for a job on the composition faculty of the Conservatory of
Conservatories and they the personnel dept. they thought that this
man or this mann who he spoke the language so strangely to their
rich accents and ears they thought that Schneidermann he meant to
apply for a job as a janitor,

Schneidermann he told the Head of Personnel that he'd
brought a letter of recommendation from Stravinsky, a *letter!*

Schneidermann he waved its stain in the air, *a letter!*

and the Head of Personnel she just told him, and without
humor or pity, executive-harshly, that here they have their own
ladders (she must have thought, and she had reason to, that the
envelope it was only a snotrag),

wouldn't hire him even as an asst. sanitation or maintenance engineer, like sorry, no openings, we wish you good luck —
but there's maintenance and then there's maintenance as Schneidermann he answered me in pure laconic Schneidermannese when I
asked him, well, how it was,

how it went (after Schneidermann he refused my help,

even

even discreet inquiries, no pull, if I had any left after getting fired
from there for rape however artistic), told him that he didn't want
to fix toilets gurgling musical anyway, that he didn't want to spend
all day tuning pianos

  (that's if they'd let him), as the bells of Saint John the
Divine they rang out powdered sugar all over our Hungarianmost
pastry up at a café in Morningside Heights, where Schneidermann
he'd met me for coffee and Western Humanism,

  up near where a — prospective — lover of mine she works
at the University where,

  teaches astronomy, astrophysics but,

  rang hollow and sweet as Schneidermann and I we talked
and talked maintenance in all of its manifestations, as if the
misunderstanding of Schneidermann's intentions it sent-a-message,

  for us,

  for me to interpret:

  like Ladder, Schneidermann said,

  and Letter, I repeated (accent! like you've got to work on
dein Akzent!),

  like Maintenance, Schneidermann said,

  and Main-ten-ance, I repeated,

  and Maintenance, Schneidermann said — like when they
had to redo the cracked clapper of the church bell over at St. Vitus
in Prague, after it died to predict the thousand-years'-flood,

  tolling now! O hark and hear the distant church on the
other side of the ocean, its bells newly cast soon striking their
noon,

  when they'll all be salting their pork plates,

  and guzzling beer — O I had friends there: Braunstein,
Schwarzstein, Grabstein

  and then *what happened,*

  what had happened — with Schneidermann bringing to the
Conservatory as he applied for the position of professor of composition and not the position of professor of the custodial arts a
score of his that it was written on the frontpage of his toilet's
newspaper,

  or on the reverse of boxed-in-cardboard-wine that Schneidermann he'd purchased at his local Spanglishmart, or else at the
ARAB STORE

and then dried out to write upon it his setting of the
poems of a poet from my own hometown:

Die Posaunenstelle it went,
     but Gabriel's ascended hasn't he? and his part with him.
     tief im glühenden, hear the trombones? Schneidermann he
asked, padding chord beneath muted trumpet?
     Leertext, but what exactly is missing and am I to be his
redactor?
     in Fackelhöhe, and what's this with the lights anyway?
     im Zeitloch: which is where we are if we'd only listen.
     hor dich ein, yes, do that
     mit dem Mund, with anything, everything
     and the mouth,
     because according to Schneidermann, well, music itself it's
the *Zeitloch,*
     the *time-hole,*
     our head,
     voids of interpretation and the actual weighed in the scales
of our ears, at least according to Schneidermann (and his interpretation):
     in the plunkings and scrapings of my fellow students at
the Conservatory in Budapest, that which conserves that which is
neglected by everyone else, at the Music Academy in Budapest I
knew Braunstein fresh in from Prague,
     later the streetsweeper,
     Schwarzstein of Brno (of Brünn),
     later the undertaker of the ghetto, to be liberated from
Łódź by the Red Army — only to be shot a decade or so,
     nine lives later in prison and by his liberators the impris-
oning Soviets (Lubyanka):
     grabbing you and sticking you in the wet mud,
     graven you on the earth — the poet of all this it was Paul,
not Peter that thrice denier and he too was one of us:
     Antschel and then Ancel and then Celan in the last stage
of his anagramming,
     an *Amsel* as Schneidermann he always called him, circling
high above a river a suicide in Paris May 1970 — the corpse a
great admirer of Schneidermann,

or

Joshua Cohen

or so Schneidermann he liked to think (his letters they
were never answered, the letters they were never sent, 6 *Avenue Zola,
Paris 15e* it was postage) — B. the trumpeter and S. the trombonist
and,

> but what's this? the house lights up and then down again?
> What's this about?
> What's the program?
> Stay interested! involved! Or there'll be no encore!
> Yes, I know my stage directions,

Avram storms stage right, undertone — they're so detailed,
aren't they? how they become more and more like Scripture,

> like fate with each passing line (death),
> just as these painlines, radial wrinkles they become more

and more pronounced on this punim of mine I hope will be seared
into your eyeballs for all time:

> the face of destiny, yes, but more accurately the face of one

who has failed destiny,

> preserved forever in a moment,
> hold-it, click! (can I see your press pass?),
> to be rendered into the most sentimental — and so

dangerous — of clichés,

> just kitsch like the photographic work of Francis Galton

who he took scores of portraits of Asians and their Asian faces, of
Slavs and their Slavic faces, of Aryans and their Aryan faces, of
Jews and of their Jewish faces and all each on a single photographic
plate in order to get the picture of their typical features, the typical
features of the typical Jewish face of the typical Jew, an image of one
for all, a record both collective, yes, and anonymous — all posed, all
staged, all worthless much like the portraiture of my youth,

> that wide-thighed assistant at the studio of Erdős Sándor

in Budapest, how she just swore that I was the cutest little Jew-
violinist that they'd ever had the pleasure to shoot (my first
erection! at least the first I remember),

> when the entire family we'd take three days to get ready

and the photographer he'd have to get it all set up it'd take it
seemed like a year of your life, take a decade to get the imported
palms angled just so, the elaborate headgear fixing your gaze
implacable as in-place,

> elbow on a pile of antique encyclopedias,

or else the pillows that you were allergic to, too — and then always one last time for your mother, all mother, to rush in and spit your hair back into composure,

then the faintest Mona Lisa of a smile held not in the mind or the mind's eye but *in time*,

for the exposure to spend itself, to earn its keep on the mantle — in the studio of a prominent photographer I knew, over here, now dead, drugs, no names, who he once asked my opinion, solicited my opinion of a project of his:

which was that the photographer he'd play music, loudly, for extended periods of time,

then,

like a child's game, the photographer he — who was violin-high-strung, Jew-neurotic — would shut off the music abruptly at any improbable point, or rather he'd have his assistant, lover, shut off the music and then he'd photograph the subject (seated in a comfortable chair, actually a divan halving the studio west to east),

immersed in the music, at the exact point of the music's stopping, to capture the reaction, the so-called return to reality occasioned by the sudden so-called silencing of music (as he the Jew-photographer put it in the artist-statement he finished before the photography it actually began).

However, though the subject he or she was expected, indeed admittedly sometimes instructed, to become immersed in and involved with the music — every other activity including conversation and the smoking of cigarettes being forbidden during sessions in the studio — often the photographer and his assistant (lover, AIDS)

would also become so immersed and involved that either the photographer he would forget to cue the assistant (drugs)

to shut up or turn off the music, or the assistant (dead)

he would, being so immersed and involved, miss the cue and falter, and so out of 50 subjects and 50 sessions, let's say for argument's sake that only about three of them

(self-portraits, the assistant assisting) went according to plan and that out of these three the photographer he framed and exhibited a triptych quasi-religious,

though most critics they regarded the massed portraits as

overly

overly-mannered, asking why so awkwardly, or were they just
ineptly posed?

and but Schneidermann he sat for him the photographer
once, at my urging, insistence, I had to bribe both:

this the only portrait of Schneidermann that I know, I have
the only extant print (should I pass my wallet around? it's empty),

but I assume that the photographer's estate it has one or
negatives of the session on file and Schneidermann himself or
absence-of-Schneidermann he or more accurately non-he probably
has one just lying around somewhere in that apartment mess of his
that I have to sort out some,

one day, and the photographer he was playing some music
for the harpsichord on the turntable I forget but at Schneidermann's insistence and so Schneidermann he knew it as well as he
knew all, some harpsichord music for him at his own insistence
and at a uniformly huge, harpsichord-dynamicless volume and
when the photographer he cued his unfortunate assistant and the
self-sacrificing-assistant — who he hated as much as I do the
sound of the harpsichord more than the sound of any other
instrument — stopped the music, the music it stopped and yet the
Schneidermann he remained unaltered, the same, later explaining
(after the photograph it was taken, and taken unsatisfactorily for
the photographer's unsatisfactory purposes and unrealistic, even
inartistic, specifications, but in all other satisfactions to me it's
fine, even luminous),

after the stopping of the music and the shooting of the
photograph, of the Schneidermann he, still, anyway, remained
unaltered, unchanged and then when asked why? — by whom I
forget — Schneidermann he just replied that when the music it
stopped, well, he'd hardly noticed,

that he merely filled in the silence in his own head,
provided the rest, the remainder, invented it or else Schneidermann
he just knew it knew all,

and in that way, well, nothing ever stops for any of us,
now, does it?

at least not for those of us with our talent, with mine, me
being the photographer's assistant that day up, Downtown, in his
studio and previously mentally prepared to take the cue whenever it
might occur, and especially against the hated harpsichord and I did,

but, as I said and as I knew even beforehand (as the photographer he inartistically knew the artistic results he wanted beforehand),

it was to no avail, to come to nothing, zero because I knew Schneidermann and I knew that Schneidermann he knew this music, that indeed Schneidermann he knew all music and that further and more importantly the moment or moments of silence following music they mean or meant nothing for a man in whom music lived,

in whom music it might as well have been born (for me),

however many billions of years ago, Schneidermann — and so that while most people they feel and even manifest signs, symptoms of extreme disorientation if not just anxiety following the abrupt, unexpected termination of music, I understand, we know, that this everyday thing:

on the taxi's Farsi radio,

at tele-ordered on-hold home,

leaving wholegrain stores and striped-tie places-of-business that this is our best metaphor, or translation,

for death, and that death — quick, irrational — should be gone to in peace or else not at all, at peace or else not at all, that our minds they should always and with a vigilance be prepared for it, for death, and the death of it, the death of death (its promise, its assurance, for us)

so that it, it never surprises us,

powering-off our flow and whenever — that we must ensure that our music it lives on, sings within louder than the without, which will anyway be done away with with as little thought (because a thinking death it's too terrible to imagine, Schneidermann he once told me after telling me that his death it was near)

as we'd accord let's say,

as I'm just remembering now — like when you enter an elevator and you're hearing muzak though just for a minute on your way up like the Ascension to the hundredth plane-targeted-floor:

hearing the first part of a sonata going up up up, hearing the last part of a sonata going down down down, the recapitulation and so missing entirely the middle, the development,

instead you've exited the elevator into something else

entirely

entirely (and almost its moral-same):

      the hum of business to do, of business being and done,

      of money money money for wallpaper but the elevator it keeps on, is the vessel that it still must be inspected regularly for safety's sake every say six or so months,

      going down down down with the quitters the losers 10 persons max. capacity and bringing others up, the select, the chosen,

      up up up to the heights, floors closer to God, exiting and even why not tipping? because I'm a fellow human being, tipping the elevator boy (a man old-as-music, with the — Western — omelets I had for brunch as his uniform's epaulets),

      the resident elevation-expert around here,

      the ferryman version 2.0 who he seemed at least as old as Schneidermann was and I'm,

      I'm in the headquarters, the HQ of my recordlabel, with these multinationals we have now it's the HQ of everyone's recordlabel and here to turn in the liner notes I'd written for an album release by this cellist I'd been engaging vaginally and orally — no names because those of us truly with no fear, at least a positive self-image, well, we don't name names (we just know, Mister Rothstein),

      or it's just that those who are set on mediocrity they should be allowed to pursue their mediocrity in as undisturbed, unmolested a manner as possible — to turn in my linernotes to an album of hers, indeed to her first, debut album that let's be honest no one is going to buy it but her parents and close-relatives,

      friends for X-mas-presents,

      holiday-seasonal-offerings,

      fellow musicians, the Hamptons dinnerparty set too and, even so, the conglomerate it's sure to feel good about itself losing money as they are on high culture,

      content with tax deductions on art I'm entering with my typewritten sheet (and I still three years later have no electronic means nor knowledge of them at my disposal),

      and I catch a glimpse of the album's cover-art, just propped up, in living-size, against a wall office-far,

      a photograph exploded: it's her almost topless, no, I blink and refocus the old myopia, shortsightedness:

her totally naked but blocked from shame by the graceful
and yet huge, lithe and yet lumbering body of her cello,
   a Guarneri 1716 which I've played (poorly),
   and I'm so disgusted and aroused at once at the sight of
this photo, the spectacle (non-spectacle),
   the publicity image and even more so — disgusted — at
what they've titled the album as:
   The Intimate Cello it's called like she's intent on sodomizing
herself with the bow, stemming her moans by biting down on a
puck,
   but here my liner notes read, the praise she'd sucked out of
me:

   The violoncello, as played by NAME WITHHELD, *is an*
instrument of pure song.

   The sheer various beauty of the immense cello repertoire — extending
from the works of Bach to those of the living American composers featured here —
has finally found its match in the sensibility and technique of

and so on and so forth as the release it features, of course,
the requisite Bach suite (the once not and now famous Bach),
   and a bunch of Americana fluff alternating with Jewish —
American — *schmaltz* Schneidermann would say if he said anymore
by composers who they include a dead man
   (but not a Schneidermann), a reformed, you must think
repentant popstar, a handful of — dabbling — jazz musicians and,
well, still I handed in my copy,
   pimped it like a good A & R man should:

   the KOL NIDRE, *by Max Bruch, speaks through the generations in*
a voice of suffering, and, ultimately, of triumph

and, God, I'm such a fake, Jesus!
   but what a great body she has! and that's just the cello!
and I left, not to the elevator no instead I took the stairs like in
case of emergency or fire break your glassiest hip, all 50 flights of
them and emerged as if a planet unto myself and rotated out of
orbit from the lobby to the street more confirmed than disheart-

disheartened

ened, knowing that I'd never stroke her, never varnish her again, no,

and also, wrist-to-ear that I had to meet Schneidermann at 3 p.m. for our never-scheduled — and yet never not-scheduled — matinee movie at a matinee movietheater today that day far to the west by the gray tongue of river that I've often thought about licking (suicide).

Because that's what we'd do, Schneidermann and I we'd go to the movies, as attendees, as an audience of two of one mind and numbed, benumbed with painkillers,

Schneidermann and I having forsaken true artistic achievement or else us having been forsaken by Schneidermann and I we'd watch matinee movies and on painkillers,

painkillers by subscription only, prescriptions refilled in perpetuity — whiskey in one contoured drink holder, COCA-COLA CLASSIC in the other: one on my side, one on his or just both in the contoured containers of the seat in the middle, the medicus between and though I'm not getting paid for saying it (though I should),

the whisky it was always JOHNNIE WALKER RED LABEL but sometimes (if I felt as poor as an idealized Jew) it was JIM BEAM as I told the Detective — good American names, NONE GENUINE, or is it authentic? the label of whichever it says, WITHOUT MY SIGNATURE,

and then JACK DANIEL'S autograph writ underneath as assurance, guarantee, feeling the relaxation manifest itself in our necks (at least my neck),

and shoulders, down to our toes (my toes),

with my shoes off and socks and their feet left to the stick of the floor's spillage and tropical-punch though now flavorless gum,

old holy socks propped up against posted regulations on the seatback in front of me alongside — one jacket-piled seat away from — Schneidermann who he's telling me in the stagewhisper that he'd use at the movies (though we were the only ones in the theater, usually were, or at least so it seemed when Schneidermann he stagewhispered to say, and anyway Schneidermann he usually didn't talk and even in a stagewhisper in the matinee movietheater unless what he had to say it was as important as all-sanctifying fire),

telling me all about his own moviehouse organist days in Hungary in Budapest in Pest because what's there to do in Buda? and in doing so illuminating the appropriate nearly Talmudically-codified-cues (in his own words)

the moviehouse organist he has or at least had available to him for the representation of (reproduction of, parodying of)

let's say birdsong and braying animals, a pratfall and a waterfall like Schneidermann and his urination problems that,

all the denouements, the suspense tropes, the love-death themes so simplified Wagnerian because that's all that Wagner he ever was according to Schneidermann:

the vocal line in the *Ring* almost seeming grafted onto the scoring, the orchestra,

as an afterthought — the same thing as the live and more often than not improvised accompaniment on the moviehouse organ merely

reflecting in Schneidermann's own word (or words, because the *reflected* according to Schneidermann, well, it's unavoidable:

dialektischer, no?), the emotions the images were, and are maybe still, intended to impart to a paying audience who we're,

who they're more eager to submit than Russian Orthodox Churchgoers — who they make wonderful, passionate if erratic lovers, especially the ones with moustaches,

ever so fine, love-bristles like brooms to sweep the stick off your face,

tines inseparable in coital sweat as she ate my ears — her name it was Sophie or Sophia (I forget)

or Sophwhatever with an *f*,

the kind of girl who she won't fall off the bed in the idiom of my youth,

the kind of woman to steal horses with, as my father he often described your grandmother — and but the reason I thought about her just now with the eyes, well, hyperthyroidal

is because she looks exactly like,

that this policewoman here sitting in the three, four, five, SIXTH row center, yes you she has to be a clone of her (we've been eyeing each other all evening, haven't we?),

who her partner,

though

though,

she reminds me of,

yes, is it?

God, *it is you*!

How did you get here? how long have you been here? how
long has it been?

God, hello!

Shalom, because sometimes you just want to say Shalom!

of her which for me is where it must end,

with you, it's amazing you showed up! thanks a life!

where it begins — you my naiad, my nymph (can we get a
spotlight?),

the only her that I ever truly loved truly and, yes, I know
that it sounds ridiculous but the ridiculous,

the stupid is most of the time true (at least at the last-
minute, in opera, in matinee movies),

you who you never walked out on me because you never
walked in on me (with your sister),

just never responded to me, never submitted, you, God it's
great to see you!

were always so great-lipped, tongues within tongues (no, I
can't hear you!),

and well-thighed, just popping everywhere brunetteness
and even when you got fat to me you looked better to me than ever
and now, well, look at you now!

She's here! yes, just arrived, I guess, must have seen me on
the news, up on the teevee, how else? how? thought you could help,
could resolve the situation we have here,

this *regrettable incident* — you must've flirted your way in,

the spectacle of me up on this parquet mountaintop thank
God with the houselights! just now flicked on like the stars you
study and teach so that I can now and finally look my public in the
glasses that (that's how I joked to an exwife, how I knew that I was
alive when the automatic lights on a sensor they went lit outside
our, her, house in Maine and when they wouldn't light above the
doorstop, automatically in my presence home from art and adultery, that's when I would know I used to joke but not joke that I
was indeed already a ghost),

anyway you're here, you've arrived, I'm not saying which

one but you,

were always so half-freckled, and even when you got fat to me you looked better than,

I've thought about you and often, been thinking — we haven't fought in a while, which must mean that I've been out of town,

yes,

of you growing up with my daughters, up up up from the student and the excellent if labored swimmer,

the, well, passable pianist with a prune for a tongue (that once),

such kisses (a daughter's sweet-sixteen-sleepover!),

lashes of the slowest glass, the dry hotness when everything in my house, that old house in Maine — Shaker — when you were up for the weekend to visit my daughter and me,

when it all shrank except the doors when you walked in so I could run out onto the lawn the spics Schneidermann he called them they never cut and scream

help me! and *thank you!* in one word in an imaginary language which means both, just like music,

and now — look at you! — all grown up, grown beyond me to your own husband, family, life,

how you would never sink yourself below me (and for once I'm not referring to fellatio),

allow me now to kneel before you — you Doctor, Doctoress now and professor of stars like mine and like Schneidermann's, but with a husband, am I right? and children?

God, you have kids!

who he's a professor of history too and the Jews, history the lowest discipline according to Schneidermann:

all this dealing with the dead, antiquity when art it's all over, democracy's done with and the darkside, well, it's starving to death (NEVER FORGET Schneidermann would laugh, we never learn!),

to make skin for the unfurling ballot, hand-stitched in gold by labor illegal and migrant into a red carpet,

God! for you to walk all over me on the way to the premiere of this movie I'm doing, I admit,

this movie I've agreed to and just this afternoon,

this

this memory for a movie that I've traded my soul for I
should tell you, yes and you're welcome to attend!

a movie I just agreed to do today — you're welcome, yes, I
did that favor, and one-good-turn-deserves — or actually yesterday
with how late it is, almost, is it? 6 a.m.,

yes, will you accompany me to it? arm-in-arm to the
premiere if I live long enough, long enough to fulfill, will you be
my date down the red tongue?

past flashbulb eyes, will you? would you and please say
yes,

you spit No.

O I could charm all the beasts but I could never charm
you!

You who you always resented my adultery even if I wasn't
adulterating you but my wives and their vows, cheating on you not
as much as I was cheating on my wives (exwives and my vows),

on the wife of mine that you would never be,

you who also and anyway always resented my relationship
with Schneidermann

(guess I've been looking for my Eurydice in all the wrong
places!) — you who never allowed me the room I said and space
you said of my own that I never even allowed myself,

would never allow myself, in our, in me and
Schneidermann's relationship you said which you were always
afraid of, and what's more that you were right to be afraid of (you
always are!),

as my relationship with Schneidermann was if not my
most passionate (this late at night into morning I'll say that that
was with you),

than it was my most deep, my most faithful, my most
important relationship and what's worse is that you knew it,

that you knew you were right (sure, usually-are),

that my relationship with Schneidermann it transcended
ours, mine and yours,

what it was and indeed what it could ever have been,
be,

relationship which as a word it doesn't exist anyway as
Schneidermann he once told me, that at least it doesn't exist in the
way that we think it and use it,

that it's indeed a fallacious misnomer of a word (whereas I always thought that *misnomer*

that it was a Hebrew word or at least Aramaic, such strange lapses!),

relationship the shibboleth of millions of overweight women marooned on exercycle islands the oceans over,

a password so necessary to the economy of the psychological profession,

an advertising slogan so vital to the linking of THIS worthlessness to THAT worthlessness,

relationship a word as Schneidermann he once told me first used by Pope in his 1743 edition of *The Dunciad* and have you ever read it Schneidermann he asked?

and no I answered, used by Pope according to Schneidermann who had read it — of course he had — to *relate* his enemy Cibber to mad busts sculpted by his father, what Pope calls Cibber's *brothers* and if so then a fraternity most strange,

relationship, a word, a noun, a linking of contempt really, of calumny even, the true meaning of which it has been revived only in our time, up on the screen in this movie that I think you've all seen it — it seems to be your taste, on-your-level — all about the ship that it's named the TITANIC and it the movie it's titled *Titanic* as well,

a movie huge and grand all about a huge grand sinking ship and a quickie love-death — *liebestod* if you know it — enacted on deck and, fleetingly, in the waters surrounding,

I know, operatic! this movie *Titanic* that Schneidermann and I we took in on one too long afternoon giving way with mixed precipitate to early evening when Schneidermann he told me afterwards over hot mocha with marshmallows and extra pink and green and yellow marshmallows (for him, the younger man treating, as always)

that he would have loved to have had a shot at playing for it (were it 50 or so years ago, the old hands),

by which Schneidermann he meant forget Celine Dion that leonine-looking but feline-sounding Frenchtalian bitch! Schneidermann he insisted, let me play the score!

me, on a moviehouse organ, Verdi-style, Giuseppe's *Requiem*-style but orchestrated and perpetrated all on a moviehouse

organ

organ, yes, Joe Green-style to pull out all the stops, to catch all the nuances that that James-Horner-schmuck missed, because as Schneidermann he explained that the moviehouse organist he can respond,

> in his toe-tapping gumming and popcorn flatulence,
> to the film, the movie and what's more,
> *to the audience,*
> and in what's now our *real time,*
> and so tell me, Mister Rothstein who it's amazing that

you're still around,

> tell me that that's not more modern than what it, the

practice, what it was forsaken for,

> the improvisation forsaken for the fixed — or is the

utterly adaptable, flexible, protean, mobile or just modular, well, are they outdated already?

> *passé* as the Germans say?
> like last season's HIP, IN, TRENDY, STYLISH and yet

now remaindered office furniture?

> borax for the corporate set straight from the most social-

ist-efficient warehouses of Sweden, an Oriental-seeming office-cubicle looking also much to these dying eyes and from offices afar like a glacier, O God maybe it even comes in the GLACIER color?

> which shade?
> do you think (ask the representative for more details,

samples, swatches)?

> altogether something to smack up against, to test your

mettle against, this partition floating amid — iceberg-frosted — glass across the winedark wall-to-wall as I,

> I walked toward this miscellaneous executive's office for

this meeting I'd refused a forgettable number of times but a meeting, an appointment that I was, finally,

> obliged — forced — to honor and this afternoon by a girl

a woman who I need to be loved by,

> that one, my love, yes I bared it, came-through
> and you're welcome,
> my true love who you'll minister to me tomorrow, won't

you? that is, if survival it's to be mine,

> yes her, you and you know how to thank me,
> you who only kissed (once),

you who would actually never be my lover no matter how I asked or how much,

begged, what I bought you (pearls, third houses, tampons),

might as well tell it, who her bestfriend-in-the-world she's in the movie-industry and could,

would I do her — her — a favor? you asked, didn't you? last-week-on-the-phone?

a favor for her oldest, dearest friend who she's just now and after a failed first career — housewife — getting into casting (as a receptionist, sorry, personal-assistant),

moving certain well-worn faces into certain well-worn roles, spreading the money around thick on faces with a spackling or margarine knife,

ensuring that we all know the same people as different people so as to stay as confused and yet as safe as our credit lines they will allow,

staying prepared and yet also and at the same time deliciously unprepared as I walked with that oldest as dearest bestfriend and into her boss' office, into the miscellaneous movie executive's office:

everything catalog-ordered perfect like I was his mother arrived for a surprise inspection, I sat down in one of the two quote unquote comfortably overstuffed leather chairs suspended high above the Park as the bestfriend who she served as his personal assistant, more accurately her breasts did that bore me in from Reception they retreated in pursuit of the hot water with lemon that I'd asked for and, please, no sugar make it saccharine so that my manhood it shrivels to scrotal tumor, yes I even said please as the manchild across from me — this was earlier today — this boy-man with longish hair platinum as a rich Nazi's, his smooth to daily-moisturized hand it was still extended, fingers splayed like well-manicured shivs, unmet by me and then retracted into a hair-smoothing gesture to mire his something-scented gel (hair), in his something-scented moisturizer (hand), and so we just sat down, slowly, and he, with impatient courtesy as much as youthful though youthful-executive exuberance, kept quiet and yet questioning as I,

I surveyed his squared palace: an altar of brushed metal

ashtrays

ashtrays though it was probably a federal offense to smoke in there, antique greenglass lamps with the brassified, brassinated pullchains from which dangled hasty yellow squarelets of sticky memoranda, photographs only of himself posed with casual caution on jetty rocks with various beautiful women and skinny boys (his nephews, as I later learned as if I wanted to), and then to my left — his right — and propped up high against the wide glareless glass tipped to falling over the Park (as if to shatter through, fall and smash a head in):

a gravestone, a headstone, a tombstone and as I was studying it — the name it was *Schneider*, *Schneider* only, he couldn't read it too well and I,

I obviously could — the miscellaneous movie executive he wound up and made me his pitch: we love you, we love you, we all love you, I'm talking L.O.V.E., huge fans, and we want you, we do, no one but you because O God are you perfect! absolutely, Mister um Laster, you're the one for this, well, there's this movie: THAT'S WHAT I WANT is the working title, it's a *ro-co* (a *romantic comedy*, as the miscellaneous movie executive he explained, self-conscious-industryspeak), and it's great, funny as funny as all hell like all seven of them it's starring Drew of the Barrymore dynasty and some guy who I'd never heard of who he's American but he seems somehow British the miscellaneous movie executive he couldn't quite explain it and, well, the long and short of the story is that the girl she's this kind of punky, spunky chick, right? and then there's this guy, a very serious blueblood Fleet Street and so on lawyer who he falls for her, head-over-loafers' heels in love with her and tries to civilize her, it's classic:

there's a totally laugh-out-loud dinnerparty scene at his parents' on Park Avenue, a great church confessional scene (the lawyer he's religious, or his family is and she's not, she's topless), and then there's this scene, what we're talking about here, involving you or we hope, a scene in which he takes her to the orchestra, the symphony, this very hall, indeed this is the pivotal scene, climax and then CREDITS — the lawyer he's a civilizing influence, or at least tries to be, you understand? that's the running gag limping: you can't change a person, can you? the miscellaneous movie-executive he didn't let me answer and so in this last great scene the lawyer he takes her to this hall, ladies and gentlemen, here, and of course he's all dressed up appropriately tuxed and she's not, she's all spunked-out they show up in a limo, stretch, pull up to the curb, enter and go into a VIP box, Dress Circle of course, undressed underdressed, this is the movies, you understand?

this was today, this afternoon, this meeting it was only some-15-16 hours ago, ladies and gentlemen, and, of course, he the miscellaneous movie executive went on: and of course we want, no we'd love it, would be honored if it was you up onstage, you high onstage in this last great scene and playing your piano (*violin*, I was about to say and was interrupted)

(music in a movie that's not overdubbed, it's called diegetic the miscellaneous movie executive he interrupted himself after I'd failed to, "a hallmark of neo-realism" he boasted I dropped out of film school before), but then she, the Taming of the Drew she's going to throw a fit, you understand? I did, she's going to pitch a tantrum in the audience and with everyone just looking on, even you, you just stop playing and stare, and listen! everyone shocked and shushed, spotlight on her screaming at him screaming at her and then just voila!

(apparently they didn't script this part yet, it was still being punched-up) they all just laugh, kiss and make up, the lawyer he proposes marriage or whatever something like that it just doesn't matter as the music it swells, you playing again and all the audience including his parents they just applaud and applaud and applaud just like mad:

yes, this'll be *the moment of truth in their relationship* — at which I interrupted, asked him an obvious question, asked him what piece I should play (on the piano, or the violin, I'm an old circus-man, both?) to be interrupted by her, by their tantrum and the miscellaneous movie executive he just shrugged what? like he would know, like why would you ask me? and something like that? like that's what we have musical supervisors for like some communist apparat apparatchik I told him, then a silence

(awkward), a tritone but a silent tritone,

a devil's interval of silence and then I, I just did the logical *thing*,

which was that I asked him and as innocently as possible, in a small-talk-sort-of-way (though I was dying),

asked as if I was asking a worthless question just to use

the

the time it would take for him to give me an answer equally
worthless in which to think about his offer, to engineer a response
to it and so I asked him,

     I was dying to ask him all about the tombstone the
miscellaneous movie executive he had tipped against the infinite
glass above the forever Park where — and the miscellaneous movie
executive he answered, immediately and eager, that it was from
Europe, and from where in Europe? I asked like an x-examining
lawyer and the miscellaneous movie executive he answered that it
was from Eastern Europe, uhuh, from Hungary specifically and
explained that in an earlier incarnation of moguldom that he'd
worked scouting locations for various HOLLYWOOD film
productions in Eastern Europe, for five years and right after the
fall of communism, God those were crazy years! he the miscellaneous movie executive went on, the fall of the Iron Curtain and so
on and so forth,

     and that after all the Prague locations they got overshot a
few years back, got more expensive, legislation and so on, that he'd
been instrumental in shifting most of the big-name/big-money
productions over to Budapest, Magyarville, Hunland, both sides of
the Danube, a great town and so on and so forth:

     beautiful as its women and the miscellaneous movie
executive he went he goes on and on with words such as CASTLE
and LIQUOR, but soon notices that I'm only half-listening, all-
staring at the stone and so the miscellaneous movie executive he
says:

     anyway, you can read it? and I answer, yes, and the miscel-
laneous movie executive he says well, you have to tell me what it
says sometime and so not yet sometime I tell him to go on, and so
he says:

     so anyway, long story short (but not short enough),

     my mother, I'm from Long Island the Five Towns she told
me that her parents they were from this asshole in northeastern
Hungary up near the Slovak and Ukrainian borders,

     and the Romanian border too I said,

     indeed the confluence of the four borders I knew where
and,

     yes, the miscellaneous movie executive he said that the
town's name it was Sárospatak (I grandfathered his pronunciation:

SHAAA, the *a* as in *father*-ROSH-PA-TAK),

and she my mother she asked me to go there, said if I had the time, which from my mother it means to do it and get some photos,

yadda yadda yadda and so one day in the last month of my gig there — I was supposed to come back to the States, moved into casting thanks to my cousin — anyway I got a company driver and a company car it pissed me off because it had all these advertising stickers all over it, the company's NAME writ large across the four-door (product-placement along the Heritage Trail),

anyway, I'd found it on the map I bought when we gassed up (on the company's forint),

and so we left Budapest (where I had a wonderful apartment, split-level-luxury,

anyway), and headed for this dot on the map that it might've just been some sweater lint name-designer,

and a few hours later from Budapest the capital (I know it's the capital I said, want to tell me in Hungarian?),

O, so you know Hungary? the miscellaneous movie executive he said: okay, so we're on the M3 and heading up to Debrecen but you pull a dogleg at Füzesabony up to Miskolc, the north-by-northeast route up through Szerencs, the chocolate-capital-of-the-East, you know (he'd dated a pornstar with a sweet ass and sweet tooth)? and then Mezőzombor up to, Sárospatak I said, yes, a few hours later of listening to the Rolling Stones and Led Zeppelin IV and we arrive, show up and scout around, nothing much to do, we ask some natives for some directions to the Jewish ghetto, the Jewish quarter of town there — there's no shul there or rabbi's house or anything like that still standing (apparently my great-grandfather he was the Chief Rabbi there), there's just a mikvah, a ritual bath (I know what a mikvah is, I told him go on), a mikvah that my friend the Chabad Rabbi in Budapest he told me about after he'd researched it with colleagues and contacts on the Internet like dubyadubyadubya.dot.wehavenofoodorclothingin-easternhungarybutwedohavetheinternet.dot.com: an old mikvah that an old couple they were living in, bought it outright from the State in 1992 during Privatization, them and their red-hatted-garden-gnomes it turned out that they kept fenced in in the garden alongside a model, a diorama that the husband of the couple he

had

had built with all his retirement and pension money and time: a non-ruined scale-model of the ruined castle to-scale, just standing there against the fence of the property it was shaped like a menorah (want to see some pictures? he asked, then went to tap at his laptop until I shut its screen for him to urge him on) —

we saw all the storks, their nests and the actual living castle, ruined in the flesh and then, well, I had my driver, Zoltán I had him ask one of the natives for the Jewish cemetery of the town and the third guy we asked, riding his rackety bicycle over this rickety bridge over this river ass-brown, this he was the oldest guy that we asked, and he knew, indeed he seemed as if he was the only one who knew where, directed us there and so it was there that we went: looked for my name, actually my mother's familyname, either Kestenbaum or Weiss, Rabbi Weiss he was the Chief Rabbi there in the 1900s apparently, Ferencz or Ferenc Weisz his name was, which is the Jewish equivalent of, which translates to Frank White but it sounds so much better — but the cemetery it was in ruins, either by the Nazis or by time, or by the locals and, well, the inscriptions were in Hebrew, are in Yiddish maybe and that's the reason that I can't read them too well, at all, they were a mess, deep in moss and rained-away — we jumped over the cemetery's stonewall, the gate it was locked all for nothing and we looked around, my driver, Zoltán always in an astrakhan hat that it looked like a mons veneris grown wild he was totally perplexed, to-be-expected, like what-the-fuck? was the deepest thing that Zoltán he could say about this whole thing in the American language (my-Hungarian-sucks), a decent guy though, don't-get-me-wrong, knew where all the willing extras and models were in Pest, the newest, most progressive bars with the Westernmost cocktails — and I wanted to take home a souvenir (all I had now was paprika and photos, for my mom, who she didn't want the stone, like not in my livingroom it clashes with the drapes), and the only stone I could lift it was this small one, at least smaller than the rest, don't know whose it is, don't know who's on it or who was under it I just lifted it because I could, threw it over the stonewall, lifted it again, took it back in the car with us back to Budapest, we stopped at a highway fastfood joint same as highway fastfood joints all over the world, right? for HOT MEAT SANDWICHES, as Hungarian restaurants they try to translate their menu into my language and

FANTA orange soda on me always expensed and we were back in
Budapest, well, I'd say by dark, and when I left for the States the
next month I took it with me, the stone, wrapped in plasticbags in
a suitcase and locked, Customs it didn't even check and now here it
is, are you satisfied and, well, will you do our movie? what-do-you-
say?

and so I told him my logic, my thinking, my deal-with-
the-Devil: told him that, yes, that indeed I would do the movie
but, well, only on one condition,

and the miscellaneous movie executive he was *all ears* as
that proverb goes,

told him that yes I would do the movie but that I would
only do the movie for the stone, that this stone it was the condi-
tional, the stone in payment was what I wanted, no other remunera-
tion required and the miscellaneous movie executive he looked
flustered, out-of-his-element and so I said yes again, said that I
would do it, again, I said, but for the stone and only on condition
of the stone,

of the stone of one Baruch Schneider, son of the father it
was illegible, overgrown with moss and where not then just snow-
eroded away, Baruch Schneider born it was also illegible, died 5670
I calculated the Jewish to the secular date in my head (the Jewish
year inscribed there it was 5670 and this Schneider he was born
late in it, so take 5670 I told him and subtract the magic number
3760 I remembered that it equals 1910 in anno domini),

and that no other money would be necessary, requested or
required, even wanted and the miscellaneous movie executive he
adumbrated all those come-on-nows,

come-off-its,

incredulous, out-of-his ordinary and so I said listen, just
give me the stone and I'll give you $3,000 personally, no strings
attached and obviously I'll also and gladly do the movie — like nu?
as Schneidermann often said, so what do you think? yes, finally the
miscellaneous movie executive he said yes and so finally I deigned
to shake his moisturized, gelled and sweating-manicure hand, told
him to wait, that I'd be back down down down the elevator (from
which the operator had disappeared, descended to lunch), past
lobby security and out the door, broke into the bank one street up
and withdrew that amount, $3,000 in cash in $100 bills I stuffed

into

into my jacketpockets all four of them and a half-hour later
returned, dropped the $3,000 cash in $100 bills on his desk,
pretensions-to-teak, and the miscellaneous movie executive he —
now unguarded — said hey like wow! okay, fine if I was serious,
which obviously I was, or else insane or what? that he'll call my
agent and today with the particulars

      (and did he, Adam?) and then I, I picked up the stone,

      it was lighter than it seemed, which is a rarity with stones
as with women,

      and I took it out to the lobby, the elevator down down
down to the L of the lobby, past security and out the revolverous
door and out to the Park,

      this was this afternoon at around 3 p.m. about two hours
prior to last rehearsal and soundcheck and I,

      well, there in the Park I found sleeping — on the
pitchingmound of a municipal diamond — a homeless man named
something I'm sure but he never told me other or what (sounds-
like?),

      gave him $50 with a promise of $50 more to run and now
as fast to a local-hardware-store,

      and return with a shovel (he said he knew where, I was too
exhausted,

      too much *tzedakah*),

      and so waited (was he coming back?),

      and waited how dumb am I under the huge bursting body
of air,

      thin-stitched garment of sky — sitting on a bench beside
the stone and against all my intuition he the homeless man who
maybe he lacked a name as much as a home he if miracles ever
happen did he returned and with a shovel glinting virgin against the
sun's plunge,

      gave him the other and my last $50 to help me dig *nur die
Wind, den solches Blatt im Wenden würfe, reichte hin, die Luft, wie eine Scholle,
umzuschaufeln* Schneidermann he hated to love those lines lifted
from where?

      wir schaufeln ein Grab in den Lüften da liegt man nicht eng were the
— up — lifting lines that Schneidermann loved: it was dark
already and I wanted a grave for my Schneidermann, and though he
wasn't a *mann* a *Schneider* he had to do, a man or a mann who he

might've been a tailor — maybe even a composer too — who he died in the same year that Schneidermann, that my Schneidermann he might have been born,

the homeless nameless man and I we walked the stone out deeper into the Park and under some oaktrees (I think),

a grove, and there taking turns on the purest synthetic materiality of shovel (it was a snowshovel, molded plastic, from the homeless and nameless what to expect?)

dug it the stone deep, deep enough into the freeze of the ground,

I, then I found the most volcanic stone around,

an igneous pebble erupted into my foot, a pebblet I then placed on the stone as per tradition or as if to hold the larger stone in place, from the wind and the rain and,

and now, if you'll look there: in America, in New York, in the Park, in the 60s, near 68th Street if I remember it right and under the nymph-abandoned, nymph-divorced oaktrees,

oaking a grove,

there's a Jewish gravestone from a small town in Hungary, which is now the only approved, official grave of my friend Schneidermann,

of the great musician Schneidermann,

of the transcendent musician Schneidermann wherever he is and whether Schneidermann he's dead or not,

even if Schneidermann he's still alive, wherever (the sofa overstuffed I always promised him in Florida? the Ever-glade?),

that is, if the Park-people, if Maintenance it hasn't already removed it to wherever they warehouse these things,

exemplar of metro-strangeness,

and the movie, well, it starts shooting next month, if there even is a next month for me now,

and now what? you're going to electroshock me or something like you did to Charlie Parker in a trench Uptown only a few years after I,

I played the violin behind him and staggered out of that studio's ragged, bottle-and-butt-strewn-nest just stunned to my very, Schneidermann he would say *pupik*?

that night I couldn't sleep and almost no night after that, either, his — high-fly — alto ricocheting between my ears because,

well

well, why sleep?

and so out I went again that night out in the early days of
this past half-century and out to pace the Park,

doing my mental laps,

to get mugged of a forged Greek passport — my name
it would have been Stavros Romaniote, born 1929 — it turns
out I wouldn't have needed anyway but bought and just liked
carrying around (you never know, I never do),

a contingency as much as my talent is, was — the Park
where I just today buried or not-buried Schneidermann under or
not under the stone of a Schneider:

a dark grave in the dark,

a grave of one piano key just standing thought-high in the
midst of the municipal recreation facilities,

a gravemarker of one piano key all that's left on the ash ice
plain,

this one pianokeyshaped headstone,

this one tombshaped pianokey: lone and so who knows
which note it once sounded? once was charged with? its duty?
which note whether pitched heaven or hellwards it once was fated
to? which note it was burdened with? condemned unto weather to?

which it memorialized or memorializes?

one disembodied death-black,

death-dark many-named and yet unnoted pianokey standing stark as rude and upright in a pile of bonechips, ice and ash in
the apocalypse of the late winter night's Park — an idol with no
worshippers or,

rather,

our death,

all death is to be the worship of this God rising and only
now,

after dark back home, back in childhood, in young-young-
young-childhood,

this the stuff-of-earliest-memories

and how I'd hide like a Jew under the sag of my bed,

or in the piano making those sounds in my mouth's sore
that I'd wished I could make with my hands (like my father, at our
black-as-cancer which is what killed my mother piano),

and how I'd just go and ruin the already ruinous piano

more, make our old upright piano even more dead, deader still as I
would steal those — sweeter-than-marzipan-to-me — keys from
it,

would steal one key from it at a time, bringing them and
always one at a time, one a night and up up up to my room and
always replacing the last one I took the last night with the new one
of this night:

I would steal a D, take it upstairs after I replaced
yesterday's C♯ or D♭, the same thing on the piano if not to the
well-tempered-ear, upstairs and up more to my room I was tod-
dling, just walking which was then mostly Adam-type-falling for
me and with the new key of the new night in my sticky-with-lint-
and-honey-hands,

with today's new key disembodied, separated from its sex
and there, in my whitewashed room I would've shared with my
sister had she lived, just trying each — disembodied — one and
just to hear whether, to hear if it indeed contained that magic, if it
concealed that magic,

to find which one was it that it was the magical one, the
special one that I always heard in my head and in

(from) my father but that I could never find when I
wanted to, if, when I tried, could never identify and isolate and just
have all to

(for) myself, to find that special warmth,

that note that it had that warmth to it (which warmth I
found only later, with and in Schneidermann),

that lowness in the high and that weight in that light and
as I got through, exhausted all the 88 keys that we had, our entire
piano's reach, how I found — and much to my loss of innocence,
which wasn't in the end a total loss, merely was innocence

contextualized as they say up at the University that it would
never hire Schneidermann even to teach Music Appreciation 101
(and maybe because Schneidermann he didn't appreciate music,
more like lived it and hated himself),

was actually and totally innocence deepened — that not
one of them had it, that none of them did, any of the keys, possessed it, the magic, or was possessed by it and also that the music
it never changed, that the notes they never changed upon my
replacement of them, even when I reordered the keys, reattached

them

them when I replaced them each night in a different order, assigned
or reassigned each as I then thought to other, different pitches
(emotions, and so on),

      that there was no missing note,

      or no note to fill up my loss,

      no breathing in the emptiness behind it all that I had
already lost and how? in all my stealing and replacing,

      detaching reattaching and ordering, reordering how after all
88 keys of this, 88 days or maybe a whole year of this maybe it
was when I was 5 years old how I,

      6,

      how I just and forever ruined my father's piano which it
ruined him too as,

      7 or 8 inexcusable!

      ruined it totally even more than ruined, made deader than
dead it was gone, rendered deadest — and so the money to purchase a new one it was saved,

      the expense we couldn't afford,

      my mother's cancer,

      collapsing and,

      dying and,

      Europe collapsing and — but still there's work to do, to
be done, to do you,

      work making the man as Schneidermann he often insisted,
the man dying and the work living on as Schneidermann his
disappearance must insist,

      what was intended to be art surviving though as nothing
more than a confession, and so — that acknowledged and Schneidermann buried even if he's not, totally, truly, wholly, dead — it's
time for me to become my own man, to be my own mann my own

      mensch Schneidermann he always said:

      unlike Orpheus never to turn back, around, behind me, in
an effort to redeem, to save,

      which is to die,

      alone,

      but not before declaring myself, me,

      as a no one,

      a non-entity,

      if an Orpheus then an Orpheus without a myth, a myth

without a hero, a Jew who I didn't even have a halfway decent
opportunity to survive,
    or to die,
    whose family — fathers, one of talent one of life — got
him out of Europe before Europe it would have gotten him out,
through a smokestack, into the air,
    how I didn't have my shot at martyrdom and so this,
among you art-idiots,
    you art-retards,
    you Americans,
    among my fellow Americans if I have to admit
(O how I envy their estate! the coffin-as-a-booth-of-
confession), whereas Schneidermann, how Schneidermann he
survived survival for much less gain!
    and so I've lost out yet again to a man who he never won,
ever and, well, explain that! Schneidermann as a certain or uncer-
tain Schneider of Sárospatak-in-the-Park and me the son of an
immigrant opportunist,
    a hack pianist who he laughed at all the — exterminated
— relatives who they laughed at him when he announced his
intention and then actually followed through with it, to move us
here,
    my father whose son I don't want to be,
    my father who should've been my Schneidermann,
    my Schneidermann who he should've been my father, the
father I am and don't ever want to be and, what's more humiliating,
the father I still will be even after my
    death,
    even after my Jewish death as all deaths are Jewish
    and my Jewish burial as all burials they're Jewish — like
those of the Greeks that Schneidermann he always told me about,
of Homer who when a hero dies in his epics he's described as the
son of someone, or at least that's how it is in the original German.
    Is there another crown my size? and can I borrow it?
    I'm having mine blocked,
    money's in the hatband to the back hung on the rack in
my dressingroom — save the redeeming stub left in your other
mouth,
    along with a will for my lawyers' 100 eyes only, stipulating

that

that human whatever your name is, if you're still there, here and I
don't want to know in Row AA, Seat 100,

　　　and some vodka and slivovitz still left on the *vanity*,
appropriate word,

　　　　　going back to my roots,

　　　forsaking the scotch and the whiskey and three encrusted
monogrammed handkerchiefs containing what could conceivably be
three children or more because, children, my seed's still strong,
have any doubts?

　　　　　but I should tie my tongue in a bowtie now,

　　　　　before,

　　　which makes me seem like a monkey anyway, a monkey
strangled by a butterfly — and so I am that I am,

　　　which I've also read and heard said to me in the original
and could repeat to you if you cared enough. But you don't. *Ganz
und gar nicht* according to Schneidermann. Like what he said.

　　　　　O accents,

　　　accents — no, instead you'll let me go or make me young,

　　　　　but not just yet, langsam, rit – ritardando, wait up:

　　　I took your ear strangely, and I'll give it back if you'll
refund me my deposit in full (I'm paid a week ahead at the Grand!
ten days in-advance!) — like when last I had sexual intercourse, it
was three nights ago, another María and, well, as I

　　　climaxed — cleaved — all I could think of it was Psalm
137:

　　　that order to rip your tongue out before singing your song
to strangers (Schneidermann he always loved that Psalm, wanted to
set it for choir and hand-organ),

　　　all those willows hung with all those harps like the fruit of
the fruitless (Schneidermann he never found time for that opus),

　　　that order to exit or exeunt Schneidermann and I but we're
not over, just yet.

　　　Let me take a bow, and then we'll get down to the business
of the unfinished:

　　　an industry in serious trouble of late, but for what reason?
why does everything require your pledge-driven-generous-support?

　　　NEVER FORGET the free umbrella! the-totebag-
complimentary! (filled with ashes) — like why can't someone or
thing just succeed honestly in this world, on his or her or its own

merit? asked my daughters and sons, asked my Schneidermann who
he should have known:

like what to expect of this — anti-art — world in this —
anti-music — universe with its string more like a noose streaming
on down from the *nut*?

Like me — I can't play this *thing*!

Me? I slept my way to the top! and now I just want to die,

and not a slow Yiddish death like you once found down on
2nd Avenue,

but fast! immediate! must divest as my portfolio analyst
who he couldn't make it tonight, sends his best regards, whitest
flowers though I'm sure he's always telling me that,

God! I want to die,

    die,

        die,

            die,

                die!

                I've smashed this into, this violin,

                and this should be a Yiddish or at
least a Yinglish word (Schneidermann he
loved to Ying),

                I've smashed it into *smithereens* (Gaelic
shards).

                A waste?

                Worth priceless, don't own it.

                Stick of a bow, snapped over my knee.

                Well, tell me why not?

Gasp

Gasp.

    Vomit.

    Not mine to waste,

    because I've turned Asian women into observant Jews, I'm sick — JAP-ish they speak:

    Mushi-mushi, is here Sarah and the like, because I've turned — would-be — violinists into auto-mechanics, into taxi-drivers, insurance salesmen, lawyers, doctors, exwives, into failures, would-be failures

    and even suicides (I ask you don't ask),

    because I've turned myself into

    myself,

    because I've watered the wine that was art, wasted my time, yours, God's and, yes, Schneidermann's all on this fermata:

    this bird's eye staring everything still, but its shell, in here, this gilded expanse I've been heating and stirring in and now peck, peck, peck:

    chickenscratch the orchestra would say (but they're underpaid and overworked or invert that),

    in the man's own handwriting Schneidermann he wrote their parts out himself though I helped some one drunk American night up at my penthouse at the Grand Oldage Home,

    the Grand Funeralhome,

    because season after seasons — inevitably premiering with Mozart and postmiering with Beethoven — O God how I've made mistakes!

    omitted notes, which ones?

    slowed down metronome markings, freely interpreted difficult measures but so what?

    They are what made me, splinters at my feet — that I am them and they are me, a mistake myself and so what are you? and what are you going to do about it?

    that I'm a fraud and that really sets you off, gets you as mad as is deemed polite, appropriate,

    makes necessary additional psychoanalysis sessions you'll owe and far too much for — because you've already paid for this, for me and own my albums, for me and my own art and my Schneidermann and his and how now you'll have to radically revise your opinions,

cocktail/dinnertable-talk,
your entire idea.
I've made my difficult passage, and now I just want to die.
I've smashed my violin that isn't mine.
Dead.

And

And so approach,
        because I'm worthless and the whole world it's mislaid its
mental apparatus,
        lost the instructions and the markings and no one knows
what's good and what's not anymore,
        and what would it matter anyway if they did? as Schneider-
mann he killed himself maybe or maybe not by maybe just allowing himself to get old and slow and tired, to rest on his laurels that
were mostly of-his-mind (and latterly out-of-it),
        to get insane and just disappear one day from our matinee
Holocaust movietheater, and from his welfare hole at nearly a 100
years old, if you take his earliest possible guess at a date his father
and his nine aunts they never told him,
        or told him eight things — and leaving behind only shit,
worthlessness, history (the first, last and only estate that Schneidermann he loathed),
        some other compositions — which? how and why? — and
this his *Concerto* that I haven't even explained yet (played),
        which will never be explained (played),
        which I never finished (played),
        which will never be properly finished, played again (and
that if Schneidermann he lived any longer he would've soon enough
thought it — unplayed — unfinished itself as himself,
        would have wanted to sit on it more, to rethink, rework,
relive),
        no *movement* in the future, understand? no directions staged
or not, no next scene, next waiting waiting waiting and then what?
        When our redemption it's
        in the waiting (according to Schneidermann).
        Is the waiting (according to Schneidermann might as well
as say me).
        Bridegroom by the door (unfinished opera's first scene),
impatient, enumerating petals.
        Bride still upstairs, always, dressing, too proud to ask for
help to fasten (duet)

        Diese Kette von Rätseln
        Um den Hals der Nacht gelegt

Yes, it's time,
        set firm in its foundations,
it's your cue, officers, your entrance,
time for you to approach the royal presence,
        it's in the to-be-evened score — you badges,
bluemen, Courtiers from the empire most foreign:
        empire of decorum, empire of politesse, empire of
fat and happiness, applause light on the palm,
                and but when this involves *death*!
        a Romantic death in which nothing's going to
resolve in the end,
        the Classicists who don't even know what Classi-
cism is anymore (my children, the suburbs),
        your comedy and tragedy masks without ears, you
ever notice?
        all these frayed veins marbled,
        all your subscriptions sold out to multinational compa-
nies for vital clients,
        expense-accounted to impress whomever flying in from
overseas, an excuse to get dressed up, groomed and perfumed and,
                no, don't obtain permission!
                get clearance!
        don't!
                come in,
        rush in,
where everyone they fear to tread.

O

O Schneidermann, why hast thou forsaken me, for whom and
what's in it for you?
        Verily, let us split the difference. Heaven or hell.
        O Schneidermann drop a cloud of a piano on me now
(you'll say a Kaddish for Rudy's next incarnation),
        God's turd (how Schneidermann he said *piano*),
        here on me now in the *anus mundi* (sadly Schneidermann's
name for America, for anywhere he was not understood and but),
        O pucker up and listen to me! you who are left,
        left alone,
        you who have survived this and expect your reward,
        your explanation,
        your justification — you who are left and haven't been
here before because the State it doesn't pay you adequate salaries,
        I propose raises all around and all the precincts they get a
night at the opera every week,
        with presentation of badge and bullets and gun and but
what good would that do? what effect?
        Instead you're usually at home asleep, or else up late to
morning and with your life on the screen,
        as 3 out of 5 sapiens or sentients prefer,
        and then the hang — suspension — for the next install-
ment, STAY TUNED or else,
        to be continued...
        within the span of your indulgence,
        unto closure, the arch arched, the end, the finale,
        a resolution without encore:
        me on the 8 a.m. news, tomorrow, which is today,
        now and as you're just trying to get-by, rush the hour,
        O allow me a stationed break in the way of advertised
sorrows for that great lover of Orpheus his name it was Thomas
Taylor,
        whom the Americans, especially Emerson loved and not
the Europeans and why?
        despite that loved by Schneidermann too,
        because no one and even now at history's end is able to
resolve preference and the empirical,
        as Schneidermann who he once set these lines so beauti-
fully and for boys' chorus so often and so quietly asserted in his

quiet,

      this Taylor, this Taylormann who he says,
      sings his Orphic ode to death:

      Thy fleep perpetual burfts the vivid folds,
      By which the foul, attracting body holds:

      No fuppliant arts thy dreadful rage controul,
      No vows revoke the purpofe of thy foul;

I'm

I'm so tired!

    how tired are you?

    that I can't even tell between the two (sleep and death, audience and audienced and),

    and O the vivid folds!

    O so tired that I can't even kill myself, so afraid that I can't even kill myself, too afraid as all poets are, as all artists are, as all prophets are,

    all afraid of not being a martyr.

    And so someone betray me besides myself! someone martyr me!

    and you're coming, yes, finally you listen,

    come! don't walk! run! to embrace a lost brother who stole the age's birthright, and you'll bear the gifts of

    silence: a honeyed key kept warm under a wet tongue,

    or under the doormat like an ebony pianokey sounding entry to every wife's house I don't belong in,

    am legally barred from.

    Make me unto myself, my true self or at least who and what I once was (young, with promise that it needed nothing else),

    someone, anyone, please! I'll make it worth your while (is my wallet still making the rounds?),

    while I can't have much time left — you all have guns, so use them, won't you?

    a big-big-boom!

        a boom-big-boom!

        the kettledrum that ends this work, the fire-truck New York, New York sound and the anvil of Mahler — but, wait!

            no!

                  we haven't even gotten to Mahler yet,

                  fully, all, and so wait!

                      hold up!

                          Schneidermann

                  yes,

            he was eclipsed,

        but Alma,

        with whom he,

    but I,

no gag, allow a man his dignity, yes:
by the shoulders,
and dignified,
okay, so three steps back and bow to the
,
because what else is there to respect except those things
that are not,
for the very nature of their nonexistence, no, their potential,
because there are some things that are, that must be left
unsaid,
unevoked-uninvoked,
and they are art,
because what can we expect of ourselves?
being as nothing from nothing,
ashes-to-ashes-to,
hanging by our fingertips from the lowest rung of the
angel's ladder (Maintenance),
and how we've all now lost that past footing the
bill — and so we scream!
everyone, all together now, aaaaaaaaa!
O my God Rilke too!
I apologize — where's my memory?
Schneidermann, what have you done with it?

Sei allem Abschied voran, als wäre er hinter
dir, wie der Winter, der eben geht.
Denn unter Wintern ist einer so endlos Winter,
daß, überwinternd, dein Herz überhaupt übersteht

which were Schneidermann's and so my favorite lines from
those *Sonnets to Orpheus*,
yet another work of his unheard — by anyone but him —
set in his head for castrato solo and 100 lyres,
and but wait, no!
Yes, so now lead me out.
I'll never remember it all but I will
lead the processional,
up the redcarpet for my coronation: a crown of stars and

not

not back through the wings,
     no,
     under the balconies, down the center aisle,
     out the door to the lobby and out the lobby's door into
winter,
     the stations,
     it's X-mas soon, treetops starring the skies,
     low doors, modest for a hall of this stature, aren't they?
     To humble the seeker seeking and finding the grandeur of
art.
     Human.
     Expected-expecting.
     Forgive me.
     Good morning!
       and yes,
           O is it snowing out?
             yes, soon...
                 soon...
                     soon...
                         O the lit air.

ACKNOWLEDGMENT

Schneidermann's most evident typographic feature, the use of the so-called *catchword*, in which the first word of a following page is caught below the margin of the page previous, intends to replicate in prose the practice of indicating musical cues on individual instrumental parts; these cues are indicated so that a musician, whose hands might soon be occupied playing, does not have to waste time — time better spent in physical and mental preparation for an impending entrance — on turning pages.

The work of literature in which I initially encountered this marginalia is *The Hymns of Orpheus, Translated from the Original Greek, with a Preliminary Dissertation on The Life and Theology of Orpheus, to which is added the Essay of Plotinus, Concerning the Beautiful*, by Thomas Taylor (1758–1835), which I own in a "facsimile reprint of the original English edition of 1792," published by the Philosophical Research Society, Inc., Los Angeles, 1981.

While the catchword's original purpose, which was to aid a binder or compositor in a book's correct pagination, has been technologically mooted, this feature might still be useful — as an aid to those who would read aloud, with or without an audience.

ABOUT THE AUTHOR

Joshua Cohen was born in southern New Jersey in 1980. He is the author of a collection of stories, *The Quorum*, and a forthcoming novel, *A Heaven of Others*. *Cadenza for the Schneidermann Violin Concerto* is his first novel. Cohen lives in Brooklyn, New York, and writes for *The Jewish Daily Forward*.

CPSIA information can be obtained
at www.ICGtesting.com
Printed in the USA
LVHW012203220822
726583LV00001B/83

9 781879 193161